(uncensored)
MEMOIRS OF A
FAB, FUNNY, FREAKY, FAT GIRL

A true story about a typical college girl

Smillee Sims

∞

Copyright © 2017 by Smillee Sims

All rights reserved. No part of this book may be reproduced or used in any form or by any means— graphic, electronic, or mechanical, including photocopying, recording, taping, or information storage and retrieval systems—without the permision of its author and publisher.

ISBN-13: 978-1544102542
ISBN-10: 1544102542

CreateSpace Independent Publishing Platform

For information regarding bookings, interviews, and/or special discounts for bulk purchases, please contact author via email at smilleesims@yahoo.com.

*To the people I've lost along the way,
and the people that'll always be there,
to the person I was before all of this,
and the person I've become,
to my mom,
to my best friend and love of my life,
to my readers and supporters,
to you all.
Thank you.*

XOXO,

Table of Contents

1 | Move-In Day: 15
2 | White Girl Wasted: 26
3 | Snow in the Fall: 45
4 | Thanksgiving Break: 60
5 | For My Ancestors: 67
6 | Shoot & Miss: 83
7 | Check Please: 99
8 | Friends and Fingers: 113
9 | Petty Queen: 118
10 | Nothing Was the Same: 132
11 | Peter, Pussy Popper?: 152
12 | Man of Omega: 170
13 | Free Fall: 197
14 | Cinematic Antics: 210
15 | Citric Sensations: 218
16 | Best Buds: 226
17 | Baetoven: 232
18 | Not Okay: 245
19 | Pony Rides: 255
20 | Birthday Gift Hell: 267
21 | Three's Company: 273
22 | 1 Year, 1 Nigga: 281
23 | Impala Encounters: 293
24 | New Year Bullshit: 301
25 | First Impressions: 306
26 | Free Agent: 319
27 | Baby Mama Drama: 338
28 | Head & the City: 355
29 | Captain Fuckboy: 364
30 | Kappa Style: 381
31 | Mitosis Osmosis: 398
32 | Dapper Dick: 409
33 | What Goes Up: 424
34 | Must Come Down: 432
35 | Love At First Fuck: 442
36 | Plan B Chronicles: 458
37 | For An Audience: 473
38 | All Tied Up: 478
39 | Valentine's Day: 488
40 | In Conclusion: 494

Preface
∞

Now, I'm pretty sure you came here because you've heard about all the nasty, freaky, disgusting things I've done to, with, and for my sexual partners. Maybe you just simply found the title intriguing. Please understand however, that sex is not the only thing that this book is about. I mean, yeah, don't get me wrong; a good 99.999% of it is, however, there are little tiny inklings of life lessons I hope you'll take from reading this. In a world so obsessed with what women should be, how they should think, act, and look like, I'm not ashamed to admit that I pretty much did whatever the fuck I wanted to, whenever the fuck I wanted, with whomever the fuck I wanted to do it with.

A few things you should know about me before we continue. For starters, I have a very, very mild fucking case of potty mouth— I apologize for that. If you're uncomfortable with it, I'm not sure what else there is to do. These are my sexual confessions, so I'm not going to be talking about roses, rainbows, and unicorns—maybe penises shaped like unicorn horns and vaginas that smell like roses, but that's about as cute as it gets.

As I've said before, this book is not just about sex; it's also about the unapologetic petty things I've done in this life (among other things). I'm not the average petty person, believe me. The word "petty" is an understatement, to be honest. The past four or five years (with all the shitty people I've met and the terrible things I've gone through with them) have truly allowed my pettiness to mature and to flourish into a beautiful ball of "fucklessness". You'll see exactly what I'm talking about soon enough.

I've hurt a lot of people and I'm working on that, I promise. I became the people that hurt me. I know I have to learn when to stop; I have to understand when enough is enough. But until then, why not make a couple people laugh in the process?

I've never actually said this out loud, but I would consider myself a recovering sex-addict. I started out a goody two shoes. I was the average prude (not necessarily because I found joy in teasing people and giving guys blue balls, but because I was deathly afraid of sex and every possible consequence that comes with it). It seems like pregnancy is the new black nowadays, and people treat STD's like they're a fable or a myth.

When I got the hang of things and figured out how to protect myself, the rest was pretty much history. For years, I followed a strict set of rules that I'll share with you now; you can choose to do with them whatever you please. I guess you can consider them Commandments of the 21st Century and they are as follows:

Commandments of the 21st Century:

Commandment #1: Thou shalt be weary of social media. It is the route of modern-day evil.

Commandment #2: Stay away from fuckboys/fuckgirls. Being a fuckboy/fuckgirl means having complete and utter disregard for people's feelings. 'Tis not an individual act, but a mentality. If thou hath never come in contact with a fuckboy/fuckgirl, thou art living thy life right.

Commandment #3: If thou art in fact a fuckboy/fuckgirl, be the absolute best fuckboy/fuckgirl thou canst be. If thou must be a fuckboy, be a caring fuckboy, or a thoughtful fuckboy; it is possible.

Commandment #4: Thou must always use protection; this includes (but is not limited to) socially, sexually, emotionally, spiritually & mentally.

Commandment #5: Having side-chicks and side-niggas (contrary to popular belief) is entirely overrated.

Commandment #6: Thou shalt never throw shade, if thou cannot throw hands.

Commandment #7: Thou must never take shit personally, or worry about people that don't matter.

Commandment #8: Pettiness is an essential part of life, but never exercise it unwarranted.

Commandment #9: Netflix & Chill is more of a test of will than an act of cinematic relaxation.

Commandment #10: Don't make someone a priority in your life if you are not a priority in theirs.

Now, of course, some people slipped through the cracks, which is mainly the reason behind this book. Life just happened. I went away to college and I managed to get myself wrapped up in the bullshit most college students allow themselves to get wrapped up in.

Since you have been familiarized with the Commandments of the 21st Century, I suppose I'll carry on. As far as my sex life goes, have I participated in some unorthodox sexual activities, in unorthodox places, for unorthodox reasons? *Define "unorthodox"*. Have I hit a few major speed bumps in the road? *Absolutely*. Has it made me a better person? *That's quite questionable*. Would I be who I am without my past? *Absolutely not*. I am who I am and there's not much anyone can do about it. Let me reiterate and tone down the proper vernacular for the people who refuse to hear me: men like to get their dicks wet, sucked, and stroked on. I like to get my pussy spat on, poked, and licked on. My pussy is my pussy and to this day, it's tight, clean, gets extremely wet, sort of tastes good, has no viruses or STD's, and (most importantly,) I've had zero pregnancy scares. It's quite that simple.

Granted, I may have gotten lost along the way, but I'm exactly where I'm supposed to be. I've lived my life (for the most part) without regrets, shame, or fear. People will think what they want to think, and say what they want to say. But, let me be perfectly clear; I could not give any less of a fuck about what people think about me (or my past for that matter) than I already do. The only way in which I could possibly care any less would be in the event of my death. I'm *human* and I *love sex*. That's seriously the only justification I need.

That being said, read the book. Let a couple things marinate. Learn a few tricks. Try some new things. Have a drink, (or two, or five, or ten) because you're definitely going to need it. If you're asthmatic, I suggest you have your inhaler on your person at all times while reading this book. Get on your knees and say a couple Hail Mary's. Have two sips of red wine at communion. Go bathe in Holy water. Go read a scripture (or five, or 23). Shit, whatever it is that you need to do to get right with your god, I suggest you do so right now.

Things might start a little slow, but bear with me; that's me trying to ease you into this shit-storm. I'm letting you get your feet wet to test the waters. I guarantee there will be moments you'll need to throw this book, or take a walk to gather your thoughts. Hell, you may even want to burn this book after the second chapter. But it'll change your life. If you've read some of these stories before, many details have been added. Be full warned: my mannerisms may change. You'll see some slang, but don't worry, white people; I've got you!

My writing style, my tone—they'll both do a complete 180, but hang in there. By the end of Chapter 3, you will undoubtedly see things in a different light. You'd be surprised how quickly a mild case of pettiness can flourish with a little help from fuckery and other people's selfishness.

You'll learn life lessons. You'll learn things you might want to try in the near future—over and over and over again. You can thank me now, or you can thank me later; either way is perfectly fine with me, honestly.

If you make it to the other end of this book, be sure to give yourself a round of applause and take a fucking bow. This book may actually be unlike any sex novel you've ever read before (nothing like Zane's chronicles or the infamous Zola story). It's certainly nothing like *50 Shades of Sadistic White Rich Guy* (I said what I said, and I stand by it).

It's not all crazy. It's not all bad. It's not all jokes, either. Keep in mind that the things you're about to read, the actions you're about to witness, the tricks you're about to learn all actually occurred. The people you're about to meet, I really dealt with (however, their names have been altered for the sake of their privacy and confidentiality—I'll try my best to keep the first letter of the fake names consistent with their real ones).

In conclusion, if you are underage, I really cannot in good conscience condone you reading this. But hey, if it's your money and you feel adult enough, have at it, young blood. If you don't even think you can fade it, I understand. Some things in this book actually might make you want to vomit.

If you have consciously made a decision to carry on with reading this book, let me be the first to commend you. I'll see you in Chapter 1. Good luck!

Part I: Head Strong

1. Move-In Day

∞

Freshman Year, September, 2011

Picture it: September 2011. It was a Friday morning. I kissed my mother and my grandparents on their cheeks, hugged each of them for an embarrassingly long time and waved as they pulled off to head back home to DC. Imagine being smothered for eighteen years by a (crazy) loving single mother, and ending up at a college three-hundred miles away from home! She could never just "drop in"; there would never be any "surprise visits". After living my entire life on a short leash, can you imagine how freeing that felt? She had no idea the type of effect that had on me.

*(Side note: This is a PSA to all parents and future parents reading this. Do **not** smother your children— because as soon as they get a taste of freedom, they're going to go all out, in*

ways you could never imagine. I just thought I'd put that out there.)

After packing up my entire life into cardboard boxes, enduring a four-hour drive, and two hours of unloading a pickup truck, I was officially a freshman at Lycoming College in Williamsport, Pennsylvania. I know, you've never heard of the school— no one has, trust me. Shit, the people that go to Lycoming haven't even heard of it; they just somehow ended up there. There were so many things to do, places to explore, majors to choose from, memories to make, drugs to take, and white boys to experiment with. It was a PWI, so you know I had to get the full experience.

(Side note: For my white folks reading, "PWI" is an acronym for a predominately white institution.)

I was finally on my own, and I was going to take advantage of every fucking minute of it. (I would later find out that there was nothing in Williamsport but dirt and grass, and more fucking dirt and grass, but that's beside the point).

I was a city girl, with a country heart, and a mild (and by "mild", I mean "extremely severe") case of pettiness. I was quiet and timid but I was still from the hood; don't get it twisted. I stayed in my lane, and I tried to mind my own fucking business. But, man was I petty as fuck. Don't worry, my pettiness never fully thrived and reached its full potential until circa 2013. It remained dormant for a long while (which we'll get to).

I got into my dorm room and unpacked my things. I printed out my schedule for the week and walked around campus to familiarize myself with where my classes would be. After that, I went out to smoke a cigarette and realized it was my last one. I nearly had a fucking panic attack. Imagine my surprise when I looked up and noticed a Rite-Aid across the street from campus! I headed over to stock up on some cigarettes.

I walked in and the entrance motion sensor dinged. The store was completely fucking empty (that tends to happen when you decide to attend college in the boonies); there wasn't even a radio station playing. Shit was a little weird

I looked to my right and saw quite possibly one of the sexiest men I had ever seen in my entire life— he was Latino (and I later found out he was actually Puerto Rican). He was standing behind the register handing someone their receipt and change. Then he looked over at me, bit his bottom lip, smirked and nodded in my direction. I awkwardly smiled, picked up a hand cart, and walked away.

I headed over to the toiletries section and picked up a couple bottles of Dove Body wash, some lotion, deodorant (all that good shit). Then I pretty much just walked around, trying to stall and waste time— praying that someone less attractive was in the back on a lunch break or something and would come up front to relieve him.

Then, for a moment, I was relieved to see a door open in my peripheral. I could tell it was a girl with her curly hair in a ponytail. Before I could even thank God, I caught a glimpse of her face. She was a stud. I cried a little on the inside because I was stuck between a rock and a hard place. I had two options, and it was the hardest decision I could've ever possibly made. They were both my weakness at the time. Both of them had neck tattoos, perfect smiles, spoke Spanish. There I was, fantasizing about sitting on both of their faces at the same time, all while standing between Summer's Eve and Clean & Clear face wash.

Long story short, I somehow got the courage to head up front because, at that point, I was just dragging it out. They both looked at me, waiting to see who I would choose. It seemed like the closer I got to them, and the clearer their faces became, the wetter my panties would've been (if I had worn any). Jesus took his time with them! It made no fucking sense how fucking beautiful these people were.

So, I walked up to the front. They both looked at each other and smiled. Then at the same time, they both called themselves trying to reach for my hand cart, bumping and pushing each other out the way trying to grab my things. I just giggled nervously.

"I can ring you up right here, beautiful," they both said, damn near falling over the fucking counter.

(Side note: I'm not entirely sure why, but every time I hear that word, "beautiful", I feel uncomfortable. For me, "beautiful" is what scratching on a chalkboard sounds like to other people. It's not that I'm unattractive or anything; it's just that my glow-up came so late in the game, I was never used to hearing it. I'm still not.)

I didn't know what to do. He was tall as hell—she was a pretty stud. She didn't have to say she was a stud; there are just certain vibes you get from certain females, and she was absolutely, 100% without a doubt a carpet-munching, strap on-using, sports bra-wearing stud. They were both fucking me with their eyes, both licking their lips, both fine as fuck. I looked at their nametags: I'll call them "Ricardo" and "Casey".

"Hmmm," I clicked my teeth and smirked. "Tough choice, guys."

I sighed, shrugged my shoulders, and shook my head. "It doesn't really matter to me".

Ricardo started ringing up my things and Casey stepped back like she was defeated. I smiled and turned my attention to Ricardo. He had a short cut, with waves, and a slight beard going on—not too thick; thick enough to tell he was a grown ass man, but thin enough to want to sit on his face to help him grow and fill it out more, you know?

I remember it like it was yesterday. I stared at his arms longer than I should have: tattoos all up and down both of them. In the span of maybe ten seconds, I could make out pretty much every tattoo. He had nearly an entire sleeve dedicated to Puerto Rico alone: the Puerto Rican flag, of course, some Spanish phrases, skulls, and what I think was a Taino symbol.

He was light-skinned and he smelled so fucking good. I don't know why, but a guy that smells amazing automatically becomes three times sexier; it's science. I could smell his cologne from across the counter. He was just perfection. I was willing to have his bodiqua babies! I really don't think you guys understand how beautiful this man was. I caught myself before I started drooling.

"Is there anything I can get you today, beautiful (there goes that fucking word again)?" Casey asked behind Ricardo in front of the cigarettes.

I brushed it off and tried to pretend like she hadn't just paid me a compliment, but she was just so fucking fine. She reminded me of why I went into Rite-Aid in the first place.

(Side note: Even to this day, my memory is all sorts of fucked up and hazy from smoking weed in high school.)

"Can I get three packs of Marlboro Smooths?" I asked while Ricardo rang my things up.

(Side note: For my Newport smokers, and black people worldwide, Marlboros are cigarettes white people smoke.)

Ricardo stopped ringing my things up as soon as he heard me say "Marlboros". His facial expression changed from a smile, to a smirk, to a subtle look of disappointment.

Casey cleared her throat.

"I'm sorry, what?" she replied.

"Marlboro Smooths," I repeated.

"I'm sorry, what?" she said again, fucking with me.

By that time, I was irritated as hell. Never play about a woman's hair, money, or vice (in this case, it was cigarettes)! There are just some things that will get you royally fucked up.

I sighed and was prepared to give her one more shot before climbing over the fucking counter my damn self.

"Marlboro…Smooths," I said slowly.

She sucked her teeth and turned around to the cigarette locker behind her.

"I'm just playing with you, ma," she said.

I rolled my eyes because I knew exactly where the conversation was about to go; I knew exactly what was about to be said at some point.

"Mami, you too beautiful to be smoking," Ricardo said.

I knew it! Somebody owes me money because I fucking called it! If I had a dollar for every time someone has ever said that to me, I'd have about $132. Every time I ask for a pack of cigarettes and the cashier looks like they want to fuck, they always use that lame ass, played out line. I pushed my hair away from my face, cleared my throat, and pulled it behind my ear.

"Thank you?" I replied hesitantly.

"No need to thank me, hunny," he said. "I'm just bein' honest."

Casey slid the door open and crouched down. She pointed at the blue pack and looked back at me.

"The blue pack, right?" she asked.

I nodded my head. "Yeah."

"Can I see some ID?" Ricardo asked.

I dug into my front pockets, then my back pockets, and realized I had left my ID on my dresser back on campus. I looked at my keys and pulled my student ID out of the lanyard, nervous as hell.

"I left my ID on campus, but can y'all take my student ID instead?" I pointed out my date of birth on the bottom right. "I promise I'm 18."

Ricardo looked at me, paused for a moment, twisted his lips, folded his arms, and did the National Asshole Stance, followed by the notorious "thinking fingers" (you know, when someone taps their lips with a few fingers to make it seem like they're making a tough decision).

I squinted my eyes and felt myself starting to pout. I tried to make as helpless a face as possible, but in hindsight, that wouldn't have helped because I've always had a baby face (even to this day, I get carded when I go to bars). Then he smiled.

He took my ID out of my hand, looked at it, then looked back at me, then looked at it again. He handed it back. Casey looked up and Ricardo nodded. She passed him the cigarettes and locked up the glass in front of the tobacco products.

"$32, even," Ricardo said. I exposed my teeth and gave an awkward smile.

"I need one more thing," I nervously added.

It seemed like Ricardo was just not feeling me at all after finding out that I had smoked.

"Can I get a BIC lighter too?" I handed him two twenties.

Casey handed me a pink BIC lighter, which ironically would've been the exact same one I would have asked her for. Her reasoning behind it, however, wasn't what I was expecting.

Let's disregard for a moment the fact that I had on some black and pink "PINK" (from Victoria's Secret) leggings, **and** let's *also* disregard the fact that I literally had on a black and pink "PINK" (also from fucking Victoria's Secret) t-shirt. She looked me up and down, smirked and bit her bottom lip.

"You look like a pink kind of girl," she said while literally looking at my groin area, smirking.

She saw me, *see her*, **see me**, <u>see her</u> looking at my camel toe. My jaw dropped. I didn't know what to do, or what to say. Ricardo handed me my change and I waited for the receipt to print out.

"I am," I replied. "How'd you figure?"

Ricardo passed me my receipt and change. Then, I saw him open a water bottle in my peripheral while I was focusing on Casey. He started shaking his head.

Casey lightly shrugged her shoulders.

"I 'ont know," she said.

She sucked in her lips and I noticed her dimples. I could've fucking collapsed right then and there on that fucking floor. **TAKE ME NOW, JESUS!** She clicked her tongue.

"You just seem like you've got a lot of ummm," she paused, "pink things."

Ricardo choked on his water. I raised my eyebrows and decided to play Casey's game.

"Some things pinker than others," I added.

All of a sudden, Ricardo spat out his water all across the counter in disbelief of what I had just said. Some of it got on my arm, but it was nothing major. I looked at him. He was holding his mouth, with his eyes wide. He bent down and got a roll of paper towels. Then an older white guy walked behind the counter; I figured he was their manager because their whole behavior changed. That was my cue to get the fuck out before I got them into trouble.

I took my bag, trying to act all professional and shit, as if we weren't just talking about my vagina.

"You guys have a good day," I said.

"You too," they both replied.

I walked toward the automatic doors, and put my hand cart in the pile. Casey and Ricardo were both looking at my fucking ass (which is honestly nonexistent, but we won't talk about that). I crossed the street and headed back to my room. On my way back, I was trying to figure out who the fuck said the things I said back at the store, because it damn sure wasn't me.

I had never said anything like that before out loud to *anyone*, especially to someone I had just met. I didn't realize it until later, but being at college for less than two hours changed me, it honestly did. So, imagine what four years did.

2. White Girl Wasted

∞

When I got back to the room, my roommate had finally shown up. She introduced herself (for the sake of the story, I'll call her "Keegan"). I helped her move in and everything. We walked around throughout the building, introducing ourselves to people. You have to start early before it's too late. You don't want to fuck around and not have any friends your freshman year of college. It was a co-ed dorm, and guys and girls weren't separated by floors! Only PWI's do that shit, by the way.

The girls in the room beside ours came over and we just clicked ("Jessica" and "Lindsay"). Lindsay was a country girl from Oregon that smoked weed like it was her major. Jessica was a rich white girl that didn't know she was white. You know the type. To be honest, she was blacker than me, and I'm from the fucking hood. They were cool as hell, though. We ended up just chilling in our room, talking for hours.

Our dorm room was right across the hall from the stairwell and our door was open. So, when a group of cute guys came walking past our door, all hell broke loose.

Long story short, they ended up coming into our room and we had a slight kickback. Okay, now that I think of it, "kickback" is an understatement; you'll see exactly what I mean soon enough.

My aunt had given me two bottles of Grey Goose as a "going-away" present and they were both the 1.75 mL bottles. Keegan had a big ass jug of that Hawaiian Punch shit—the one with the guy surfing on top of the fruit, you know which one I'm talking about. Jessica had some Cherry Pinnacle. "Allan", one of the guys, had some weed, Lindsay had some EZ Widers (rolling papers mostly white people use, because niggas use blunts), Keegan had some Solo cups and we were in business! So, you can pretty much assume some shit was about to go down that had no business fucking going down.

(Long ass side note: I'll be honest, I may or may not have had a slight (and by "slight", I mean "almost addicting") brush with weed toward the end of high school. But, let me tell you something, and I need you to really, really listen to me. White people don't party like black people do. They don't drink or smoke like black people do. White people that party get drunk, wasted, and maybe even high. But white people that party at PWI's are unapologetically incapable of giving a fuck about consequences and repercussions. Everything is in excess and to the extreme. They don't party to have fun, or make memories with their friends and loved ones. They do it to get **fucked up**. *I'm talking "pissing on yourself, puking on yourself, giving a blowjob, and puking on yourself again" kind*

of fucked up. I'm talking "losing a shoe, fucking on the dance floor, breaking a body part and not noticing until the next morning" kind of fucked up.)

Flash forward an hour or so. Everyone but me was drunk and high as fuck. We played "Kings" then "Never Have I Ever" until most of the second bottle of Grey Goose was gone. They were fucked up and apparently, I was the most (relatively) sober one in the room because I was pretty much an angel my entire life. Let's just say that I was the only virgin in the room, okay? But the things they were admitting to doing made my fucking head spin. Some of them admitted to fucking in front of their parents, to being in orgies, to having a train run on them, to being fucked in the ass—guys were admitting to having their asses eaten. It was just a mess, you guys. I would've never imagined what was about to happen.

Mind you, this was only my first night at college and I was about to witness something I had never seen in my entire life. We started playing "Suck and Blow" (if you've seen the movie, *Clueless*, you know exactly what I'm talking about). It's pretty much a drinking game where you have to pass a card or piece of paper around but only with your mouths (don't worry; you sit boy-girl-boy-girl in a circle). That's about where shit got weird. I gave Jordan (the only black guy in the room) the card with my mouth. He looked at Jessica, and she started puckering up. He turned to pass her the card but purposely let the card go from his mouth. The rules say that when the card drops, the two have to kiss and whatever number is on the card is the amount of shots they both had to take. This was different. Of course, they started kissing, and they *kept* kissing. And they *kept* kissing. And they *kept* kissing. And they <u>*kept fucking kissing*</u>. And out of nowhere, her boob was out, and then the other.

All of a sudden, his lips were wrapped around one of her nipples, and his hand was up her fucking skirt. I put my index finger up politely to interrupt them.

"Sir?" I said and cleared my throat. "Ma'am?"

Everybody else started laughing and cackling. I cleared my throat again. They were still kissing. I cleared my throat once more, this time for a continuous five seconds, but to no avail. It was already too late.

I was not ready! Eventually, she was on her back, with the skirt on her stomach, no underwear, no shirt, and no fucking bra. In my mind, I was thinking "**Jessica, where is your mother!?**" No one else in the room seemed at all fazed. I was the only one who showed a hint of surprise and confusion.

I looked around and everyone else already had their phones out recording it. You know how black people take their phones out when someone's fighting to put it on World Star? That's exactly what it fucking felt like!

I was dumbfounded, speechless, flabbergasted, bewildered, dismayed, floored, stumped; I was fucking thunderstruck. *My heart!*

At that moment, I understood that white people (and black people that grow up around white people) really don't give a speck of a sliver of a fraction of an atom of a half of a pinch of a dash of a scrap of a shred of a piece of a fuck. **You guys don't even know each other's last names! Jordan, you don't even know her favorite color and you're just going to puncture her vagina with your tongue? Okay, I guess.**

This was some real life *Girls Gone Wild* type of shit. I never realized it, but the college section on PornHub was real! It was all real! It's not staged like most people would think. It all happened so quickly. I was in the middle of it. Where did I go wrong in life for me to end up hosting a porn-casting party? I couldn't move. I couldn't think. I forgot how to breathe for a moment.

I was so shocked; it took me a while to smell the popcorn in the microwave. No, literally. Keegan actually consciously stood up, took out the popcorn from her food bin, walked over to my microwave, plugged it in, opened the door, placed the popcorn into the microwave, closed the door, pressed some buttons and popped fucking popcorn—not just one fucking bag, multiple fucking bags! She passed them around just like we passed around the weed.

You would think that it would've stopped there, right? Nope. Jordan actually stood up, unzipped his pants, pulled his dick out through the hole in his boxers, and started fucking Jessica in the middle of my dorm room. Lord, Jesus. **What is going on right now!?** All of a sudden, the door opened, and another group of guys walked in nonchalantly like it was a private movie screening. After a while, there were at least twenty people cramped up in my dorm room watching this shit go down.

One of the guys had sent a text to a lot of people on campus. It had gotten so crowded in our room that they eventually just said "fuck it" all together, and left the door open. **This was move-in day. MOVE-IN DAY!** People walking by the room ended up stopping in the doorway and watching from the fucking hallway. **How is this okay!?** I knew deep down in my heart of hearts that I was not high or drunk enough for that shit. Jordan yanked her by her leg and threw it over to turn her onto her hands and knees. People were cheering and clapping. Camera shutter sounds were going off, white lights were flashing. I felt like I was on the set of a low-budget porno. Someone even brought a fucking Bluetooth speaker in to set the mood!

Before I knew it, most of the people on our floor were in or outside our room. Meanwhile, I was too busy sitting there trying to get right with my God and they were all apparently used to this shit! I was moving my eyes around the room looking for Ashton

Kutcher. Homeboy never came out to tell me I was being Punk'd. Bummer.

Jordan got about thirty or so pumps in while fucking Jessica doggy-style before an obviously drunk (and possibly high) white guy walked in (making the room **even more crowded**) and dapped him. (I later found out his name was "Sean".) I couldn't make out exactly what they were saying to each other because there was a lot of noise going on: Jordan's thighs and Jessica's ass cheeks slapping, popcorn bags ruffling, music playing, people yelling, screaming and chanting.

Sean and Jordan were having a full-on conversation. You know when you're having an intense conversation, and you start talking with your hands and bobbing your head subconsciously? That's what the fuck was going on! Keep in mind that Jessica was still taking back shots in the middle of my fucking room! Everyone was focused on the two of them fucking, while I was the only one worried about that poor child's knees (and her future arthritis) for being on the marble floor (like I was her fucking grandmother).

You guys, I was so nerve-wrecked by the situation that I ended up all the way near the back of the room, in a corner, standing on my bed. But because I'm always such a thoughtful host, I passed someone a decorative pillow that I got from Wal-Mart. That person passed it to another person who passed it to another person who handed it to Jessica—and God-willing, that pillow got to that child and she was able to use it as a knee cushion (but I threw it away right afterwards).

I noticed that Sean started taking off his t-shirt. In my mind, I was thinking **well, the air conditioning is on full blast and it's freezing in here, but maybe he's claustrophobic and he gets a little warm when he's surrounded by a lot of people, which would be completely understandable. Kinetic energy makes heat, so, you know.** Then he reached for his belt buckle, unzipped his khaki shorts, and took them off. Then I started thinking to myself **well, maybe his thighs get really, really hot, or maybe he has hypertension and it's really serious in his general thigh area.** Then he pulled his dick out of the hole in his boxers as well. Yeah, I couldn't justify that action—I couldn't give this guy the benefit of the doubt. I felt my mouth opening wide.

Jordan pulled Jessica's hair so that he could whisper into her ear, while still fucking her. She looked over to Sean and nodded her head, mascara running down her face, lipstick smeared all over her lips. **Oh, my God! They're about to tag team poor Jessica! She needs some milk! Someone, get her a Gatorade!** Jordan started slowing down his strokes and eventually slowly pulled out. He kept jerking off, which I thought was weird as fuck, considering he was surrounded by a couple dozen people; fucking is one thing, but jerking off is another. Then he tucked his dick back into his boxers. Sean got down on his knees, slapped Jessica's ass, spread her cheeks, and shoved his dick inside of her. She let out a piercing gasp of a moan. Not one condom had been used—**not one fucking condom!** Take a moment to let that marinate, please. (Would you believe me if I told you that there was a huge herpes, gonorrhea, syphilis, **and** chlamydia outbreak all throughout campus shortly thereafter? Good, because that actually happened. Those kids gave not one fuck.)

    Then Jordan popped back up, started rubbing on his dick through his boxers, and pulled it back out. It was pretty sad because Jessica was actually moaning louder with Sean than she did with Jordan, but that's none of my business. Come to think of it, a black guy being out-dicked by a white guy is low-key depressing, but that's also none of my business.

    Sean kept throwing the dick and Jessica kept catching it. Jordan got down on one knee and grabbed Jessica's hair again. He started slapping her in the face with his dick. Sean was holding her by her waist; he was doing damage to her uterus, and Jordan was doing damage to her throat. Collectively, they were just destructive as hell.

    When it all came down to it, she stopped moaning. The moans were eventually replaced with grunts, actually. If only you could see how red that girl's ass and thighs were. You would've felt sorry for her too—poor little Jessica. Out of nowhere, Sean and Jordan high-fived; **they fucking HIGH-**

FIVED! I guess it's true what they say: friends that fuck together are stuck together.

She was being gagged and stabbed at the same time. It's a pivotal moment in life when you can say that you've actually witnessed, with your own two eyes, someone being "Eiffel Towered". This poor child was being raw dogged on her first day at college and I was nervous about two attractive people at a Rite-Aid? Who the fuck did I think I was? This went on for at least thirty minutes. I'm not sure if that speaks volumes about Sean and Jordan's stamina or Jessica's pussy. But eventually, things died down, and she got completely quiet. She could no longer hold her arch. It had just become a sad mess. Most people started filing out, and the room became less and less crowded. My God is a good God, is he not?

Jordan ended up standing back up and started slow-jerking his dick near Jessica's face. Sean started pounding harder from behind, but slower still. Jessica kept falling forward. Sean pulled out, and came on her ass. Jordan came in her hair and on her face. Homegirl did not complain one time—what a trooper.

Once the three of them were done with their business, someone in the hallway passed in a roll of paper towels from the bathroom because, team work. Jordan took the roll and ripped some off for him. He handed it to Sean and wiped himself off. Sean cleaned himself off and handed it to Jessica. **They had just given that girl a cloudy shower and**

neither one of them offered to clean up their mess! They had just made it white rain all over this bitch and they just threw her a roll of paper towels?! Savages!

The room smelled like popcorn, liquor, and (what I later became familiar with as) sex. You know that musty smell that disperses throughout the air after you've finished fucking (whether the two of you just got out of the shower or just came from the gym)? That shit fucking stinks, and it smells even worse when it's not your sex that you're smelling. Jessica tried wiping herself off but it didn't work because she was fucked up out of her mind and high off her ass. It was so sad.

After a while, it was back down to the original people that were in the room, with the addition of Sean. He and Jordan ended up somewhere on the floor, drinking the rest of the Grey Goose. I walked over to Jessica to check and see if she was still fucking breathing. I crouched down and put my hand near her face. I felt a light warm breeze, so she was good.

I looked over and saw light reflecting off the floor, and realized it was cum. I heaved in my mouth a little bit and ran over to my closet. Thank God my mom stole some Clorox wipes from her job, because they had me three different types of fucked up if they thought I was going to clean up a mess that three entire, whole ass, other people made.

I threw the Clorox wipes in Sean and Jordan's direction and dug out a towel from my closet.

I picked up the bag from Rite-Aid and walked over to Jessica. Then, I wrapped the towel around her and helped her up. Lindsay walked over to us and picked Jessica's clothes up and took them to their room. Keegan stayed back and cleaned up the mess we had made when we were drinking earlier. Fortunately for me, Jessica and Lindsay's room was directly across from the bathroom. I guided her to a shower and started the water up.

She let out a gut-wrenching scream because the water was cold.

"Stop screaming, Jessica," I begged. "Just step back and wait 'til it gets warm."

She looked at me and made the ugliest crying face I've ever seen in my entire life (and I've seen some **ugly** bitches; I've also seen ugly bitches crying). Then she just started bawling. This cry was so serious that she had to stop for a moment to catch her breath. Her mascara started running down her face some more.

"Why are you crying, Jessica?" I asked.

I reached under the shower to test the temperature and took the towel from her.

"I'm gonna die!" she screamed out.

"You're not going to die, Jessica," I reassured her. She looked at the shower.

"I'm gonna drown," she whined out.

That was when I realized that her level of drunkenness was far beyond my expertise. Of course, in high school, I was always the babysitter for my friends, but never had I ever had to deal with an eighteen-year-old who thought she was going to drown, standing upright, in a fucking shower. All I could do was let out a long sigh.

"You're not going to die, Jessica," I said. "Look."

I turned her body to face away from the shower head.

"Are you dying, Jessica?"

She nodded her head, leaned it back and purposely gathered the shower water in her mouth. Then she spat it out.

"I told you," she said, coughing the water out. **REALLY, BITCH?**

I tried my hardest not to laugh, but a little giggle came out.

"You're not dying, Jessica."

I looked over to the undressing station and noticed there were already other people's shower caddies in there. So I picked up a random person's body wash because I didn't want to use mine, fuck it.

"Give me your hand, Jessica." She had fallen asleep, in the shower, **standing up**! I poked her in the shoulder.

"Jessica!" she flinched and opened her eyes in a panic. "Give me your hand."

She reached her hand out and I squeezed body wash into it. She looked at me and pulled her hand to her face with her mouth open. **This bitch was about to eat the fucking body wash!** I grabbed her arm.

"Jessica, stop! Look at me, Jessica."

She turned her head to me.

"Rub your hands together and wipe them all over your body, Jessica. Like this." I had to literally act out what to do. Her eyes squinted. She started washing herself.

"Here's some more body wash," I said.

She reached her hand out and I squeezed some more into it.

"You **have** to wash your thing," I said.

"My thing?" she asked standing there, rocking from side to side, water draping her wet hair in her face. I pushed her hair back.

"Your pussy, bro." She looked at me confused. "Just pretend like you peed, and—"

"I did just pee," she replied and smiled.

I looked at the shower floor, and sure enough, there was a river of yellow liquid going down the shower drain. I stepped back and put my hand over my forehead. This bitch was really fucked up. I tried thinking back to what could have possibly allowed her to have been tag teamed. Keegan wasn't that fucked up. Lindsay wasn't that fucked up. I definitely wasn't that fucked up. Then it hit me. She had a Four Loko in her hand when she and Lindsay first walked into our room earlier that day, before the guys came in.

It was at that moment that I vowed to never touch a Four Loko in my life, ever. And if I did, I promised to never mix it with anything, white, brown, or otherwise. Don't get me wrong, there have been plenty of times that I've blacked out and did some shit my friends had to remind me about the morning after. Shit, one time I got so fucked up, I woke up with acorns in my pocket—there aren't any, nor have there ever been any acorn trees in my neighborhood. I refused to be in Jessica's situation.

I closed my eyes and said a silent prayer because this shit was out of hand. She started jumping up and down, kicking her pissy puddle everywhere, titties flapping all over the place.

"Stop it, Jessica!" I yelled out, and she did. I knew that was God giving me some help. She started to behave.

"Pretend like you're wiping your pussy with toilet paper, but over and over and over again, okay?"

"Okay," she giggled out. I looked away and let her do her thing for twenty seconds.

"You finished?" I asked.

"Mhmm," she replied. I bent down and took someone's shampoo out.

"Gimme your hand again, Jessica."

She reached out her arm without incident, and I squeezed the shampoo into her hand.

"This is shampoo. Wash your hair, okay? Then you can go to bed."

She smiled and started rubbing her hands in her hair. I helped her rinse her hair out then I turned the shower off. I got her out and dried her off. I walked her to her dorm room. I had assumed that the bed Jessica's pile of clothes was in front of was hers. I looked in the storage bin under the bed and found a t-shirt and put it on her. I saw a pack of water near Lindsay's bed.

"Lindsay, can I give water to Jessica?" I yelled. She could hear me next door.

"Yeah, go ahead," she yelled back.

I got one out, opened it, pulled the blanket back, and sat her down.

"Drink this," I told her.

She shook her head.

"Well, at least drink half of it for me please, Jessica."

You guys, it took her five whole minutes to drink half a bottle of water. I made her stick her finger in her mouth to make her puke because I didn't want her choking on her vomit in her sleep. She shrugged her shoulders and did it. I saw her neck expand. I've been puked on enough times in my life to know exactly what was about to happen.

I jumped back and grabbed the trash bin by her desk. I don't think I've ever reached for something so quickly in my entire life. I was Kobe with the trash can. The puke just kept coming, then it would stop—and just when we thought it was over, it would start back up again. After a few minutes, it was finally over. I made her drink the rest of the bottle.

"If you have to throw up again," I said, "do it in this trash bin, okay?"

She nodded her head trying to keep her eyes open. I had to talk to her like a toddler.

"If you have to throw up again, where are you going to do it, Jessica?"

"The trash can," she said, rolling her eyes.

It took everything inside of me not to curse her Thotty McThotterson ass out right then and there, but I didn't, because I had God in my heart.

I lied her down on her side, tucked her in, and put the trash bin off to the side. I told her to bang on the wall if she needed anything and that I would be back later that night to check on her. I walked across the room, turned off the light, and closed the door behind me.

When I went over to my room, Jordan and Sean were passed out on the floor. Keegan and Lindsay were still cleaning up. We just decided to let the boys sleep there until the next morning.

"She okay?" Keegan asked.

"Yeah, she should be," I replied.

Jessica was a free butterfly (and I really commend her for that), but baby girl needed Jesus; baby girl actually needed every single deity that exists in every single religion, to be honest.

(Side note: she has a family of her own right now—married to a man in the Marines and everything.)

    We pretty much spent that whole night getting to know each other more. We talked about our families, our heartbreaks, our majors and aspirations. We didn't really talk about Jessica because surprisingly, none of us liked to talk about people behind their backs. Every hour or so, one of us would go and check in on her. Jordan and Sean didn't wake up until we physically shook them and kicked them out. We decided to call it a night at around 6 am.

    We had to be up by 9 to get to breakfast by 10. Keegan, Lindsay, Messy Jessy, and I walked into the cafeteria. As soon as we swiped in for breakfast, you could hear a fucking pen drop. Not because the cafeteria was empty, but because everyone stopped doing what they were doing to gossip and whisper. Jessica was too hung-over to even care, and the rest of us were honestly just hungry.

    Freshman seminar was at 11 so we had to rush. We found an empty booth, sat down, and got up to get food. Jessica refused to get up and practically spent most of breakfast with her head down on the table, asleep. She didn't want anything but orange juice. When we got settled, I could see a group of people walking over to the booth in my peripheral.

    Lo and behold, it was Jordan, Sean, and the other guys from the day before. They literally pulled up a table beside our booth, brought their food over, and ate with us. I didn't know what to make of the situation. This was some white people college drama they only depicted in movies. None of us ever spoke about what happened on move-in day after that.

Sean and Jordan were soccer players, so they had known each other for months because they had training camp on campus most of the summer. For some reason, they thought all of us were really cool and chill (even Messy Jessy). After a day of team building exercises and a pointless scavenger hunt, we all pretty much stuck together and became really good friends (of course, Jordan and I were the token black friends, but that's neither here nor there.) As you can imagine, the move-in day incident definitely caused some turmoil throughout our entire group. Jordan, Sean, and Jessica had an ongoing love triangle right out of an X-rated Disney movie. They were in love with the girl—go figure.

I could already tell freshman year was about to be filled with unnecessary drama and fucked up situations. I was right.

3. *Snow in the Fall*

∞

It had been a month or so into school, and I had finally gotten used to the motions of college and being independent. We partied and turned up every night. Typically, my daily schedule included me waking up at 6 every morning, and then going to class from 8 to noon. After class, I'd eat lunch with my friends until around 1, and then I'd have a nap break until another class at 2. After that class ended at 3:30 pm, I'd head off to the library and do homework from 4 pm to 7 pm. By then, it was time to get fucked up and pre-game.

All of us hosted a party once a week in our tiny ass dorm rooms. Most nights, there would be between twenty and thirty people. On Mondays, Keegan and I would host. On Tuesdays, Lindsay and Jessica would host. On Wednesdays, Sean and Jordan would host. On Thursdays, "Braxton" and "Michael" (the other guys) would host. On Fridays, we pretty much just chilled and played it by ear—we bounced from one place to another.

Sometimes, we'd go to the frat houses, or to the commons (apartments off campus), but everyone knew the soccer house and the football house were the places to be. You don't attend a PWI if the sports teams don't have houses like sororities and fraternities do. Both houses had been on probation for over a year because of an incident. And the last day of probation had finally come!

I was finishing up some homework in the same private room in the library I always used when Jessica started banging on the glass door.

I jumped and looked to my left. When I realized who it was, I took a sigh of relief.

"It's open, dumbass," I said quietly, trying to finish typing up a paper.

She laughed and turned the handle.

She then sat on the table I was typing on and dangled her legs. She pulled out a Marlboro (I told you, cigarettes white people smoke) and asked me for my lighter. I looked at her up and down as if she were fucking insane.

"Jess, you know you can't smoke in here, right?"

"I know, I know. Just let me see it."

Please tell me why my dumb ass gave her my lighter like she wasn't going to turn around and end up doing it anyway! She lit her cigarette and put the lighter back into my pocket as I was typing. At that point, I didn't even care. Besides, I was almost finished and no one was in the library on Fridays anyway. I started packing my laptop and notebooks up.

"Guess whaaaat," she said.

"What?" I replied.

"No, you have to guess," she said. "That's the only way it's fun."

She stood up and started twerking and sticking her tongue out.

"Chicken butt?" I replied sarcastically.

"Seriously, Tiy. C'mon, guess."

"You finally decided who you want to be with?" I said slyly.

She laughed.

"Yeah, right," she replied.

I pursed my lips and clicked my teeth.

"Well, shit. At least give me a hint."

She rolled her eyes and twirled.

"Okay. We'll do a riddle," she said. "Look out the window. What do you see?"

She took a puff from her cigarette.

I reached my hand out and she passed it to me. I took a puff.

"Ummm... people walking?"

"Nope," she said. "Try again."

"It's raining?" I took another puff.

She gasped. "You're so close, but no. Guess again."

"Shit, I don't know."

"What's the opposite of rain?" she asked.

"Sunshine?" I took another puff and handed her cigarette back.

"No, the other opposite, babe," she said. I was pretty much ready to give up.

"Snow?" I asked.

She put her cigarette out on the brick wall in the study room and stuck her tongue out again.

"So, it's supposed to snow tonight or something?"

She nodded and smiled. I was confused. I didn't know what that meant. It was barely October.

"What about snow?"

"Shhh!" she put her finger over my mouth. She reached in her pocket and pulled out a small baggy.

"It's snoooooooooowing!"

She shook the bag and plucked it. It was half a gram. My jaw dropped. I smirked and looked side to side.

"Is that what I think it is?"

She poked her lips out and nodded.

"Who did you get it from, Jess?"

"Don't worry about it," she said.

Then she opened the baggie, put it to her nose, and sniffed lightly. She smiled.

I started shaking my head then she put it to my nose. I shooed her arm away. I got a whiff of it, though. It sort of smelled like nail polish and gasoline—way too strong for me to actually consider trying it.

"You're trying it tonight with us, right?" she asked.

"No, I have to babysit you bitches, remember?"

She started pouting and whining, like the big ass baby she was.

"Puhleeeeeese? Pretty please?" I shook my head. "Pretty, pretty pink pussy please, with cherry-flavored thongs on top?"

"You need Jesus, you know that, right?"

She sucked her teeth. "Just think about it, Tiy."

I scoffed.

"Yeah, okay," I said, not paying her any mind.

We got back to our dorm. I showered, washed my hair, and shaved every inch of my body (even though it wasn't necessary). By the time I got out, those bitches were already drunk. That was nothing new because I always took the longest to get ready anyway. Big girls have to put in extra effort. That's just the law of the land.

Jordan walked in when I was getting dressed, I gave absolutely no fucks because neither of us was attracted to each other. He was kind of like an annoying, lost, perverted brother I never wanted. I blow-dried my hair, flat ironed it, and did my makeup. At the time, it really only took me maybe ten minutes to do my makeup. I was new to the whole makeup thing, and I had only started using it recently after senior prom. Back then, the only thing I used was Black Opal's stick foundation and some mascara. I was not aware of the other necessities such as primer, concealer, powder, setting spray, and eyeliner. My makeup skills didn't flourish until late sophomore year.

By the time I finished, a drink that Keegan had fixed for me was waiting on my desk. I thought long and hard in the shower—I created a pro/con list in my head. I went over worst case scenarios and best case hypotheticals. Then I figured, for once, I was not going to be the responsible one. Being the designated "sober" friend was truly draining. I wanted to get white girl wasted to see what the hype was all about. So, I broke my cardinal rule. Not only did I drink whatever was in my cup, I took at least three shots of Henny.

On top of all of that, Jessica bought me a Four Loko because I had never tried it. I remember it plain as day. It was the grape flavor. It tasted like ass and cough syrup, with a dash of grape soda. Mind you, I had just finished drinking the white mix Keegan made me, had shots of Henny, **and** was almost halfway finished the entire can of Four Loko. In hindsight, that probably wasn't the smartest thing to do.

Out of nowhere, everything changed. I was fighting to keep my eyes open, and my stomach and throat began tingling. I couldn't stop laughing and giggling. The room was spinning. I was officially fucked up, and that's where I fucked up.

Jessica pulled out the coke and I was ready!

"Oh, shit!" Jordan yelled out and rubbed his hands together. "It's like that?"

Jessica picked up my dresser mirror, then took the cards on the coffee table out. We all sat around it in a circle. She poured some of the coke out onto the mirror and separated it into five or six white lines.

She pulled out a straw and asked for some scissors. When she got them, she cut the straw into three.

She grinned and looked at everyone then snorted a line. She grabbed her nose and held her head back. Then after what felt like the longest five seconds of my life, she finally exhaled.

"Oh my God, you guys," she started snickering. "This is some good shit."

I watched in amazement as her eyes watered and grew wider—more attentive. She passed me a piece of straw.

"Go ahead," she said.

I took a deep breath, leaned in and snorted a line in one swoop. The inside of my nose burned like hell and it left a chemical taste in the back of my mouth. I held my head back and I let it melt down the back of my throat. I felt nothing at first. So I played it off like it didn't faze me. Everyone else did a line. When we had all finished one-by-one, they all looked at me.

"Tiy, your nose is bleeding, bruh," Jordan said.

I tapped above my lip and realized he wasn't lying. I darted to the bathroom, ran into a stall, gathered some toilet paper, and ran to the mirror. I cleaned it off my mouth, rolled a piece up and stuffed it into my nose.

Then all of a sudden, **I felt my fucking pupils dilate. I could feel my blood flowing through my body. I heard my lungs expanding.** I felt extremely calm, but aware and paranoid at the same time—it's hard to explain.

I got back to the room and everyone else was relatively calm.

"Are you okay, baby?" Lindsay asked.

"Yeah, I'm fine," I replied, even though I wasn't.

I had goose bumps for no reason, my heart rate sped up, I felt like I couldn't breathe, but like I could at the same time. For some reason, I started dancing; there was no music playing. I started babbling about nothing; it was just bad. I made out with everyone in the room, and I mean *everyone*. Even the two love birds. I was gone. Fortunately, Jordan got a text from Sean that the party had already started.

We had eventually decided to make our way across campus. We were fucked up! We were all paranoid, and kept telling each other to shush. Here's an accurate description of the events that followed: we all held hands going down the stairs—literally, one by one, with our backs up against the railings so that we wouldn't fall, like a class of preschoolers on their way to the playground. Then, when we got outside, we all walked in a straight line on the quad as quietly as possible because we were trying not to get written up by campus security. The more we tried being discreet and inconspicuous, the more we ended up looking guilty as fuck.

(Side note: Before I even address the party, I feel like I need to say this. Let me be clear: no one parties like white kids party.

Let me be even clearer: **no one** *parties like* **white college kids** *party. In simpler terms, it is just complete and utter messy chaos. When white kids party, they low-key try to end their lives, or to end up in a coma, at least. They do it to kill as many brain cells as possible. They do it to fuck and forget about what happened the morning after. They could be sucking dick in a gas station bathroom or doing a line on a toilet seat in an IHOP men's restroom Friday night, and come Monday morning, be bright-eyed and bushy-tailed at 6 a.m., ready for advanced chemistry class.)*

We had finally reached the soccer house after what felt like a thirty-minute walk. As soon as we walked in, the funk and heat hit us like ton of bricks. By that time, I was already coming down from the coke but I felt my feet for the first time that whole night. Fortunately, I was still drunk enough to notice the discomfort, but not feel any pain. Six-inch heels and drunk big girls don't match, unless they know what they're doing. When I say that the entire party was problematic, please don't take it lightly.

I looked to my left, and there were naked bitches walking around with platters of drugs—**platters**. No; they did not have on underwear or bras. These bitches were entirely birthday-suit, butt-ass naked. In one corner, people were playing beer pong, and "Quarters". In another, people were literally having sex. I looked around and people were jumping off of tables and out of windows—**out of fucking windows**! I turned to one window and saw people (*not* <u>one</u> person, **multiple** people) falling down onto a fucking trampoline from off of the second floor. I want to say that was the moment I realized that those kids really didn't give a fuck about their lives. Granted, I did try coke earlier that night, but still.

We danced for hours. Subwoofers filled our ears with Dubstep (white kids love Dubstep, by the way), "Ass" by Big Sean, and songs by the fucking Ying Yang Twins; that should explain the music selection for the night. Then again, what else can you expect from white kids in the boonies?

Let me tell you about how drunk I was. During that entire semester, I never danced with white guys because they just never really did it for me. They were cute, but their dancing skills were sub-par. It just dried me up. That's not racist; it's just how it is, okay? I saw how they danced with other girls and I refused to be subjected to that type of sadness. At the moment, though, I was too drunk to care anymore. I knew I was in trouble when I started twerking and grinding on multiple white guys that didn't know how to stay still. They couldn't just take the ass. At black parties, black guys usually hold girls by the waist and stand there, whereas, at white parties, white guys can't fucking stand still. That was one thing.

A girl walked up to me and we randomly started making out. There goes another one. This is where it gets interesting. Never have I ever, in my entire life, been attracted to feminine girls. I mean, don't get me wrong; I can appreciate their bodies from afar, but I've never actually acted on it because it just dries me up. So the fact that I had just made out with some of my closest friends *and* some random bitch I didn't even know really took the cake. I was officially white girl wasted. The room was spinning. The floor was sticky in one spot and slippery due to vomit, vodka, and God knows what else in the another.

I think the moment I realized I was in a fucked up spot and just could not hang any longer was when I glanced over at one point and saw a guy puke his brains out in the center of the floor. Said guy proceeded to kiss the girl he was hooking up with right before he had puked. The smell got to me and I felt the urge to hurl chunks right then and there.

Then I legitimately had a conversation with myself in my head.

"Self?" I said to myself.

"Yes, self?" I replied.

"Are you thinking what I'm thinking?" I asked.

"White people are crazy?" I responded.

"No, the other thing," I suggested.

My sanity and drunkenness had had a conversation and mutually agreed that it was time to go. I had to leave because the level of fuckery was far too extensive for my capacity. I looked around for my friends and saw Jessica making out with **both** Jordan **and** Sean. She kissed one then the other, then the other again. I was told Keegan and Lindsay had gone to the bathroom together. So I said "Fuck it, I'm out".

I made my way through the crowd and stumbled out the door. I managed to make it across the street without incident. I somehow, by the grace of God, found myself nearly approaching my dorm. By that time, it was 4 am and I could still hear the music blaring from all the way across campus. Surprisingly, I didn't receive a fine from campus security for public intoxication at all—and I had puked a couple times on the sidewalk on my way back. I even fell down in the fucking grass on the quad and stayed there for a good thirty minutes, just looking up at the stars. I just had to get my barrens straight.

When I got closer, I noticed a guy sitting on the bench outside, smoking a cigarette. His hair was covering the side of his face. He was looking down at his phone, so I couldn't make out who it was.

I staggered over to the bench and plopped down beside him.

"Hey, can I bum a smoke from you?" I asked.

He held his head up.

"They're Marlboro's" (I told you, white people love Marlboros) he replied. "They're the only kind I smoke."

I shrugged my shoulders. "That's fine."

He dug into his pockets, pulled the pack out, and reached it out to me. I literally felt like a four-year-old getting offered candy from a mall Santa. I gasped and put my hands over my mouth as if it were a present. I was so happy; scratch that, I was drunk.

I scooted in closer, pulled one from the pack, and put it into my mouth.

"Can I borrow your l—" and before I could finish my sentence, he was reaching to light my cigarette for me. What a precious fuckboy!

I pulled a drag from the cigarette and tried to look at him closer.

"Where do I know you from?" I asked.

He looked at me and flipped his blonde hair from his face.

"I think you're in my theater class," he side-smiled and shyly replied. "You're Tiy, right?"

I nodded my head in surprise. "Yeah, how'd you know?"

"Everyone knows who you and your friends are," he said. "People talk," he added.

I scoffed.

"Don't worry," he dragged from his cigarette. "Nothing bad about *you*. I heard you're the quiet one".

Even while drunk, I felt uncomfortable talking about people, especially about people I was friends with at the time. So I tried to change the subject.

"What about you?" I asked. "What's your name?"

For all intents and purposes, and for the time being, I'll call him "White Boy Timmy". He fit almost every single stereotype you could possibly think of when you think of a white guy. He had blond surfer hair and flipped it more than an "unbothered AKA". He wore cardigans, skinny jeans, and Vans. His ears were gauged and according to his Facebook page, he was into My Chemical Romance and Fall Out Boy.

He didn't talk to me like I was a token black girl, he was more so curious about who I was and what I was all about. Not once did he say "yo", or "girl", or refer to Hip-Hop or black culture. He didn't try to act "hip", which was refreshing because the people at Lycoming all seemed to when it came down to communicating with the few black people that attended. He seemed comfortable being himself around someone different and actually talking about issues. He was pretty philosophical, actually.

We talked about stars and astronomical constellations. We argued over scientific theories and fucking time travel. And to wrap it all up, we spoke about race relations, and Pangea. It was both intense and eye-opening for the both of us.

He was obviously high (he smelled like weed and laughed incessantly) and I was drunk as fuck. We were still able to talk about seriously complex issues, which was all-around cool.

We got each other's numbers but never really spoke that much afterwards. I'd see him in class, of course, and in passing, but that was about it. I later heard he had a girlfriend, which I never really cared about. But when I found out who it was, I was a bit disappointed. I was never attracted to White Boy Timmy or anything like that. The thing is, his girlfriend (who happened to live on my floor, by the way) was a racist bitch who had it coming (and very, very soon).

She was one of the most blatantly and carelessly disrespectful people I'd ever come across. She had never said anything to me personally, but she was a topic of discussion at a few Black Student Union meetings. I was just waiting for my chance to put her in her place, and eventually, the opportunity arose.

Alright guys. This is where things are about to take a terrible turn. From this point forward, understand that I am not the average petty person, as I've stated earlier in this book. Fuck hurting your feelings; I go after your pride. I come for your ego. I draw blood and ruin lives. If you want a cup of this tea, go grab your sugar cubes now.

4. Thanksgiving Break
∞

Let's flash forward to Thanksgiving break. Keegan invited me to stay over her house for the week. Even though we had been talking about it literally the entire month of November, I'm still not quite sure her family knew or remembered that I was supposed to be coming over. Her house was a filthy, disgusting, atrocious mess. It smelled like cat vagina and wet dog balls. Trash was all over the place, clothes were thrown across chairs and couches. The carpet had piss stains. The smell alone made my fucking soul dry-heave!

To be frank, I was pretty bummed. The white rich kids from my high school had maids to handle that. But regardless, what family allows their house to look and smell that way? Whenever we got the chance to go into town or leave the house, I was the first one out. That's how bad it was. I don't think I ever appreciated fresh air as much as I did during that week.

One night, we went over a couple of her friends' house to "chill", which (unbeknownst to me) meant entertaining a lame fuckboy while Keegan fucked the other one in another room. Now, I knew Keegan was cool, but I didn't realize most of her friends back at home were all black. She was a dainty, white girl from Reading, Pennsylvania. She lived in the boonies. I won't lie; I had some assumptions, but she was really down with the homies. Anyway, we pulled up to this mobile home, and I was left wondering just what the fuck Keegan was getting me into.

We walked in and there were two black guys. One's name was "James"; the other's name was "Aaron". Upon entrance, I was hit with the familiar aroma of weed. It took every bit of me not to cum right then and there in the doorway. I had spent most of my first semester of freshman year away from weed (granted, I did try coke that one time but that's neither here nor there).

I'm not going to lie; for a trailer, it was a pretty nice setup. The interior decor was stupendous. The living room/kitchen/dining room had nice lighting. The feng shui was out of this world. I was really digging it.

Anyway, we all ended up playing video games and smoking weed. Long story short, Keegan and Aaron excused themselves and went into a bedroom, giggling. When I say that within sixty seconds, the entire trailer started shaking rhythmically, I'm not exaggerating. Aaron was giving Keegan some "welcome back dick". It seemed like every time I looked to my left, James kept getting closer and closer.

"So tell me about yourself, beautiful," he said.

I tried my hardest not to curve him on account of him being such a gracious host—you know, with the weed and all. But to think that anything would come of it was another thing.

"Well, for starters," I replied, "I have a boyfriend" (which, I mean yeah, was a lie, but it seemed a lot less harsh than saying "I don't find you attractive, so back the fuck up").

He put his hand in my hair and twirled a couple strands around his fingers. I moved my head away from him and scooted further to the other side of the couch.

He inched closer, "So you can't have any f—" I cut him off.

I knew where this was going because it's the national fuckboy follow-up line.

"Actually no, I can't," I replied.

"But you can never have too many friends," he added.

He put his hand on my thigh and started sliding it closer to my crotch. I felt my heart racing. I grabbed him by the wrist and threw his hand back at him.

I cleared my throat.

"I'm good on the friends part," I said. "Thanks, though."

He just would not stop. He gathered my hair into his hand and moved it to the other side of my neck.

He licked his lips and whispered into my ear.

"You sure about that?" Then he grabbed my boob—big fucking mistake.

I slowly turned my head to him and blinked ever-so calmly. I glanced down at his basketball shorts and saw his little dick print, and then I chuckled.

I tried not to smile. "Can I ask you something, James?"

He licked his lips again.

"Go ahead, beautiful," he said.

"If I wanted to, say, cheat on my boyfriend," I clicked my tongue sarcastically and slapped his hand away, "don't you think I would do it with someone who didn't have a baby dick?"

He sucked his teeth and backed off.

"Fuck you, bitch!" he replied. "Don't nobody want your fat, ugly ass anyway!"

I chuckled again because it had become pretty obvious that he was butt-hurt.

I put my index finger on my bottom lip then pointed it at him upside down.

"But you was just tryna fuck, though, little dick nigga." I tilted my head and smirked. "Why're you mad?"

He ignored me and continued playing the video game. I laughed all the way to the bedroom and banged on the door. I didn't even wait for a response, I just flung it open.

Keegan was on her hands and knees getting fucked from behind. They both stopped in their tracks and looked at me.

"We need to go," I said, "right now." They were both breathing hard. "Finish up whatever the fuck you're doing, and I'll meet you in your car."

I looked at Aaron, stepped in, and hugged him (mind you, his dick was literally inside of Keegan).

"Ummm...It was nice to meet you, Aaron," I said. "Thanks for having me."

I walked back to the door and closed it behind me. I grabbed her keys from off of the table and looked at James (who was trying his hardest to ignore the fuck out of me, by the way).

"Bye, James," I said tauntingly.

He didn't look my way, but he raised his middle finger at me while he was still playing the game. I rolled my eyes, walked out, and slammed the door behind me. I got into the car and waited for Keegan.

You would think that that was the last time somebody had me fucked up in a major way, but it had only just begun.

The day before we headed back to campus, Keegan and I went to the movies with her brother and sister. Everyone in the Black Student Union club group chat was talking about Becky posting some racist ass shit on Facebook. Because we were at the movie theater, and Keegan lived in the boonies, I couldn't get to Becky's page and the fucking screenshots weren't coming through. Once we got back to her house, I ran in to connect to her Wi-Fi.

I won't get into exactly what she said; just know that the word "nigger" had been dropped multiple times. At first, I called White Boy Timmy's phone. He seemed like the logical person to get in contact with. The phone rang a couple times and then I was sent to voicemail. I called once more and the same thing happened. So I figured I'd shoot White Boy Timmy a courtesy text.

Long story short, I resorted to texting him to warn his girlfriend to take down the disgusting things she had posted on Facebook earlier that day.

"Handle your girlfriend, before I do."

That's all I texted. It wasn't sent as a threat, but a warning. Apparently, she had his phone because she ended up being the one that texted back.

She replied with something along the lines of "Or what, bitch? Why are you texting my boyfriend?"

We texted back and forth about the situation—and of course, being the rational person that I am, I gave her multiple chances to redeem herself. Scratch that, I gave her chances to save herself. Unfortunately, she did not take the bait. She continued with further pejorative comments about me and people that look like me. It took everything in my being to remain calm. But the moment she called me a "nigger" was the moment I was going to make her regret everything she had said. Becky obviously was not aware of the pettiness that would later occur, nor was she aware of the bad karma she had just brought upon herself.

I made her aware of the fact that I'm not, nor have I ever been into arguing over the phone. I had evolved from my hood rat ways, and I take pride in that. I brought it to her attention that I'm more of a "face-to-face kind of girl". Call me "ghetto". Shit, call me "crazy" (which she did), but if you ever call me a "nigger", it's a wrap! That's it. El fin. If I know where to find you, you might as well run, hide, and start new life. It's that serious.

I guess it's safe to say that I had already begun planning, plotting and scheming one of the most intricate revenge missions I've ever had the pleasure of watching unfold.

5. *For My Ancestors*
∞

So, we got back to school Sunday night. I did my nightly rituals to get ready for the next day. I woke up the next morning feeling so refreshed. You know that feeling you used to get when you woke up in the mornings and you smelled your mom cooking pancakes in the air? So carefree, so inspired. Well, I smelled an ass beating on that glorious Monday morning. I stretched, I yawned, I smiled. I looked up and saw Keegan coming back in the room after a shower.

"Good morning, love," I said extremely hyper.

"Why are you in such a good mood?" she asked.

"No particular reason," I replied.

You have no idea the amount of energy you get from knowing that you're about to ruin someone's life. I felt my ancestors above cheering me on and singing Negro Spirituals as I lie there. It was beautiful. I was atoned. I showered, did my hair, and went on my merry way to class much like I normally did. 11:59 am rolled around and you could not imagine the amount of ecstasy I felt knowing that I knew that Becky bitch would be in the cafeteria like she normally was every single weekday.

Noon hit and I was the first one out of the classroom. I always sat in the back (on account of my far-farsightedness), so that should say something about how quickly I was moving. I had a certain kind of pep in my step, for sure. I was so wrapped up in getting to Becky that I never even texted or looked for any of my friends to accompany me to lunch. I cut across the quad so fast; you would have thought that I was running from someone, or after someone. I was just in a different world. I had a one-track mind and the finish line was Becky's face. I was determined to do some serious damage to her—whether it physical, mental, or emotional. All three works too.

I was so excited that I dropped my backpack at the door and cut in the line to get my meal plan card swiped. The cashier handed me my card back. I put it in my back pocket, stepped in, and walked around the entire cafeteria until I found that bitch. I ignored people that were greeting and trying to hug me. I told you; I was on a mission.

Just when I thought I wouldn't find her, I circled back around and lo and behold, there she was! She was sitting down beside the bagels and waffle machine, surrounded by other Beckies. Did you think that the fact that she was surrounded by her friends deterred me from going over there? Honestly? Truly? Guess again.

I felt myself grinning, but there was nothing I could do to change my facial expressions into something a bit more appropriate. It was almost as if I were possessed by something greater than me. My eyes locked on her. I felt my blood pumping. I felt the veins along my wrists pulsating. I felt my hands trembling and my ears growing hotter. Hot head is a bit of an understatement, now that I think about it. I had to take a moment to calm down because I was scaring myself. I figured counting down from ten in my head would alleviate the situation, or at least de-escalate it. Eventually, I had stopped shaking.

So I moseyed on over there and greeted the other Beckies at the table. I was socially cool with most of them; they knew who I was on account of my scandalous group of friends.

"Do you ladies mind if I talk to Becky for a moment outside?" I asked, pulling Becky's chair from underneath her.

They just looked at each other awkwardly. Becky kept trying to push my arm away with her boney elbow. She looked up at me as if I were crazy (which I am). Then, she turned her head back to the table as if to continue the conversation I had interrupted when I came over. Now, I don't know about you, but being ignored just simply does not sit well with me.

So I politely tapped her on the shoulder to remind her that I was still there. She started coming up with excuses and at first, it sort of sounded like how adults sound on the Charlie Brown show.

All I heard was "wah, wah, wah, wah."

I couldn't make out exactly what she was saying. But when I heard the word "nigger", I snapped. All hell broke loose! All of a sudden, I was whaling on her, you guys! I heard the blows landing—the sound of flesh pounding into flesh. I really surprised myself because typically, I'm not at all a violent person; racism just brings something out of me. I don't really remember what happened, but I remember grabbing her by her blond hair and punching her over and over again. I had never before anyone go from white, to red, to blue so quickly in my life. It had gotten so bad that we started trampling on top of some of the girls at the table. Then I heard keys jingling, and footsteps running up behind me, pulling me off of her.

We ended up in the security office, with a big black security guard sitting between us. The head chief of security walked in, looked at us and shook his head.

"Ms. (Becky's last name)," he continued, "are you going to be looking into pressing charges?"

She and I locked eyes. I started getting nervous and sweating. She squinted her eyes and looked back at the head chief. Of course, she took advantage of trying to play the victim (which, she technically was). She began lying and claiming that I walked up to her and randomly started punching her in the face.

I jumped up and lunged over the guard toward her, but he picked my big ass up and put me back into my seat.

"Yo, calm down," the guard sitting between us said.

"No!" I replied. "She called me a nigger."

"No, I didn't," Becky replied. "I would never say that word."

"Unfortunately, Ms. (Becky's last name)," the chief said, "I've spoken to a lot of the students, and all of their stories validate what Tiy just said."

Becky's shoulders slumped. She looked defeated. She was caught in a lie.

Thank God none of her friends were really rocking with her, because all of them told the truth, even about the part about Becky calling me a nigger.

"Right now, Ms. (Becky's last name), there is nothing I can do," the chief said. "My hands are tied. If you do choose to file charges, you will need to take a trip to the local police department."

He looked at me. "As for the both of you, this is a warning." I looked up. "If either of you is involved in another altercation, that will be your last day on this campus. Do you both understand me?"

We nodded and he dismissed us one by one. He told me I could leave first and that was that. I don't know what happened or what was said when I left but Becky avoided the hell out of me for the rest of the semester.

A few weeks later...

It was December. Things had definitely died down. Sometimes, Becky and I would cross paths, but we somehow managed to avoid having any further incidents. Translation: whenever she'd see me, she'd change her direction immediately.

Little did she know, a bloodied nose was not the end of it. We had just barely scratched the surface. I was waiting for any and all opportunities to further ruin her; that day had finally come. Hell hath no fury like an angry black woman out for revenge. Remember that. The physical damage had already been taken care of. The emotional damage was yet to come. That took time. That took planning.

The events that would later take place happened as if they were right out of a college dramedy. Cue the suspenseful music. After beating up Becky, I spent the next three weeks trying to set up a deal of the century, and it cost me a date with Lindsay.

You know how they say God never comes when you want him to, but he always comes on time? You have no idea!

One day, after drama class on the last week before finals, I walked up to the teacher assistant and worked my magic. It wasn't because I needed help writing a screenplay or questions on iambic pentameter; it was because I saw an opportunity and I snatched the fuck out of it. I remember Lindsay telling me about a cute theater guy that kept liking all her photos and statuses on Facebook named Will. Will happened to be the T.A. for the drama department. Guess whose class Will led when the drama professor chose not to come to class. I think you're catching on.

I broke it down to him. I asked him if he knew a girl named Lindsay, and it rang a bell. His eyes lit up.

"What would you say if I told you she's one of my best friends?" I asked.

He raised an eyebrow. "I'm intrigued."

"Now, what would you do if I told you I could get you a date with her?"

At first, he didn't believe me, but then I pulled my Blackberry (yes, I had a Blackberry at the time, don't judge me) out and showed him texts between us that proved that we were pretty close.

"I'll do anything!"

And just like that, I had him! After I told him what I needed, he thought he was getting over on me, but he was just a mere pawn in the elaborate chess game that was Mission Sabotage Becky.

Final exam week was upon us. I had held up my end of the bargain, and now it was his turn to hold up his. Will was in charge of assigning partners for the final dialogues. I persuaded him to make it so that I would have a certain partner, who many of you may remember. I'm going to give you a moment to guess who that partner was.

If you guessed "White Boy Timmy", then come on down! You are the next contestant on *The Pettiness is Right!* Doesn't it sound like a blockbuster movie just waiting to be in theaters?

Long story short, I walked up to White Boy Timmy at the end of our last class. It was a little awkward on account of the fact that I had recently beaten up his girlfriend.

"Dude, I know this puts you in a fucked up position. But we have to study and memorize this dialogue."

He nodded his head, "That's fine with me. But why would it put me in a fucked up position?"

"Because you're with Becky."

He shook his head, "Me and her have been done for a couple weeks now."

I was a little saddened. I figured my scheme would not go as planned. I thought all my hard work would have been all for naught. Being that Keegan had already taken her finals, she was already gone. So I told him that I had the room to myself and that we could totally run lines together that day.

So, he came over and reminded me how cool he was. We were laughing and joking around, trying to be serious while reading our script. We couldn't help it. While we were sitting on the bed, he was showing symptoms only emblematic of the fuckboy syndrome. It's very hard to explain, but he was giving off subtle hints here and there. Every time he received a text message, he turned his phone away from me so that I couldn't see who it was.

Being that the dorm that I lived in had a heating problem, and I have always literally had cold feet, I asked if I could put my feet under his butt. At the time, I wasn't trying to flirt at all. But something deep in my pit told me to pretend like I was interested.

And sure enough, it worked. Out of nowhere, he asked me a question I thought would take him all night to ask.

"Have you ever gotten head from a white guy?" he asked.

I swallowed a gulp of spit nervously. At that time, I had never gotten head from anyone because I was an angel, relatively. Fuck, I was still a virgin.

I flattened my lips, and shook my head.

"No, I'm an angel," I replied and smiled.

He flipped his surfer hair. "Do you want to?"

I didn't know what to do! It was all happening so fast! I was starting to think I couldn't go through with my own plan.

I pursed my lips.

"Fuck it," I replied. "What do I do?"

He laughed.

"You're so cute," he said. I rolled my eyes. "Just lay back and relax."

I took a deep breath and did what he told me to do. I felt my body shaking. No one had ever gone down there but my gynecologist (and even then, her hand had gotten locked in between my legs on multiple occasions).

He tried to slide my underwear off but it was just not working out for him. After what felt like forever, he had finally gotten them off and I clenched my legs together and placed my hands over my face. Don't ask why girls do that; we just do. It's a reflex of some sort.

White Boy Timmy was just not having it, you guys! He yanked my legs open with such force that had I not known how to fight, I would have been afraid.

"Tiy, relax!" he said. "I'm not going to hurt you."

So I listened and relaxed my body.

When he got down there, he blew on my pussy. He pushed back the hood and started sucking on my clit. The entire sensation changed my life. Fireworks went off, I swear! After that moment, I was never the same. My entire body went numb and I could not move. But I felt every single thing.

White Boy Timmy was going to town on my pussy. He was spelling his name out with his tongue on the clit, swirling, fingering—literally doing all the right things. Have you ever had head so good that it stopped time—**stopped fucking time?** This was the type of head that you had to get out of your clothes for.

For whatever reason, my dumb ass got the nerve to tell him to spit on it. I never realized how big of a mistake that was until he did.

I ended up taking all of my clothes off because it had gotten too hot! All of a sudden, he started motor-boating my pussy. White Boy Timmy was killing it, you guys! My first time getting head and it was from a white guy who knew exactly what to do with his tongue. What were the odds?

His phone was beside me on the bed, charging. For whatever reason, in every dorm on campus, the electrical sockets were all oddly high up on the walls.

Mid-pussy eating, he received a text message. His phone dinged, so he stopped. He then picked his phone up to reply, turned the volume off, and put it back down beside me. Then he went back to work. I felt his phone vibrate while he feasted on me. I'm a pretty nosy person (always have been, always will be, but only if it concerns either me or my pussy) and I honestly don't give a fuck (never have, never will).

I lifted my head up slightly and snuck a peek at his phone. Imagine my surprise when I saw who was texting him. It was that Becky bitch (even though less than an hour before, he was feeding me some bullshit story about how they had broken up)! Even better!

"Hey babe," she texted. "What are you up to?"

Let's just say that at that moment, I was a little livid because it had hit me that he was still with her. But, then again, this was amazing news (well, not at all for him, and certainly not for Becky)! He had lied to me and above all of that, used me to act out on his curiosity. I was going to make him regret every bit of the lie he had told me, just like I made that bitch regret ever having a Facebook page.

It's understandable that his life would, in turn, need to be ruined as well. You get that, right? Please tell me I'm not some insane, crazy person unnecessarily out for vengeance! I don't think I could live with myself.

Okay, maybe I could. In other news, the scheme was back on! I had a limited amount of time to act on it. I could move forward with the initial plan, and to be honest, I was a little too excited about it. Like, scary excited.

Because I like to consider myself "Princess Petty", of course I had to live up to my name. I picked up his Red Samsung Rant phone and prepared for the kill.

Would you believe me if I were to tell you that I slowly slid the phone up, clicked on the camera icon, and snapped a candid photo of him eating my pussy?

Would you also believe that I sent that photo to his darling Becky with the caption "he's a little busy"? If you thought that I was incapable of doing such terrible things, you obviously have no idea how much pride I take in my pettiness.

Within a matter of fifteen seconds, his phone started blowing up! I squeezed it hard, trying to muffle the vibrations. Becky kept fucking calling. Keep in mind that White Boy Timmy was still down there!

By that point, I couldn't understand how the fuck White Boy Timmy hadn't caught lockjaw, but I had to tap the fuck out. I rolled over. He grabbed me by the waist and turned my entire body around so that I was on my knees, facing the wall. My ass was in the air.

"Stay just like that," he yelled out.

He began eating my pussy from the back, guys! That shit was golden! Deep down in my spirit, I knew in my heart of hearts that my ancestors were up there, doing both the Electric and Cha Cha slides! All of a sudden, I felt him rubbing on my asshole. My body went limp and I fell forward.

He grabbed me by my waist again and lifted me back up. Keep in mind that Becky was still calling. My hand was still clutching onto the phone. Fortunately, my moans were doing a pretty good job at cancelling out the noise from the vibrations, but eventually I turned it off just to be safe.

I was low-key speaking in tongues. White Boy Timmy had a face full of pussy. People were banging on the walls and on the door. This head was epic! This head was historical. This is what Dr. Martin Luther King, Jr. had died for—okay, not really, but it was still amazing.

I hadn't noticed how far to the edge my body had gotten until I fell off of the bed and hit my head on the marble floor. White Boy Timmy really meant well. He tried to catch my big ass but the damage had already been done.

After he helped me up, he literally tried fingering up against the wall, while I was still trying to regain my balance and catch my breath.

"No!" I moaned out. "I'm done with your crazy ass."

I panted, fanned myself, and pushed him away with the other hand. I backed into a corner. He came back toward me and tried to slip his hand right back in between my legs.

I slapped his hand away.

"No, _____ (his real name)," I said. "You should really go."

He backed away, thought about it, and took another step.

"I'm serious," I said.

He sucked his teeth and readjusted his boner. He ran his fingers through his hair and picked up his script.

"By the way," I said, "your '*ex*' has been calling for the past twenty minutes. But don't worry; I told her you were busy, though."

His eyes grew wider. He grabbed his phone and yanked his charger out of the wall. He pushed me out of the way in hopes of doing some damage control.

"Don't be so dramatic," I nonchalantly said with an evil grin.

White Boy Timmy was gone, you guys! He moved quicker than Flash! He moved quicker than a white woman locking her doors when she sees a black man walking on a sidewalk. He moved quicker than a cop pulling a gun on an unarmed black teen because he "feared for his life". He moved quicker than that girl in the State Farm commercial should have when she reached for that dollar on the fishing rod! He ran so fast, the papers on my desk caught a whiff of the air and scattered to the floor. I could hear him running down the steps. He ran so fast, the pictures on my walls were fucking shaking. To say the least, he moved pretty fucking fast.

After I fully processed what had just happened, I hopped in the shower. I got dressed and placed a chair in the center of the room, facing my door. I sat down with my switchblade in hand, waiting for Becky to come through my door for about an hour. But she never showed up.

The last day of drama class rolled around. I was sitting in class, talking to my homies, when in walked White Boy Timmy.

For a couple seconds, the room grew silent. He had not one, but *two* black eyes. When he sat down, a part of me wanted to feel really bad for the guy. But then again, he had lied to me. So the other part of me really wanted to gather his tears in a cup and drink them.

How the fuck did Becky beat his ass, when I never caught any hands from her? When the professor called our names, he looked at me and I looked at him. I cleared my throat and smiled. We walked up to the front of the classroom, did our dialogue, and sat back down. I think the saddest part was the fact that **no one** commented on his black eyes, you guys! Oh, it was so sad! The news spread faster than a syphilis outbreak.

Fortunately, we got an A. It could have been because Lindsay ended up fucking Will, but I won't question God's will. After that day, I never heard from White Boy Timmy or Becky again.

When we got back from Christmas break, I found out that both of them had transferred to another college in the city. (I later found out that they graduated from the same school in May of 2015 together.) I guess the moral of this chapter is *don't be racist*. Also, don't be liar. In any and all circumstances, pettiness always prevails. This was just the beginning of my pettiness fiasco. That was the day that the savage in me was born, and it's been inside of me kicking and doing well ever since.

6. Shoot & Miss

∞

Freshman Year, 2012

It was second semester and first semester grades didn't look quite as good as I wanted them to. So, I had to make a lot of sacrifices. The first sacrifice I had to make was friends. I had to make the decision to cut myself off from a lot of people. A lot of drama had begun to unravel between Jessica, Sean and Jordan, and I wanted nothing to do with that destructive love triangle, so I distanced myself. I had love for them, but I didn't need the added drama coming my way.

Lindsay ended up rushing to join a sorority, and Keegan transferred at the last minute. So, I had the room to myself, which allowed me to focus on college and college only. Because of that, I spent most of my time alone, focusing on grades and whatnot.

I met a girl named Ava in Spanish class, and we hit it off pretty well. She was a twenty-one-year-old freshman that took a couple gap years to travel. She seemed pretty level-headed, but boy, did she know how to fucking drink.

One night, to celebrate midterm grades, Ava and I decided to go to a local club called Synergy (which was actually lame, but was the only club the both of us could get into because I was only 19). Synergy was having a foam party. That night, she and I got drunker than we should have with her fuckbuddy, Alex. We drank white, brown, and some jungle juice Alex had brought over from his frat-house. It was lethal and ptotent!

He was a red-headed fuckboy (but a fuckboy nonetheless) who was talking to another girl at the time. Ava was in love with the guy, but he treated her like shit. That's just how fuckboys are; they're magical, mythical creatures that can hypnotize girls with charm and blatant disrespect. No matter how bad of a vibe I got from him, she didn't want to hear it. So, I stayed out of her business and she stayed out of mine.

Long story short, we ended up in the club and for a while, I was the third wheel. Ava and Alex were practically fucking on the dance floor, just with clothes on. Now normally, as I've stated before, white people can't dance. But if you add some cheap Vodka and Tennessee Whiskey on top of that, it's just a mess. It looked like Alex was fingering Ava, but I couldn't tell because the foam was up to our stomachs.

I had been ready to go home from the moment we made our way down the stairs and walked out of my dorm. That's how boring it was. The club was packed; I just wasn't feeling it at all. Around that time (circa 2012), white people fell *in love* with Dubstep music. I am a **black** girl from the <u>hood</u>. I could not, for the life of me, get jiggy with it.

    I was dancing with some white guy. Well, I was *trying* to dance with him. I was throwing that ass back and he didn't know what to do with it. He danced behind me, jerking my hips around and moving all off beat. It was so sad! After a while, I got fed up and stopped dancing. Eventually, homeboy got the hint and walked away. I pulled my phone out, trying to make the time pass. We were *in a club*, in a fucking **<u>college town</u>**! How sad is that?!

    All of a sudden, I noticed the scent of a familiar cologne. My knees weakened. I felt someone put their hands on my waist and their dick on my butt. I could tell he wasn't white. I just knew it. It wasn't necessarily the size of his dick, but the way in which he held me. He didn't seem hesitant or afraid. I didn't turn around; I just kept dancing. I waved my phone at Ava to get her attention. She was dealing with her "situation", but she had finally looked over. I sneakily put my thumb up and down to figure out whether or not the guy behind me was cute. Girls do this all the time. Pleasantly, to my surprise, she nodded her head immediately, which meant that he was fine as fuck. She knew my type and she got it right every time!

    I slowly turned my head and I saw his face. It was Ricardo—the sexy ass Puerto Rican guy that worked at the Rite Aid across the street from campus! He was fine as hell—so fine that I think the only appropriate measure of expressing his "fineness" would be to list off some analogies to help you fully understand his fuckability. He was honey bun in a microwave for exactly eight seconds fine. He was freshly baked hot fudge brownies with vanilla ice cream on top fine. He was lobster and shrimp stuffed crab drizzled in Jesus' cum fine!

I smelled Henny on his breath—or it could've been my breath. I don't know; I was fucked up. That's how much I drank. I can't even tell you how I managed to stay standing for so long. Hennessey does things to people. With it, *Hennything* is possible. That was the night I realized that if you're drinking Hennessey, you might as well top that off with a Plan B pill, because you're getting pregnant, baby girl.

I turned around, wrapped one arm around his neck and guided one of his hands up my dress with my other hand. I felt his warm hands against my lips and I quickly became wet.

He started fingering me in the center of the floor. We were literally surrounded by hundreds of people. He started biting me on my neck and whispering Spanish into my ear during the music break. I understood everything he was saying, which only got me wetter.

"I want to stick my tongue in your pussy," he said in Spanish, still fingering me.

"Is that so?" I replied.

"Ain't that what you want me to do?" he asked.

I felt myself about to cum, and I leaned my head all the way back then came back up.

"I want you to do whatever you want to do to me."

The music started up again. He began kissing me on my neck and flicking his fingers faster and faster. Then I came. He slowly pulled his hand from between my legs, stuck his middle finger in his mouth, pulled it out, and licked his lips.

He mouthed the words "come here" and I obliged him. He kissed me and I hesitantly pulled my head back. He smacked his teeth and grabbed me by my hair. He put his fingers in my mouth and I tasted myself for the first time. I fell in love with it. Then he sloppily shoved his tongue down my throat. At that point, I didn't care because I was so hung up on the way I tasted. I licked my lips again and touched them. I leaned into him and put my lips to his ear.

"Come back to campus with me," I yelled over the music.

"Okay, cool," he said.

He had to go get his things from the table his friends were at and told me he would meet me at the door.

I walked over to Ava to tell her I was leaving.

"With who?" she asked as if she were my mom.

I scanned the club with my eyes and pointed out to him. He was dapping his friends at their table. She asked how well I knew him.

"Good enough," I replied.

I guess she was too drunk to process my answer, and I was too drunk to give a fuck. He was fine as fuck and you know how that goes.

She shook her head and made me promise to call her as soon as I got back on campus. I promised her, gave her a kiss, and headed to the other side of the club. (I never fucking called her back. I'm a terrible friend and I hate myself every day because of it.)

When I got to the front, he was waiting there for me, with his abs poking through his soaked white t-shirt. I saw every rip, every single fucking beautiful cut.

I don't think you guys understand how beautiful this man was. Everything about him was perfect—the way the waves rested on his short hair, the way the light reflected off the water on his tattooed arms. I could've cried but my pussy did it for me.

We made it to my dorm and nearly tumbled down the stairs trying to make out.

"Get a fucking room," someone yelled out as they passed us on the stairwell.

We stopped, chuckled, then went back to kissing. It was a disgusting, sloppy drunk kiss that forces you to catch your breath. He banged me up against my door and started kissing me all over. I tried to put the key into the lock but I just couldn't find the hole.

After literally thirty seconds of me trying to get the key in, alas! Once we stumbled in, he didn't give me a chance to get completely settled at all. He held me by the face with both hands, kissing me. I threw my keys, kicked off my heels, and dropped my phone on the floor. There were absolutely no remnants of a fuck to be given, which was typically the case whenever I was drunk. He guided me to the bed then threw me onto it.

"You ready?" he asked as if he were about to Magic Mike rock my world.

He stumbled back and began slowly taking off his shirt. He was too drunk to flex his abs, but he was naturally ripped that he didn't even need to. I motioned at him to come closer, and he did. He slowly climbed on top of me and aimed for my mouth again. I turned my head and his lips landed on my cheek. I've never really been the type of girl able to kiss a stranger. I don't know where that started; that's just how I am.

"So, you want to play hard to get?" he asked. "We can play that game."

He licked his lips again and let his eyes melt down my face, then my neck, and finally my chest. He smirked.

"Do you want me to touch you?" he asked, waiting for me to reply.

I never said a word. I was so enamored with his face that I could only focus on fantasizing about what his lips would feel like munching on my pussy. I'm not going to lie; I was far too familiar with playing the innocent act. That was my go-to game plan. For whatever reason, guys love that shit.

There's just something about tainting innocence that really gets their dicks hard.

I'm not quite sure how he knew I was still a virgin; he just did. He must have seen it in my eyes.

"Tell me when to stop," he said.

"Okay," I murmured out and chuckled.

He nodded his head and glanced back down at my body. He slowly slid one sleeve off my shoulder and then the other. He helped me get my arms out and pulled the dress down to my stomach. He kissed on my shoulder—then on my collarbone. I felt the warmth of my wetness between my legs, causing my lips to stick to one another every time I readjusted my body in reaction to his kisses.

He pulled my dress down my thighs, past my knees, and before I knew it, it was off. He lifted my body up and unclasped my bra from behind. Then he laid me back down. He pulled one of my boobs out and wrapped his lips around my nipple. He pulled the other out and lightly pinched, tugged on, and twisted it. I cringed and he flicked his tongue across my nipple. The more I cringed, the faster he would flick it. What made it even worse was that he was dry humping me through his pants. I felt his dick poking me. I felt it growing larger and larger the harder it got.

I watched him pull his hand to his mouth, spit on it, then place it between my legs. I gasped sharply. The slick from his spit colliding against my clit only intensified the sensation. My back arched in ecstasy.

He pressed up against my clit harder, massaging it in a clockwise motion (then counter-clockwise, and clockwise again), all while he continued sucking and licking on my nipples.

I placed my hands over my mouth and moaned into my palms. He grabbed the both of them with one hand and pinned them both above my head. He wanted to hear me scream. He wanted to hear me cry. He wanted to hear me moan. We made eye contact for an uncomfortable amount of time as he fiddled with my swollen clit. I watched him watch me make faces of pleasure. The best ones are the ones that look like you're in pain. I pushed my head back into my pillow and screamed out. Every time I tried to bring my legs together, Ricardo would slap them back open.

I looked down at him and saw sweat trickling down his forehead. That's how you know he's really putting in work. That's how you can tell he's only focused on you and you only. Sometimes, my body went into the London Bridge position trying to get away from this nigga.

Out of nowhere, he lifted my body up, put his thighs underneath my back, and ordered a mouthful of pussy (heavy on the juice, by the way). He was eating me out from a 45° angle. Have you ever been eaten out from a fucking acute angle? It's quite ravishing, to say the least.

At that time, the beds had been arranged as bunk beds for a while. I reached my arms up and grabbed onto a railing. I started doing pull-ups but he paid it no mind because he was glued to my pussy at all times. At one point, he ended up on the floor, on his knees, while I was holding onto the side of the bed. I slid down further onto his face. His arms were holding up my thighs, which meant his face was consequently buried in my thighs.

For some reason, I had gotten a little too comfortable and let the side of the bed go. All of my weight was on his shoulders, and he was taking it like a champ. I ran my fingers through his waves. We had almost tipped over, but he stood completely up and sat me down *on the top bunk*! He was comfortably eating me out from at least five feet in the air. Have you ever gotten head from someone that took you higher, philosophically and physically—someone that made you feel like you were on drugs? He rubbed his face into my pussy, smothering himself, willingly.

I don't know if it was my fear of heights or the intensity of the situation, but I lied on my back. My body trembled—violently. He slowly lifted my legs up while still eating and traced his fingers along the backs of them—from my ankles, to my calves, down to the back of my knees, and down my thigh. He then used his fingers to open up my pussy. He pulled back the hood of my clit, exposing it. He started sucking on it, lightly lifting and bobbing his head with every slow sucking stroke. His lips were warm up against my smooth clit.

I gasped for a brief moment and listened to the clicking noises as his fingers maneuvered in and out of me. I kicked his arm out and forced my cream out as well. I let out a high-pitched squeal. Then I grunted—it wasn't sexy at all, but it didn't stop him. He slowly forced a finger back in and I moaned out. He eased in another. He pulled them out and stuffed them back inside of me, over and over again. He stirred my creams and juices inside of me, mixing them. I lifted my body up and he finally pulled them out. I watched him separate his fingers while the cream retracted between the two. It oozed down his knuckles and the back of his hand.

"Oh. So you're a creamer *and* an oozer," he said excitedly.

He drove his fingers into his mouth and closed his eyes in a trance. He moved his tongue around the outsides of mouth as if he had genuinely enjoyed his meal.

He opened his eyes and reached his fingers out to me, offering a sample. I looked at his face, then his fingers, then his face again. I grabbed onto his wrist with both hands and guided his fingers into my mouth. He must've been into how nasty I was willing to be with him because he grabbed me by my waist again and brought me down to the bottom bunk. (I honestly think you guys keep overlooking the fact that he was picking me up on multiple occasions, effortlessly. He was fit, but I was easily twice his size.)

He looked at me for permission. I nodded my head and bit my lip. He dug into his pocket and pulled a condom out. I swear I blinked and within two seconds, he was out of his pants *and* boxers. He crouched down and licked my pussy again. I heard the condom wrapper drop to the floor and the condom pop onto his dick. He never flinched. He stood and lifted one leg over his shoulder. He bit my calf and slapped his dick on my pussy.

And then...

He puked *everywhere*! It was literally **projectile vomit**! It slid down my leg and into my pussy. It splashed onto my stomach and into my hair. I felt it glide down into the crack of my ass! He just stood there, rocking. I panicked. I legitimately freaked out. The worst part was that it wasn't chunky; it was straight fucking liquor!

"Oh my G—," I choked on my words, gagging and pushing my vomit back down my esophagus.

I took a deep breath and remained frozen.

"Why!" I screamed out with a broken voice.

I jumped up and ran past him to my dirty clothes hamper. I pulled out my hair towel and wiped the vomit out of my pussy and ass. That was priority #1—first and foremost. I wiped it off my stomach. I pulled out another two towels from my closet, wrapped one around me, and gave him one to clean himself off with.

I checked my pillows and surprisingly, they were safe. So I threw them onto my desk. I stripped my bed and wrapped everything up into the fitted sheet.

"I'm so sorry" he murmured out, slumped on the floor.

"Chill out," I replied, breathing through my mouth. "It's cool. Just—"

I couldn't even look at him without wanting to gag. I sighed.

"Don't worry about it," I added. "I'll be right back."

I tossed the towel I had wrapped around me and the one with the majority of the vomit into the fitted sheet. I pulled out some shorts and a t-shirt to put on. I grabbed my laundry card and a few laundry pods. I ran down the steps trying my hardest to continue breathing through my mouth because the smell alone made me dry heave. I got to the laundry room, separated the ball of laundry into three different washing machines, and chose the "very hot" cycle for each and every load.

I headed back upstairs and regretted the events that had led up to that moment. When I got back to my room, he was still on the floor. I grabbed the towel I gave him and laid it across the bottom bed. I slapped him a few times (which I will admit, I enjoyed) to wake him up. I got him into the bed, grabbed a crochet fleece that Keegan had made me for Christmas, and threw it over him. I put a trash bag into my trash bin and put it off to the side of the bed near his head.

I poked him in the shoulder and pointed it out to him where the trash bin was. He nodded and put his head back down. I got out my Clorox wipes and cleaned up what was on the floor. Even when drunk off my ass, I still somehow managed to be someone's fucking baby-sitter. Even when a nigga was eating me out, I still ended up being his fucking mother. I can't make this shit up!

I sprayed my room with Lysol disinfectant spray and air freshener until the fumes burned my nose and made my eyes water. Then I opened up both of the windows. The chilly air blew in and saturated the room.

I ripped my clothes off and literally ran to the shower. It took *two* showers to get that fucking vomit smell off of me. I washed my hair four times—*four fucking times*! By the time I got out and walked into my room, he was out like a light. I felt his snoring vibrating through the floor. He was getting some good sleep.

I dug out a cami and some leggings. Then I ran downstairs to put my laundry into the dryer. By the time I got back upstairs, I was too dizzy to do anything else. I grabbed my phone, climbed up on the top bunk, and took my ass to bed.

When the sun was just shy of rising, I woke up to a tickle in the back of my throat. I jumped off of the bed and nearly broke my fucking ankle. I sprinted (not ran; sprinted) to the bathroom to puke my guts up. The entire floor was silent except for my retching echoing throughout the halls.

I think I held the toilet seat tighter than any man has ever held me in my entire life (and I've dealt with some smothering ass, clingy ass, crazy ass niggas). I gagged so hard and with such force that it gave me a headache and made my face hot. My ears rang. When I flushed the toilet, I heard the stairwell doors slam open, followed by loud footsteps vibrating down the walls. I wiped my mouth and rinsed it out at the sink. I didn't even care to rush back to my room because I knew it was him that was leaving in such a hurry.

I figured it would be a good idea, since I was up, to go ahead and run down to get my things out of the dryer. When I got back upstairs, I threw everything but the comforter onto my desk. Then I wrapped myself up in the warm blanket and lied down on the bottom mattress. When I checked my phone, it was around 5:30 am right before I closed my eyes. When I opened them back up, it was 6 **pm**. I checked my phone and I literally had over 50 missed calls and texts from Ava freaking out. When I finally decided to call her back, security was already keying into my dorm room.

I want more than anything to tell you all that that was the lowest point in my life—that there were no other bad decisions made on my part with the assistance of alcohol. Then again, you wouldn't be reading this book. I guess you can say that that day was the day I promised myself that I would never drink again.

7. Check, Please

April, 2012

It had been weeks since I had stepped foot in Rite Aid after the whole "puke in the pussy" incident. I was scarred; I think I still am, honestly. I didn't think I could handle seeing Ricardo the same way. I mean yes, don't get me wrong; he was still beautiful, but there's just something about having someone's stomach acid drip down into your pussy that really kills the vibe.

One day, I persuaded Ava to walk with me to the Rite Aid across the street from school just in case I needed her to go in to get me cigarettes. I didn't want to see Ricardo.

She stepped in, looked to the right, and walked down an aisle looking for the Puke Bandit. He was nowhere to be found. She gestured at me that the coast was clear. I sighed relieved. I stepped in and looked at the checkout section. Casey was standing behind the counter smiling at her phone (which should've been a warning to stay away from her, but I digress).

I walked up to the counter. She noticed me, smiled, and tucked her phone away in her back pocket.

"Hey," she said. "Wassup Tay! How you been beautiful?"

I cringed.

"Tiy," I said.

She squinted her eyes.

"Huh?" she said.

"It's Tiy," I explained. "My name…it's Tiy."

"Oh," she said. "He *did* say 'Tiy'. I just smoke too much weed. Sorry about that."

She laughed and I awkwardly laughed with her. I knew exactly who she was referring to as "he", but I tried to avoid it.

"Please tell me you're not here to get what I think you're here to get," she said.

I gracelessly smiled. She sucked her teeth, stepped back, and folded her arms.

"Come **on**, bro," she said. "How many times do I have to tell you that you're too cute to be smoking?!"

I pouted awkwardly and locked eyes with Ava.

"She won't listen," Ava casually said, looking through the makeup display right beside me. "I've been telling her to stop since we met."

I sneered at her. I gave her the most dedicated, thoroughly-thought out and planned "Bitch, shut the fuck up" face.

I scoffed and sucked my teeth.

"Y'all act like I smoke seven packs a day or some shit," I said. "I barely smoke *two* cigarettes in a day!"

Casey poked her lips out and looked to the corner of her eye.

"Alright," she said. "I have a proposition for you."

I folded my arms and tilted my head.

"I'm listening," I said calmly.

She turned around and opened the tobacco window. She reached in, pulled something out, and locked the window behind her.

She placed a cheap vapor on the counter. Of course, she picked out a pink one.

"Alright," she said. "So, check it. You get *maybe*, what? Like 10-15 puffs per cigarette, right?"

"Twenty, actually," I interjected.

She rolled her eyes.

"Okay, twenty, fuck," she said, corrected. "With this vape, you get like over 600 puffs! That's like three or four times as many you get from a whole pack of cigarettes, plus it's only six bucks. No carcinogens, no tobacco, no nicotine. Just water vapor."

I rolled my wrists twice to get her to finish telling me the proposition.

"I guarantee that if you try this out for one week, I can get you to quit cigarettes," she said. "That's part one."

I dropped my head downwards to get her to finish up.

"And what's part two?" Ava asked for me.

I looked over at her again, spreading my arms out in annoyance.

"If you let me take you out on a date, I guarantee it'll be the best one you've ever gone on."

I pursed my lips, trying not to smile.

"And what's in it for me?" I asked flirtatiously.

"Well," Casey said. "For one, you get me—the fuck?"

I smirked.

"Uh huh…" I replied.

"And if the vape doesn't work," she said, rolling her eyes, "I'll buy you a whole carton of Marlboros from Sam's Club."

I placed my elbow into one hand and pressed my chin into my index and thumb finger.

"You, Miss Casey," I said, "make a pretty convincing argument."

She scrunched her lips up and raised her eyebrows, nodding her head in agreement.

"Duh," she said.

I stood there for ten seconds.

"A whole carton?" I asked.

"Yah," she said, nodding.

"Of Marlboros?" I added.

She sucked her teeth.

"Yes, man," she said annoyed. "The deal is only on the table for ten more seconds. Make up your mind."

"But that's like $60, bro," I said nonchalantly.

She looked her at her watch and held her hand up. She held up five fingers, then dropped one, then another, and another.

"Tiy!" Ava yelled out.

"Okay," I said, smirking. "You've got a deal."

I sighed and smiled. She stuck her hand out. I reached mine out and we shook on it. She reached into her back pocket with her other hand, unlocked it, and handed it to me. I locked my phone number in and we had a deal.

She side-smiled and her butt-chin poked out.

"So, what are you doing tonight?" she asked.

"Well, it's a Tuesday, and I have no life," I giggled out. "So, nothing."

"How does six sound?" she asked.

"Six sounds perfect," I replied.

"Bet," she said calmly.

She finally rang the vape up.

"Your total is $6.42," she said.

I handed her a ten and she gave me my change and receipt.

"So, six o'clock tonight," she said, reminding me almost as if I had already forgotten.

"Yes," I chuckled out.

"K," she said, licking her lips as Ava and I walked out.

"Oh," she shouted out. "Which dorm you in?"

I stepped back.

"Asbury," I replied. She nodded.

5:30 rolled around and I got a text from her letting me know that she was leaving her house and was on her way to me. I had a last minute outfit change. I decided on an off-the-shoulder pink top, with a distressed jean skirt I had gotten from Forever21. I paired them with some wedge flip-flops and took down my pin curls. I really got dolled up for this girl! In hindsight, looking back at it, I looked an absolute fucking mess, but it was cute in 2012!

    She was outside my dorm by 5:56. I was already outside, trying to get used to that pathetic fucking vape but it just was not working out. She honked her horn. I put it away and jumped in.

    "Hey beautiful," she said, smiling.

    She looked even better outside of her Rite Aid polo. She was looking rather scrumptious, actually.

    "Damn, I don't get no hug or nothing?" she asked jokingly.

    "I'm sorry," I said, snickering. "My bad."

    I awkwardly reached out for a hug. She pulled me in.

    "Girl, stop acting shy," she said. "You know damn well you 'ont act like this around your friends."

    I relaxed my body and held her temporarily. Her wet hair hit my cheek. She smelled good, though.

    "You look nice," she said loudly.

    I flipped my hair from shoulder. I lied back into my seat and looked down at my outfit to remind myself of what I was wearing.

"Why, thank you," I replied cornily. "You don't look too bad yourself."

"I try, I try," she replied.

"Where are we off too?" I asked.

"It's a surprise," she said. "You'll see."

I pouted. I've always hated surprises—it's just how I am.

"We'll get there soon enough," she assured me. "I promise."

I smacked my teeth and moped.

"Okay," I replied then sighed.

I sat in the passenger's seat, waiting for her to pull off. She just stared at me—almost as if she were waiting for me to do something.

"What?" I asked shyly.

"You forgot something."

I tapped my pockets and realized what she was talking about. So I pulled the seatbelt over my body and locked it in its latch. She sped off.

We pulled up to a nice Italian restaurant. When she got out of the car, she closed the door behind her. As soon as I reached for mine, she locked me in. She didn't unlock the doors until she came to my side.

She pulled my door open.

"See, you so damn fast," she said. "I was gonna make you get out of my car when you first got in so that I could open the door, but I didn't want to be late for our reservation."

I side-smiled and thanked her for opening my door. We walked in and the maître d' greeted us at the front.

"Hi," Casey said. "I called earlier. We have a reservation for 6:30—under Ramos."

"Certainly," the maître d' replied. "Just two, right?"

She nodded. We followed her to our booth.

"How long have they been open?" I asked.

"Just a couple weeks I think," she said.

"Oh, okay," I replied. "So tell me about yourself."

"I mean, what you want to know?" she asked, leaning back.

"Are you from here?" I asked. "What are your hobbies? Are you in school? How old are you?"

Casey chuckled out. I saw a girl with a pitcher or water and ice.

"Welcome to Santino's," she said, pouring water into my cup. "I'm Maggie—I'll be your waitress for the evening. Can I start you two off with a refreshment or an appetizer?"

She turned to Casey and stopped in her tracks. Casey was frozen.

"Oh, hey," she said. "What's up, Maggie? How you been?"

"Hey Case," Maggie replied, pouring water into her cup. "I'm good. How's **Ashley**?"

Maggie looked over and scowled at me.

"She's…good," Casey replied and gestured her hand out to me. "This is umm…my friend, Tiy. She goes to Lyco."

"Oh, okay," she replied mischievously. "So, what'll you guys have to drink?"

"I'm actually good with water," I replied, dragging out my words. "Thank you."

She nodded her head.

"Case?" she said.

Casey just shook her head while fiddling with her utensils.

"I'm good," she replied.

Maggie tapped on her note pad.

"Any appetizers?" she asked.

Casey and I locked eyes. We shook our heads simultaneously.

"You guys need more time?"

We nodded.

"Okay," she said. "I'll be back in ten, fifteen minutes for you guys' orders."

Before she stepped away from the table, I noticed her pulling her phone out of her apron. She nodded, looking down at it as she walked away. Something was about to happen and I felt it in my bones. I grew up around ghetto bitches and my fuckery senses were tingling. Right then and there, it felt like Casey was hiding something from me.

I pointed my thumb behind me towards Maggie.

"What just happened?" I asked unamused.

"Nothing," she said. "That's just my ex's best friend."

I pursed my lips up because I knew she was lying. No one's ex's "best friend" is going to ask how said ex is doing if they know they're already broken up. But shit, it was free food, and I had already missed dinner in the cafeteria so I was going to ride it out as best I could.

About fifteen minutes later, Maggie came back and asked us if we had decided on what we wanted. I figured since it was an Italian place, they must have had Alfredo, so that's what I ordered. I didn't even look at the menu. Casey ordered mushroom risotto.

It got a bit awkward—too quiet. Then, she finally broke the silence.

"Well, to answer your question," she said, "I'm actually from Jersey. I moved out here with my mom and my sister a couple of years ago. I'm taking a few courses in bio at Penn College. I'm 20 and I like smoking, if that counts as a legitimate hobby."

I smiled. She had actually listened to my questions. I mean, yeah, she seemed like a fuckgirl, but a funny fuckgirl, with weed, or at least a consistent plug. Maggie walked over with a tray of our food resting on her shoulders. She placed our food in front of us and asked if there was anything else she could get for us. Her entire tone had changed. We were good, so she walked away.

From my seat, I saw her walk outside, light up a cigarette, and either place a call or answer one. She kept nodding her head and pointing into the restaurant behind us.

"Do you want to try some?" I asked Casey.

She grinned and scooted over closer to me. She held her head back and opened her mouth wide. I rolled my eyes, twisted some alfredo onto my fork with a spoon, and fed it to her. She chewed and I wiped the side of her mouth off for her.

"You have to try some of my risotto," she said to me.

I mimicked her and held my head back, waiting for her to place the food into my mouth. Then she did it—I was a bit skeptical at first, but it really wasn't that bad.

Half way in, I was so full. I couldn't even drink the rest of my water. A bitch was hungry, okay? I lied back and sighed.

"I'm so full," I said exhausted.

"I'm not," Casey said excitedly. "I kinda wanna taste you."

And before I could say anything, her hand crept up my skirt. She massaged on my clit and it took everything in me to maintain my composure in that restaurant. The torture only lasted about thirty seconds. She pulled her fingers to her nose and slowly dropped them into her mouth. She licked her lips and I lightly panted.

Then Casey looked up.

"Shit," she said.

Casey scooted back over to her side and her breaths sped up. The restaurant door swung open and a blonde came storming towards our booth. She leaned onto the table and into Casey's face. She was red. She seemed a bit angry.

"Hey babe," she said enthusiastically. "You want to know something crazy? Maggie called me telling me you were here with some black chick, and I thought that was funny because one: I'm not black, two: I was on the phone with her, and three: you told me you were working the night shift tonight."

I just leaned back and watched shit unfold. All I needed was popcorn.

"I'm sorry," she said, blinking. "Who are you."

"Oh, me?" I asked confidently. "I'm Tiy. You must be Ashley. Maggie brought you up earlier, but Casey," I said, pointing to her, "said you were her ex. I'm gonna go ahead and take a gander and say you're not an ex."

She slammed her hand onto the table loudly with her words.

"**BUT WHY ARE YOU HERE?!**" she yelled out.

"Why am *I* here?" I repeated. "That's something we need to ask your girlfriend, but I think the most important question is <u>why weren't you?</u>"

I pulled my cup to my face and slurped water into my mouth with my straw. Her nostrils flared. I slipped my wedge flip-flops off one by one.

"Oh," I cleared my throat and snapped my finger. "You might also wanna ask her why she was fingering me under the table about thirty seconds ago."

Her eyes pierced into my soul. She started trembling. Casey's jaw was on the floor. Ashley grabbed my hair and pulled me out of the booth. I grabbed a butter knife and slashed her arm. It was a cute little scratch, really, but she screamed out and let go of my hair. She grabbed her arm and checked for blood.

Then, she looked up at me and charged. I stepped back, grabbed her by her blonde hair, and slammed her face onto the table. She barely grazed her forehead on it, but she just *had* to be overly-dramatic. She held her forehead, turned around, and fell on top of me. She started clawing at my face and got a couple licks in. I pulled my skirt up to my stomach and spread my legs open. I wrapped them around her and turned over—we flipped positions. I grabbed her by the throat and slammed the back of her head into the carpeted floor.

She tried punching me in the stomach, so I punched her in the throat. She started wheezing and grabbed her throat.

I stood, picked my shoes up, grabbed my purse, and looked over at Casey.

"You," I said panting and pointing at her, "are a piece of shit."

I pointed at Ashley on the floor still holding onto her neck.

"And **this**," I said, "is all your fucking fault."

I stepped over Ashley on my way out of the restaurant. She grabbed at my ankle and I kicked her in the face. It was like a love tap.

I walked to the end of the corner and hailed a cab. The ride back to school with $20. I never went back to that Rite Aid after that. One day, when my mom visited me, we went to the Sam's club and I bought a carton of cigarettes that lasted me until fucking December of that year.

You know, I never understood that—why people immediately attack the person they find their partner out with like it's not their partner who owes them loyalty. I could've handled the disrespect that she had thrown at me, but I was not going to put up with her putting her hands on me. I'm nice, but I'm not that fucking nice.

8. Friends and Fingers

∞

Remember that promise I had made to myself a couple chapters back—the one about not making shitty decisions while intoxicated? Yeah, about that. Let's just say that that promise was very short-lived considering the fact that Ava and I ended up fucking one night when she came to me, crying about that fuckboy Alex I warned her about from the get-go.

"She's his girlfriend now," she cried out.

Alex had chosen the girl he was also talking to over Ava. They had just made it Facebook official. When she confronted him about it, he just blew her off and blocked her on everything.

"He wasn't shit from the beginning," I said. "And you know that."

"I know," she said, choking on her words. "I just thought he wanted to be with me."

She was in a terrible place emotionally and I just wanted to make her feel better.

We ended up drinking nearly an entire bottle of Tennessee Whiskey (without chasers) that night.

I tried to comfort her, you know? I did friend things. I insulted Alex, we laughed about how small his dick was, I hugged her, I kissed her on the cheek.

She looked at me a little too long. I looked at her a little too long. Then she slowly inched her face to mine. I giggled and pushed her back.

"Dude, what are you doing?" I asked.

Then her shoulders slumped and her head dropped.

I wanted to make the pain go away. She had been crying so much that her eyes were puffy.

I poked my bottom lip out and hugged her.

"Don't cry, buttercup," I said with my arms wrapped around her. "You're beautiful and amazing. He's just a fucking idiot."

I let my grip around her go. She wiped her nose and smiled. She looked up and we locked eyes again. I drank another swig of Jack.

"Fuck it," I said and jumped on top of her.

I kissed on her neck and she moaned out. Then our lips met and I tasted the salt from her tears. My fingers ended up inside of her warm pussy. Her red hair smelled like strawberries and cream. I pulled my fingers out and helped her out of her shirt and bra. I flipped my hair to the side and rubbed on one nipple while sucking on the other.

I began kissing down her stomach and on her inner thighs, but I was too much of a pussy to actually eat hers. I was drunk, but I wasn't that drunk. I looked back up at her and got a whiff of her pussy. It didn't stink; it just smelled like pussy. At the time, I was a pillow princess, and had never gotten the chance to appreciate the taste and smell of pussy yet (it happened much later).

After I kissed her thigh, I made my way back up her stomach. I came back up and kissed her. I ended up on my back and she had actually started eating me out. It wasn't too shabby. It sort of tingled from the alcohol on her breath. She even poured some down my pussy lips and took a pussy shot. That was the night I knew what it felt like when guys go to the barbershop and have aftershave slapped onto their necks. She got lost in the sauce and her mouth disappeared into my pussy lips on more than one occasion. It could've been because we were totally fucked up and everything felt like it was in slow motion.

A part of me enjoyed it; the other part of me didn't because she wasn't a stud or a dyke. For the most part, I just wanted it to be over. I wasn't really completely into it. Feminine girls have never really done it for me. They never get me wet. I've never dreamt or fantasized about them. I've never even felt moved or compelled to flirt with the likes of them.

(Sideline: For someone who has been involved in lesbian relations and relationships, I understand some of my readers won't/don't know/understand the differences between "stud" and "dyke". For starters, a stud is a masculine female who has made it up in her mind and accepts the fact that she is, and will always be a woman. She is content being one. Studs are rarely ever open to penetration of any kind (including penises

and strap-ons), but it can happen. Hell, you might fuck around and actually see a stud in makeup for shits and giggles. Studs often dress like men and share the same mannerisms and gestures of them. A "dyke", however, believes in all her mind that she is a man, or man-adjacent. She will refuse to ever be the bottom (or submissive one) in a relationship. She has likely never had sex with men, even in adolescence. For dykes, a sex change isn't completely out of the question.)

I guess I tried it out for the sake of "experimenting", which is pretty much emblematic of college. Ava was a girly-girl—a fem who, without the inclusion of drinking and heartbreak, would never have ended up eating my pussy in the first place. Her tongue was smooth but her teeth kept scraping up against my clit. She was literally eating my pussy. That should've been a hint that she was absolutely, 100%, without a shadow of a doubt straight. But, like I said, booze and heartbreak will make you do things.

I pulled her by her red hair and put her face to mine. One thing led to another, and by that, I mean "we ended up scissoring" (for those of you that don't know what "scissoring" is, hold up peace signs with both your hands, then intertwine them at the openings).

Don't judge me, okay? It just happened. I had a brief lapse of judgment, and by the time I realized what had happened, it was already too late. After going on a date with Casey and, not only finding out she had a fucking girlfriend, but also having no other choice but to beat her ass, I realized that the dating pool was pretty much filled with fuckboys and fuckgirls. All hope was lost. That was around the time that I realized that people were pretty shitty, so I gave up on them as a whole and stayed away from them as much as possible. Ava was the first person I had dealt with in a long while.

To say that the incident sort of put tension on our relationship would be kind of an understatement, so I'll leave it at that.

I learned the hard way that liquor will make you do things you thought you never had the balls to do. It can make you go crazy, lose friends, even hook up with someone who'll eventually puke into your pussy. I wish I could say that that was the last time I had ever done something with someone I considered a friend, but I can't because my life is incredibly filled with unsurpassed fuckery and bad decisions.

9. Petty Queen

∞

Sophomore Year, September, 2012

Sophomore year rolled around. It pretty much came and went almost in an instant. I was a loner and I was honestly fine with it. I kept to myself a lot. Of course, I would see Lindsay, Ava, and Ashley around campus, but those encounters ended with nothing more than a couple "hi"s and "hello"s. When my first semester of sophomore year started, I made it up in my mind that I was going to transfer closer to home. College in the boonies was boring. Everyday felt mundane and everyone knew everyone. There was nothing there but dirt, grass, and more fucking dirt and grass.

Everywhere I turned, there were old friends who weren't in my life anymore. I couldn't get out of there soon enough. I maintained my grades and focused on transferring only. I applied to a few universities, and got into all of them. The problem wasn't me not getting accepted. The problem was me affording it, or me not being able to, for that matter. I got into AU, Georgetown, UMD, Towson—the list goes on. Things were looking up. But then, when I found what tuition would cost, I felt my heart sink into my chest. They weren't trying to cough up any scholarships.

∞

Sophomore Year, January 2013

At some point, my heart told me I belonged at an HBCU. I needed to be closer to my people.

(Side note: For my white readers, don't worry; an HBCU is a historically black college or university, that's all.)

So, I applied to Bowie State University, and got in with no problem. The tuition was just right, the location was perfect, and the men were gorgeous. Okay, I'm getting a little off topic. I sent in my acceptance forms and committed to attending in the fall.

∞

Summer, 2013

My last day at Lycoming was one of the happiest moments of my life, to be honest. I packed my shit up into cardboard boxes, loaded them onto a truck, and headed back home to DC.

I was so happy to be home. The night I got back, I called my friend, "Brittany" up to see what the move was. She was my **hoe ass, thotty ass, slutty ass** friend. (Just for your information, "Brittany" was the sluttiest name I could possibly think of, so we'll just have to make do with that.) I know it may seem like I have some animosity toward her, and you would be right in assuming so. Anyway, when I asked her what the move was, she told me there was a party in Clinton, MD and that we should go together. So, I signed up for that night's antics, not knowing that it would be the reason I would later become the savage that I am today.

I got dressed, and waited for Brittany to pick me up. Brittany was always on time, so if she said she would be there at 10:30 pm, she would be there at 10:29 just waiting to honk her horn. She was a slut, but she was an early slut. (I know the animosity may have caught some of you off guard, but we'll get there soon enough, I promise.)

So, we drove over to the party, and it was already crowded. I twerked on a couple dicks. I grinded on a couple pussies (studs). It was beautiful. I missed ratchet ass, ghetto ass house parties. It was just something about Gogo music drowning in my ears that made me feel at home. It had gotten too hot, so Brittany and I decided to go and rest on the walls for a little bit, where the fans were.

I looked across the room and saw a tall, caramel macchiato, beautiful creature of a fuckboy. I asked Brittany if she knew who he was. She told me his name was "Brendan".

He caught a glance of me and the rest was history. I felt like it was all happening in slow motion.

It seemed like we were in a music video. He was on the wall, I was with my crew (slut). He was watching me. I was watching him. Slowly, he walked over (just like in Beyoncé's "Yes").

I'm going to say this before it's too late: just for future reference, do not, I repeat, **do not** get involved with a guy or a girl you met at a club or a party. You'll soon find out that they are either a piece of shit, unambitious, or dumb (or all three).

I maintained my cool. He said hello to me, and I smiled and waved awkwardly as I always do. He seemed to be a good guy, so I gave him my phone number. Two weeks later we were dating—two weeks after that, I was in love with him. He always pressured me to have sex, but I wanted to wait until marriage.

Surprisingly enough, a lot of his friends were some of my childhood friends, I was cool with a lot of them. It had all gotten too serious too quickly. Just when I thought I was ready to give him my virginity, of course he would find a way to fuck it up.

One day out of the blue, one of his friends, who went to middle school with me, texted me. For the sake of the story, I'll call him "Jay". He asked me where I was and told me that he needed to talk to me. He stressed that it was urgent. At first, I thought he was being over-dramatic like he always was, but it was different this time. I agreed to meet up with him at his mom's house.

I feel kind of ashamed about how terrible I looked. My hair was in a messy bun, I had on absolutely no makeup, some homemade shorts, and an old t-shirt. At that time, I didn't really care because he was my mans (for my white readers or readers that aren't from the DMV area, "mans" is specifically a term of endearment meaning "brother", "friend", or "confidant").

Anyway, I caught the bus all the way to his house. When I got there, I hugged his mom and his little brother. She asked me how school was going— you know, the basic "catching up" questions any friend's mom would ask. After we spoke for about ten minutes, she let me go on my way. I asked Jay's little brother where he was and he pointed up the steps. When I got to the top of the stairs, I knocked on the door.

(Side note: Jay had always had a crush on me since we were in middle school, but I never gave him any rap, at all. Also, for my white readers, "rap" means "to entertain" or "to flirt with".)

"Who is it?" he called out.

"Tiy," I replied.

He opened the door. (Oh. My. God.) Have you ever realized that you chose the ugly one in the group of friends? I had never before seen Jay in that light. He had on basketball shorts, no shirt, abs and tattoos for days. He was one of those guys that gave absolutely no fucks about his future. He had two or three tattoos on his face—tattoos on his arms, hands, chest, and back. He even had tattoos on his fingers and elbows. (I don't understand, nor have I ever understood why that is a thing.) He had truly accepted the fact that he had no future and nothing going for himself.

He stood there, abs protruding all over the place, rolling up weed. He had that natural V-cut. I had considered him a brother up until that moment. I never saw him without a fucking shirt on. I saw his dick print peeking through his basketball shorts. I could tell it was huge, but I tried my best to ignore it because I was in a relationship. Honestly, to some extent, I kind of felt uncomfortable with him being that sexy. For the most part, Brendan and all of his friends had the same body type, but I only paid attention to Brendan for obvious reasons. But Jay? He was chocolate, which is and always has been my weakness.

Like I said, because I'm not a cheater, I cleared my throat and sat beside him nonchalantly pretending to be unimpressed.

"What's up?" I asked. "What's the big emergency?"

He put his jay down.

"If I tell you," he started, "you gotta promise you won't tell Brendan I told you."

I rolled my eyes, but deep inside, I knew bad news was on its way. He took a deep breath and reached for my hand. I pulled it back and folded my arms. I was nervous.

He sighed.

"You know Brendan and I are like brothers," I nodded, "but you're too good for him, Tiy."

I squinted my eyes. "What do you mean?"

"Look," he said. "Brendan's been cheating on you since day one."

I swallowed a gulp of spit and tilted my head in disbelief, looking up at the ceiling. I saw red. Have you ever been so entirely livid and ten seconds later, completely calm—like scary calm?

"Are you serious?" I asked, begging him to tell me it was a joke.

He never gave me that. I was in denial the first couple minutes, but then it hit me; Jay had known me for years and never had a reason to lie. He pulled out his phone and showed me text message threads between him and Brendan. All of the incriminating evidence was right there: pictures, names, all of that shit.

By now, you should know that I was already scheming. I was low-key heartbroken. Now, you guys know I'm a petty person, but was I petty enough to let Jay eat this Pillsbury Dough, honey-glazed pussy?

I. Sure. Was.

Once I left his house, I went home and made a fake Twitter page. I then searched the internet for fake photos (don't judge me, I'm crazy). I know most of you would have just confronted Brendan, but that's not in my nature. I'm a petty person and petty people have to make an effort to ruin someone's life. You can call me childish, you can immature, but you can't call me someone who never gets revenge—that's for sure. I also promised Jay that I wouldn't out him.

I followed Brendan's dumb ass—liked and retweeted a couple tweets. He followed me back and immediately slid into my DM's. It was about to go down. We conversed. I asked him if he was single, and unbeknownst to me, he was. That was news to me. His dumb ass really fell for that trick. I had given him a shot to redeem himself, but once he fell for it, there was no turning back. It had to be done.

I thought he was playing it smart when he suggested that we FaceTime. Of course, I came up with some bogus excuse. I told him that I didn't have an iPhone. You would think that he would suggest that we Oovoo, but he was a dumb ass.

I downloaded a sideline app and registered for a free phone number. I told him to call me and he did. So I switched up my voice and he fell for it.

"So, why are you single?" I asked.

"Because my ex was a crazy bitch," he replied. Okay, it was true, but I was still his girlfriend at the time.

An hour or two in, we started having phone sex. Then we started having phone sex every single day. He sent me pictures of his little dick. I sent him fake pussy pictures. I didn't really know how to feel. He was cheating on me, but he was cheating on me, with me. How is one supposed to feel about that situation? I didn't know if I should kill him or fuck him.

A week goes by. We had planned on finally meeting each other in person. I (the fake me) was supposed to meet him at his house one day. The same day, I (as myself) asked him to come over my house because I had missed him so much. He told me that he had some errands to run with his mom, and that he would "see what he could do". If that wasn't the straw that broke the crazy camel's back, I don't know what the fuck was.

When he and I (the fake me) were supposed to meet up, he got stood up. He called and called and called and called, so I ended up deleting the app. Then he called me (the real me) and told me that he didn't have to go with his mom anymore.

I told him that he could still come over and he told me he would be there in twenty minutes. So I was at my house, practicing my speech, trying to figure out how I was going to scar him emotionally. Twenty minutes goes by really quickly when you're trying to figure out how to use as many curse words as possible in the span of ten seconds.

The doorbell rang. I looked through the peephole and it was him. The time was now. I had to get into character. There was no turning back. I took a deep breath and opened the door.

"Baby!" I yelled out, pretending to be excited to see him.

I had to act like I still gave a fuck about him, even though he fucked me up mentally. I developed an entire personality just for the sake of being petty. That's a completely different level of fuckboy. I gave him a hug and kiss and everything.

We walked down to my basement and sat on the couch. He was telling me about his day, but I had tuned out everything that he was saying. It was going in one ear and out the other. Mid-sentence, I cut him off.

"Mhmmm, that's cool," I said. "But babe, who's Brena?"

(Side note: Brena was the fake name I had used for the Twitter page. But let me tell you how much of a fucking idiot he was. Brena is my middle name. He never connected the dots.)

I swear to God, as soon as that name left my lips, his eyes grew wide and he immediately started sweating. He licked his lips—and I knew he was thinking hard. The only reason light-skinned niggas lick their lips is to lubricate their lies. I felt my nostrils flaring in anger. He began stuttering and scratching his head. Now, you know when a guy starts scratching his head, he's about to lie. He parted his lips to say something. I stopped him once more.

"Lying only makes it worse," I said to him with the most serious of serious faces. "If you tell me the truth, we may be able to work things out".

It was a lie, but I needed him to believe that there was still a chance between him and me. He avoided eye contact and tried so desperately to figure out what to say to me. He opened his mouth to start talking and I knew he was about to lie. So I cut him off again and placed my index finger over his lips.

I pulled my phone out, unlocked it, opened up the Twitter app, clicked on to the direct messages tab, and handed him my phone. He held it and began scrolling through it confusedly.

"Brendan, who is Brena?" I repeated.

He looked at me. He looked at the phone. Then he looked at me again and sucked his teeth.

"I knew it was you the whole time," he said.

I remained entirely still for thirty seconds, just looking at him calmly. Then he started laughing.

All of a sudden...

I hit his ass with a two piece! No biscuit, no drink, no wedges, no dirty rice—no sides at all! We ended up on the floor and I started pounding on him. It was scary because I'm not at all a violent person, you guys. It's just that when you put me in a fucked up space, that's not good for you. I blacked out.

The fact that I even hit him was the scary part to me. I started screaming at him. We stood and I threw more punches. I cried endless tears. I asked him how many times had he cheated and how many bitches there were.

He reached out for a hug. I mushed him in the face. I kneed him in the dick and everything. He started yelling at me, swearing up and down that he was sorry. It was tumultuous, to say the least. I put my hands at my sides and started bawling my eyes out. He kept trying to hug me, which only made it worse. He grabbed me by the arms and fell on top of me. He pinned them up beside my head. I kept crying like a little bitch. He kissed me and I bit his lip as hard as I could. He was still hanging in there, trying to fight for "us".

Then he kissed my neck. Then he licked my ear. Fuck! I kept moving my head to block the kisses.

"Bae, I know you want it," he said. "Calm down, please."

Long story short, he ripped my thong off and started eating my pussy. This was the day that I learned that guilty pussy-eating was the best type of pussy-eating. It was gentle, but it was so sad at the same time. I loved it at first, but it was weird. I had never had anyone begging for forgiveness by way of eating my pussy.

He started massaging on my thighs, sucking on my clit, and moving his head in an infinity motion. It felt good—I was still crying. I'm not sure if it was because I was sad, hurt, angry, or because it genuinely felt good. He shoved a finger in and started massaging the insides of my pussy.

Have you ever had an epiphany when you're high? For me, getting head is like getting high. I realized I hated his ass—genuinely hated him and every bone in his body. I hated everything that made him *him*. I started thinking about all the shit I saw in Jay's phone. Meanwhile, he was kissing my pussy and asking for forgiveness after every kiss. At that moment, I had realized that he didn't deserve it.

I remembered how petty I was and how easily he had gotten off. He had no idea. I did one of the nastiest things I could have possibly thought of doing. Go ahead and guess what that was.

I pushed with all my might. I wanted so badly to shit in his mouth, you guys; I really did!

But God said "Chill!"

He did, however, bless me with a queef and a fart, so I took any blessing as a sign that he agreed that Brendan deserved it. A little pee came out too. The savagery meter was broken, entirely. Did I feel good about what had happened? I absolutely did. In hindsight, though, I don't think it was necessary.

We literally started scrapping. We were in a real fist fight. After he realized what I had done, he actually started throwing punches. Fortunately for me, I knew how to defend myself. I blocked every single punch but one or two. I started crying again.

Sooner or later, we stopped fighting and he tried to hug me again.

I peed in his mouth, farted and queefed in his face, but he couldn't see that I didn't want his ass. Thank God my mom was walking in the door from work. We heard her walking around upstairs and he ran out the basement door. As soon as I caught my breath, I made my way upstairs and snuck past my mom. I posted his little dick all across social media: Tumblr, Twitter, Facebook, Instagram; the list goes on.

I called Jay crying and told him what had happened. He, his older brother, and cousin ended up jumping Brendan. I never heard from his ass again and he blocked me on everything.

(Side note: I recently found out that he and Brittany have two ugly children together. She even gave him herpes, but they're still rocking with each other. How cute. ☺)

Part II: Car Seat Chronicles

10. *Nothing Was the Same*

∞

Junior Year, September, 2013

It was September and I had just transferred to the illustrious Bowie State University. School had been in for a few weeks. I mostly kept to myself. I didn't speak to a lot of people. Honestly, I was just irritated that I would need to take an additional semester because most of my credits had not transferred. At that time, I didn't know anyone. I remembered specifically one guy (named "Malcolm") from a college program I did a ways back went to Bowie too. I made a post on Instagram about Bowie, and because Instagram Direct messaging hadn't existed yet, he commented his phone number on a photo from 100 weeks in my past.

That was the first hint of shadiness from God, but did I listen? Of course not. We eventually started texting and made a plan to meet up one night. Unfortunately, my dorm (CMRC) didn't have visitation the first two weeks of school, so we figured we'd just catch up in his car.

I knew damn well Malcolm had a girlfriend, and I respected that. I respect relationships. I always have. I respect people enough to expect them to tell me the truth. My gullible ass actually believed he wanted to be just friends. Silly me.

I was so convinced that Malcolm and I would be just friends that I didn't even bother to put makeup on. That's how much I wanted a friendship from him.

(Side note: If I don't put makeup on for you, I'm not interested in impressing you; it's simple.)

It was a little chilly outside for it to have been a fall night. He wanted meet up at midnight. That was the first sign that he was a fuckboy. That was strike two, but my stupid ass still agreed to meet up with him. Right before he showed up, I smoked a cigarette. I did so to prevent him trying to make any moves or kiss me. Most guys get turned off by the whole cigarette scent, so I'd like to think I was being proactive.

He pulled up and I hopped in his fancy car. I don't remember what kind of car it was because I'm not at all impressed by fancy things—I've never been into name brands. When I closed the door behind me, he gave me a hug.

"You smell like cigarettes," he stated in a disgusted tone.

"And you sir," I said grinning, "would be absolutely correct in coming to that conclusion."

He decided to lecture me about how smoking and how girls smoking isn't attractive. Toward the end of his spiel, he turned his heat on full blast and suggested that I take my jacket off because it was going to get a little hot. That was strike two and a half.

(Side note: His fucking windows were rolled all the fucking way down.)

"Nah, I'm good," I replied.

I tried changing the topic.

"So, how's grad school going?" (He attended the grad school on campus.)

"It's good," he answered. "You sure you're not hot?"

I kept trying to disregard his advances.

"Nope," I replied, even though my back was sweating. You know how guys are.

"Why are you sitting all the way over there?" he asked. "You should come closer."

I rolled my eyes.

"I'm cool," I replied.

We started catching up. Then the conversation got a little inappropriate. I looked at the clock on the dashboard, then at the nonexistent watch on my wrist.

"Now, would you look at that," I said. "It's past my bedtime."

"It's only like 1 in the morning," he responded. "Where you rushin' off to?"

"Oh, ya know," I said. "Gotta get my beauty rest."

He reached for my face. I tilted my head back.

"Chill!" I exclaimed. "What are you doing? Don't you have a girlfriend?"

He sighed like he knew that question was coming.

"We don't need to talk about her," he said. "The only thing that matters right now is you and me."

I turned my lips up in confusion. He couldn't have possibly had me that fucked up. I had never before heard such fuckery in my twenty-something odd years of living.

"What the fuck do you mean, Malcolm?" I demanded.

"It's not even like that," he assured me. "She broke up with me a while ago."

I took the bait and believed him. Oh, I never even got the chance to tell you guys what old boy looked like. I mean, he wasn't ugly. Actually, he was kind of cute in a teddy bear kind of way. I was going through a big boy face at that time in my life and I have no shame about it; I never will.

It took me a long time to realize that he was lying. It took me an even longer time to realize that the chances of a big guy having a big dick were one in a hundred million (him included).

"Oh," I replied in a relieved tone.

"Yeah, we don't even speak," he added.

We spent some time reminiscing about old shit. Then my dumb ass got the nerve to admit to him that I had had a crush on him once upon a time. He licked his PEL's (pussy-eating lips) and his face changed.

"You still do?" he asked. I twisted my lips up.

I snickered and cleared my throat.

"No, boy," I replied in a pretty unconvincing tone.

No matter how determined I was in trying to persuade him that I didn't like him, I low-key did. There's just something about an intellectual man that does something to me.

"Oh, you don't?" he asked as if it were a challenge.

"Nope."

I smiled and shook my head slowly.

He licked his PEL's again. Then he leaned in and I leaned back. He grabbed the back of my head and I pulled back.

"Stahhhhhhhp!" I whined out.

I didn't want him to, though.

He leaned in closer and started kissing me. He snuck his hand into my leggings. He was surprised when he realized how wet I was. I didn't have on any underwear. When I say it literally takes nothing for me to get wet, I mean that shit. I could be irritated as fuck with you, and still manage to get wet. I could be ready to write you off completely and a waterfall could still be happening in between my legs.

As soon as he put his hand in my pants, he stopped kissing me.

"Damn," he said, then went back to kissing me.

He used his thumb to rub on my clit. Then his index finger found my hole and he slowly slid it in. He dug his finger in more to drench it. He slid it in some more and I started to back up because it started to hurt. I guess my hymen was still intact and he was pressing up against something that did not want to let him in. He pulled his finger out, then slid two back in, and pulled them back out. He continued rubbing my clit with his thumb. He started kissing and biting on my neck. Mind you, this was literally behind the student center parking lot, where a lot of people parked. Even though it was late, there was a lot of traffic. Even when headlights would flash in, he wouldn't stop. He gave no fucks at all. He was my kind of guy.

I felt like I had to pee (which I later found out was actually my body telling me it was about to squirt).

Long story short, I came all over his hand. When he pulled his hand out, my juices were melting down his wrist and arm. When I saw his hand, I felt so bad. It had gotten on his sleeve. It was just a mess. Then he rolled his sleeve up and sucked every single fucking finger clean. I didn't know what to do with myself. A part of me was worried about how freaky he was; the other part was kind of turned on. He stuck his hand out.

"You want some?" he asked.

My jaw dropped. I was paralyzed by how nasty he was. I yanked his wrist and sucked every single finger too. I let his hand go, then put my own hand in my pants and tasted myself (I'm pretty competitive, if you couldn't tell). We looked at each other in silence. I think we were both stunned by what had just happened. I was out of breath.

"Can you play some music or something?" I asked, panting.

"I know exactly what to play," he replied, smirking.

He rolled the windows up and started playing *Nothing Was the Same* by Drake!

(Side note: Coincidentally enough, no matter who it is, or where I am, almost every time I sucked dick, a song from that album usually played. That just happened to be my dick sucking album by chance.)

"Tuscan Leather" played in the background and he started unbuckling his pants. **This would be the first time I had ever sucked dick!**

I was ready! Any girl that claims that she's never watched porn and studied the art of the blowjob or practiced sucking dick is a filthy fucking liar. Bananas and I have an understanding. In my mind, I planned on choking, gagging, stabbing myself in the throat with the dick. I was finally about to see what all the hype was about. So he unzipped his pants and took a little bit of it out.

(Side note: I don't know if it's in us genetically, or if it's because we're just hungry, but big girls are typically more excited about sucking dick—law of the land; way of the world. It's just science.)

I turned and bent over into his lap, ass in the air. I took it by the hand and tried to pull it all the way out. With his dick still in hand, I slid the rest of my hand into his zipper to get it out. I tugged and his whole body jerked in agony.

"What are you doing?!" he asked.

"I'm tryna take it all the way out," I replied. "Help me take it all the way out."

"It **is** all the way out!" he exclaimed.

I immediately regretted my decision! **Abort mission!** Malcolm played me over a marshmallow?! I was practicing sucking dick on a banana, but it turned out I could have cut the banana into three and one of those pieces would have sufficed. I was so upset. It was my first time sucking dick and it already sucked—no pun intended. I couldn't gag. I couldn't choke. There was no swallowing of the dick. I didn't want to spit on it because then it would be too slippery and I wouldn't be able to grip onto it.

So, I took a deep breath and put on my big girl panties. I wrapped my mouth around it, at least tried to. The zipper kept scraping up against my cheek. I was kind of bummed that I wouldn't be able to practice my deep-throating skills.

I was struggling to make suction and to make ends meet. It was just not working out. I wanted to jerk him off and suck his dick, but I could only choose one at a time. It was just sad.

He started groaning and out of nowhere, he panicked. Then he pushed my head away and started zipping up his pants. Thank God!

I wiped the spit off my mouth and looked up. It was 4040 (campus security) pulling into the parking lot. They were on the other side of the parking lot driving the opposite direction, but God was giving me an opportunity so I just ran with it. I put my jacket back on and hugged him.

"It's been real!" I said, then dipped the fuck out.

On my way back to my room, a part of me was trying to make excuses for him, you know? Maybe it was just too cold outside. Maybe he was nervous.

Two weeks later, we finally got visitation in my dorm. We chilled a few more times and tried the friend thing. We watched movies and did homework together. We laughed. I told him about the drama going on in my life. He gave me pretty good advice.

One day, he decided to be open and honest with me. Not only did he still have a girlfriend, guess who my next door neighbor was, you guys. I couldn't make this shit up even if I wanted to. My life is literally a book of fuckery and it is never-ending.

The only time Malcolm would come to my dorm was when he knew she was in class or working. At that point, I didn't care because I just wanted a friendship genuinely. He claimed that she cheated on him and kept breaking up with him because he was "too much of a good guy". He even told me that one time, she got an abortion and didn't tell him until afterwards.

Of course, my stupid ass would actually believe every single word he said to me. It got too deep, too serious, too quickly—I think I sort of felt bad for him at a time. He was telling me his entire fucking life story. Eventually, I knew he was lying because some shit just didn't add up.

One day, one of my suitemates told me she saw him with some ugly chick and that they went into the apartment right beside ours. Right then and there, I knew it was his girlfriend and that he was completely full of shit. I had seen pictures of her on Instagram. She wasn't the prettiest flower in the rose bed.

I honestly didn't care because I cared about him as a friend, or a brother, or a brother whose dick you sucked—or a brother whose dick you *tried* to suck. I never brought it up; we just kept the entire situation strictly platonic.

One night, I called him up crying over the fact that Brendan had actually moved on. He rushed to my dorm. I was drunk and high, trying to drown my sorrows.

I remember him hugging me. He started kissing on me and I didn't stop him. Then all of a sudden, he was sucking on my nipples. He ate the soul out of my pussy. I came in his mouth at least twice.

Somewhere in between horny, hurt, and irritated, I asked him if he had a condom. He looked surprised that I would even ask him that because I would have normally blown him off. He pulled out a Magnum.

I remember laughing out, but only for a moment.

"Malcolm, your dick isn't gonna fit in that Magnum, bruh," I said out loud without even considering his feelings.

Have you ever said that to a grown ass man? Literally—have you ever looked into a man's eyes and said anything remotely close to something like that? Have you ever seen a man's pride die? It was so incredibly sad and I felt terrible, you guys! His shoulders dropped in discouragement. He sucked his teeth and reassured me that it would.

"Just turn around and put that ass up," he said. "Don't worry about me."

I waited and watched him put the condom on. I wasn't about to put my ass up for anyone, especially if said someone surely could not fit a condom meant for big dicks. Malcolm made a mountain out of a molehill and slid the entire condom on (all bunched up and everything) just to teach me a lesson.

So I gave in and turned around. I put my ass up as earlier requested. I couldn't stop giggling. He put one hand on my hip and slapped my ass with the other. The dick slid in probably half an inch.

"Is it in?" I asked perplexedly.

"Yeah," he replied.

"Is it *all* the way in?" I asked.

"Mhmm," he said.

But I felt nothing at all. The hymen was still intact, literally. He pumped one time before my roommate came banging on the door. She wanted me to do her hair.

"Gimme twenty minutes," I yelled out and looked back at him. "Actually, give me two."

I turned around and he was jerking off. Mind you, I never even felt him pull out, to be completely honest. He couldn't get hard again. The big man upstairs was really looking out for me. If we're being truthful, my tampons go in deeper than he did, so there's that.

He had given up trying.

"I can't get it back up," he said. "If you give me head, maybe I c—."

I cut him off.

"It's cool, it's cool," I said. "Can't say we didn't try."

I pretended to pout and tried to make it seem like I was saddened by the minor (and I *do* mean **minor**) speed bump. I fake yawned and picked up my phone to check the time.

"Damn," I said. "I got a test in the morning."

"Oh, okay," he replied and pulled his pants up back up.

He gave me a hug and leaned in for a kiss. Of course I turned my head away and it landed on my cheek. I was beginning to sober up. As soon as I heard my apartment door close, I blocked him on everything. **Everything.** After all that work, I was still a virgin. I was so upset.

(Side note: I figure I'd share with you all that Malcolm graduated with me in December of 2015 from Bowie's grad school. He sat in the row directly ahead of me. When we were standing, he turned and we locked eyes for a couple seconds. I busted out laughing. A while ago, I unblocked him on Instagram and found out that his then-girlfriend gave birth to their daughter in October of 2015. She should've watched him put the condom on like I did; now she's stuck with his ass. But that's none of my business. No tea, no shade, no pink lemonade.)

∞

October, 2013

After the whole Malcolm disaster, I told myself that I would just stay away from Bowie niggas altogether. On the whim, I decided to log into my Tagged profile page after years. I don't know why I did it—I probably felt like my juice was drying up and the list of contenders just wasn't as impressive as I was used to. I noticed that this guy named Mike had been trying to link up with me for the longest time. He went to Allegheny but he was from Laurel, MD.

(Side note: I don't really know why, but I was in a thot mode and for whatever reason, it was in full-throttle. It could have been because I felt lonely and needed to validate my worth. It happens. It's life. It could have been because I was acting out of curiosity. I don't know. I had at least a dozen niggas on my line and I led all of them all. It just felt good to feel wanted, you know? I got bored. I think I entertained so many of them because for once, I found the guys at my school attractive. Pulling niggas just came easily to me even though I never tried.)

So after messaging each other back and forth, I gave him my number. iMessages turned into FaceTime calls. I got to know him as a friend. We talked about everything—about what we wanted to be, where we saw ourselves years from now. I don't think I was really attracted to his intellect; he wasn't really the brightest highlight in the makeup bag. I was, however, attracted to his willingness to actually listen to me and my problems. He was always honest with me.

We tried countless times to figure out when and where we wanted to meet. I made plans to visit him but it didn't really work out that. Then we decided to meet up at my school one night. He drove five hours to see me, but when he had gotten to my school, it was too late (because visitation ends at midnight during the week at most HBCU's).

I always felt nervous meeting someone for the first time, especially after talking to them for some time. It could've been because I was worried I would disappoint them. I don't know. This led to me getting the nervous shits, which *always* seemed to happen a couple hours beforehand. I shat, then I shaved while I showered. This ritual would later be known as the infamous "Three S's".

(Side note: You can't shit after you've showered, but you can shave while you shower. That's the only exception.)

When I got out, he still hadn't called or texted me. I thought he had stood me up. I waited for two whole hours. I even fell asleep. I was awakened by my phone ringing. He told me he was outside, so I hopped up, sprayed some Pure Seduction on (also a ritual) and met him outside.

I got into the car, and was immediately a little disappointed. He looked nothing like he did on FaceTime. It could've been the lighting. It could've been because I was usually on my way to bed when we FaceTimed. I felt bamboozled. Don't get me wrong. He wasn't ugly or unattractive; he just wasn't cute to me, at all. But when he smiled, his dimples made my heart melt.

"Wassup with you?" he asked, dimples piercing into his cheeks.

I pursed my lips and shrugged my shoulders shyly.

"So, I don't get no hug?" he added.

I smirked and rolled my eyes, then leaned in and hugged him. He had just gotten a fresh cut and his short hair stabbed the side of my face. But boy, did he smell like Heaven. Oh my fucking gosh, he smelled amazing. If Shemar Moore dipped himself into a tub of lavender and bad bitches, then ran through a mist of Calvin Klein, that's what I imagine he smelled like. Mike smelled amazing!

"I'ont get a kiss?" he uttered.

I folded my lips on top of each other as if that were an answer. He shifted his head forward and raised his eyebrows in search of an answer.

I side-smiled and gave in. I scrunched up my lips and aimed for his cheek. He purposely repositioned his head so that I would land on his lips. We were eye to eye and started making out. I'm not going to lie; his lips tasted good (that's a fat girl observation, by the way), but when more of his saliva was in my mouth than my own, I pushed him back and wiped my mouth.

"You gotta chill!" I called out and shifted myself back into my seat.

He grinned and shifted the gear.

He wanted to go on a tour around my school, so I obliged him. After about fifteen minutes, we ended up on the opposite side of campus, near the MLK Building (almost every HBCU in the fucking country has an MLK building and/or a Harriet Tubman building; Bowie had both). He turned the engine off and plugged the aux cord into his phone. He placed his arm on my head rest and just watched me.

"Yo, you cute as shit," he said.

I pointed at my chest and played dumb.

"Who?" I asked. "Me?"

He nodded his head.

"Stamp," he affirmed.

"Nah," I replied. "I'm ugly for real."

He flared his nostrils, tilted his head, and gave me that "come on now" face. He sucked his teeth and let out a long ass, unnecessary ass, exhausting ass sigh.

"Tiy, you know damn well you're not ugly."

I contemplated ways to change the subject immediately. I exposed my bottom teeth awkwardly, slanted my eyebrows, and shook my head in disagreement.

"So," I said, "how was your day?"

After a while, it was obvious he found me attractive, which actually made me pretty uncomfortable. I don't know why, but there's just something about being complimented that really gets to me. I always tend to get uneasy once someone has uttered those dreadful words: "pretty", "attractive", or "beautiful" (the worst one). A part of me knew that Mike really liked to me.

For the most part, he actually looked at my face when we were conversing, instead of my tits, which was something I had never really experienced. It was pretty refreshing. However, we had both established that neither of us was looking for anything at that time—at all. We were both focused on school and being a fuckboy and fuckgirl.

We hit it off so well, though. We just clicked—and we balanced each other out (he was from the suburbs, and I was from the hood). I don't know if it was because I found his conversation enticing, or because my only intention getting into that car in the first place was to have a mouthful of dick, but that's neither here nor there. (I was going through some things, you guys. I was just in self-destruct mode. I was stressed about school, and money, and family. It was a downward spiral, honestly, truly.)

Eventually, his dick was out, he was holding my still wet hair in a ponytail, and *Nothing Was the Same* started playing in the background (I told you!). Now, I won't go into much detail (simply because for a while, I considered him one of my best friends), but as far as dicks go, let's just say that it wasn't the longest strand on the scalp, (if you know what I mean), but it was a thick, healthy strand. Fuck it; it was a chode, okay? It was short, and thick. It was a Vienna sausage. It was an Orange Crush soda can. It was a fucking C-battery. Are you happy now?

Surprisingly, his dick smelled good, though (also a fat girl observation). It kind of smelled like Gain, and tasted like nothing (which was a plus). If I can't say anything good about his dick, I can say that it smelled and tasted pretty decent. It could be because big girls just naturally have heightened senses, and I was probably hungry, but there you have it.

He came in a matter of two minutes. I felt my mouth fill up with a warm, salty-sweet and thick liquid. I didn't know what to do! I was low-key (high-key) freaking the fuck out on the inside. I had never practiced what it would be like catching cum. I had never had to make the choice between being a spitter or a swallower until that very moment. I asked myself if I should spit it out, or stop being a little bitch and take the "L", opening up Pandora's box. I opened up the box—or opened up the back of my throat and drank him down (whichever sounds best to you).

He leaned back in his seat out of breath, with his hands intertwined behind his head. I felt my stomach churning. That was the moment I knew I had fucked up. You know how they say you should never swim on a full stomach? Well, if you're going to have someone's kids swimming around in your mouth and stomach, it'd probably be a good idea to eat something beforehand.

I saw patrol lights reflect off of his face and sure enough, Cockblock Central (4040) swooped in to ruin the night. He put his seatbelt back on and started the car up.

"What you wanna do?" he asked as we pulled out of the parking lot. "You hungry?"

The fat girl in me that hadn't eaten all day was hungry, but the girl whose stomach was doing backflips really just wanted to be hugging a fucking toilet for the rest of the night.

"Nah, can you just drive me back to my dorm? I'm not feeling good."

We said our goodbyes and he told me to feel better. I ran up four flights of stairs because I didn't feel like waiting for the elevator. I'm a big bitch; we don't do running and we *certainly* don't do stairs. I got back to my apartment just in time. I pushed the bathroom door open and hurled my body past the sink. I almost didn't make it. I spent the rest of the night puking up water and cum. That was the night I found out that an empty stomach and swallowing cum don't mix well. That was arguably one of the worst nights of my life. But did it keep me away from dick? By now, you probably know me well enough to know the answer to that question. I never really possessed the ability to make smart decisions.

Part III: FWB

11. Peter, Pussy Popper?

∞

November 3rd, 2013

We had just finished up with midterms. It was like any other Friday night. I had made a face-sitting appointment with a guy from my roster. Normally, they would come over, we would chill, and we would converse. They would eat my pussy then try to fuck, and I would turn them down. They said pretty much anything in hopes of getting pussy. When I would initially tell them that I wasn't interested in hooking up, they would try to hit me with "just let me taste it", with every intention of fucking; but the gag was, they were never going to.

Of course you would think that it was because I was so hell bent on remaining a virgin, but it was mainly because I honestly didn't give a fuck about anyone else but myself at the time. I know that sounds pretty shitty on my end, but I was convinced that every nigga was the same. I hadn't even had the chance to lose my virginity and I had already gotten used to people lying to me. So, I used them to get what I wanted before they had the chance of doing the same to me. I told you, I was a fuckgirl. I'm not ashamed to admit that. I think everyone goes through that fuckperson phase in life— when they feel like everyone is trying to play them.

On this specific night, Mike was supposed to come over. So, after finishing up homework (on a Friday night, might I add), I proceeded to the "Three S's" (in case you forgot: shit, shower, shave). He was going to be home for the weekend and promised me we would hang out.

When 1 am rolled around, I still hadn't heard a word from him. I called to make sure he was still coming. There was no better way for him to prove to me that he was an even bigger bitch than I had initially thought he was than for him to come up with some bullshit excuse as to why he wouldn't be able to make it. He claimed that he was doing laundry at his mom's house and that he wasn't sure whether or not he was going to come through.

Do you remember Commandment #3 in the beginning of the book—when I spoke about being a caring fuckboy? In this sense, Mike was (and still is to this day) a caring fuckboy. I think deep down inside, he knew that if he had come over, we probably would've fucked, and he didn't want to be the fuckboy to take my virginity. I had recently told him that I was still a virgin, and he starting acting differently. It wasn't in a bad way; he just eased up on the sexual innuendo. We had become pretty good friends in as little as a month, and he had started to see the good person beneath my fuckgirl exterior.

Normally (had it been a weekday), I would have blown it off because I had a lot of other options, to be honest. But for some reason unbeknownst to me (because the school has a lot of potential), Bowie's campus, on the weekends, is always dead as fuck. There were barely any parties, and if a party did occur, 4040 would shut it down almost immediately. Most people just went home Friday nights.

I figured I'd make a post on Instagram and Twitter to see if anyone wanted to chill. I sent out a tweet and posted a video on Instagram to weigh my options.

Within two minutes, at least ten niggas had posted their phone numbers under photos a billion weeks old, and twelve niggas were already in my DMs on Twitter. I got a text from an unknown number with the 👀 emoji. After asking a series of questions, I later found out it was Malcolm. He claimed that he had missed me so much that he downloaded a free phone number app just to contact me. Typical.

So, besides the fact that this doorknob dingaling ass nigga had the nerve to go out of his way to text me even though he had a girlfriend, I continued browsing through the profiles of the people that had reached out. One guy did catch my eye. According to his Twitter page, he was into photography, was from Baltimore, and also transferred to Bowie that semester. We'll call him Peter. After messaging back and forth, I invited him up for a *real* nightcap. After Mike bailed on me, I wasn't really in the mood for, nor was I interested in doing anything sexual with anyone.

About ten minutes passed and I heard a knock on my front door. I got up and walked out of my room toward the kitchen. When I opened the door, he was standing in the doorway, staring at his phone. When he looked up, I felt a little giddy, not because he was cute or anything, but because, at the time, I was madly in love with Kid Cudi and everything about his music (it was a tie between him and Childish Gambino), and Peter looked just like him. If only Cudi were a tad darker, a tad chubbier, and a bit more *colorful* (which we will fucking get to), he'd be the spitting image of Peter.

Immediately, I had gotten a vibe that he was a little *extra*. I had gotten the feeling that he fancied a little extra sprinkles on his cupcakes, if you know what I mean. It seemed like he preferred sausage to bacon, if you catch my drift. It seemed like he preferred bananas to strawberries. He was obviously gayer than a double-sided rainbow with cotton candy at both ends (or so I thought). It was his demeanor, his mannerisms, his tone.

I let him in and we stepped into my room. I sat at my desk and he sat on my bed. We introduced ourselves, of course. He told me about him and about his hobbies. He mentioned that he was from Baltimore. It was pretty much the standard stuff. We spoke about our favorite musicians. He spoke about Beyoncé—fucking Beyoncé! Honestly, it was refreshing because it felt like I didn't need to act sexy or flirt with him. We spoke about sex and about the fact that I was still a virgin momentarily. In my mind, I had obviously misinterpreted what he had said on Twitter an hour before as flirting. In my mind, I just knew this guy was obviously gay. There's no way he could have possibly been attracted to me in any way.

We essentially had an actual conversation, with words and meaning. He didn't call me beautiful, which was a relief. He did, however comment on my hair, and my nails. I was happy. Shit, I was fucking ecstatic. Here with another guy friend I could add to my friend roster. A decent 90% of my friends are gay or bi (including myself), so I felt pretty comfortable around him.

Of all the fucking DVDs that I own (200+), he chose "Easy A" for us to watch. It was official; Peter was Kinsey 6 gay, I just knew it. Sure, I doubted my assumption when he asked if he could wrap his arm around me. Sure, it was a little strange when his hands repeatedly brushed up against my ass, but gay guys love ass! Sure, it was a little weird that I felt his dick up against my ass (and for a moment, I thought it was hard), but he had on some sweatpants, so of course I would feel his dick.

When the movie was over, we called it a night and he gave me a hug goodbye.

∞
November 4th, 2013

Imagine my surprise when the next morning he asked if we could watch another movie together that night.

"Of course," I texted back.

"This time, can we make out?" he replied. "Lol."

Lol? Lo-fucking-l?! I was stuck! My mind was in a thousand different places at once. Could my Gaydar have been misleading me! For two fucking hours, I let this nigga pretty much hold me and put his dick on my butt without caring because I was under the impression that he was gay—two fucking hours!

"Huh?" I messaged.

"Lol, you know," he typed as more gray dots popped up. "Kissing. Fondling."

"I didn't know you liked me like that," I suggested.

"Of course I do," he sent. "You're funny as hell. You're beautiful."

There it was. Just like that, I was finally on the same page as he was, and it wasn't glitter-coated like I had initially assumed.

That entire day, I ignored all of Mike's texts and calls and did the laundry that had been stacking up in my closet. I got a dub of weed from the plug and spent the rest of my day thinking about my life choices. I smoked two and a half jays all by my lonesome. When it all came down to it, I figured I would go ahead and throw it at him. Why the hell not? Every other nigga on my line was fucking it up anyway.

It could've been because I was high as fuck. It could've been because I was the only one of my friends who was still a virgin (and I was the oldest by at least a couple months, so there's that). I wouldn't say that peer pressure got to me; a large part of me wanted to experience the dick that I had graciously allowed to rest on my ass-cheeks for two hours. Blessing me with the dick was the least he could do, right?

I just wanted to see what all the hype was about. I was almost twenty-one and contrary to popular belief, having your pussy eaten almost every night by fellow fuckboys was entirely overrated. I had dedicated two or so years to practicing and I was finally ready to lose my virginity. I called Peter on the phone. Before he could even say "hello", "hi", or "hey", I cut him off. I tended to do that when I was high.

"So like… do you wanna fuck?" I asked.

"Wait," he hesitated. "What?" He snickered thinking I was joking.

"Do you," I paused for an obnoxiously long amount of time, "wanna fuck?"

"Yes?" he answered in a high-pitched, confused tone. "When?"

I told him that 8 o'clock would be good for me. Then I ended up falling asleep eating Domino's Pizza and watching a fucking Golden Girls marathon; don't judge me, I just like the Golden Girls, okay? In a sense, Blanche Devereaux and Rose Nylund are indeed my spirit animals. Come to think of it, so are Sophia and Dorothy. It had to have been no later than 2 pm. When I opened my eyes and checked my phone, it was well after 8. Peter had been sending me a slew of question marks and 👀 emojis. I rubbed my eyes and unlocked my phone.

"Hey," I texted him. "Sorry, I fell asleep."

Grey dots popped up immediately.

"It's cool. When should I come over?" he replied.

We had agreed on 9 o'clock, sharp then got off the phone. I sat up and proceeded to the "three S's". I called my best friend at the time (Brittany) to ask her for some advice. I put her on speaker and hopped into the shower. We were literally having a conversation about blowjobs, anal, and all sorts of shit as if there weren't three other people living in the same apartment as me and the walls weren't paper thin. But did I give a sprinkle of a fuck? You've probably already gathered that I did not. She told me that I should douche beforehand. I started freaking out because, for one, the idea of a douche grossed me the fuck out—and two, I didn't have one.

"Well, do you have a water bottle?" she asked as the crackling of shower water echoed throughout the suite.

"Yeah," I answered. "Why?"

"Well bitch, hurry the fuck up and go get one!"

Now, you can assume that because I was in such a vulnerable place and hadn't really had any experience in the field of having my vagina poked and prodded by someone's dick, I went along with whatever she was saying. In hindsight, maybe she wasn't the best person to call considering the fact that she now has two children (by a nigga that doesn't even love her), but I digress. I hopped my big ass out of the shower, ran butt-ass naked to my bedroom, pulled out a water bottle, and ran back to the bathroom. Mind you, three other people lived in that very same fucking apartment, and they had guests on the regular. But, like I said, I gave no fucks at the time.

Would you believe me if I told you that she taught me how to make a homemade douche? I kid you not. I couldn't make this shit up even if I tried. She told me to pour the water out then to fill it up with warm water. Then she told me to add in a few squirts of Summer's Eve and shake it up.

(Side note: Now before I continue, there is something I need to address. Ladies (and guys, I guess) there is a huge difference between Vagisil and Summer's Eve, okay? Summer's Eve is for <u>maintaining</u> a healthy pH balance, and Vagisil is for

fixing an unhealthy pH. So if you see Vagisil in someone's restroom, just know that they are going through some things and it is not pretty.)

Would you believe me if I told you that she expected me to shake it up, spread my legs, open up my pussy lips and squeeze it into Nikki? (Oh, by the way, "Nikki" is what I refer to my pussy as because she has a mind of her own.)

I'm not going to go into a lot of detail, but let's just say that the inside of my vagina smelled and felt like roses, daises, unicorns, and some other shit. Fortunately, I had already Naired away my pussy hairs the night before, and that whole area was pretty much smoother dick. Sometimes you've gotta do what you've gotta do. I'm not afraid to admit that that shower was a pivotal moment in my life. Unbeknownst to me, after I stepped out, I was never the same. Actually, I was never the same when I willingly, not only made a homemade douche, but used it, but that's neither here nor there.

I hopped out and twerked a little bit. I was embarrassingly happy. I felt squeaky-clean. Nikki was bald, my skin was clear, my hair was growing and flouring, my homework was done, all of my laundry was washed, I was about to be dicked down for the first time. Life was good. I did not have one fucking care in the world.

I dried off and put on what would later be considered the "In-House Dick-Getting Attire" (that's a real thing, by the way—it goes by many names). This consisted of a Victoria's Secret matching bra and thong set, a pair of black leggings (or booty shorts if you're feeling frisky or the weather is appropriate), a pair of footie socks, a crew neck sweatshirt (or a tank top/cami, t-shirt, or sports bra when applicable), and a messy bunny (or high ponytail if desired).

I sat down at my desk, and spun my makeup carousel trying to figure out what "Dick-Getting Makeup" look (also a thing) I wanted to go for. I was eager to find foundation I wanted to be wiped off during the course of a blowjob. I didn't choose my Lancôme foundation because that would've been too fancy (and that shit literally costs $50). I didn't want to go with Black Opal because the guy that agreed to pop my cherry deserved more than that, you know? I had finally decided on a happy medium and chose my Mac Studio Fix foundation in the color NC45. It was perfect for the occasion.

At 9 o'clock on the dot, homeboy texted me saying that he was outside my door. I hopped up out of my seat, reached for Pure Seduction (by Victoria's Secret) and sprayed myself from head to toe. That's the final touch, and then you're officially ready for the dick-down (kind of like a touchdown, but a touchdown in your guts).

I got all giddy inside and practically ran to the dick,

(I mean door). I looked through the peephole, inhaled through my nose, and exhaled sharply from my mouth.

I opened the door. Of course, the awkward hellos happened, which were followed by the awkward hugging. When we got to my room, he kicked his shoes off and plopped onto my bed. He tapped his hand on the bed suggesting that I sit beside him. I looked down and watched my feet walk over to him.

Moments later, my knees were kissing the floor. I can't really remember a lot up until that moment because I was still pretty high. He helped me unbuckle his pants. He pulled down his boxers and out plopped a veiny monstrous cock. It was long and thick, with a slight upward curve. It was the type of length that made me incredibly worried. I'm not too proud to admit that the better half of my first semester at Bowie was spent sucking on Tic Tacs—so it was different. This was all new! His dick fucked me up. For the first time ever, I was being exposed to someone whose dick was longer than my middle finger. Game. Changer.

It was a work of art. It was brown, with extraordinarily deep purple hues. The veins spiraled around his dick like a piece of abstract art or like licorice strands before you pull them apart. I don't know why it made me hungry, but I felt my mouth water and my begin clit throbbing.

I took no chances. I reached my hand out and wrapped it around its girth. I caught a whiff of it and it smelled like a garbage can after six straight days of rain. I was bummed, but it was already too late to turn back. I spat on it, spat on it again, and then again to dilute the smell. I made sure we locked eyes. I slowly guided his chocolate-dipped Eckrich sausage into my mouth. I spent six or seven strokes specifically focusing on the tip and slowly made my way down to the base.

He let out a quivering sigh. I watched his stomach contract. I made sure my suction was on point and the slobber was kept up to par. He reached for my messy bun and pretty much took the lead. Every time my lips touched the base, everything went black. Yes, there is such a thing as too much. Of course I gagged, but I kept myself from making that infamous gagging face. As he guided my head, he closed his eyes and tilted his head back with his mouth wide open. Then he completely lied back.

I grabbed onto his thick thighs for leverage occasionally and dug my nails in when the scent got a little too much or when I felt like I was going to die. A part of me tried to make myself believe that it wasn't his dick smelling like that, because the garlic sauce that I had poured onto my pizza earlier that day was still sitting on my desk.

The head was so wet that my fingers started pruning. That should say something about the dedication I had at the moment. He yanked me by my messy bun and forced me to stand. He walked around me, pushed onto my shoulders and I fell down onto the bed. He pulled my leggings off, then spread my legs into a split and got down on his knees. He didn't have the sense to push the skin back on my clit, but he stuffed his face with my pussy after pulling the thong to the side. He motor-boated his face into Nikki, and I grabbed onto his uncut bush with both hands (I tried to run my fingers through it, but that didn't really work out). I wish I could say that it was the best head that I had ever gotten, and that I saw shooting stars, fireworks, and felt the earth moving, but the head was especially mediocre.

It seemed like he knew what he was doing, though. Well, he didn't eat pussy like a gay guy. It felt like he had done it before. Peter slid a finger into my creamy pussy and finally found my clit with his mouth. He started sucking on it, which felt really good, but still, no stars and no cigars. Then he started flicking his finger inside of me like that would do something. Guys (or girls), if you're going to finger someone, do it with a purpose.

Eventually, he was stretching a Magnum condom over his dick. He got onto the bed and climbed between my legs. He took his dick in his hands and rubbed the tip on my clit (which made me wetter). Then he looked up at me.

"You sure you want to do this?" he asked before sealing the deal.

"Yeah," I said, nodding my head and flaring my nostrils. "But be gentle. If it hurts too much, that's it."

He bobbed his head and glanced down at his dick. He tried to slide it inside of me, but my walls just wouldn't allow it. I felt the pressure of his dick pushing up against me and trying to get inside, but my walls refused to relax. I felt my skin trying to stretch further than it ever had. Not even my juices alleviated the situation.

"You gotta relax," he stressed. "I'm not gonna hurt you, I promise."

I had to think calm thoughts. I had to make my pussy calm; I had to make my pussy feel at peace. I had to relax my body and just let go.

Then, it happened. His dick pierced into me. He sighed and started moaning. My hymen was in shambles. It felt like my insides were being ripped apart and shredded. My body grew stiff in agony. I wrapped my legs around him, but that only forced him further inside me. I scratched on his back but that only encouraged him.

I winced and sharply breathed in through the grip of my teeth.

"Wait, wait, wait, wait," I called out.

He eased up, pulled out, and rested on his calves.

"Oh, shit!" he said worriedly. "Did I hurt you?"

I shook my head but didn't move my body at all. I just lied there looking up at the ceiling and held my index finger up.

"Just…" I paused for a moment "Give me a moment."

Thirty seconds passed and his dick was still erect. I fanned my hand at him, signaling him to hop back onto the pony. My mother didn't raise a punk ass bitch, so I was going to get through this, even if it meant having the outsides of my vagina burn from being stretched and literally cracked open. My juice only perpetuated the situation because the wetter I got, the more it burned.

"You sure?" he inquired.

I nodded my head again.

"Yeah, let's go," I replied.

He slowly thrusted back in and sighed pleasurably. I centered my focus on his bulging dick rubbing up against my walls inside of me, and not so much on the skin surrounding my pussy that burned like a bitch. When I did that, I actually fell in love with the sensation and the macaroni sounds. It was like I was sucking him in. He let it get to his head too much and started trying to shove his entire dick inside of me.

He had me fifty shades of fucked up if he thought that Nikki was going to be able to accommodate his entire eight inches like it was just a cakewalk. No, sir. I pushed on his stomach to hint that his airplane was coming in a little too hot. He was going to town—it was too painful.

The burning was overwhelming—not to mention the part about him stabbing me in the guts. Every slow stroke he gave, the further I tried to run away, the closer he got, and the deeper he went. It was a vicious cycle. I was on the verge of crying but I bit my bottom lip. He put his weight on his hands while slowly stroking inside me. He must've loved Nikki because it seemed like every time he stroked, the louder and more drawn out his moans became. We locked eyes and his face lowered down to my mine. He tried to kiss me. I turned my head and he landed on my neck. He started sucking on it and whispered into my ear.

"You like this dick?" he said, panting.

I just nodded my head while tears fell down into my hair. I looked at him and he made what I would like to consider the "National Cumming Face". His nostrils flared, his jaw dropped, his breath paused, and his head started trembling. I felt his dick pulsating slowly inside of me as the condom filled up with a warm liquid rhythmically. The pulsating stopped and he fell down on top of me.

We cuddled for about ten minutes and he asked me how I liked it.

"It was cool," I assured, "but it hurt really hurt."

"I'm sorry about that," he said. "I just couldn't help it. But it won't hurt after a while. You just gotta get used to it."

It was the beginning of a friends-with-benefits situation. I was never really attracted to Peter, but he was attracted to me. He was actually pretty cute, in a "he may or may not be gay" kind of way.

Once he left, I had to change my sheets because there were a few blood stains underneath where I lied. Afterwards, I brushed my teeth for ten minutes straight, then took a bubble bath because my entire body ached. As I lied in the bathtub with candles burning and a Miguel Pandora radio station playing in the background, only then did it finally hit me that I was no longer a virgin. All the songs started to resonate with me on a spiritual level. I lost my virginity November 4th, 2013—and I haven't been right since. I thought that Malcolm had opened up Pandora's Box, but that box had nothing compared to the one Peter had opened. It was only the beginning.

12. Man of Omega

∞

Mid-November, 2013

I had been fucking Peter regularly for about two weeks. By then, I was completely, without a doubt, 100%, unequivocally addicted to sex. I kept him on speed dial. We had fucked almost every night after I gave my virginity to him. He had been acting weird lately because he kept hinting that he wanted to be more than friends, which would later be the pattern guys would follow after I'd have sex with them. To this day, I'm not sure if it's a blessing or a curse. So I was on the hunt for new dick—to start anew. I was officially a newly-inducted member of the sexually-active population and he had unknowingly, unintentionally, single-handedly created a monster.

One day, my cousin Alysha wanted me to do her hair. So I caught the MARC train and metro to her house. I probably finished her hair around 7 pm. She was supposed to take me back to campus that night, but if she had, you wouldn't be reading this chapter. Her boyfriend, Jaylen, walked into the apartment and they started talking. I don't really know what they were saying because I was on the phone with Peter trying to make a dick appointment and he was being utterly difficult.

Alysha looked at me.

"You tryna stay here tonight for a kickback?" she asked.

I shrugged my shoulders because Peter was playing games.

"Yeah," I said. "I'm down."

Alysha went to go drop her son off at his father's house because he had custody on the weekends. Jaylen and I went to go get weed and liquor. We ended up having to scoop up some of his friends because his best friend was back in town.

So we ended up in Randallstown, Maryland. We pulled up to a house. It was all pretty much downhill from there.

"Oh, God," I thought to myself. "More fucking Baltimore niggas." This had fuckery and foolishness written all over it. An entire fucking slew of niggas came pouring out of that house. Honestly, I'm not going to lie; they were all cute (hoe thoughts) and they all had the perfect faces for seats (more hoe thoughts). But I knew deep down that from the looks of things, they were all fuckboys (*especially* if they were all from Baltimore).

"I'll be right back," Jaylen said.

He got out of the car and walked up to the group. They did that dap and back-punch shit niggas do instead of hugging each other or shaking hands. They spoke for a while. I stayed in the car, smoking a cigarette. The windows were up because it was too fucking cold outside. His back was to me but the other guys were facing me.

I noticed one of them pointing and nodding in my direction inquiring about who I was. Then they went into the house and came back a while after. Jaylen and three of them came toward the car. The other four in the group got into a car across the street. Jaylen got in and told me that he had to say hello to his homie's mom because it had been a while. I still don't really know why he felt the need to tell me that because I didn't give a fuck.

Two of his friends got in on my side, and the other one got in on Jaylen's side. He started the car and introduced us.

He pointed at one dude.

"Tiy," he said, "this is Mark."

Mark waved.

Jaylen pointed at the other.

"And this one's Patrick."

Patrick nodded his head, then Jaylen pointed to the last one. He parted his lips.

"And I'm Kirk," the last guy said.

Kirk reached his hand out for mine and I gave it to him. He smiled.

"Nice to meet you, beautiful," Kirk said.

I smiled awkwardly.

"It's nice to meet you, too."

(Side note: I feel the need to let you all know that my type for the longest time had and always had been dark-skinned, but Kirk was light-skinned with green eyes. I knew he was

trouble—that he had broken hearts and punctured vaginas up and down the DMV area. Is that racist?)

He licked his lips and acted like a typical light-skinned nigga. He even flashed the "National Light-Skinned Nigga" face (he put his chin between his thumb and index finger, tilted his head, squinted, and side-smiled).

I turned back around in my seat and lit another cigarette. That was the biggest mistake ever. All hell broke loose.

"Aye yo," (Baltimore niggas love the word "yo", by the way) Kirk said. "Chill. You look too good to be smoking, sweetheart."

"Bro, forget it," Jaylen said. "I said something to her about it when we first met. She just don't give a fuck. Let it go, please."

I looked at Jaylen and somehow managed to maintain my composure.

I turned my palms upwards and pointed at him.

"But aren't you like an alcoholic?" I asked. "Do you have any idea what your kidneys look like, homie?"

Then Jaylen and I started arguing as if I was the one in a relationship with him instead of my damn cousin. Then Kirk felt the need to add in his two cents once more.

"But that shit's not cute, sweetheart," he added.

That was when he fucked up. "Come on down, Kirk," I thought to myself. "You're the next contestant on "The Shade is Right!"

"First of all," I said, "when I smoke cigarettes, I don't do it to be "*cute*", my nigga. It's not that type of party. And second of all, when I drink, I don't do it to be "*cute*" either, so what's up?" I poked my lips out, ready to argue my point.

Kirk just sighed. I turned to the other guys and they were on their phones. Then I turned back around and took the most satisfying, drawn-out puff from a cigarette I've ever taken.

"Raise your hand if you don't think smoking is cute," I said. I looked in the rear-view mirror and noticed that everyone in the car except for Mark had their hand up. He was too into his phone.

"Now, raise your hand if you really think I give a fuck," I said. Nobody bothered to raise their hand. They knew they couldn't win, or wouldn't hear the end of it.

"But raise your hand if you smoke weed," I added.

Everyone raised their hand. Then we all burst out laughing.

Patrick cleared his throat.

"Yo," (there we go with that "yo" shit again) he said, "you funny!"

"Yeah," Kirk jumped in. "You cool as shit".

I smirked a little and took another drag from my cigarette.

Then, Mark actually contributed to the conversation.

"Where you from, yo?" he asked.

"DC," I replied.

Mark started laughing.

"DC niggas is clowns," he said.

(Side note: If you don't know anyone from Baltimore, "clown" is a very ambiguous term. It can mean one of two things: either it means "funny"/"hilarious", or "whack"/"weak". There's no in-between. But based on his context, I assumed he meant the latter).

Someone had asked me what school I went to, and I told them Bowie. They expressed to me how they had friends there, but I didn't care because most of the people that attend Bowie are from Baltimore, so it wasn't ground-breaking information, you know?

We pulled up to a gas station to get some rellos (short for Cigarello, white people). Mark hopped out of the car.

"How come Mark is so quiet?" I asked. "He always this shy?"

"Nah," one of them said. "He just got out—that's why he actin' weird, for real."

"Out of what?" I asked. "School? The Army?"

Everyone in the car started laughing because apparently whatever I had said was the funniest thing ever.

"Prison, Tiy," Jaylen said. "He just got outta prison."

I felt my eyes grow wide in disbelief.

"For what," I asked. "How long was he in there?"

"Armed robbery," he replied. "And two years."

I cleared my throat.

"I'm sorry, what?" I asked worriedly.

Jaylen and Kirk chuckled.

"Yeah, he robbed a gas station or somethin'," Patrick said. "I can't remember, though. I wanna say it was a 7Eleven."

"Nah," Jaylen said. "It was just a gas station."

I pinched the bridge of my nose for seconds then rubbed my forehead, just soaking it all in. I was in shock—I swore it was just a joke they were playing on me.

"Okay, let me get this right," I said, "because I *clearly* didn't hear y'all correctly. Y'all telling me that he literally just **got out of jail** for *armed robbery* and for whatever reason, y'all think it's appropriate for him to go into a gas station by himself?"

No one said anything.

"Makes sense," I added sarcastically.

A couple minutes passed and I tried to shrug it off. Then I asked them if they knew whether or not that particular gas station sold 4Lokos. They told me that it did. So I hopped out of the car to get me a couple.

I stepped in, picked up some 4Lokos from the fridge in the back, and walked up to the other register. Mark stood beside me at the other register. Then he looked over and reached for my things.

"I got it," he said.

I thanked him for the offer but politely declined.

"I said I got it, yo. Damn."

I was not trying to argue with him. I just stood there as they rang my stuff up with his.

He bought Coca-Cola, Sprite, Jolly Ranchers, Twizzlers, Skittles, and Starbursts.

*(Side note: Now, if you're not black, these items may sound like typical soft drinks and hard candy. But I assure you they are nothing of the sort. For black people, especially if they buy Rellos **and** those specific sodas, it's about to go down.)*

It was awkward. I thanked him and he nodded. He pulled a roll of money out of his pockets, sifted through it for the correct amount of money, and handed it to the guy behind the counter.

"You know Kirk is gonna try an' smack at you, right?"

(Side note: For my less urban-exposed readers, the term "smack" means to flirt with/holler at/woo/hook up with/smash/bang/bone/screw/fuck—all that good stuff.)

"Oh, Lord," I uttered. "Why me?"

"He has a thing for pretty, light-skinned big girls," Mark stated.

I felt a war going on inside of me. I mean, don't get me wrong; he wasn't ugly, at all. Actually, he was cute as fuck, but he was light-skinned and from Baltimore. Those are my two no-nos. I considered actually giving him a chance on our way back to the car, though.

Let me break this down for you: when we walked back into the apartment, Alysha had not gotten back yet. So essentially, there were eight guys, and one girl. If you subtract Jaylen, there were seven guys and one girl. Fuck no. Jaylen introduced me to the other four guys. As soon as I had the chance, I headed to the kitchen to put my drinks into the freezer. I darted to my other cousin's room to get a pair of shorts because they kept the heat in their apartment on 5000°. Then I went to Alysha's room and waited for her because that was just too much damn testosterone around me.

About thirty minutes later, I heard the front door open and close. I heard music blasting and started smelling weed, but she didn't come to the room for a good ten minutes. That bitch didn't even text or ask about me.

She walked into the room and looked confused.

"Why are you in here by yourself?" she asked.

I lowered my eyes at her as if to say "Bitch, you know why." She laughed and grabbed my arm.

"C'mon," she said. "It's not gonna be just two girls, I promise."

That sort of made me feel better. We walked down the hallway and turned the corner. They were passing around at least six jays. Two of the guys were in the dining room making lean. That was when I realized that they weren't playing any games. Hood beverage essentials were spread out all across the living room table: SOLO cups, a bowl of ice, Henny, Sveka, Jack, Jager, a plethora of chips, Kool-Aid in a jug, Rock Creek sodas, and some wine coolers.

I looked over at Kirk and he started cheesing. He tapped on the couch beside him and Alysha pushed me over to him. He was obviously fucked up. I sat down and gave him the most unbothered, uninterested, unnecessary frown I think I've ever given to anyone.

A jay came to me and I took a couple puffs (puff, puff, pass is a real thing) and started coughing. By the time I passed the second jay to the next person, I was gone. A jay came around every thirty seconds. This went on for twenty fucking minutes. I was so high that I had to pace my breaths and let the tingling perforate throughout my entire body.

I looked to my left and a group of girls walked in. I literally felt my face slowly forming a smile. Then it finally hit me that they were all ugly. I looked over at Alysha and spread my hands out in confusion.

"How is this helping?!" I yelled across the living room.

Everyone looked at me, wondering what I was talking about, but we were all too high to even care.

If anything, that made the entire situation a whole lot worse. Kirk wouldn't feel the need to flirt with ugly bitches. But then again, I didn't care at the moment because I was too busy being hot and cold at the same time. All I could do was laugh. I couldn't even be upset.

Someone turned the bass all the way up on the iDock. It was so loud that the Kool-Aid was actually shaking. The kickback had officially turned into a party. The entire apartment was smoky. I started seeing niggas tripping and falling over one another. I stood up to get my drinks from the freezer. Kirk slapped my ass. I sat down on his lap (not because I wanted to or anything, but because I was honestly too fucked up to stand and he threw me off balance).

I yelled across the room at Alysha again and asked her to get my 4Lokos out of the freezer. She brought them over and dropped them into my arms. Kirk was holding me by my hips and grinding under me. I put two off to the side of his feet and popped the top on one. It was all over for me. I literally drank it all the way down in under thirty seconds. I reached down and popped another one open. I started hearing my heartbeat—or maybe it was the music, I don't know.

I stood up and turned around, spread my legs and sat back down on Kirk's lap, facing him. I started grinding on his dick.

Then they turned the lights out and the countdown to the fuckery began. By now, you should know that I'm not really like that, but when I'm inebriated, I do some dumb shit. I mean honestly, after reading what you've read thus far, can you name one instance when I did something stupid completely sober?

I wrapped my arms around his shoulders and starting kissing and licking on his neck. He smelled so fucking good, even better than Mike. He wrapped his arms tighter around my waist, then traced his hands back to my ass and slapped it. He started moving his hips under me. Then he yanked my hair back so that I couldn't move my neck. He pulled me in and started biting and sucking on it.

Then he slid his hand into the leg opening of my shorts and managed to pull my thong over to the side. He pulled the skin on the clit up, then slid his other hand into the other leg opening and started rubbing on my the exposed clit—that was strike one.

Keep in mind that there were almost twenty other people in that living room with us, but it was dark. The only light came from peoples' phones. Also keep in mind that Patrick was literally sitting right beside us, and Mark was beside him.

Kirk pulled is hands out. I thought he was done, but he wasn't. He leaned back and readjusted his body. He reached for my shorts again and started unraveling the drawstrings! He inched his hand under my stomach and shoved it down into my thong. He put his thumb into my pussy and massaged my asshole with another finger—that was strike two.

He had already wrapped his arm around my back, so I couldn't go anywhere. He was strong as fuck. I was seriously in the living room moaning and stuck. Had the music not been blasting, it would have legitimately sounded like the set of a porno. I felt people dancing behind me because they kept bumping up against my back.

He tugged me by my shirt and pulled me in closer.

"Yo, shut the fuck up," he said near my face.

He put his lips against mine and I pulled back. He yanked my shirt again and kissed me. You guys should know by now that I'm not into kissing someone that I don't give a fuck about.

I pulled his hands out of my shorts and got my phone out of the side pocket. Then I leaned over and popped open my last 4Loko. I could see him reaching for his pants. He pulled his fucking dick out and took my phone from me like I was a toddler. He grabbed me by my wrist and put my hand on his dick. His dick wasn't even hard and it was seven inches long.

"Strike three," I thought to myself. "You getting fucked, homeboy!"

I guided him to my other cousin's room. As soon as we walked in, he pushed me onto the bed. He took his shirt off. He had abs for days—abs for fucking **days**! His fucking abs had abs. Then I noticed a branding on his chest, but I couldn't make it out because I didn't have my glasses on. Then I moved in closer and realized it was an Omega symbol branded on his chest. And then it hit me.

"You're a fucking Que (pronounced "Q", or "cue") dawg?!" I asked.

He smirked. "Most of us in here are."

It had all made sense: his lack of fucks, his aggression, his dedication to fuck, his obsession with my ass, his looks, his game. He was smooth as hell—I just hadn't realized it was because he was a man of Omega Psi Phi. To be completely honest, I didn't even care that he was most likely an absolute fuckboy because Nikki was hungry.

They say that men of Omega Psi Phi are "wholesome"—that they're "faithful" and "loving". I cannot deny that these things are all true—but the gag is that it's only true for the ones that have graduated from college and are no longer living the hoe lifestyle—the ones that are settled in their lives. It's only true for the ones that want to settle down and start a family. The young ones, the puppies, they're **all** sluts, but the girls can't help but to love them. When we see them, instead of running the opposite direction, there's something that forces us to chase them around like a snack, or a dessert, or a Thanksgiving dinner—like a fucking deer in the headlights. They are addictive—they're like fucking high fructose corn syrup: you know it's bad for you and that there's no way it could possibly end well, but we do it anyway.

I was so high that it really didn't matter that he was a Que; he could've been an A, B, C, D, E, and I still wouldn't have given an F.

I was in for a rude awakening. He looked down and licked his lips.

"You got some pretty ass feet," he said.

Confusion washed over me. Before I knew it, he was sucking my toes. I tried to tug my leg away from him, but he dug his nails into my leg and clenched harder.

"Don't do that," he demanded. "Let me be a dog."

I looked at him confused. Then he barked. What the fucked had I gotten myself into?

At the time, I thought it was just something that all Ques said and did. I thought for sure he couldn't have been serious. But boy, was I wrong. He continued sucking on my toes, pulled his dick, out and started jerking off.

He then kissed my inner ankle, then my shin, my calf, my knee, my thigh. He bit my inner thigh, hard. Then ripped my shorts off; he literally ripped them off (I had to pay my cousin $30 for those fucking shorts). He clamped down onto my thong and pulled it off with his teeth. I would soon find out that the infamous neck roll is not to be played with or underestimated.

"Take your shirt and your bra off," he commanded.

I did not argue, not even a little bit. This shit was fucking happening. He stood, grabbed me by the waist, turned me around, lifted my big ass up, wrapped his arms around my stomach, and flipped me over. I was upside down. My knees (and tits) were in my face (which sort of made it hard to breathe, but I digress). My thighs rested on his arms and my ass was underneath his chin.

"Open up your legs!" he yelled. He kissed my ass (literally—both cheeks), licked my crack, then my taint (the skin between my ass crack and pussy)! Then, he made his way to my pussy! I could hear him swishing my juices around in his mouth with his spit, gathering it.

All of a sudden, warm spit started oozing down my crack, down my back. Spit was dripping down my stomach, then between my boobs. Then he started rolling his neck. He stuck his tongue so far into my pussy that I actually felt his teeth scraping against my clit. Then he pulled it out and shoved his tongue down into my asshole. He pushed it all the way in; he literally started tongue-fucking my ass. I lifted my legs and curled my toes. He pushed my legs back down into my face. I kept asking myself what I had done to make him so upset. It hurt a little bit, but it felt fucking amazing at the same time. He spat again and dove into my pussy. He didn't ease into it; he just started jackhammering my pussy with his tongue.

Spit was splashing everywhere! Then he stopped. Some spit was sliding down my stomach.

"You better catch that shit," he said then went back to eating.

Then it dripped down further and he stopped.

"Catch it," he repeated.

The further it dripped down, the louder he yelled "catch it".

So, it had finally slid down between my tits, and I caught the spit; I fucking caught it with my mouth. I don't think he understood how far down the rabbit hole I was willing to go with him. I loved the taste of myself, so telling me to catch it was only doing me a favor.

He started sucking on my clit and stuck his fingers in my pussy and rubbed my asshole. He hummed on my clit. I came in a matter of twenty seconds. The cum had eventually made its way down my stomach again and I was prepared to catch it before he managed to say anything. It slid down further and I wiped some of it up with my fingers and shoved it into my mouth.

"Open your mouth," he called out.

I opened my mouth and stuck my tongue out. Then he went to my pussy, slurped up some cum and spit it down into my mouth. I swallowed it. He didn't understand how down I was for all of this, so me catching glimpses of his surprised face made the entire situation even more invigorating. He rubbed his entire face in my cum and in my ass—he started tongue-fucking my pussy again! I went numb and started sliding down, but he caught me and reinforced his grip around me. Then he went back to work. I came again and felt tears falling down my temples, into my hair.

I tried to push his head away, but he swatted my hands. Then he had eventually gotten fed up and put my hands under his knees! More cum started sliding down my crack He slurped it up, spat it out, and slurped it all up again!

It was all true! The rumors about Ques eating ass and pussy, and changing lives one tongue-fuck at a time were all true!

Cousin Cockblock came swooping in, banging on the door. I knew it would be Alysha, because she would be the only person to come looking for me. The music was still blasting, so her voice was muffled. He held me up and shifted his weight so that he was on his back and I was on his face (bars). He tapped me on my leg and I slid off of his face onto his chest.

"Grab my hair and put my face in it!" he said.

So I slid back onto his face and grabbed his hair. I took my other hand, pulled his dick out, and tried jerking him off. He slapped my hand again. Keep in mind that Alysha was still banging on the door, trying to get in. We just ignored her.

I reached for it again, but he yanked that arm and put it under his head. I was literally holding his head in my pussy with both my hands. He slid his head further down and shifted my body up a little. His nose was rubbing on my clit and his tongue was in my pussy. I started fucking his face and it was glorious. He pulled his hand around to his face, put his middle finger in his mouth, and snuck it into my asshole. Back then, I didn't really know how to feel about ass-play. I just went along with it.

All of a sudden, I felt like I had to pee. So I let his head go and tried to push off, but he clenched onto my thighs. I could not move or go anywhere. The harder I pulled away, the more he pressed down.

"I'm about to cum!" I screamed out. "I'm about to cum! I'm about to cum!"

He pulled down harder. It became way too intense. I let his head go, eased up, and started rubbing on my clit. He started licking everything as if he were trying to clean me up with his tongue.

Then all of a sudden, I pulled back and this clear, warm liquid came spraying out of me. I slapped my pussy and started crying and moaning. Then I tried to push off of his face, but he just rubbed his face in it. I went limp and lied back on his stomach. I tried to catch my breath. Meanwhile, his face was still down there. He was still slurping, coughing, spitting, and tugging on my clit with his lips. That was the first time I had ever squirted.

When you cum that hard, the only you can do is think about every single decision you've ever made in your life and how you ended up there. He smiled, and lifted me up off of him. He licked his lips, wiped his mouth off on the blanket, put his shirt back on and reached for the door.

I held my head up.

"Soooo," I said panting, "you not gonna wash your face off or anything?"

He looked at me, frowned, put his fingers back in his mouth and shook his head.

"Nah."

He ruined my life because he had changed it completely. He had opened a door that is rarely opened and didn't even grant me the dick. He shut the door behind him. I lied there for a couple minutes. My stomach started hurting. I jumped up and ran to the bathroom. I threw up everything then I rested my cheek on the toilet seat. I had vomit in my hair. Shit was serious.

I guess the whole maneuvering around forced everything up. I jumped in the tub, washed my hair and showered. I had to have been in there for at least 45 minutes. I got out and found some sweats and a shirt in my cousin's drawer. God was really looking out because I also found a new toothbrush in her bathroom mirror cabinet. I got the blanket off the bed and ran out to throw it into the washing machine. I crawled up into a ball on the bed. I thought I could roll with the big dogs, but I just couldn't. I dosed off.

When I woke up Alysha was in the bed smoking a jay. All I could do was smile. She knew exactly what had happened. She saw it on my face. Then she told me almost everyone had stayed there because they were too fucked up to drive. I looked at my phone and it was 4 o'clock in the morning.

Apparently, Jaylen was already in bed, but she just wanted to check on me and get the tea with her nosey ass. As soon as she left the room and I heard her bedroom door close, I jumped up and sprinted toward the living room. I snuck around the corner and everyone was snoring. I felt like OO7 trying to step over niggas. I tapped Kirk on the shoulder but he snored louder. Then I shook him and still nothing happened. I put my hands in his sweatpants and started stroking his dick. It woke up before he did.

"Wassup?" he groaned out.

"Nigga," I said with a blank face. "You know why I'm here."

I kept jerking him off, then he flinched and grabbed my hand.

"You tryna yeah?" he whispered quietly.

I nodded my head sternly.

"Well, duh," I replied.

He smiled at me, crossed his hands behind his head, and gestured toward his dick with his eyes.

"Prove it," he said and smirked.

I looked behind me. Everyone seemed to still be asleep. Then I whipped his dick out and got down on my knees.

"Go ahead," he rushed me. "I'm waiting."

I took a deep breath and womaned up. I shoved his dick in my mouth without hesitation.

As soon as I wrapped my lips around it, and swirled my tongue ring around the tip, he went crazy.

"Oh shit", he mumbled with his voice shuttering.

Sure enough, he cuffed my neck with one hand, and grabbed my hair with the other, pushing my head down. I'm not sure if he was trying to make me go brain dead or not, but it hurt. I was sucking it slow and steady. It wasn't necessarily because I wanted to; weed just slows me down, no matter what I'm doing.

I guess Kirk knew that the more you choked a bitch, the sloppier the head would be. I wanted to cough, but I couldn't. I wanted to gag, but I was scared I would wake someone up. My chin was wet, my pussy was wet, the couch was wet, his sweats were wet. It was just a wet, beautiful mess. Tears started rolling down my cheeks. Every time he'd press down, then eased up and pressed down again, it felt like I was dying each time it hit the back of my throat. All of a sudden, someone sighed, and Kirk slapped my forehead. I pulled off of his dick. I grabbed my forehead wondering what the fuck it meant. I'm not sure if it was a reflex or if it was because he was genuinely nervous.

I turned around and saw one of the guys stand up and scratch his balls. We kept still and watched as he stumbled down the hall and into the bathroom. He wanted me to keep going, so he pressed down on my neck again. I kept it stiff.

"Ummm," I whispered, "what are you doin'?"

Long story short, we ended up back in my other cousin's bedroom. I pushed his hand-happy ass onto the bed like he had done to me hours before. I yanked his sweats off in one swoop and went back to work, for real this time.

He gathered my hair into a ponytail. Then, he put my hair into two pigtails. For a moment, I thought he was going to start braiding my shit up since he wanted to act like an indecisive hairstylist. He yanked me up, and pushed me down over and over again. I probably got whiplash from the whole incident. Then I got fed up and took control. I wasn't about to have this nigga disrespecting my throat **and** my edges. No sir.

So I took a page out of his book. I let his dick go (still sucking), pulled his hands out of my hair, and held them at his sides. I started sucking on the side of the dick. Then I wrapped my tongue around his dick and guiding my head up and down. I kissed on the veins and let spit gently trickle down. I began jerking him off while sucking on the tip. He started panting, shaking, and grunting. I wasn't quite sure if it was a fuckboy thing or because my head was just exceptionally bomb that early morning. I could tell he was about cum. His dick started throbbing. He somehow managed to pull his hands from my grip and pushed me back. He paused for a moment, and let out a few labored breaths. Then he shook his head.

"Shit!" he yelled out. "You gotta chill out, babygirl."

I guess he was surprised that two could play that game. He reached for his sweats and pulled out two condoms. Who was about to blessed with the holiest of all penises? I was, in case you were wondering. He walked back over to me, grabbed my arm, stood me up, turned me around, pushed me forward, bent me over, and pulled my pants down. He slapped my legs open.

I didn't have underwear on because I didn't have a spare pair considering I never planned on staying at Alysha's house in the first place. I forced me up onto the bed and I arched my back just enough to look like an advanced algebra equation on a mid-term exam. Take a brief moment to stop reading this, and google: $f(x)= 2x^2+5x+3$, to appreciate the art of the arch, you guys! I was dedicated.

There I was, ass in the air, waiting for him to slide it in. I looked back. He slapped my ass and told me to look forward.

"**YES, DADDY**," I screamed in my head.

So I turned back around. He took his dick and rubbed it into my juices, slid it down, rubbed it against my clit, slid it back up, and rubbed it on my asshole. Then without warning or ease, he shoved it into my pussy. There was no mercy. He pierced my cervix or something. He dipped his dick into my soul without even saying a prayer. I literally yelped out.

I reached for a pillow to scream into but he yanked it out of my hands. He wanted to hear me scream. He wanted everyone to hear me.

"Yell for me, baby," he said. "Let it out."

Each stroke was a poke to my guts and all I could was scream and moan. My mind didn't really enjoy the idea of being impaled by an 8 or 9 inch dick, but Nikki loved every bit of it. I felt so accomplished in life—I was taking it like a pro and he was making space. I could feel the ridges of his dick. He had a curve in his dick like Peter, but his curved to the side. It made all the difference. We were loud. If they didn't hear me moaning, they definitely heard the headboard banging on the wall or the sounds of his thighs slapping against my ass.

Imagine adding seven different cheeses to macaroni then putting it into the oven for forty-five minutes, then taking it out, adding four more cheeses, and then stirring. That's what it sounded like. I never even thought I could get so wet for a guy I gave absolutely no fucks about. But he surprised me—shit, I surprised myself.

Kirk kept telling me to stop clenching and to ease up, but I just couldn't help it. I started fucking him back—it still hurt. These weren't normal back shots. This was a war: *The Battle of the Arch*. We were fucking each other like we hated each other, even though we had literally met less than 12 hours before. He was sweating and I was sweating. It wasn't because of the heat, but because of the amount of energy it took me to maintain that arch. He started slapping on my ass ruthlessly. Then he started choking me from behind. This wasn't a regular choke. It was an "I'm trying to end your life but make you cum at the same time" type of choke. I had to calm down and slow my breaths because I was on the verge of passing out.

I was loud. I knew I was loud. The people in the living room knew I was loud. Alysha and Jaylen knew I was loud. I didn't give a fuck, though—not one fuck, two fuck, red fuck, blue fuck (not a damn fuck—just a complete lack of absolute fucks. The concept of fucks seemed foreign to me).

My fucking elbows were sweating and I didn't even know that elbows could sweat. He rested on my back to catch his breath. Then he pulled out and ate it from the back. I went limp again and fell forward. He picked me back up, grabbed my hair, and went back to eating. Then he slapped my ass again and shoved it back in while spreading my cheeks. I felt spit oozing down. He started slow-stroking and guided the spit into my pussy. He was fucking me like he was breaking up with me but trying to steal me from my new nigga at the same time, you know?

I found out in the worst way that that fuckboys had the best dick, or the worst best dick (whichever makes more sense). Kirk had the type of dick you needed to take a shot beforehand and then smoke a jay and a cigarette afterwards. Another ten minutes of him abusing Nikki went by. By that time, I stopped screaming because I had lost my voice. Then he came, but kept stroking. The last stroke was the most deadly. He pumped so hard that I fell forward and the condom slipped off inside of me. Literally, the suction from Nikki was so intense that it yanked the condom right off. We panicked. He slowly pulled it out, tied it up, and threw it away.

I turned over and put my hair in a bun and he came back on the bed and lied beside me. He fell asleep as soon as his head hit the pillow. I got in the shower again and came back and lied beside him.

When I woke up, the sun was out, the birds were chirping, grass was being cut, and Kirk was gone. Eventually Alysha and Jaylen broke up so I never got a chance to ask him about Kirk after that. Because Peter could never compare and was being a little bitch because I wasn't ready to be exclusive, we never fucked again.

13. Free Fall

∞

Late November, 2013

About a week after the Kirk incident, in came this guy who I'll call Carlos. He started liking and posting 😊 emojis under all of my pictures on Instagram. Out of nowhere, his number popped up on a photo posted in the past.

He was Dominican and black—beautiful specimen of a man: tanned and almond-hued, curly hair, a beard for sitting. I texted him and sent him the 👀 emoji. Then he decided to FaceTime me without making an appointment. Something inside me told me to accept the call, so I picked up. I pretended to be shy and innocent, but you all know the truth.

"First off," he began, "let we start by saying you're gorgeous." I smiled. "I really want to get to know you for real."

I put my hand over my mouth playing coy.

"Thank you."

We stayed on FaceTime the entire night and the rest was pretty much history. Long story short, he wanted to "get to know me", which really meant he wanted to shove his face into my pussy, but I was still pretty new to the game. I agreed and suggested that we watch a movie. Mind you, this was before I started to build up my five-star roster, and before I realized I had the juice (or coffee).

For about a week we texted, FaceTimed, and flirted (all the cute shit). He too had PEL's (pussy-eating lips) and every chance he got, he'd lick them. Then one day, he asked for a picture of Nikki and it was all over. Little did he know, once you open up a photo of Nikki, it's like signing a contract and agreeing to allow me to sit on your face.

The day had finally come for us to "Netflix and Chill", which, unbeknownst to me, actually meant "fucking", but we'll get there. For whatever reason, he was already in my building, which was great because I really didn't want Peter to see me with another nigga. It just would have been drama I did not need.

I tidied up my room a bit, lit a couple candles, and proceed to the "Three S's" the way I normally did. I plugged up my phone to my iDock and played my newly constructed "Sex Songs" playlist on Spotify. Yes, I actually made a playlist for getting dick.

(Side note: In case you were wondering, the playlist consisted of the following songs: "Inside My Love" by Delilah, "All The Time" by Jeremih, "Bad" by Wale and Tiara Thomas, "Body Party" by Ciara, "Tonight" by John Legend and Ludacris, "Bed" by J. Holiday, "Love Faces" by Trey Songz,

"Neighbors Know My Name" also by Trey Songz, *"Hold On, We're Going Home"* by Drake, *"Pussy Is Mine"* by Miguel, *"Pony"* by Ginuwine, *"In Those Jeans"* also by Ginuwine, *"It Won't Stop"* by Sevyn Streeter and Chris Brown, *"Bed Peace"* by Jhene Aiko and Childish Gambino, *"They Don't Know"* by Rico Love, *"Wet The Bed"* by Chris Brown, *"No BS"* also by Chris Brown, *"Trading Places"* by Usher, and last, but certainly not least, *"Look Back At Me"* by Trina.)

So, I hopped in the shower and spent the better half of the playlist twerking and I still hadn't washed my ass yet. Girls truly get lost in the music. I hopped out of the shower—Nikki was bald, legs were shaved, hair was washed. I kind of felt like a born-again virgin, who was about to get her guts fucked. I put on some trap music to sice my head up. I was about to get some new dick and I was excited.

I, of course, dried off and put on some "In-House Dick-Getting Attire" (with shorts substituting the leggings, and a high ponytail), followed by some "Dick-Getting Makeup". I went with Black Opal makeup. I couldn't chance it. You don't get top-shelf makeup unless you have top-shelf dick.

He was supposed to come around 9 pm, so I figured I had time to blow dry and flat-iron my hair since it was only 8 o'clock; but no. For the first time ever, a nigga actually showed up **early**. I got a text asking what my room number was, so I ignored it and tried to hurry up and do my hair. When I started blow drying it, my phone started ringing. It was Carlos, and he was ready to come over even though I hadn't finished getting cute yet.

"Did you get my text?" he asked.

"Oh, you texted me?" I tried to play it off. "Oh, I see it now. It's 404A."

"Okay, I'll be up there soon. I'm on the 4th floor anyway."

I started freaking out, so I just decided to fade wearing a hoodie and let my hair air dry. About five minutes later, there was a knock on the kitchen door. Carlos was really persistent and dedicated to the cause (of having his face being a seat). So, I reached for some Pure Seduction and I ran to the door. Then I ran back to my room to grab my phone to make it look like I wasn't excited.

So I opened the door, pretending to be nonchalant (even though deep down, I was pressed) by looking down at my phone. I looked up, and up, and up. Carlos had to be at least 46 ft, 890 inches tall. He was disrespectfully tall. He was unnecessarily tall—like tall for no reason. Mind you, I'm barely 5 feet tall, so everyone pretty much looks like a gargantuan to me. When I looked into his eyes, I felt myself grinning and I eighty-sixed that shit immediately. I toned it down to a smirk.

"Oh, hey," I said, smiling.

He looked me up and down and bit his lip. I could have fainted right then and there. He had a curly high-top haircut, will a side part. I remember it as clear as yesterday. He had on a jean jacket, some joggers, and some black Jordan's (I'm not sure which kind because I'm not really into name brands). He wasn't big, but he was bulky, thick, solid (I later found out it was because he was taking steroids at the time). His PEL's were perfect—not too big, not too small, just big enough to slurp my goods up, spit on my pussy, and suck on my clit. His lip line was sharp!

He put his phone in his pocket and hesitated coming in.

"I don't get a hug or nothin'?" he said with a Bronx accent.

Never understood why niggas feel the need to ask that very same question every time. It must be what's taught on the first day at the learning annex.

Just like that, my panties were wet. I opened my arms wide and he stepped in. He wrapped his arms around me and lifted my big ass up in the air—**in the air**! It was new to me. Big girls aren't used to heights at all, so I was dumbfounded.

"Damn, you smell good," he said.

"Thanks?" I replied confusedly.

He hugged me again and sniffed my hair.

That dick appointment fragrance (Pure Seduction, Vanilla Lace, or Love Spell) always does the trick. That was pretty obvious considering the fact that his dick immediately got hard. He smelled good. I don't know what it is about a guy that wears cologne (other than Axe Body Spray) but it gets my panties moist and it makes them three times more attractive; it's proven science.

Carlos closed the door behind him and turned the lock. He followed me to the bedroom. I stepped back and let him walk in first, then I closed the door behind us and locked it. When I turned around, he was right there in my face. Shit.

He pushed me up against the door, helped me out of my hoodie and started kissing on my neck. I had to control myself, so I pushed him back. He came toward me again and kissed me on the lips. Fuck.

The fact that he was a good kisser only made shit worse for me. I really wanted to get to know him and he could tell it was pretty important to me. So, he eventually stopped and readjusted his dick in his joggers.

"So..." I wiped my mouth. "What movie do you wanna watch?"

"At this point, it don't really matter for real," he said. "Whichever one you want is cool with me."

He wasn't about to get off that easily.

"I have over 200 movies," I said. I reached for my DVD cases and handed them to him. "You choose."

He sighed in a defeated tone. He probably thought that we were actually going to watch a movie. He stubbornly flipped through the movies and said that he preferred that I choose the movie.

So I gave in and picked my favorite movie, "Zombieland". He sat down and I walked over to the DVD player and put the movie in. Then I sat down in the chair at my desk. He was obviously not entertained.

"Yo, stop playing!" he demanded. "Bring your sexy ass here. This is your bed."

I rolled my eyes and slowly walked over to the bed. He figured it was the perfect opportunity to kiss on my neck again. I kept trying to ignore his advances.

"Chill," I moaned out. "The movie hasn't even started yet. Back up."

He stopped and backed up. I sat beside him, barely. I made sure that there were at least two to three feet of distance between us. I didn't want to rush things. He sucked his teeth.

"For real, stop playing," he said. "Just sit beside me."

I slowly but surely scooted closer to him.

"Do you mind if I put my arm around you?" he asked.

I didn't even move my head, but I glazed my eyes over in his direction and shrugged my shoulders.

"Nah, go ahead," I replied.

He smiled and pulled me in closer. Then he lifted his arm back up.

"Matter of fact, I was in the gym today and my back hurts," he said. "Can I lay down?"

"Yeah, that's fine," I replied annoyed.

I knew the fuckery was on its way. He lied down on his back.

"I can't see," he said. "Can you lay down with me (there goes that fuckery I was referring to)?"

I lied down to shut him the fuck up because he was ruining my favorite fucking movie. I had my back to him. He asked if he could put his arm around me one more time.

"Go ahead (nigga, damn)," I replied.

He pulled me in close again. I felt his dick throbbing behind me.

Then all of a sudden, he started rubbing on my booty, then slid his hand down toward my crotch area. He started rubbing as if I hadn't noticed. Then he stuck his hand down my shorts and into my thong. Oceans, lakes, rivers, ponds, waterfalls and flash floods— none of them could compare at that moment. You know when you first get a fresh wax or shave, and everything just feels fucking fantastic? That's what happened. Then he spread my pussy open with his index and ringer fingers and started playing with my clit with his middle finger. I started moaning into my sleeve because I didn't know if any of my roommates were in the apartment.

Before I knew it, he was on top of me. He pulled my shorts down and almost yanked my legs out of their sockets. He slid my thong to the side and pressed his warm tongue against my clit. His beard stubble tickled me and only made me wetter. He had eventually pulled my thong off. I never know how good it felt to have a beard/mustache scratching up against your clit while someone shoved their tongue as far as they could into your vaginal cavity until that moment. It was lit like a candle.

He stopped and looked up.

"Damn, you taste good as shit," he said.

He continued and began grunting. I kept running. He kept pulling. I kept pushing his head away, but that only made him push his tongue in deeper. I think he was trying to sing lullabies to my G-spot or something, I don't know. I came once. Then he stopped, wiped face, and told me to stand. In the mist of my discombobulation, he wanted me to stand! My legs were shaking and it took me a couple tries, but I did it!

"Ima get on my knees," he said, "and I want you to put both your legs on my shoulders, facing me."

My face froze.

"I can't do that," I assured him. "If you're trying to do what I think you're trying to do, you're gonna *die*, nigga!"

"Nah, Ima be ite," he said. "Just c'mon."

I took a deep breath and put one leg on one shoulder, then I held onto his head and put my other leg over the other.

"Close your eyes," he said. My dumbass actually did it!

All of the sudden, I felt the wall scraping up against my back. I literally stopped breathing. I was up in the air, holding onto a prayer and the ceiling.

He was eating my pussy out directly from the source. He was all up in my strawberry salad! It felt amazing for a moment, up until he tried balancing my ass with one hand and putting a finger in my asshole at the same time. That was where he fucked up.

We lost our balance and I leaned forward a little too much. The ceiling fan slapped me against my forehead, not once, but twice! It felt as though everything happened in slow motion. I jerked back and fell sideways onto the bed.

You know how they say your entire life flashes before your eyes right before you die? I saw my funeral—people gathered and mourning the death of Smillee Sims who passed away untimely by way of cunnilingus. Carlos literally had killer head; he really did.

I would love more than anything to say that that was it, but it wasn't. I bounced off of the bed and hit the floor. On the way down, my head hit the wall and the wind was knocked out of me, literally. I could not breathe. I felt like my ass was in my chest.

He gasped, flipped the light on, jumped off the bed and came down to me.

"Oh my God!" he exclaimed. "You good?"

He tried to help me up but I didn't want him to touch me.

"I'm okay. I'm okay," I said. "I just…need a minute."

He opened up the door and ran to the kitchen. I heard cabinets and drawers opening and slamming shut. I heard ice rustling around in the freezer. He ran back with a sandwich bag full of ice and gave it to me. I placed it on my forehead.

"You want me to leave, don't you?" he asked.

"No," I replied. "I'm okay, really."

"That's not the first time something like that has happened to me," he said.

It took me a moment to process what he had just said.

"And you thought it was a good idea to try it out again, huh?" I asked sarcastically, holding the bag to my forehead.

I felt a knot forming and pulled the ice away from my face. His eyes got big and he started pacing in the bedroom. He was nervous as hell.

"It's fine, Carlos," I told him. "I heal quickly. I'm okay, I promise."

He crouched down, held my face up by the chin, and examined me. Then he sighed and let it go.

"So, what you want to do now?" he asked.

"Honestly?" I replied. "I just want you to fuck me, like a normal person."

He sneered.

"No gymnastics," I added. "No circus acts. No special shit."

"You do?" he asked surprised. "You sure?"

"Yeah," I answered and pointed at my forehead. "You kinda owe me."

We laughed.

Carlos helped me up onto the bed. He eventually put a condom on. He walked over to me, leaned in, and kissed me again. This time, I didn't turn my head. His dick was pretty big, so I guess that was the big payoff. They always say that good things don't come easily; and it didn't because we fucked for an entire hour. The only breaks he took were when he needed thirty seconds to recuperate after cumming and to change the condom. His stamina was impeccable. He was able to recover and prepare for the next round in seconds.

I had only fucked two guys before him but it was entirely different. He was acting like he was trying to hurt me, but trying to apologize at the same time, you know? It had to have been the Dominican in him. When he gave me back shots, he alternated between hard and soft strokes, just to make sure I was okay—because, versatility. Every time I came, he came. We were in sync. The chemistry was crazy. He was dumb as hell just like I was and I thought it was pretty cute.

We eventually started "talking", and by "talking", I mean "fucking each other like it was a hobby and misinterpreting amazing sex for emotional chemistry". It felt new and exciting every time. Then he started to like me as a person, and it all went downhill from then because I was a fuckgirl, only interested in dick at the moment.

14. Cinematic Antics

∞

Early December, 2014

So I guess you can say that Carlos and I had been talking (fucking) for a while. I didn't think either of us had intended on moving forward with anything more than sex up until then. But it had become obvious that we truly cared for each other.

I realized that it had gotten too serious when he started telling me about how he enjoyed my company and then he said that God-awful word: "exclusive". That was when I knew I had fucked up. Like I said, I was too busy being a fuckgirl.

One day, I was on a fuckgirl move, trying to set up a face-sitting appointment with a prospective hoe, then I got a call from Carlos to be ready in forty-five minutes.

Because I'm so stubborn, I asked him why.

"Don't worry about it," he said. "Just fucking get ready."

I didn't know how to feel about the tone. However, it sort of turned me own. I didn't know if I wanted to punch him in the dick, or choke on it at that moment. Sometimes he was a sweetheart, and sometimes he was daddy-material.

By now, you should already know my routine. I blasted some music, showered and washed my ass. I got out, twerked for a couple minutes, and brushed my teeth.

I got dressed in my "(Winter) Dick-Getting Attire" which consisted of a matching bra and thong set from Victoria's Secret, black leggings, North Face jacket (black), and some UGG boots (or Bearpaw boots if you're balling on a budget). I figured we were just going to his house to fuck, so I didn't bother putting any makeup on. Literally, as soon as I sprayed my choice of dick appointment fragrance on (that particular night, I switched it up and used Vanilla Lace), he was calling me to tell me he was outside.

I moseyed my way downstairs to his car. I got in, we kissed but it was kind of awkward because we didn't (correction, I didn't) want a relationship. He pulled off. His left hand was steering the wheel and the other was gripping my thigh, literally. So we pulled up to Bowie Town Center. I was livid, worried, and confused at the same time. I was expecting to go to his house so that we could fuck so I dressed for *that* occasion.

"I'm not dressed for the fucking movies, Carlos," I said. "I don't have on any makeup, my hair looks a mess."

He turned the car off and grabbed me by my chin (that was his thing).

"You look beautiful, Tiy." He kissed my forehead, then my cheeks, my nose, and finally my lips. "You actually look better without makeup to me."

I sighed and grabbed his wrist and lowered it away from my face with attitude.

"Chill," I said. "Don't do that. I really—"

"Well, we here, now," he said, interrupting me. "Let's go."

He opened his door, got out, walked over to my side, pulled my door open and waiting without saying a word.

Carlos always had the distinct talent of switching up from a sweet guy to a bad boy in an instant. I don't know why, but that always turned me on.

Fortunately, it was a weeknight, and the theater was dead. He bought two tickets to "Anchorman 2", which we in turn argued about because I didn't bring money because I was under the impression that we were going to his house (which he knew) and because I hate when people pay for me (which he also fucking knew but disregarded).

We walked into our theater and there were only four or five people there. He looked at me and gave a grimacing smirk; I looked at him and gave a devious grin. We didn't even have to say anything to know where we were both going—all the way to the back in the corner! We walked up the steps and as I walked in front of him, he slapped me on the ass. I gasped, looked back, and saw him biting his bottom lip. He had started it and he didn't even know it.

He sat down in the chair by the wall and I sat beside him. When he went to get popcorn, I pulled my phone out to spill all the tea to Brittany. Just when I saw the gray dots finally pop up, Carlos was already walking back in.

He sat beside me and handed me a soda. I was low-key mad because I told him I didn't want anything. I don't care what anyone says; I'm the type of girl that doesn't like people paying for her, even on dates. It's how I was raised.

So the movie started and he put his arm around me. I couldn't help but stare at his PEL's. He caught me staring at him in his peripheral.

Then he turned to me.

"What?" he asked, smiling.

I didn't say anything. He licked his lips and looked back at the screen. He took his arm off my shoulder. Carlos reached for the popcorn. I thought he was about to eat some, but nope. Carlos picked up the popcorn and put it in the seat beside me. I grew more confused.

He told me to take my jacket off. So I took my motherfucking jacket off. It's a shame how turned on I was. I was honestly trying to pay attention to the movie and be a good Christian girl, but no. Niggas just don't give a fuck where you are when they're horny.

As I continued watching the movie, he lifted my shirt up and slid his hand into my leggings. Thank the Lord in heaven that had I shaved the night before because I didn't have time to do so before he picked me up. Completing the "Three S's" is a commitment in and of itself. He started massaging on my clit and I started moaning under my breath. I started getting louder, but I couldn't help it. I'm just all around a loud person.

A white chick sitting beside some guy (who I'm assuming was her boyfriend or husband) glanced back at us. Carlos stopped moving his hand. She whispered into his ear and he turned back for a brief moment. Then he continued and I let out another moan.

"Shut up, yo," he said in his Bronx accent.

So I tried my hardest to shut the fuck up. He looked at me then looked at the rest of the room. Then he used his other hand to pull down my shirt. Mind you all, I had on a V-cut shirt and my boobs are easily a triple D cup. It took some effort to get my boobs out, but he succeeded. Then he looked back at the room again to make sure no one was looking. As Ron Burgundy reported the news, I cringed in my seat. I was fidgeting, gasping, grunting. Trying to keep a moan in is sort of like trying to keep in a fart: painful.

As he fingered me, I was on the lookout for security. I've always been a paranoid person. He pulled his hand out and started sucking on his fingers as he always did (because big girls just taste sweeter).

"Take your pants off," he said.

"I'm sorry, what?" I replied.

"Take your," he paused, "fucking pants off."

Do you really think I would let him eat my pussy right then and there in a public place with people in it? What kind of person do you think I am?

Of course I did!

I sighed and took off one UGG, then slowly took my leggings off of one leg and left the other leg on because I am a lady. Then I slid the boot back on. Carlos and all of his 6 feet slid down out of his seat, lifted my leg up over the seats in front of us, and slid my thong to the side. Then he started eating my pussy, guys!

He stopped for a moment and looked up at me.

"Put your jacket over your leg so nobody can see me."

I picked my jacket up, flapped it open, and let it fall down on top of him. I looked up at the ceiling and bit my lips trying to keep the moans in. There was so much going on in my mind at the same time. I was wondering about what it would be like to go to jail specifically. Normally his head was amazing, but the fact that it was in a public place intensified everything. He shoved two fingers into my pussy and started finger-fucking me. I loved every moment of it. The seat was soaked.

Then he tried to put a finger in my ass and I accidentally locked his head in between my legs. He slapped my thighs and I eased up on his nasty ass. There is always a time and a place for ass-play; it just was not then and there.

One of the employees walked into the cinema room and I stopped breathing.

"Don't move," I mumbled out quietly.

Then he turned his flashlight on and moved it around in the room. He flashed it at me and gestured so that I would know to put my feet down. So I slowly let one foot down, then slowly let the other one down and kept the coat over my knees. He nodded and walked out. God was truly looking out for us. Come to think of it, being ashy also saved my life. Think about it: If I had remembered to put lotion on that night, the light from the screen would have reflected off of my leg and we would have been in jail.

I gave Carlos the go-ahead to come back up. By then, it was twenty minutes into the movie. We didn't want to try our chances again so we watched it for an hour. I picked my jacket up and put it over me pretending to be cold. Then I reached for his zipper and pulled it down. He was paranoid too because of what had just happened.

"Chill," he whispered out and grabbed my hand.

I unbuckled his pants and pulled his dick through the pee-hole in his boxers. I lifted my jacket over my head, leaned over, and went to work. I spat on the dick one time and immediately went to deep throating. I was trying to make him cum as quickly as possible. I didn't have time to play games. I was quietly gagging and spitting. Then out of nowhere, he held my head down and cut off my breathing for a good fifteen seconds.

Apparently someone got up and left and they didn't take their coat with them so we knew they were coming back. Then he let go and I went back to work. I knew I had a limited amount of time to get the job done and I was committed. I had a deadline. I don't think I've ever sucked and jerked a dick so fast in my life. I was doing all the right things: jerking, twisting, sucking. Slurping and spitting were at minimum for obvious reasons.

All in all, when it was all said and done, I managed to get the job done in two minutes (which was an accomplishment for me because it normally took him forever to cum). I swallowed his cum, wiped my mouth off, and took the jacket off my head. I re-positioned my body, fixed my hair, and put my head on his shoulder. We literally slept for the rest of the movie. We had tired ourselves out! We didn't wake up until the ending credits started rolling and the lights came on.

15. Citric Sensations

∞

So we got up and headed to his car. He held my hand and it was just so cute and adorable. In my mind, I was sort of saddened because I knew that this cute shit would have to come to an end sometime soon. I just knew I would fuck it up. I always did. I told you, I was a fuckgirl.

Don't think I'm a mean person. He had just gotten out of a relationship, and I wasn't looking for a relationship. The two don't mix. So because I felt bad about the blowjob being rushed, I asked him if we could take a trip to Wal-Mart. I had a trick up my sleeve.

We pulled up and parked.

"You want me to come in with you?" he asked.

"I mean, you could if you want," I replied.

We walked in and I headed straight for the produce section. I picked up a couple grapefruits, headed to the toiletries section, grabbed a travel toothbrush/mouthwash/toothbrush set, and then I headed to the register to check out.

When we got back in the car he was so oblivious and it was cute.

"Ewww," he exclaimed. "You like grapefruits?"

I just smiled.

"Nah," I replied, "Not really."

"Then why did you even," he stopped in his tracks.

He was about to ruin it. I shook my head implying that his best bet was to shut the fuck up. We pulled into his neighborhood and I didn't see his brother's car (they had their own townhouse).

"Where is Miguel?" I asked Carlos.

"He's working the night shift at the hospital," he replied. His brother was a nurse.

Even better! If the neighbors didn't know his name by now, they would soon. We walked into his house and headed upstairs to his room. He sat down and reached for his nightstand to pull out a condom. He started rushing and I hadn't even gotten settled yet.

"Slow down," I said and stood up. "I'll be back in a minute."

"Okay?" he replied confused.

I went back downstairs, headed to the kitchen, pulled a knife and cutting board out with intentions of "grapefruiting" him. For those of you who don't know what "grapefruiting" is, it's an act in which your man can feel like he's fucking you and getting head at the same time, which we'll get to later. I cut the two ends of the grapefruit so that it could lie flat. Put it in the microwave for eleven seconds exactly and headed my ass back up the stairs.

I walked in and Carlos was already naked, lying down on his back. His dick was already hard. He was scrolling on Instagram as per usual.

"Damn, you could've waited for me," I said sarcastically.

He put his phone down.

He chuckled.

"My bad, yo."

I rolled my eyes and started taking my leggings off. I knelt at the foot of the bed and lightly tugged on his legs.

"Come here," I said in a sweet and innocent voice.

I started pouting and tried to be cute. When he came to me, I realized that I had forgotten to cut a circular hole into the grapefruit so I darted downstairs half-naked to the kitchen. He was probably thinking I was crazy (which I am, but still).

I grabbed the knife out of the sink, rinsed it off, and cut a hole in the center. Then I ran back upstairs out of breath.

I looked at him.

"Why you cut your grapefruit like that?"

"I'm going to use it on *you*," I replied and flashed my tongue ring.

He was shocked and confused at the same time. He had no idea what he had gotten himself into.

"What you mean?" he asked.

"Just lean back," I said, "and come closer to the edge."

He listened to me for once and actually did it. I stretched the grapefruit's center out so that it could fit onto his dick— not too tight, not too loose. I looked at his dick and slid the grapefruit onto the tip through the hole. I glided it down and my mouth followed. He came back up and I pushed his chest with my other hand.

I stopped sucking.

"Lay back down!" I yelled at him.

I was over there trying to change his life and he kept fucking it up.

I moved the grapefruit up and down his shaft, lightly twisting it while my mouth was handling the tip. He loved it. I felt him curling up his toes at my knees and my entire body literally lifted off the floor. I was dumbfounded but excited because I'm not a little chick.

While I was sucking his dick, just ten seconds in, I already tasted pre-cum in my mouth. So I pulled the grapefruit off and he jolted.

"Don't cum!" I screamed out. "I still want to fuck."

"I won't, I won't," he replied. "Just don't stop! Put it back on!"

So I slid the grapefruit back on and went back to sucking his dick. Grapefruit actually tastes pretty good when you're stabbing the back of your throat with someone's dick. Because I had been fucking him for a while, I knew how long it typically took him to cum off of head. Tell-tale signs that he was on the verge of cumming included trembling legs, slow breaths, and him punching the bed. His legs started shaking and I felt betrayed.

I slowly twisted the grapefruit up and down and started sucking on his balls. I felt his dick starting to pulsate and I knew it was time. I continued stroking the grapefruit and the cum flooded out of his hole. I kept stroking, I kept sucking. I swallowed it as it was coming out, so that when he stopped cumming, there would be no mess to clean up or handle.

"You know you lied, right?"

I stood up. I slid my thong off and stepped out of it. He jumped up, grabbed me, and threw me on the bed. I was so fucking wet.

My juices were already sliding down. He pushed my knees into my face and tried to slide the tip in. I kicked him in the stomach.

"What the fuck are you doing!?" I yelled. "Put a fucking condom on, Carlos!"

He tried to play dumb.

"What?" he looked down. "Oh, shit. I almost forgot. Haha."

"Haha shit," I replied, unamused. "Stop fucking playing with me."

He sucked his teeth, leaned over, and reached for the one on his nightstand. He opened it with his teeth and slid it on in a matter of two seconds, I kid you not!

He was ready. He put my knees in my chest, slid the tip in, and stroked slowly. Still holding his dick with one hand, he pulled it out, slid it in, pulled it out, slid it in (you get the picture). Then he grabbed my ankles, put them in the air, and started whaling on Nikki at Sonic speed!

I kept pressing on his stomach to remind him that he was still making space in my pussy.

(Side note: Making space just means that he was one of the first people to enter my vagina, so things still felt a little painful.)

"Don't do it so hard," I whined and moaned out.
"Just relax your pussy," he retorted.
But I was relaxed! I had only lost my virginity less than a month before and he was fucking it like I had been fucking for decades. Apparently, when a vagina feels threatened, it strangles anything within three feet of it. I started breathing slowly and tried to communicate with Nikki to try to get her to ease up. She was strangling his dick, but Carlos did not complain at all. He loved it, in fact. I came to the realization that he just did not give a damn about my walls. That was pretty obvious. He knew how to take it easy on me (because he had done it before), he just decided not to. What had I done? Why did I bring a grapefruit to a cum fight?

He put my legs down, stretched one out to the side, and put the other one on his shoulder. I started rubbing on my clit and looking him deep into his eyes. We had some intense eye contact going on. I felt myself about to cum. Just before I reached the top of the fucking mountain, he pulled out, turned me over, and slid back in from the back. He slapped me on my ass and proceeded to disregard my walls.

I didn't really know how to feel considering the lack of fucks he gave. I had to get my arch right to feel every ridge of his dick. I made sure that E equaled mc^2, and that y equaled $mx+b$. He literally fucked me from the back for twenty minutes. Of course, he took four or five mini breaks in between so that he wouldn't cum. I grew annoyed because I came at least five times. He kept pulling out and pausing. What was he waiting for?

He pulled out.

"Ride my dick real quick," he said.

"I'm sorry, what?" I replied.

I looked to my side and he was already on the bed beside me, jerking off. I got on top and straddled him. I started rocking back-and-forth, grinding, bouncing up-and-down. I had only been on top for a minute and a half, and I had already caught another nut. After I came, I lied on his chest with his dick still inside of me. He held me by my waist and started fucking me from underneath.

I started yelping and groaning. The more he stroked, the gushier it got, the louder the clicks become. I kept tilting my body over to the side to sneak my way off his dick, but he wasn't having it.

"Nuh uh, don't run now," he said and gripped onto my waist harder.

"I'm…a…bout…to…cuuuuum" I cried out.

Each bounce chopped my words up. I pushed on his chest, sat up, and spun around with the dick still inside. I leaned onto his thighs. Keep in mind that I'm a big bitch. We can only ride for a good five to ten minutes, at most—and that's without getting back shots for twenty minutes beforehand. I was dying inside. So I started grinding my hips and bouncing as best I could with the energy I had left over. He finally stopped being stubborn and came.

I hopped off, looked at him, and noticed he was already half-asleep. Nikki always put him to bed. I got a warm washcloth, took the condom off, and cleaned him off. Then I got in the shower and went to bed beside him.

About a week later, he asked me to be his girlfriend and gave me an ultimatum. I just wasn't ready and he couldn't accept that. He ended up moving to Pennsylvania and starting a new life there.

16. Best Buds

∞

Mid-December, 2013

Despite him making me look like a dumb ass the night I met Peter, Mike and I were best friends. Well, he was my best friend. He always said that he could never truly be friends with me because every time he saw me, he wanted to fuck. I told him about every nigga I was dealing with and he always seemed to give me the best advice. It was refreshing to get the male perspective because guys would always try to play me. He was the only nigga that kept it completely open and honest with me, no matter what.

When I confronted him about the night that he stood me up, he told me that he didn't want to be the one to hurt me. He said that he would have preferred not being my first, because he knew that he was a fuckboy, and he didn't want that on his conscience.

I had gotten used to the idea of us strictly being friends. I valued our friendship so much that whenever he would ask to come over, I made very clear rules and circumstances in order for him to be invited. One night in particular, one of my roommates and I went in half on an eighth of loud. By the time Mike showed up, I was high and drunk. In shorter words, I was in a different mindset and you know how that goes. I stumbled downstairs to sign him in and made out with him right there. When we walked in through the second door, Peter was walking out to put money on his laundry card. He looked like he had seen a ghost. I busted out laughing.

"Who was that?" Mike asked.

"Oh, nobody," I answered. "Just the guy I lost my virginity to."

"The gay one?" he asked.

I stuck my index finger up to my mouth and smirked.

"Shhhh. That has yet to be proven," I said. "But yes."

We cackled all the way to my apartment. Mike followed me into my room and closed the door behind him. When he turned around I pulled him by his coat collar and shoved my tongue down his throat. He was thrown off and didn't know what to do with my energy, so he pushed me back.

"Tiy, Chill," he said, wiping his mouth.

That snapped me back into reality. I offered him some weed and the rest was pretty much history.

I kissed him on his neck, then his collarbone. He took off his shirt. He was bulky—not fat. He was solid.

I was so high, I licked his nipple and he freaked out. He pressed his hands against my shoulders to get me off of him.

"Chill with that gay shit, Tiy," he murmured. I laughed out.

I pulled the drawstring on his pants and helped him out of them. I shoved my hand into his boxers, and pulled his Vienna sausage out. I put it near my chin then slowly spat down and let spit trickle down his dick. I started slow-jerking and twisting his dick, and rubbing on my clit through my leggings at the same time. My thong was drenched.

Because I was high, everything seemed like it was in slow motion. Everything was intensified. I rubbed his dick across my lips and slapped it on my cheeks. He leaned back. I stuffed his dick into my mouth and started humming. He moaned and he breathed out.

"Oh, shit," he uttered.

He put his hands over his forehead. I massaged his warm dick inside of my mouth. His entire body quivered and without warning, his cum splashed in the back of my throat. I swallowed it down.

I got up and I stepped out of the room to go brush my teeth. When I got back to the room, he already had a condom on, ready to fuck. I snickered.

"Damn, you ready already," I suggested.

He stood up, grabbed me by the sides of my face, and kissed me. Then he guided me to the bed and pulled my leggings off. He fell in between my legs.

He rubbed on Nikki on top of my thong! I dipped my head back and arched my back in ecstasy. Then he leaned back and pulled them off like a gentleman. He swiped the back of his hand into my juices—then rubbed on my pussy with the fronts of his fingers. When he was satisfied, he slid a couple in and started caressing my insides. He twisted his fingers. Then, he moved his fingers rapidly in and out. *Click! Click! Click! Click!*

I started squirming and running away. The closer I got to the wall, the faster his fingers moved in and out of me. Then there was nowhere else I could go. It was torture. I shrieked. I started sounding like a barking puppy.

He cut the speed down drastically, slowly pulled his fingers out, spread them apart, and licked the cum and juice strands that separated between them.

I giggled and held my weight up by my elbows.

"This is not what best friends do," I proposed.

"But you got that macaroni," he replied and smirked. "So it's different."

I scrunched my lips up and tried not to smile.

"I mean," I paused, "I guess."

Me always being wet was no new information.

He stuffed his fat dick into Nikki. He groaned out when he finally had enough leverage to start stroking. I don't want to say that he was a two-pump chump, I'll give him thirteen (and that's me being generous). He came, and I didn't. This entire time, he had talked his stroke game up, but when it came down to the wire, it turned out I had more cigarettes in my pack than he had pumps to give. I was over it. I made a mental note to never let him fuck again and to this day, we haven't.

I rolled another jay, gave him dibs to the first few puffs. He took it in his hand and puffed one time. Then he started coughing and wheezing. He handed it back to me. He was tripping. It was good quality weed and I was offering it to him for the free—the fucking free!

It became clear to me that he, apart from being a good friend, was a poser and a liar, and a lame. That dried me up completely. He didn't even eat me out, you guys! And that almost never happened! I realized that he did not smoke as often as he let on when I first met him.

I took a few drags and reached my hand out to give it back to him. He waved his hand and shook his head. I took a few more puffs and reached for my ashtray to put it out. When I stood up, he slapped me on the ass. I didn't even react because I was annoyed as hell—another "Three S's" down the drain—another unneccessary body to add tto my body count. I walked across the room and put the ashtray onto the window seal. When I turned around, he was knocked out.

I lied beside him and ended up fingering myself until I made myself cum. I fucked me better than he ever could, honestly.

After that night, he too kept hinting at wanting to be in a relationship with me. He fucked up our dynamic and it got entirely too awkward. Nikki was that addictive sometimes, I guess. There was just something about her that forced guys to put their prides aside and try to take me off the market. Ninety percent of the people I've slept with have either been dropped and blocked when they suggested we start dating, or have actually become my boyfriend or girlfriend. Mike was the last person I fucked in 2013. I decided that I was ready for a relationship, just not with him.

I was over lame niggas, but that didn't stop me from dating one.

17. Baetoven

Junior Year, January, 2014

I had recently gotten a job on campus in the Residence Life office. My schedule was hectic with the newly added job (in December).

Just like every other fuckboy that came into my life, a phone number popped up on an old photo of mine on Instagram. I'll call him Stanford.

(Side note: Everyone on campus called him "Big Texas" due to his size and the fake accent he picked up one summer at his aunt's house down south. He was born and raised in Baltimore, but he stuck with the accent. He just loved the attention—never really understood how that worked out.)

Carlos had stopped talking to me so I no longer felt bad about being single, acting single, and doing single shit. Mike kept being awkward and tried persuading me to be his girlfriend every chance he got. Eventually, he stopped talking to me because he was apparently "in love" with me, and seeing me with different niggas wasn't ideal for him.

Stanford told me that he was a freshman, and at first, I didn't want to waste my time. I was technically a junior and fucking a freshman seemed so taboo to me because I was focused on school and work.

Long story short, he got my attention. He was from Baltimore. You would think that that would have been a hint to stay the fuck away, but then again, you know me. Even though he lived in the dorm beside mine, I never really had the time to meet up with him. But I gave him a chance, just like every other fuckboy that had come into my life.

Winter break had started and our conversations started happening more often. I was intrigued by how mature he was and by how articulately he spoke.

One day, Jennifer, a girl I had met on campus who had become one of my best friends, came over my house. While she was there, Stanford FaceTimed me. He noticed her voice in the background and asked who it was.

"My friend, Jennifer," I told him.

"Is she a music major?" he asked.

Jennifer and I locked eyes. I flipped my camera to show her face. He put his hand over his mouth because he was surprised apparently.

"Oh, shit! What's up, Jennifer!" he yelled through the phone.

"Who is that?" Jennifer asked. I walked over to her and showed her the screen. Her jaw dropped. Come to find out, they had a class together and he tried to talk to her for the longest time but she gave him no rap.

Jennifer was like that. She was a very sweet girl, but her only flaw was that she was shy and timid. She was very picky, and had never had a real relationship in all her 21 years, but she would complain about being single all the time, which I never understood. She sort of reminded me of myself, only she was a virgin and I was not. She was still innocent and those days, for me, were long gone. We were almost the same person—personality-wise.

January rolled around and it was move-in day for the rest of the campus. I had dreaded seeing him that entire day because I knew he would have to come to the office to get his keys at some time or another. When check-in was wrapping up, he was one of the lasts to show up.

He walked in, he saw me, I saw him, my heart stopped and I darted to the back of the office. He was cute, and tall, and brown-skinned, and chubby—he had a beard, and dimples. He had beautiful PEL's. I didn't know it was the devil's work until it was too late. He was too perfect. He was my type, to the T. I told you guys, I was going through a big boy phase.

About ten minutes later, he texted me.

"Lol," he sent. "Your forehead big ass shit!" Then he sent a ☺ emoji.

I replied with a plethora of 🙄 emojis.

We closed up the office. I was on my way to my dorm, smoking a cigarette. Then I noticed him sitting on a bench outside of my dorm. It seemed like he was waiting for me. That was another hint God was trying to throw at me, but I disregarded it also. He had a conniving smile on his face, stood up, reached his arms out as if to hug me, then he grabbed my cigarette and threw it down on the ground. Then, to add insult to injury, he stepped on it.

I stared at him for an uncomfortably long period of time because it took me a while to process what had just happened. He couldn't be that stupid. He couldn't be that crazy. He couldn't value his life so little. He hugged me and I kept my arms at my side.

"You're too beautiful to be smoking, Tiy," he said.

It all felt like déjà vu. I was convinced that every Baltimore nigga had attended the same learning annex before being sent out into the world.

I could have told him that I didn't smoke to be cute, but that I smoked so that I wouldn't have to kill anyone's child (referring to him), but I just smiled. I felt like that would just have been a waste of time and it would go over his head.

"So what you bouta do?" he asked.

"My mom is about to take me grocery shopping," I replied.

I lied because Nikki wasn't prepared for company at the moment. I had to give myself a head start.

"But if you wanna come over around 8," I said, that's cool with me."

About two and half hours later, after a much-needed execution of the "Three S's", I invited him up to my room.

He was eating my pussy within five minutes. He later told me that he had never done that with anyone because he didn't trust girls enough, whatever the fuck that meant. He claimed that there was just something about me that allowed him to do so. The crazy thing is I've heard that countless times from countless niggas. He spat and brushed his tongue up my pussy as if he were trying to clean up his mess. I feel like you and I are close enough for me to disclose the fact that falling in love with head, instead of the person, is a real thing. I fell in love with his mouth. The head somehow glazed my eyes over and blinded me to the fact that he was a six-foot-tall piece of shit.

(Side note: He flirted with everyone, and I recently found out that he supposedly cheated on me with some gargantuan, Shrek-looking bitch named Tweety—she looked like a man, though and was not at all his type so I didn't know how to process that rumor.)

His tongue-fucking skills were unparalleled, unsurpassed and unexpected (at that time). He was The Pussy Whisperer—The Clit Bandit (whichever sounds better). By the time I met him, I became aware that STD's were not a myth.

We got campus-wide emails about various outbreaks so I took advantage of every single STD screening that was offered on campus. I was nervous as hell. I had been extremely careless and naïve. By the grace of God, I never caught anything, and that was a miracle in and of itself. So I started to wise up and begin practicing "safe head". I told him that I would need to use a condom on his dick if he wanted me to suck it. He sucked his teeth and worked his magic on me.

I think I was hypnotized by the way his lips moved or the way his fake Texas accent rolled off of his tongue or something of the sort because I was on my knees, holding his dick in my hands and I have no idea how that happened. He put his hands on the back of my head and tried choking me on <u>nothing</u>— okay, maybe two inches, maybe two and a half, hard. His dick was miniscule, small, tiny; there, I said it. It feels so much better that it's out there.

(Side not: This is not coming from a bitter part of me at all, by the way. I've since let go of feelings of animosity toward him.)

I wouldn't say that his dick was non-existent, but when it was soft, it pretty much just looked like an over-sized clit, or and "inny" belly button, and that's just me being honest. When it was hard, he had a solid three inches (four inches if he pushed back his

FUPA, which he did often to maintain pride). He kept slapping me in the face with his strawberry short cake with the crust on top (his dick was always ashy, I later found out it was because of his diabetes).

Eventually, I started gagging, not because his dick was big, or long or "too much for me to handle", but because the smell nearly made me cry.

Girls, have you ever sucked a guy's dick so small or so smelly, that every time you sucked it, you felt your soul dying and your pussy drying up? Guys, have you ever eaten a girl out who just didn't smell and taste fresh, which inadvertently made your dick soft? I dated him for ***six months!***

Every time we had sex, it felt like time was moving half as fast, and he was moving half is slow.

Before we started dating, I found out that he was talking to someone else. I had completely cut him off. I blocked him on Instagram, Twitter, iMessage. One day, because my roommate's never locked the fucking front door, he just burst into our apartment.

He begged me for fifteen minutes to unblock him as I separated my laundry on the floor ignoring him. When I didn't respond, he got fed up and left. That night, I tweeted about going on a smoke break outside. When I sat down on the bench outside of my dorm, I looked up and saw a figure coming from the dorm across the way from ours, toward me.

It was Stanford. He was crying like a little bitch. He had a habit of snatching my cigarettes away from me so I was prepared for him. When he reached for it, I put my hand behind my back.

"Stop," I said, stood, and walked away.

I took my last few puffs from the cigarette.

"Can I help you, sir?" I asked, looking down at my phone.

"I need to talk to you," he urged.

"We're talking now," I stated, walking towards the entrance of my dorm.

"Well, can you sign me in so we can talk?" he begged.

I declined because I knew that that would lead to us fucking and his little dick was not worth the trouble.

"Then, can you talk to me out here?" he begged.

I looked at my watch and waited for the long hand to hit the twelve so that I would be able to give him exactly a hundred and twenty seconds.

"You got two minutes," I said. "Annnnnndddd, go."

I put my hands at my side and pulled the hoodie over my head.

Tears started streaming down his face. He begged me for a second chance. I told him that before I would even consider being in anything with him, *especially* a relationship, he would need to tie up some loose ends (and by "loose ends", I meant cutting the other bitch off or leaving me the fuck alone). I made it very clear to him that I don't play first or second; I play only. I don't beg for attention that isn't even mine. That's not the type of life I wanted to live. I refused.

When he finally cut her off, I agreed to date him. Within two weeks, he was my boyfriend. The other bitch hated my guts.

(Side note: This has absolutely nothing to do with the story, but the tea was too sweet for me to keep all to myself, so I thought I'd divulge that information to you all, because I'm a messy bitch. That very same girl, let's call her Cici, had musty, fishy pussy. She even used benzoyl peroxide to clean her pussy out. Because of that, Stanford refused to fuck her or eat her out. He felt bad for her because of certain health issues she had, which I won't share. I just thought that it was funny that she was more worried about Stanford and my relationship than she was about the ongoing bread factory fermenting between her legs, but to each his own, right?.)

Every time she saw me, there would be a problem. Because I worked in the Residence Life office, I was able to see any and all complaints filed by students in reference to issues in their dorms. She even filed a false complaint against us for "having sex too loud", which obviously was a lie considering the fact that I could count on my hands how many times Stanford actually made me cum in our entire relationship. Honestly, I wouldn't even need my entire hand. I could've done her like I did Becky and embarrassed the hell out of her, but I had grown. Instead, I kept my page public and posted obnoxiously cute little videos of us together. Stanford and I laughed about it and then I would sit on his face.

I fell hard for him. It could've been the head that I fell hard for, but we'll keep it cute. There was just something about him, you know? He was territorial, which, in hindsight, was not ideal for a healthy relationship, but was extremely sexy at the time. He got jealous easily and was actually proud and happy that I was his, which was new for me because I spent so much time trying to be kept a secret by men I was fucking. He showed me off to his friends and it was different. We were just an adorable couple that ignored the problems in our relationship.

February, 2014

There were so many things we did in places we should not have done them. One day in particular, Stanford and I were watching television in the living room. Two of my roommates were in class and the other one normally slept before her shift in the cafeteria. He was asleep but I was up and horny. So, I slowly unzipped his pants and began tugging on his clit/dick. I put my mouth on it and started lightly massaging and sucking on his skittle. After a while, his dick had grown three inches. Then I started stroking it—well, I tried to, at least. It was just sad. He actually came, and I caught it all. Stanford tended to have at least half a cup of cum in his nuts at any given time and it tasted disgusting. The guy tasted like acetone nail polish remover. He woke up and reached for my pants. Then he pulled me up, helped me out of them, and sat me down on the couch. Then he pulled my legs open and fortunately I didn't have on thongs, so it was an open buffet.

He dove in and aimed straight for the clit. I hit my head on the wall my roommate shared with the living room—you know, the same roommate that was actually in the apartment sleeping. Then he took his phone out of his pocket and handed it to me. That meant that he wanted me to record it. We recorded more than a few videos during the course of our relationship, some of which he probably still has in his possession.

(Side note: Up until two years ago, he would threaten to use them against me—he said that he would post them and expose me if I kept treating him like a shit which he actually was. That whole posting videos and exposing girls is so pathetic to me. It's childish and it's a lesson I learned the hard way.)

I recorded as he sucked my clit in between his lips and swayed his tongue against it. Then he started tongue-fucking me and I was a goner. With his tongue still inside me, he held onto my waist, and stood. He forced me into a headstand and locked me into his arms. By that time, his phone had already fallen onto the floor. I tried keeping in my moans because my roommate could have awoken at any time.

"I'm cumming," I said quietly. I purged my cum out of me and he started slurping even louder.

My legs stiffened up and locked him in a hold. I pulled my body away from him and fell out of his grip. I landed on my back. I was exhausted and had immediately regretted waking him up.

Just when I thought it was all over, he pulled me into the kitchen. Then, he picked me up by my underarms and placed me onto the counter top. He looked down at my thighs and licked his lips. He got down onto his knees and ate my pussy right there in the kitchen, where we baked cupcakes, floured chicken, and prepared macaroni! We were disrespectful as fuck. Speaking of macaroni, Nikki and his tongue joined in harmony to make that oh-so-beautiful sound. Technically, you're never supposed to shit where you eat, but can you *eat* where you **eat**? Can you *be* a meal where you *prepare* meals?

One leg was pushing up against the dish drain, my hair was laid across the bread box, my other leg was dangling over the dishwasher. My arms displaced pots, pans, and salt/pepper shakers. I would often alternate from lifting up my body to soak in the strokes of his tongue and hang onto cabinet knobs.

I slid back onto the wall behind me and I noticed Nikki leave a trail of creamy juices like a snail. He looked me dead into the pits of my soul and followed the trail with his tongue…**all the way to Nikki**.

Then he yanked my legs around him. I wrap my arms around his neck. He stuck his tongue out and I sucked on it. We kissed so deeply.

All of a sudden, we heard someone keying into the door! He helped me down off the counter, grabbed my leggings, and we sprinted to my bedroom.

18. Not Okay

∞

May, 2014

I had been dating Stanford for a couple months. He had severe separation issues and was low-key bat-shit crazy. I never realized how bad it was until he started wanting to watch me use the bathroom often (which is all fine and dandy, but if you're just sitting on the counter watching me do my business, that's a problem). I even caught him (more than once) sniffing my dirty panties from my hamper. I didn't know how to handle being suffocated all the time.

He didn't have the best relationship with his mother and I felt for the guy. I tried taking care of him emotionally as best I could, which would explain him needing to be around me 25/8. It took a toll on me.

I carried his medicine around, did his laundry, and even some of his homework. I forced him to go to his classes and to study. It got annoying. I didn't have time to worry about myself even though I was *drowning* in my own depression.

Don't get me wrong, I loved him, and I was in love with him, I just hated the feeling of having someone up under me, all the time. I was in college, not at a daycare (although some students belonged in both). I hadn't signed up to be anyone's mother, but there I was.

I think a part of me felt obligated to be with him because he tolerated my attitude and loved everything about me—literally everything: the way my sweat smelled after the gym, the way I looked without makeup on, the way I snored (seriously, and I snore like a grown ass man, by the way).

When I woke up in the mornings, Stanford would be in my bed, clenched onto me. When I'd get in the shower to get ready for work or class, he was still in my bed. When I got off of work and wanted to take a nap, he was there. When I did my homework, he was there too, not doing his, though. He was unambitious and it seemed as though his only priority was me. For a while, a selfish part of me was okay with that. I don't know—he just had a hold on me.

That was our relationship for six whole months. He knew my schedule, my friends, my hangout spots, my hiding spots. He stalked Peter, Carlos, and Malcolm on Instagram. For whatever reason, he got the idea that he was my father and that I needed to check in with him all the time. That was funny because he paid not one fucking cell phone, light, or tuition bill of mine. It's also funny because my father's a deadbeat dad, but that's neither here nor there.

Instead, he asked me for money all the time. Don't get me wrong, if you're with me, what's mine is yours, and I will always be there for you emotionally, physically, financially, no matter how much I have to suffer the consequences, but if you're not working to better yourself, or if you're okay with being stagnant, that doesn't sit well with me.

He made me "quit smoking", which really meant me sneaking a smoke in corners and carrying perfumes in my purses all the time. It got so bad that I hid cigarette boxes and lighters in between my tits in my bras: **whole ass fucking cigarette boxes!**

Our sex life, although terrible, was adventurous. We'd fuck in the library study rooms, I'd (try to) suck his dick in book aisles in the library, even in elevators. He was just bossy, jealous, smothering, overbearing, and overprotective. On top of all of that, he was bipolar (and this is coming from someone who majored in psychology the first two years of her college career).

I felt like I was in prison every moment I was with him. Of course when we argued, I said some things that got under his skin, but he put up with my bullshit and stuck by my side.

We lasted all the way until the beginning of summer. I had permission to live on campus (in a dorm called Hailey Hall) because I had still worked at the Residence Life Office and they needed my help during the summer. I would have done anything to stay on campus—home life wasn't really fun.

I was living in a full dorm all by myself. So, of course, I asked him to come stay with me (which I technically wasn't supposed to do).

The first night he came, I hadn't seen him in a couple weeks, so of course we were going to "fuck". We made out and ended up on the floor. He ate on Nikki for a moment and all of a sudden, started ferociously fingering me. He was determined to make me squirt because I told him about the Kirk incident. He felt some type of way about me never squirting for him—but he never realized it was because he never satisfied me.

After about fifteen minutes of him fingering me, I was so fucking tempted to just pee on his hand and call it a fucking day. By that time, I was dried up because I wasn't feeling it. I fake-moaned and somehow managed to make myself cum by rubbing on my clit while his fingers were inside of me. My creamy cum gushed out, but no squirting occured.

I ended up kicking his fingers out because it was just so fucking sad. He ended up between my legs and "fucking" me. Our go-to position was missionary because that was the only way he could give me maximum dick. We had tried back shots before, but it angered him when I didn't even bother fake-moaning.

He came and fell on top of me, pressing all his weight on my stomach, out of breath. His sweat poured over me like regret.

I just looked up to the ceiling as he literally fell asleep inside of me. I pushed him off and lied in the bed, ruing ever allowing myself to end up with someone like him. I thought about the nostalgia of having to deal with that for the rest of my life, but I just couldn't leave him. A part of me knew he needed me.

The next day, Mike called me out of the blue asking me to help him on his sociology paper. Stanford was in the shower. When he got out, I was searching the web for the history of sociology. As he dried his body off, he glared at me.

"Okay," I said, "so the father of sociology was Auguste Comte."

"Who you talking to?" Stanford asked, putting on deodorant.

"Why?" I asked, annoyed.

Mike sucked his teeth.

"Yo Tiy," he said, "I'ma just talk to you later."

Stanford saw red. He charged at me and tried grabbing my phone from my hand. My heart stopped. I slid from his grip and onto the floor. I looked back and he was sliding off the bed, evidently prepared to chase me. I picked my phone up off of the floor, dashed to the door, grabbed my keys, and darted out, slamming the door behind me.

We were on the fifth floor. I contemplated pressing the down button for the elevator but then realized I didn't have time to wait when I heard the door creak open and slam against the wall. I ran toward the stairwell. I was too frightened to look back, but I heard his feet stomping closer and closer to me. Sweat trickled down my forehead. When I looked back, his eyes were empty—they were blank. It wasn't *him*.

I turned back around and thrust the stairwell doors open. He chased me all the way down to the third floor, through the third floor hallway, up to the fourth floor and fourth floor hallway, and then down to the second floor. Out of breath, I reached for each door knob, but to no avail. The first door was locked. The door across it was also locked. I made it all the way down to the opposite end of the hallway and I finally found a door unlocked. I pushed it open and stepped in.

As soon as I slammed the door behind me and pressed the lock on the door knob, Stanford began banging on the door incessantly. The walls shook; I felt the knocking in the floor and in my chest. I was petrified. I stepped back slowly and caught my breath. I stared at the door, praying the hinges would not give in to his some 300 odd pounds. He jostled the doorknob.

I watched the shadows of his feet spread apart. I thought he had given up—that he had calmed down and realized the situation escalated far too much. Then came a dark yellow river creeping underneath the door.

I tip-toed toward the door, spread my legs far apart, and looked through the peephole. He was holding his dick, aiming it towards the floor, smiling, almost as if he were proud of what he had done.

An array of thoughts ran through my head. He was peeing on the floor. I was genuinely speechless. I mean, yeah, he had had bipolar episodes before when we were together, but none like that one—none that made my heart pound and certainly none that had me seeing the devil in the man I loved.

A part of me knew he would never bring himself to hurt me, but the other part of me looked down at my wrists and saw bruising. I just didn't know, you know? He was troubled—not all the way there in the head, but I thought I could fix him. I thought me being there for him was enough to pull him out of the darkness that he had lived in for so long. That was my problem. For the first time ever, I had realized what a savior complex was and how I had ignored mine.

When he was done his business, he stepped away, took a deep sigh, and just walked away. I heard the hallway door open and the elevator ding go off.

I was dumbfounded. What had happened? There were so many unanswered questions. Was he leaving? Were we through? Was he sorry? Would he have remembered? I found a mop in the maintenance closet and cleaned up as best I could without shoes on. I took the steps upstairs because if he was upstairs, I didn't want him to be warned by the elevator that I was coming.

I slowly eased the key into the knob and clicked it in one millimeter at a time. I held the handle and turned the key ever so slightly. I opened the door enough for me to slide in. I crept around the wall and saw him sitting on my bed, crying. I dropped my keys and stood there, frozen. He looked up and gasped. I stood up and gently stepped toward me, reaching his arms out. Our bodies touched but I didn't move. He walked toward me and squeezed me softly.

I remained unresponsive and my hands stayed at my sides. I felt his hand running through my hair as he cupped the back of my head, breathing me in.

"Baby," he choked out, "I'm so sorry."

His breaths were slow and deep. His tears moistened my cheeks. He kissed my forehead and held me tighter. I had still said nothing. There was nothing I could say—there were no words to describe how I had felt.

We stood there, in the middle of the floor and in silence for at least ten minutes. We had eventually ended up in my bed, with my head on his chest. As I lay there, I thought about all the ways to end it with him, all the things I needed to say and do. I was determined to get him out of my life, no matter how much I loved him, or how much I thought he loved me.

But I stayed— for a while, anyway.

I loved him. I wanted him to get help. I wanted to be there for him but I didn't know how to without sacrificing who I was.

Fortunately (and yes, I *do* mean "fortunately"), I got fired that week for having him there, even though there was no contract actually stating that I couldn't have guests.

I knew that if I had stayed working in the Residence Life Office, I would see him more than I needed to.

I wasn't good for him, and neither was he for me. We were never quite the same. We cooled off. Our conversations got low. And one day, to his suggestion, we decided to end it, cordially. He told me that I deserved someone better than him and that I was too good of a person. I didn't argue, or disagree, or cry about it. It was all true. We were just two puzzle pieces forcing ourselves to fit into one another.

Stanford in turn ended up transferring to Morehouse College to become a better man, I suppose. He tried keeping in contact with me but I had already let go. He even tried a couples times to stir up drama in my later relationships, but it didn't really work out well for him.

19. Pony Rides

∞

Summer, June, 2014

It was summer and I was unemployed. For some reason, I just couldn't find a fucking job. Jay and I had reconnected after almost a year—yes, the very same Jay that had eaten my Pillsbury Dough Pussy and jumped his best friend for me. Jay told me that the Target he was working at was hiring and that he would put in a good word for me.

I was hired! Working at Target was *interesting* because every time Jay and I were on lunch breaks together, he ended up eating me out in the back storage room. I had to stop it. It's not that I wasn't attracted to him; we were just in two different places mentally. He sold drugs and I had no intention of being anyone's fucking trap queen. He was just too much to handle. I sucked his dick a few times, but that was always pretty much as far as it went. We almost fucked once, but one of our coworkers caught us and we never tried again.

Our friendship was more of a brother-sister relationship, if you take out the endless pussy-eating and dick-sucking part.

One night, Jay's mom had invited me to his house for his sister's welcome back party. She had just returned home from the Army. For the sake of the story, I'll call her Bianca. (Doesn't that shit just roll off the tip of your tongue?)

She was gorgeous and she knew it—very feminine features, but at heart, she was a nigga. She could get any girl she wanted and she was never ashamed to admit it. She walked like a nigga, dressed like a nigga, thought like a nigga. She was basically just a really pretty nigga with long, curly hair. She had the perfect body, perfect skin, and perfect fucking metabolism (she literally ate all the time and never gained a fucking pound).

I had seen her in pictures, but the whole time I knew Jay, I had never met her. Jay's father went to go pick her up from the airport. Then, he texted us to tell us that they were down the street. We turned off the lights and everyone had to find a place to hide. I hid behind a curtain and lo and behold, here came Jay trying to start some shit up. Other family members were behind the couch, under tables, shit like that. Jay grabbed my boob from behind and started kissing on my neck. For a moment, my knees went weak and I got a little wet; then I snapped back into reality and pushed him back. I had literally told him a week earlier that I was done with whatever it was that was going on between us.

We heard the key moving around in the lock and then it happened. She walked in, dropped her bags, and flipped on the light.

We all jumped out.

"Surprise!"

She cracked a smile and stole my heart. Her family ran up to her and hugged her—giving her kisses and cards and endless love.

I stuck behind Jay shyly as we walked over to Bianca. They hugged.

"What's good, bro," she said as they did that dap and back-punch shit.

"Ain't shit," Jay replied, then hung one of his arms around my shoulder.

I lifted and pivoted my shoulder to force his arm to fall off. I had to send a message that we were not what she would have inevitably assumed we were.

She looked at me and a part of me died.

"And you are?" she asked and licked her lips.

I felt my mouth open, but words refused to come out.

"T—," I stuttered.

"This my homie, Tiy," Jay added and put his arm around my shoulder again.

I rolled my eyes and dropped my shoulder again. I reached in and gave her a hug.

"Welcome back," I said nervously as I sniffed her hair (I'm a weirdo and she smelled amazing). "It's nice to finally meet you."

We let go.

"You too," she responded.

We locked eyes for a brief moment, and then more family members came over and ruined it.

Long story short, Bianca and I hung out every night after I got off of work, and Jay low-key hated me for it. But he was talking to some white girl at the moment (which we *will* get to), so it was no big deal because he was getting his dick wet.

She was feeling me, I was feeling her. Within a couple weeks, we were "dating". I was a pillow princess for a while but my time would soon come. We started getting serious, really quickly. About a month in, we had only fooled around, nothing serious really.

One day, she called me while I was leaving church.

"I got something for you," she said. "Come over."

So, I got a ride to their house. When I got there, I was outside at least five minutes knocking on the door and there was no answer. I couldn't even call to curse her out because my phone had died by then. So, I walked around the back, down a huge hill, in <u>high heels</u>! Fortunately, they always left their back door open for some reason.

I slid the door open and stepped in. I heard Lil' Wayne blasting in the background, which explained a lot (but I was still pissed off).

Her room was in the basement, so she probably didn't hear me banging. I walked into her room, gave her a hug from behind, and kissed her neck. Wait a minute; did you really think she was getting off that easily after I was outside sweating my vagina off? She was playing a video game which I believe to be called "Madden" or "2K" (it was a basketball game), but I'm not sure. I was already irritated—yelling and cursing and screaming. She was at least 6 feet tall and I was yelling at her as if I weren't 5'2" (which I am).

The entire time I was lecturing to her, she was still playing her fucking video game. So I walked over to the TV. Guess what I did. Unplugged. That. Bitch. I sure did. She frowned at me and threw her controller across the room. I blew it off because I knew she was a big teddy bear. She began getting closer to me. For a moment, I thought she was actually going to hit me. I backed away slowly and then she picked my big ass up (that's what the Army will do to you)!

She slammed me onto the bed. Then she walked to the middle of the room and pulled the ceiling light switch. It was pitch black.

"Hold on," she said.

She reached for her phone started playing "Pony" by Ginuwine! I kid you fucking not. I just lied on the bed confused as hell. As the song played in the background, she walked over to her nightstand and pulled something out. I couldn't really tell what it was because she had blackout curtains. In a matter of 2.11 seconds, I was completely butt-ass naked. She came around the foot of the bed and dropped something onto the bed beside me. All I heard was a big ass thump on the mattress.

I grew nervous. What the fuck was this bitch thinking? What was she doing? She reached up and put her long hair into a ponytail. Then she was ready. She pulled my entire body by my legs toward her. I began arguing and fussing again, but she wasted no time. She dove into the pussy head first! She spread the lips open and spat the meanest spit anyone has ever spat into and/or onto Nikki.

Have you ever had head so good that you started moaning, then screaming, then crying? It was that type of fucking head! She knew exactly what she was doing. No one, I repeat, no one eats pussy like a stud eats pussy! She was doing everything right—two in the pink, one in the stink. I could feel the area that was under me completely soaked. She was munching on my clit—not too hard, not too soft, just right like Goldilocks.

Out of nowhere, she literally rubbed her entire face into Nikki. **Do you know what a nose feels like in your pussy!?** Do you know what an eyelash feels like rubbing up against your clit? She kept trying to blow out air in order to breathe. It was just messy and I enjoyed every sticky, warm, wet, oozing, sloppy moment of it. After I came a couple times, she came back up and kissed me. I licked up everything that I possibly could.

She was still rubbing on my clit, outrageously fast. I kept trying to push her hand away, but she was not backing down. I somehow got the energy to push her ass to the side and got on top.

"You got me fucked up if you think you're about to have all the fun!" I said. "It's my turn now."

In the mist of me trying to prove that I was no longer a pillow princess, I began struggling to take her sports bra off (which was the only fucking thing she ever fucking wore). I had gotten so annoyed that I just ripped the shit off, right down the middle.

I started sucking on her titties and tried easing my finger into her goodies, but she caught me off guard.

"I'm not with that gay shit," she said. (I can't make this shit up!)

*(Side note: So, fuck the fact that she pretty much dedicated her entire life to being a nigga and playing the part. Forget the fact that we were **two girls** doing some pretty gay shit. Her biggest issue was me trying to finger her? Just let that sink in. I didn't know if she was joking or not, but it truly blew my fucking mind. For some reason, studs (or at least the ones I've encountered) don't really like penetration.)*

"Shut the fuck up!" I replied.

I was down there, trying to prove that I wasn't a little bitch. Being a pillow princess is boring. The time had come for me to become a woman (in my own right)! It was going to be my first time eating pussy, so I over-analyzed everything. I was trying to figure things out as if it were an algebra equation.

I took a deep breath and just did it. I tasted her and she tasted amazing. To this day, I still don't know how to describe it. That was when I realized that I loved eating pussy. I began sucking on the lips and remembered that the clit is pretty important. I thought to myself: **WWWBTD** (what would White Boy Timmy do)? I pulled the hood back and got to sucking.

Her entire body lifted. It was a bit scary, but when her pussy rose up, so did I. It got to the point to where I'm sure if someone would've walked in, they would have thought that she was about to do a backflip, or play London Bridge, or was being possessed (whichever gives you the best mental image). Bianca was flexible as fuck! Her body lowered back down and then she said the magic words.

"Sit on my face."

"Why?" I stubbornly asked.

"Just sit the fuck on my face, bae!" she said. "Damn!"

So I sat the fuck down on her face. She pulled all my weight down onto her, pulling down on my thighs. I was so afraid that I was going to suffocate her because, even though she was taller than me, she was petite. She began moving my body around on her face by my waist.

Then she stopped sucking on my clit (I literally heard the pop) to take a breath.

"Grind on my face," she demanded.

I pushed on her stomach, trying to disperse the weight, moving left to right, front to back, all around. I wanted to give her what she wanted. Then she started making my body bounce up and down!

"Bounce!" she said, muffled.

So I began dutty wining all on her face, you guys! I couldn't hold myself up any longer because I was so weak. I leaned over and began eating her pussy. The 69 was sensational, but difficult. It was my first time 69'ing with a girl. There were a lot of firsts that night. I lifted back up (still on her face) and took it all in. Have you ever had your clit sucked on from a 180° angle?! Well, it kind of hurts, but it also feels good.

Keep in mind that "Pony" had been on repeat for at least twenty minutes! So I leaned back over and started rubbing on her pussy. Then, I got the dumb ass idea to slap it. I had seen it in porn, so I thought she'd be into it. Big mistake. She wasn't.

(*Side note: Never, I repeat,* **NEVER** *do that to a stud!*)

Bianca kneed me in the face. I didn't know if it was a reflex or if she was just trying to get back at me for inflicting that type of pain on her. It was an excruciating sort of pain, but the pleasure far outweighed it. After my body processed what had happened, I got up and stood on my feet.

"I want to try scissoring," I said with my knuckles resting on both sides of my waist.

She smirked.

We started going at it. Her juices were splashing everywhere, my juices were splashing everywhere. Granted, it only lasted for thirty to forty-five seconds, but it was amazing: our clits pressed up against each other, our pussies sticking to each other and being pulled apart. She decided to stop and get up. I don't know how I ended up forgetting about the thing that she put on the bed twenty minutes before, but it all came back to me.

I saw her silhouette moving around. I could tell she was looking down. Then, I heard the unmistakable sound of velcro unhooking. I didn't know what the fuck was going on.

"Get on your knees and face that way," she said to me.

I instantly became nervous and started sweating.

I obliged her and got on my knees.

"Open your legs up a lil'," she added.

So I did that too.

I thought that she was about to rock my world and did what White Boy Timmy did and eat my pussy from the back.

But nope. She shoved an **eight-inch** silicone dick all the way into my pussy. I screamed bloody fucking murder. I swear she reached my soul. I fell and damn near got into a fetal position. She ran over to the windows and opened up the curtains

"Why would you do that?" I cried out, hugging my knees.

I was literally sobbing. She started panicking.

"I'm so sorry, bae." She said. "You okay?"

"No," I shouted out. "Bitch, you just shoved a fucking broom handle into my guts! No, I'm not okay! What the fuck do you think!?"

Then I saw her face and could tell it really meant a lot to her. So, I manned up and got back into that position.

I looked back at her.

"Take it **slow**," I said.

She nodded and smirked. She bent over, rubbed my clit, and spat. Bianca slowly slid the dildo in inch by inch, and began slow-stroking. I felt my eyes go cross-eyed. Then she began stroking to the beat, you guys! *If you're horny…let's do it… Ride it…my pony.*

You know how when someone knows you're about to cum so they speed up? She started fast-stroking and I felt my cum sliding down my inner thighs. All of a sudden, the dick started vibrating! She was moaning, I was moaning. It was just a beautiful mess—sounds of macaroni in the air. It was just so romantic.

She was throwing the dick hard as fuck and I had to prove I wasn't a little bitch. I began throwing that ass back harder. She was fucking me, and I was fucking back.

"Don't stop," I yelled out.

She kept stroking. She started cumming and I pushed her out of my pussy. I turned around, spread my legs, rubbed on my clit mercilessly and squirted,

everywhere. I saw her jaw drop in the sunlight shining in through the window.

I began to stand up and she pushed me back down.

"Where you going?" she asked.

"Ummm...I'm about to take a shower in your bathroom," I said between breaths.

She reached for a towel in her drawer and put it on the bed where my mess was.

"Lay down with me for a lil' bit," she requested.

She sat on the bed (strap-on still on) and we cuddled (until she fell asleep, then I showered).

That was the day I fell in love with the strap-on. Bianca opened up a new world for me. She would soon open up another.

20. Birthday Gift Hell

∞

Summer, Late-July, 2014

I had been with Bianca for a little less than two months. Like I said, everything was moving fast. Of course, I had fooled around with other girls before her, but for some reason, I truly loved her. Because of her, I learned that I loved eating pussy, and I did it every chance I got. For that, I'm eternally grateful to her. But, much like everyone else I had ever dated, she was just another piece of shit waiting to be flushed down the toilet.

Her birthday was coming up, so I wanted to make it really good. I asked her what she wanted. I figured she would've said some Jordan's or a video game, but she said that she would need time to think about it because she wanted it to be good.

A week went by. We were at her house, chilling, all booed up. I was lying on my back on my phone (as usual). She was laying on my stomach, watching that God-awful channel, ESPN.

"Bae," she said grinning. "I know what I want for my birthday."

I put my phone down and got up. I rubbed my hands together, thinking it was going to be good and I would finally be able to spoil her.

She leaned in, looked at me, and slid her hands into my panties. She was sliding her finger in and out, rubbing her thumb on my clit. I was deafened by the pleasure.

(Side note: Whenever I'm getting fingered our eaten out, I pretty much agree and say "yes" to anything, and she knew that shit, and tried to use it against me.)

"I want a threesome," she mumbled quietly.

I opened my eyes and stopped moaning dead in my tracks. I don't think I've ever clenched my pussy so tight! The entire idea completely dried me the fuck up. I pulled her hand out of my panties.

I backed up, trying not to knock her face in. It took everything for me not to completely Rocky Balboa her shit! I took a deep breath and tilted my head in disbelief. I think I was more shocked that she had the audacity to ask me what she asked me more than what she had actually asked.

I kept silent for ten seconds. I rested my chin on the back of my knuckles and gave her the floor.

"So," I said, "you wanna run that by me again?"

My face went from confused to livid in a matter of milliseconds. She gulped.

"I—I," she stuttered. "I think I want a threesome for my birthday."

I repositioned my body closer to her and pulled my hair behind my ear (because I obviously wasn't hearing her correctly).

"You want a what, now?" I asked.

She cleared her throat.

"I want a three—"

"I'm sorry, you want a what?" I asked again as she certainly didn't get the memo the first time that she had me three different kinds of fucked up if she thought I would ever agree to being in a threesome.

"A thr—," I cut her off again and took in another breath.

It became clear to me that she really thought I would not peel her muffin cap back blue. I looked to the upper corners of my eyes and pretended to actually give it some thought.

"No," I said.

She hit me with the puppy dog eyes. I tried to fight the urge and not look her in her hazel eyes.

"Baby, please!" she begged repeatedly and began kissing me on the neck.

I kept pushing her away, but she just kept coming back and I could no longer resist it. Bianca knew she could get anything she wanted with a sports bra on, puppy dog eyes, and neck-kissing. She kissed me on my neck again, then my collarbone, then my chest. She pulled my tank top down and licked a nipple. She laid me down, then kissed on my ribs, then my stomach, and my naval. Then she kissed me right under my naval, and she pulled my pants off (of course I helped her take them off while I pretended to be mad at her).

Then she licked my clit through my thong; then she started sucking on it. She slid them to the side and looked up at me, grabbed my waist, and pulled me down.

She slid a finger in, then crammed another in and twisted. She pulled the hood from over the clit and began sucking it at the same time. Then she stopped, and slid the thong right back over my pussy.

She watched my face and chuckled. I looked up at her feeling betrayed. Then, she ripped my thong off and spread my legs open into a split (the last time I did a split, I was a cheerleader, so I think I was caught off guard by how flexible I still was).

(Side note: She single-handedly ruined at least ten pairs of my thong/panty inventory!)

There I was, wings spread; she started tongue fucking me, licking my insides. There was no leading into it; she just went straight into tongue-fucking me (there was foreplay, but that lasted maybe ten seconds before she impaled Nikki with her tongue). She pulled her tongue out and kissed the clit one time.

"Can I have one now?" she asked.

"No," I replied and pushed her head back into my pussy.

She kissed it again, slid a finger in, then started munching, and came back up.

"What about now?" she asked.

I shoved her head back down again. She started sucking on my clit brutally. It hurt a bit, but felt good at the same time, to be honest. She turned her fingers up inside of me. She reached my g-spot and started massaging on it. She was fingering me with a purpose. I felt myself about to cum. Then she stopped everything.

"What about now?" she asked.

"Okay, fuck!" I yelled out. "Don't stop!"

She shoved her head back down there and continued. Long story short, the arch of my back pretty much looked like $y= -x^2+8$ (look up the equation to understand the severity of the head I was getting). I ended up wrapping my legs around her head and she lifted me up into a headstand! She began jackhammering my pussy with her tongue.

She kept me locked in her hands, upside down. I kept trying to push her head out, and to get her arms from around me, but it wasn't working. I felt the soul in my pussy being sucked out and I became weak.

Then I came, and she finally let go. I ended up laying there exhausted, out of breath, hair everywhere. I looked at her.

"But I have to choose the person," I managed to get out.

She sucked her teeth and raised her eyebrows.

"A girl?" she asked.

"Nope," I said. "I'll be damned if you're going to be fucking another fem. The only person that's going to be sucking dicks or dildos will be me."

She nodded her head in agreeance. I have no idea how she ended up agreeing to it, at all. But she did. I figured suggesting a guy would deter her from wanting a threesome, but no. She was actually with the shit to my surprise.

21. Three's Company

∞

I knew the perfect person. He was just fuckboyish enough to be comfortable with being a part of a threesome. I'll call him David.

I met him in high school and he used to sell me weed. We both eventually cleaned up our acts and went to college. Look at God! Won't he do it?

I texted him the very same day asking him to call me. So he finally called me and I asked if he was free some time that week "to chill". Then I explained the situation. It's kind of sad how quickly he agreed to doing it, even after I told him that Bianca was a stud. He even offered to spark us up.

(Side note: For the people that aren't from the DMV area, to spark someone up means to provide someone with weed, often for free.)

So her birthday had finally come and we planned on everyone meeting up at Bianca's house (I was already there because I low-key lived there). The doorbell rang, repeatedly. He just could not wait. We headed up the stairs to the front door. When we opened it, he was cheesing so hard that it made **my** cheeks start to hurt. He walked in, he hugged me, Bianca dapped him; it was awkward, but it was funny as hell. Shit started to feel more like a business deal than anything else.

So we headed down to the basement and walked into her room. We started smoking weed. I don't know what fucking strain it was but the shit was potent for no god damn reason! I swear Bianca and David both sprouted wings and turned colors (which is weird, because I've never hallucinated while smoking weed). I was fucked up, she was fucked up, he was fucked up.

David stood up and started dancing, like his life depended on it. There was no music playing. Let that marinate. I was really happy for him, but he was hogging the jay.

About ten minutes later, it got awkwardly quiet. David had finally sat back down on the bed. I was consequently siting between the both of them (and I hated every minute of it). I was waiting for Bianca to call it off, and for her to say she was just playing, but the time never came.

"Soooooo," I said, "about the weather."

I can't really explain to you guys how awkward it was. I cleared my throat and began telling him the rules Bianca and I had come up with (and by "Bianca and I", I mean "Bianca"). I couldn't suck his dick or engage in a kiss with him longer than two seconds. He couldn't touch Bianca. There could be no ass play or recording of anything at any time, and he was only allowed to fuck only after she had.

According to her, she was more interested in watching my face while being pleasured than actually being in a threesome.

(Side note: That's just how she was. She even liked to watch me play with myself on occasion.)

While I was telling him the rules, his excited eyes did not change. He was ready; he did not care about the circumstances. He honestly had a pretty shitty deal, but he was down for whatever.

"Deal?" I asked.

It seemed as though all of what I had just said went in one ear and out the other.

"Bet," he answered and clapped his hands one time. "Let's do this."

I looked over at Bianca and she was already getting her strap-on out of her "special drawer" (a drawer full of toys). David started taking his pants off. I want to say that that was the lowest, most demeaning point of my life, but it unfortunately was not.

Bianca walked over to me and pushed me back. She yanked and spread my legs open. Then she dove in.

I'm guessing David didn't think we were really with the shits, considering the fact that his eyes grew big and his jaw dropped while Bianca was eating me out. He began inching closer and closer. Then he put his hand on my leg and pushed down. When Bianca came up and wiped her mouth off, David took his shirt off and went down. I could not fucking believe it! Sooner or later, they had a routine going on. One would go down for twenty seconds then come back up, and handed the steering wheel to the other.

Bianca ended up sitting beside my head, watching David eat my pussy. He would suck everything up, then spit it back out and keep eating!

All of a sudden, I was sucking on Bianca's dildo while David was eating my pussy. Then he put my knees into my face and began eating my ass. My body ended up looking like a less than symbol, or a greater than symbol, depending on the angle one would be witnessing this from. Typically, I'm against ass-play, but his tongue was wide and long, so I was willing to let that reservation subside. Honestly, if you have a long and wide enough tongue, you can pretty much put it in any hole of mine you want (but you have to know what you're doing).

I'm not sure if it was bomb because I was high and everything was heightened or because he was genuinely really good at what he was doing. Bianca pulled me up, and bent me over the bed. She started throwing back shots. David walked around the other side of the bed and sat down. I started rubbing on his dick and pulled it out of his boxers. Then he slapped his dick on my face. Bianca lost her shit! She literally pushed David off of the bed, onto the floor. Meanwhile, she was still fucking me from the back.

"Chill out, cuz," she said out of breath. "Don't do that shit."

"Okay, okay, okay," David replied annoyed, then got back onto the bed.

He ripped my cami off and started sucking on my nipples. He put his head underneath me, while his feet dangled off the side of the bad. He tried to whisper into my ear.

"Put your mouth on it for a second," he said.

I looked back at Bianca. I was trying to do him a solid and jerk him off but Bianca looked at me like she was going to kill me in my sleep. So, I turned my head back. David somehow got the balls to try to shove a finger into Bianca's pussy through the gap on the strap-on. He really did not value his life at all. She pulled out, lifted me up off of him, then back-slapped him in the face.

"Back the fuck up," she said.

He went to the other edge of the bed and just sat there. That was when shit got extremely weird. Bianca went back to fucking me and David just sat there, staring and beating his dick. Trust me when I say that beating is an understatement. He was beating it like he was angry with it, or like it stole money from him. He started grunting and breathing fast. Then all of a sudden, he would just stop and continue staring. Then he would go back to it, and then stop again. You get the picture. At one point, he put it back into the pee hole, rubbed on his dick, and started grunting again. He pulled it back out, and starting jerking off with an intricate flick of the wrist.

He began turning red in the face and stopped breathing. Then he came on me—no seriously. He came **on me**, purposely.

It seemed as though he was aiming it right at me. It got on my shoulders, on my face, on my back, in my hair. My fucking hair! It got on the leggings that were in the middle of the bed. A tiny bit of it got on the tank top, but it seemed like it was splashed all over *me*.

Normally, I wouldn't have even freaked out if we were together, because I love cum. I love it. I've swallowed enough cum to start a fucking sperm bank, for Christ's sake. But the catch is that I have to be emotionally involved with that person, not some random nigga. Bianca started laughing and I felt my jaw clench up. I couldn't speak.

He began apologizing as if it wouldn't take me hours to get his kids out of my hair. Cum in the hair is the fucking worst. It was too thick and it stank! I was just trying to be a good girlfriend but ended up getting cum all in my hair. When it happened, it all came out so fast. But it seemed as if everything was in slow motion at the same time. I ran out of her room, threw my clothes into the washing machine, jumped into the shower, and scrubbed everything, everywhere. When I got out, he was gone. And then I got a whiff of my hair and gagged. I hopped back in the shower.

When I get out for the last time, Bianca looked at me and started laughing again. Then when she saw that I was truly serious, she tried to hug me, but I did not move or respond to her affection. I was over it.

Two weeks later, I broke up with her because I found out she cheated on me—story of my life. If you can avoid it, never, ever, no matter the circumstance, agree to a threesome. It's not worth it. It's all around a fucked up situation.

I pretty much spent the rest of my summer alone, focused on myself and money. Of course, Jay wanted to be more than friends; I was just mentally and emotionally not prepared for the fuckery.

Part IV: Emotional Rollercoaster

22. 1 Year, 1 Nigga

∞

Senior Year, 2014

It was mid-September and school had only been in session for two weeks. I was working in the cafeteria, had an internship, doing hair on the side, and a full-time student. I was stressed, but managed to maintain my sanity because I've always been pretty good at managing my time. I was actually happy. I was getting money. I was going to the gym, eating healthy and losing weight. My edges were growing back like they never left me. My curl pattern was flourishing. My hair was bouncy and lustrous. My skin was luminous and glowing. I was getting right with the Lord, saying my prayers every night. And in the blink of an eye, a fuckboy managed to enter my life and fuck it all up for me! C'est la vie.

At the time, I was friends with Jennifer and another girl. Let's call the other one Desiree. I had known Desiree my entire life because our parents were best friends, and on top of that, dated for a while. But for the longest time, we hated each other. Well, she hated me. I never really knew why. I was chill as fuck even in the second and third grades. I had met Jennifer the year before during homecoming and we just clicked. We were inseparable.

(Side note: I introduced Jennifer to Desiree on my 21st birthday that very same year. I had a party at a local Club in DC called Ibiza. We became a clique. Jennifer was the sweet and innocent one, I was the slut, Desiree was fucking crazy. We balanced each other out.)

Desiree was not in school at the moment, so she would often visit Jennifer and me on campus twice or thrice a week. One day in particular, Desiree and I were waiting for Jennifer to get out of class. We were between the Student Center and the Performing Arts Building, just hanging out.

(Side note: Let me just say this; Desiree wasn't bad-looking, but she wasn't good-looking either. She wasn't ugly, but she wasn't pretty either. Okay, she was pretty ugly. I can't even lie to you guys.)

A group of guys came walking past us toward the performing arts building. Now, Desiree was ugly but she was confident as hell, extroverted and she knew she had the juice. Scratch that; she had lemonade. She made the best out of her unfortunate situation.

She was ugly, but not *ugly* ugly. She was like ugly pretty, or pretty ugly—the best of both worlds, honestly.

Being the strong, independent, ugly woman she was, Desiree moseyed on over to the group of guys. She was one of those girls who was bowlegged, and thought it was cute. I wasn't even mad at her.

I heard one guy from the group call out my real name, then another one called me by my social media name (Smillee). On that day, I didn't have glasses on nor did I have contacts in. I couldn't see faces, but I pretended like I knew exactly who they were and awkwardly waved.

A part of me felt confused mainly because I made it my business to stay in the cut, out of drama, and in the books. I was confused as to how any of those boys knew my name.

About five minutes later, Desiree walked (well, bow-leggeded) back over to me smiling at her phone. She looked back and waved. Being the nosy, messy bitch I was, I demanded that she spill the tea.

"His name is Orlando," she said as she sat beside me.

She asked me if he could come to my on-campus apartment one day so that they could hang out. (For some reason, she lied and told him that she attended Bowie.) I didn't care. I was just excited for her because she had recently gotten out of a relationship with a nigga who never claimed her in public.

Weeks later, in early October, there was a function on campus. Of course Desiree and Jennifer came through afterwards. She and Orlando would finally have the chance to hang out like they had been discussing.

I signed them into my building and we ended up watching a movie. Out of nowhere, Desiree caught an attitude and threw her phone across the room. When I asked her what was wrong, she explained to me that Orlando was ignoring her texts and calls. He had promised her that he would come through that night, but he never showed. Homeboy just stood her up.

So after some investigating, I find out what his Instagram handle was and went to his page. When I saw his name and picture, I then realized it was the same guy who was trying to talk to me a year before when I first started talking to Stanford. I sent him a DM cursing him out—basically telling him how much of a piece of shit he was for standing my friend up. He had been ignoring her messages, texts, and FaceTime calls, but in a matter of thirty seconds, he had replied to me.

"I'll come up for you," he messaged.

All I could do was shake my head. I just knew that this was about to get messy. I didn't want him to come up for *me*, I wanted him to come up for the girl he had been promising to see for so long.

Twenty minutes later, we heard a knock on the front door. Desiree hopped off the bed and looked in the mirror to make sure that she looked "okay". Did she proceed to the "Three S's" beforehand, you ask? No, she did not. I must admit that I was a little disappointed.

She went into the kitchen, Jennifer and I stayed in my room. We wanted to give them privacy, but we turned the volume down because we were nosy as fuck. We heard the door creek open then close.

"Tiy and Jennifer!" he yelled out, obviously drunk. "Why're you guys hiding?"

I was confused and left wondering how he knew my name because my real name was not on any of my social media pages. We heard footsteps approaching my bedroom door. He stumbled into my doorway, then he realized that I didn't have any pants on and covered his eyes. I honestly didn't even give a fuck.

"If y'all don't come out, I'm coming in," he said.

I looked at Jennifer and we could both tell that he was belligerently drunk and we didn't want Desiree out there by herself. So we agreed to come out. We figured we would finish up some bottles I had stashed away in my closet. I put on some booty shorts and wrapped myself up in my blanket and followed Jennifer out into the living room. Desiree and Orlando were sitting on one couch, while Jennifer and I squeezed into a sofa chair.

It was too fucking quiet and awkward so I got up to get my computer from my bedroom. It was just so sad, guys. He was pretending to be interested in her, but it was just not working out the way I thought it would.

After I sat down and got settled, I realized that Orlando had spent the better portion of his visit staring at me. It was awkward. After searching for a song to play on my computer, I finally decided on "3005" by Childish Gambino. Unbeknownst to me, Childish Gambino ruined my life.

As soon as he heard the beat drop, he looked at me again and started smiling. He got up and sat on the table right beside me.

"What you know about Childish Gambino?" he asked. I bunched my face up.

"Nigga," I replied. "What the fuck you know about Childish Gambino?"

He inched closer and pulled out his Android phone to show me his music collection. He had all of Childish Gambino's albums and mixtapes on his phone; I showed him my iTunes collection because I did too.

"I knew I liked you for a reason," he said.

The room got dead quiet, and I fought the urge to facepalm.

I looked over at Desiree and she was not entertained. I never knew someone's eyebrows could drop that low in anger. Orlando and I eventually started arguing about which Childish Gambino album/mixtape was the best. Desiree was still mad even though she had no reason to be at the moment.

I didn't want him. Don't get me wrong, he was cute and exactly my type (skin so dark it could pass for purple, nice smile, fresh cut, dressed nicely, spoke articulately), but I take loyalty very seriously and I had no interest in flirting with him at all.

I didn't have makeup on, my hair was in a ponytail, I had my hair-dye t-shirt and some raggedy ass shorts. If I truly wanted him at the time, my attire would have been a completely different story. You should already know: if there is no makeup, there is no spark. I didn't even have on Pure Seduction!

Fifteen minutes went by and we were still arguing about Childish Gambino and Odd Future. Desiree was giving me the evil eye, Jennifer was looking back and forth at me and Desiree. I was trying to curve Orlando's advances.

Eventually, we ended up playing King's Cup. After a while, Orlando looked at his phone and said that he had to go. He walked over to Desiree and gave her a side hug. Then he gave Jennifer a normal hug. Then he walked over to me and hugged me for at least five seconds; normally, five seconds isn't a long period of time, but it felt like forever. I felt him breathing me in.

He walked out the door and looked back at me as I was preparing to lock it. When I turned around, Desiree was grimacing at me, and that was it. She complained about how he came there for her, but spent the entire time talking to me. She started calling me every name in the book for no reason. I was just being me. I looked a mess on purpose, and she hated me for it. It took everything in me not to be petty and to tell her that he never came for her in the first place, but I bit my tongue.

It should come as no surprise that after that, Desiree and I pretty much fell off. She started subtweeting me on Twitter and making subliminal posts on Instagram about loyalty. I was done with her crazy ass. At one point, she even involved my mom, over a nigga I didn't even want in the first place. It was war.

A couple weeks later, it was homecoming and I was going to turn the fuck up. I was completely drunk. I literally drank that entire day. Something told me that I was going to need it. I was still trying to get over Stanford and Bianca. Jennifer, a few friends, and I were standing in line to get into the after-party. Imagine my surprise when I saw Orlando's alcoholic ass walking over to us with a smile on his face. He came over and hugged Jennifer, then licked his lips and hugged me. I didn't even move my arms.

"How's Desiree?" he asked.

"I don't know," I said. "You tell me."

"We stopped talking a while ago," he replied. "We don't really talk like that."

I nodded my head because I was over the conversation. The more we talked about it, the more upset it made me. Fortunately, the line started moving (thank God).

"Save me a dance," he shouted out cornily.

I rolled my eyes and didn't even look back.

We walked into the gym and it was lit. It was crowded and hot. There was so little time, so many dicks to twerk on, and so many faces to sit on. We headed over to the center of the crowd as we always did because that was typically the most fun. I looked to my left and there was someone extremely tall standing out from the crowd in the bleachers. The lights flashed on his face and I knew exactly who it was.

Would you like to guess? Are you able to generalize the kind of luck I have in my life? Of all the people to have been attending the after-party, Stanford (a guy who didn't even go to the school anymore—a guy who went to a different school in a whole ass other state) was there.

(Side note: Stanford had transferred to Morehouse to be a thot, so I couldn't comprehend why he was even there.)

My night was ruined to say the least. Fortunately, I was drunk, so a huge part of me didn't give one teeny-weeny little fuck; the other part of me was ready to leave. I looked over, we locked eyes, and I could tell he was about to start making his way toward me. I looked at Jennifer.

"We gotta move."

"Why?" she asked. I pointed toward Stanford's direction. "Say no more."

We ended up moving to the right side of the gym. I was dancing with a couple niggas and my ex was there, so you know I had to make it extremely nasty. The twerking had to be on point, the ear-whispering had to look convincing. I had to look like I was genuinely interested. I was twerking my life away, do you hear me!? Then I felt a tap on my shoulder. It was Stanford; he made it his mission to get into an altercation with every nigga I was dancing with. My friends and I took that opportunity to move again.

By that point, we were in the front near the stage and I was dancing with another nigga. He was whispering in my ear. I was setting up a face-sitting appointment. Then all of a sudden, Stanford came over again! He asked the guy I was dancing with to step back.

"Nah," he replied.

Then there was another altercation/argument. I was just praying that security would come through, scoop him up, and kick his ass out like they do to the hood rats that fight during homecoming every year. We moved again. I was so close to successfully setting up a face-sitting appointment and like everything else, he fucking ruined it.

All of a sudden, I felt someone's arm wrap around my waist and I was ready to twerk. Then I looked up and noticed Stanford standing in the crowd, making his way over to me again. I stopped dancing and homeboy walked away. Stanford walked over to me, smiling.

"What?" I demanded. "What the fuck do you want?"

He remained calm. He was looking good—had lost a few pounds and cut his beard differently, but he was a piece of shit, so I looked past that. He asked me to come talk to him for five minutes. Meanwhile, my friends were looking at us like we were a soap opera. I agreed to walk over there. We stood in a corner and I looked at my watch. Then he hugged me.

"You got 4 minutes, and 43 seconds," I said, looking at my watch.

"You look good," he replied. "How you been, Tiy?"

I was not fazed. He kept asking me questions.

"Are you talking to anybody new? Do you miss me?"

I held my ground and didn't feed into his charm. I was so proud of myself. I looked him dead in the eyes.

"Let me cut this short," I said. "Answer my question and we will move forward from there."

"Okay?" he replied nervously and nodded his head.

"Stanford, how many bitches have you fucked since we broke up?"

He sucked his teeth. "Twelve, but—"

I didn't know what to do. I was flabbergasted. My heart sank into my chest and I could not breathe. I was hurt, but I kept it inside like I always do. At the time, he didn't know what he did, nor did I. He flipped on a switch that took forever to turn back off. He had turned the thotness on and he didn't even know it.

"I miss you, Tiy," he said. "They didn't mean shit to me."

"There is nothing left to talk about, Stanford," I said as I began walking away. He reached for my arm and I looked back at him. "I want nothing to do with you. Delete my number."

Long story short, I was ready to get the fuck out of there. Granted, I had an *entire* (brief) relationship with another person right after we had broken up, but twelve people? Twelve? I felt like I needed to catch up just for the sake of not feeling hurt anymore.

23. Impala Encounters

November, 2014

The next day, I was going over my contact list of hoes trying to figure out who to send my "hey big head wyd" text to. Then, out of the blue, I received a DM from Orlando. He was flirting, as always. For the longest time, I kept curving him because he used to "talk" to someone I used to fuck with at one time, but considering my desperate need to be petty, I looked over that. Long story short, we made a plan to hang out on a Monday night. Visitation was over, so I couldn't sign him in. By now, I'm sure you know the routine.

For the first time in a long time, I proceeded to the "Three S's". Afterwards, I put on my (Fall Season) "On My Way to the Dick Attire", which consisted of black leggings, a black baseball cap (preferably by Nike), some black Adidas or Nike slide-ons, and a t-shirt (preferably black). The all black allows you the opportunity to be completely inconspicuous and at one with the night. I did my makeup and put on some Pure Seduction body spray and lotion. By then, he had texted me and told me that he was outside.

I headed outside, walked around the side of my dorm, and saw a champagne-colored Impala sitting idle, with the engine on. When I got into the car, I hugged him and pretended to be shy and what not. But, little did he know, his dick was about to be in the back of my throat. We talked for a while and he was trying to persuade me to let him drive to the other side of campus, to the MARC train station parking lot. That's how he was. He made me think that I wanted to. (He seemed very caring and genuinely nice, but he was the type of person that used his charm to manipulate people. But I didn't find that out until it was too late.)

"I want to get to know you mentally, physically, metaphysically, emotionally, spiritually," he spouted.

A part of me feels entirely stupid that I didn't know that he was just talking bullshit because I didn't even know myself that well. He was charming. So we finally ended up on the other side of campus in the Kiss and Ride parking lot (technically off campus). The MARC train station was between us and the school. Then he started kissing me. I was caught off guard because I hadn't really needed to enforce my "no kissing" rule for months. He reached for my leggings then looked at me dead in the eye.

"We don't have to do this if you don't want to," he said, pretending to actually give a fuck about what my response would be. "I'm not like those other niggas."

I allowed him to proceed. When he saw my thong, he freaked out because they were purple and purple was his favorite color, but purple on top of pink that you're about to suck on is a color way more exciting. He slid my thong to the side and seemed surprised that there was no hair. But, as you already know, I like to keep Nikki bald.

"You did all this for me?" he asked.

It took a lot out of me not to reassure him that I only did it for his dick and head.

So, he went down and tried to eat me out. I say "try" because the head was terrible, which I expected from a Jamaican man (because they don't eat the "pum pum"). After he was done, I told him to put his chair back. I pulled his joggers down a little to get his dick out so that I could get to work. Out flopped a thick ass pig in the blanket. I had never seen an uncircumcised dick before then. I was a little in shock. He later explained to me because he was Jamaican that circumcision wasn't really a huge thing down there. I took a deep breath and somehow got my mouth all the way around it. I found out pretty quickly that I was a pro at sucking uncircumcised dick because he shivered, quivered, and stuttered. Apparently, licking on the tip while pulling down on the skin is an amazing sensation because that area is super sensitive. When he was about to cum, he stopped me by grabbing my ponytail to get me off of him. According to him, it was too intense.

(Side note: When we were together, he had to do that often because I never knew how to stop. Even after he came. I'm still like that. Giving head is just so fun to me.)

    He let my ponytail go and I went back down. He moaned, over and over, every time he slow-stroked his dick down my throat. Then he came. Spitters are quitters, swallowers are followers, and slurpers are just better at every aspect in life. So, I slurped up everything, then swallowed. I knew it was dumb and irresponsible, but there was just something about him. Maybe because his dick was big as fuck or because of his beautiful ass complexion. Maybe because he was initially nothing more than a rebound and I needed to prove to myself that I still had the juice. It could have even been because I missed sucking dick that could actually reach the back of my throat. Stanford was a grower, not a shower. I was dickmatized.

    After much conversation, he managed to persuade me to get into the back of his car. He savagely climbed his way to the back, but because I'm a lady (and too big for that shit), I got out of the car and entered through the back door. If I'm ever going to get dicked down, I'm going to get dicked down right. Keep in mind that I was only in my thong at the moment after he had taken my leggings off. So I jumped into the back seat and I was ready to get my guts fucked by this monstrosity of a dingling. I knew it was going to hurt extremely bad because it had been a long while since anything had been up there. I wanted him to tear me apart. I wanted him to tear my shit all the way up.

He yanked my legs and got a little aggressive. I was in love with every minute of it. He turned my entire body around and slowly slid it in. Still to this day, I don't know how he got the condom on so quickly. You know that paralyzing sigh guys let out when they first stick it in and he finds out that it's wet, warm, and tight? That happened. He fell down on top of me before he could get his balance. Then he started ramming me. The back of my head kept hitting the the door knob over and over and over and over and over and over again. By then, I had already had a concussion. For a moment there, I could have sworn I saw Jesus for a second and he was shaking his head at me.

Then, he told me to turn around and I did. Then he guided his rod into me. He began slow- stroking, and the sticky clicks echoed throughout his small car. Every stroke seemed like it added a year to my life but took a year at the same time. I started moaning, which turned into screaming. My forehead kept hitting the window. Then he flipped me over onto my back again. I was still concussed, so I placed my hand behind my head. When I felt the door knob behind it, I got the idea to open the door. My head dangled and I saw my breath as I gazed up at the stars. He was literally fucking me out of his car! In this case, multitasking was an understatement.

We were fucking so hard that when the cold hit our skin, smoke came off. The windows were fogged up, it was just the most beautiful form of condensation I think I've ever witnessed. I think that was the moment I fell in love with him (and by "him", I mean his "dick"; it seemed to somehow overshadow the fact that he was a terrible person). I told myself before I walked out of that bedroom that I wouldn't get invested, and there I was ready to go back to Jamaica with him to start a family—shit, maybe even help get him a green card. That's how good the dick was. I had already cum and he continued slow-stroking. It was torture.

He fell on top of me again, and held me by the back of my hair, grinding his hips and moving his dick inside of me. I looked back up at the stars and made peace with God. Then he pulled me back into the car. I slammed the door behind me. He bounced his dick in and out of me. He started moaning and it was a glorious feeling. Honestly, men's moans should be bottled up and sold to the general public (or placed in an art gallery). I felt his warm cum squirt into the condom that served as a barrier between the two of us. He slowly pulled out. We sat there in silence for a good five minutes. All of the sudden, we saw red and blue lights flashing outside of the car.

My heart stopped. He jumped up front and threw my leggings back at me.

"Don't move," he said. "Just act natural."

Meanwhile, I was sitting in the back wondering how he thought that was possible. He had literally just snatched my soul from me and he wanted me to act calm. I slid on my leggings as if my life depended on it. We heard the car doors shut and saw flashlights on either side of the car. There was a tap on his window. We both rolled our windows down. They flashed the flashlights in our faces while I was pretending to be in my phone. I eventually realized that my phone was upside down, but that's besides the point.

"Can either one of you tell me why the windows are fogged up and why you're on this side of campus," the cop on Orlando's side asked.

"Oh, sorry about that sir," Orlando answered. "I'm anemic (which was true) and we had my heat blasting because I getting very cold."

"But why are you over here?," asked the cop on my side.

"Well," I said, " visitation is over and I wanted to see my boyfriend because I hadn't seen him in months. He just got back in town." I said, lying out of my ass.

They asked to see our IDs. Orlando handed me my keys because my student ID was on the lanyard. They went back to their car for a couple minutes. Then they came back.

"Son," one said. "You don't have a full license, do you?"

I thought we were done for. I was really about to go to jail for some bomb ass Jamaican dick and he was about to go to jail for some bomb ass BBW pussy; I had come to terms with that fact. But by the grace of God, eventually they handed us our IDs and told us to get going. Orlando pulled off and we ended up behind my dorm again. We stayed back there for another thirty minutes just talking. By that time, it had to be 3 am.

"I've got to go," I said. "I've got a class at 8."

He kissed me again. I opened the door behind me and dipped out. Two weeks later, we were dating. I brought him home for Thanksgiving (even though I never really invited him, he invited his damn self because he misinterpreted me asking him what he was doing for Thanksgiving). My family liked him, and my mom loved him even more. We were complete opposites; he had a lot of friends, I didn't fuck with anyone but my best friend. He was an extrovert, and I was an introvert. He used to be a gym rat and ate healthily for the most part, I lived a fairly sedentary life, and barely ate. I hadn't realized that the emotional roller coaster he was going to take me on would later perpetuate everything about my life.

24. New Year Bullshit

∞

December 31st, 2014/January 1st, 2015

It was December 31st. Orlando texted me and told me to get ready because we were going to celebrate at his organizational brother's house. Orlando wanted to introduce me to a few of his friends. As soon as I saw that text, I dreaded it. For some reason, I just hate meeting my partner's friends; I always have and I probably always will. It's just an all-around awkward situation. All I wanted to do was bring in the New Year with him, and simultaneously cum as the ball dropped, but no. It was so important for me to meet people that didn't really fuck with him in the first place (I'll get to that later).

He was the type of person that liked to socialize and go out. I, however, am the type of person content with spending time with the people I love.

So, we pulled up into an apartment complex in Bowie, Maryland. It was Thomas and Asia's house. Thomas was Orlando's "brother" and Asia was Thomas's fiancée. I had already met them before earlier when Orlando and I first started dating. They were having a kickback—which basically meant that everyone would get shitface drunk and gossip about people and things I don't give the slightest fuck about.

When we walked inside, we were apparently the first two to arrive. Orlando walked to the kitchen to put the pizzas we bought in the oven, and the soda in the fridge.

I hugged Asia and Thomas. They were fun to hang out with normally, even though they were friends with a complete and utter dickwad, but that's besides the point. I was dating him, so what does that say about me? We waited for people to come through. Thomas (Orlando's best friend) invited me to their wedding, which would've been in June or July of 2015 (I can't remember). Orlando was the best man, so of course I was invited to be his date—how sweet.

People began showing up and coming in. All of them were graduates of Bowie. Orlando and I were the only ones that had still attended. I was obviously the youngest person there.

(Side note: I don't know why, but I always seem to attract the alcoholics. Bianca drank too much, Stanford drank away his Depression, and Orlando just didn't know when to stop. I had never really been a drinker myself since the Que incident. Almost every relationship I've ever been in was with an in denial alcoholic.)

People started introducing themselves to me at that fuckboy ceremony. I stayed quiet because I'm awkward like that. I was ready to go. The night was filled with drinking games and it lasted for hours. The entire apartment reeked of hard liquor. Niggas were chugging Henny as if it were water (that's when you know you have a problem).

Normally, I would never hang out with a crowd like that because I was so focused on graduating. I've always been quiet and low-key. I do yoga and sip tea. My drinking days were far behind me. The whole drink until you puke shit is a Freshman taboo. It's just not my cup of tea.

(Side note: Everyone in there was a Kappa, Alpha, Delta, or AKA. Orlando was a prospect for Alpha Phi Alpha. He wanted to be one so bad, but his priorities were fucked up, no matter how many times I tried to help. At one point, he was failing every class because he just didn't want to go or do the homework. I had a talent for a dating losers who didn't know how to better themselves.)

Everyone kept trying to get me to drink, and I would politely decline because the hangover has never been worth it. I finally surrendered and agreed to play one game. I looked over at my boyfriend and he was stammering around drunk as always. They were all yelling and laughing. It was too crazy for me to have fun. I had calmed down over the years, so I wasn't really interested in being there at all. Bitches were running back and forth to the bathroom because they had drank more than they could handle; it was just a mess.

I was irritated because I didn't have my license and Orlando was the one driving that night. There was a disgusting jungle juice they made that I got drunk off of with one cup. Then I joined in on the shenanigans. The only reason I joined in was because before Orlando and I got out of the car that night, he begged me to socialize. He wanted me to pledge to one of the sororities on campus and to befriend some of the girls that were there. I wasn't going to, but I was friendly enough not to come off as a bitch.

All of his friends were Greek and that just was not my style. It was just so overrated to me. Don't get me wrong; if that's what you really want to do, I'm not knocking you at all, do your thing. I just felt like I didn't belong there.

After a while, I sat down on one of the couches and started talking to Jeremy (a Kappa), and Melony (an AKA). I had asked them how they met because I assumed they were together. Jeremy was practically babysitting Melony, so I thought he was the annoyed boyfriend. Apparently they weren't; they were just really good friends.

Jeremy told me about how he lived in New York and had some acting gigs. His life seemed pretty interesting. Meanwhile, Melony was slumped on the couch, laughing hysterically—you know, the typical annoying drunk bitch activities.

At around 3 am, it was finally time to go. Orlando was fucked up and I wouldn't have been comfortable allowing him to drive me all the way home (to DC), then to have to drive by himself all the way back home (to Bowie). So I ended up staying the night at his house. When I walked into his room, I was disgusted. It was my first time being in his room and it was atrocious. I saw him differently. Like I said, we were complete opposites. I was a neat freak, who cleaned her room at least twice a week. Orlando pretended to be obsessively compulsive when he would come to my room (on campus), but by the way his room looked, that was just another thing he was lying about. He held me in his arms, and I turned my head away from him because his breath reeked of liquor. It made me want to vomit.

It was my first New Year in a relationship and it was ruined because he wanted to spend the time with his friends, like he always did (but I won't go into detail about that).

25. First Impressions

∞

February, 2015

Orlando and I were on the rocks because things started not adding up. He got into a fight with one of his "brothers" because he thought that Orlando was flirting with his ex-girlfriend. I just didn't know what to do about the situation. After the fight, one of Orlando's friends, Toby (who I had a huge crush on before and after Orlando and I broke up) told me that I should talk to Orlando about the situation, but every time I brought it up, he always found a reason to change the subject. Then he'd always take that opportunity to bring up niggas that I used to talk to that I still communicated with during our relationship, but I always kept it respectful.

(Long ass side note: I had nothing to hide. Orlando had a fingerprint to my iPhone, he knew all of my passcodes, he even read my text messages and DMs and I didn't care. Whenever I'd get the chance to bring up a girl who liked him or a girl he used to talk to, it was always a problem, so fidelity was definitely something that sat on my mind all the time. I honestly think that the only thing that held us together for so

long was his dick. And I'm not saying that to seem rude, or to be shallow or anything like that.

People say that sex isn't the most important thing in a relationship, but it definitely was for Orlando and me. I never realized how dependent on sex I was until it was too late. This was the dicksand nobody warns you about. It's the addiction you develop when nothing else in you life is going right but the dick. Our sexual chemistry was crazy. Whenever we were mad at each other, we'd fuck and make up. Whenever we'd have an argument, we'd fuck and make up. Whenever we were bored or didn't have anything to talk about, we'd fuck. Honestly, it got to the point to where if I hadn't seen or touched or really spoken to him in days, I didn't miss him, I missed his dick. Come to think of it, I wasn't really in love with him; I was in love with his dick. It fit me perfectly. I knew how to make him cum and he knew how to throw the dick.

As far as emotions go and having a conducive relationship, Orlando didn't really have emotions. He spent the better part of our relationship making me feel like shit for wanting to hang out with him. He would blame me for being upset with him for ignoring me, which made no sense at all. I would text him and hours would pass, and I'd think that he was just busy at work or in class, but as soon as I would see my notifications feed (for other people because I'm not a fucking idiot), sure enough he would be liking ugly bitches's posts and shoe photos, blatantly ignoring me.

He was just a shitty person. Why did I stay with him? It would be much easier to say that I don't know—but it was the dick. I could also say that it was because I hated being single; for the longest time, I was in a relationship back to back to back. Did I love him? I loved who he pretended to be. You know when you're with a shitty person, but you believe in all your heart that it'll get better or that you don't deserve anyone else? That was what our relationship was.)

In the last couple months of our relationship, I was really trying to make it work between us. One night, he had stayed at my apartment on campus. Of course we fucked—that was the only time we actually got along. As I said, sex was the epicenter of our relationship.

The next day, we woke up and showered. We got into his car but he refused to tell me where we were going. He liked to spring shit on me fast, even though he knew I hated surprises and always needed to be in the know. We went to IHOP and for some sad reason, I was just happy that he was spending time with me. Silly me, I didn't know I had to beg to hang out with my boyfriend, but that was always the case.

While we were there, I barely ate. I low-key had an eating disorder. I never had the time or energy to eat, even though I worked in the fucking cafeteria. At one point, I lost twenty pounds in a month and he didn't even notice. I don't know, I was just depressed as fuck.

After we finished up, we (yes, we) paid the tab because I made a big fuss out of it; that's just how I am. When we were in the car, we were holding hands—the real cute shit. That was the moment he fucked up because I became horny.

From that moment, I knew wherever it was we were going, I was going to get some dick; it was not optional. I didn't give a flying fuck about the circumstances, or who would see, or where it would be. I did not care. You can honestly ask anyone I've ever been in a relationship with that it literally takes nothing for me to get horny. If you touch me anywhere near my pussy, or around my pussy, you're getting fucked. That's just the name of the game. He told me that he wanted me to meet someone, but he still hadn't told me who it was or where we were going.

We eventually pulled up to a house on the DC/Maryland line. I couldn't help but wonder what the fuck was going on.

Orlando pulled his phone out and called someone.

"Yo, dog," he said. "We're here."

(Side note: By the way, Orlando thought that he was Randy Jackson from circa 2004 with that "yo, dog" shit. Who even says that anymore? Even though he was Jamaican, his American accent was decent. He must've learned his accent from 80's and 90's television shows, though.)

He hung up the phone and unbuckled his seatbelt.

"Alright," he said, "c'mon."

"What do you mean 'c'mon'?" I replied. "Whose house is this? Where are we? Why are we here?"

He explained that it was his friend's house whose mom had recently passed and that he was worried about him because he was going through some things. We were going to drop him off at his job (Best Buy), in Bowie. I was irritated, but I completely understood that he wanted to be there for him. They were apparently really good friends; he was even the guy's daughter's godfather.

I was always nervous to meet any of his friends. He knew a lot of people, and everyone on campus seemed to know him. I would always be nervous to find out that I knew that person or that I fucked that person before. I eventually put my anxiety to the side and we knocked on the door. A guy named Vance opened up and they hugged. Orlando introduced us, his friend looked at me and hugged me. Fortunately, I had never met him before. Vance punched Orlando in the arm.

"She's cute, bro," Vance said.

"Yeah," Orlando replied. "I know."

Keep in mind that I was literally standing right there, while they were talking about me as if I weren't.

Vance didn't have a shirt on and I was confused as to why. He had a towel wrapped around his waist.

He was obviously not ready to go to work. I grew irritated because Vance was getting in the way of my dick time. I just wanted to fuck my boyfriend and he was taking his sweet time. When we walked in, I sat down on the couch. Orlando sat beside me. It was kind of strange that Vance was walking around the house the entire time nearly naked, disregarding the fact that we had literally met less than five minutes before. He headed upstairs and came right back down two minutes later. He handed Orlando the remote control.

"I'll be ready in about an hour," Vance said.

I was literally gushing and that was plenty of time to handle it. I was starting to think that Vance underestimated the fact that I was completely willing and able to whip Orlando's uncircumcised dick out on his couch right in front of him. They were best friends, so I'm sure Orlando told Vance about all the nasty, disgusting, filthy things we did. Orlando even told more than one of his friends about that one time I grapefruited him.

(Side note: Yes, I grapefruited Orlando as well and he absolutely loved it.)

"Can I get a blanket or a fleece or something?" I asked.

"I got you," Vance replied and ran back upstairs to bring me down a blanket.

He was so sweet. He seemed like a genuine person—like the type of guy I would've dated had Orlando and I not been a thing.

Vance went back upstairs. Orlando and I looked at each other and smiled. We got closer and snuggled up. Then he turned on the Discovery Channel. That was literally one of two channels he watched; it was either that or Animal Planet.

I put the blanket over me and put my legs across his lap. Then I purposely started moving my thigh. He grabbed it.

"Babe," he said. "Chill out. Not right now, yo."

I heard everything he said, but I was blocking it out at the same time. So I stopped and five minutes later, I was back at it again with the fondling!

I honestly feel so bad for guys; all they want to do is spend quality time with their girl and all girls want to do is fuck. It's tragic.

I slid my hand down into his joggers and started rubbing on his dick. He grabbed my hand and looked at the stairwell to see if Vance was anywhere near. Then he let my hand go and leaned back. I pulled his dick out.

Then we heard Vance's heavy-footed ass stomping down the stairs. I pulled the blanket over his dick and we tried to act normal. He came and sat down on the other couch. He still wasn't ready. Orlando tried his best to sneak his dick back into his pants. I glanced at Vance.

He started watching TV with us like he didn't have a job to be at. I took my legs off of Orlando's lap and put my head on his shoulder. I was acting like the innocent girlfriend who just wanted to spend time with her boyfriend and enjoy getting to know his friend while they caught up (but we all know the truth). Vance stood and headed toward the kitchen.

"Y'all hungry or anything?" he asked.

We told him that we had just eaten.

I started pouting like the big ass baby that I am. Orlando looked at me and tried not to laugh.

"What's wrong?" he asked.

"I'm horny," I mouthed.

"What?" he replied while trying to make out what I had said.

I put my lips to the side of his face.

"I wanna fuck," I whispered into his ear then licked it.

Yes, I took advantage of the fact that whenever I would lick his ear, he would instantly get an erection; I felt no shame. I started kissing on his neck and he cleared his throat a couple times.

"Yo," Orlando shouted out to Vance. "Can we go upstairs real quick, bro?"

Vance peeped his head out from in the kitchen while eating a bowl of cereal.

"For what?" he asked while chewing his food. "To lay down, or *lay* down?"

I started laughing.

"To *lay* down," Orlando replied.

"Oh ard," Vance said. "Y'all can go to my nana's room."

"You think she'll notice?" I asked.

He took another bite of his cereal.

"Considering she's dead, nah," he replied then walked back into the kitchen as if he hadn't just given the go-ahead to fuck in his dead grandmother's room.

Orlando stood.

"Yo," he said. "You sure, bro?"

Vance walked back out to the living room and nodded his head.

"Ima be a while anyway," he said. "I should be done by the time y'all finish."

I smiled and looked at the back of Orlando's head. Of course, I was a bit off-put by the entire situation, but Nikki was as care-free as a free bird. Orlando led the way up the stairs and opened the bedroom door. I closed the door behind us and watched as Orlando put his phone and keys on the dresser meticulously side by side. He reached out for my phone and I gave it to him.

Orlando grabbed me and pulled me in. We started kissing. He slammed me up against the door and slipped his hand into my leggings.

"You don't have to be so rough!" I thought to myself. "I am a lady!"

But I liked it. When he slid his hand a bit further in, he found out just how wet I was.

"Oh, shit," he said. "Get on the bed."

I inched back on the bed. He started taking off his tight ass shirt.

He came toward me and kissed me so passionately. Then he pulled his head back.

"Lay back," he demanded.

I did. He pulled my leggings off one leg at a time then slid my panties over and started rubbing on my clit. Then he slid a finger in. I felt his eyes watching me as my facial expressions changed in ecstasy. I looked at him and he licked his lips. My jaw dropped. He pulled his finger out and began untying the drawstring in his joggers. I helped him pull them down. He climbed up on top of me and held his dick as he tried to stick it inside of me.

I backed up obviously unamused.

"Where's the condom?" I asked.

(Side note: I had never let anyone enter me without a condom because I didn't trust anyone with my body but me. That, on top of the fact that he was cheating on me was also a factor. It was a huge issue in our relationship—the condom part, not the fact that I swore up and down to him that he was keeping something from me. I didn't trust him. I never had a reason to. It seemed like everything that came out of his mouth was a lie. And after a certain period of time, I just used him for sex. We were never really in love, just in love with who and what we pretended to be. I do think he loved me once upon a time, but the good things in my life always seem to end in fire. The only

person I can blame for staying with him for so long is myself. I was desperate to be in love.)

He sucked his teeth, bounced off of the bed, and pulled one out of his pocket. So he put the condom on. It took him a while because his dick was pretty big (which was pretty much the only good thing about him). So he climbed back on the bed and started kissing me (he was such a boring kisser). As he kissed me, he slowly slid Russel, the Fuck Muscle (his dick) in. He started grinding his hips and thrusting his dick deeper into me. He slid his hands underneath me and pulled me down by my shoulders. I tried to be mindful and positioned my body in a way that my juices wouldn't flow out onto the bed out of respect for Vance's house.

Was it a sin? Was it illegal? Was fucking on a dead person's bed morally unjust?

I wrapped my arms around him and started scratching on his back. Then I lifted my head up. On the dresser, there were a plethora of pictures of an old woman with a child that resembled Vance. It was her, looking right at us.

I dropped my head down onto the pillow. Guilt draped over my body. To alleviate the situation, I got an idea into my head.

"Babe," I moaned out. "Fuck me from behind."

He sighed, pulled his dick out, and slapped it on my clit a few times. I felt my juices smearing around as he rubbed it from side to side. Then he slid Russell back in and pulled it out.

"Okay, turn around," he said out of breath.

I turned around and looked back at him while he fucked me. He grabbed me by my neck from behind. Then he got a hold of my hair and started riding me like a stallion, but he did it so respectfully.

"Harder!" I whimpered out.

I noticed that it was eerily quiet, but the claps echoed throughout the room. The headboard started clapping up against the wall to the beat of the back shots. He had finally stopped being a little bitch and pulled my hair hard enough so that I couldn't move my head. I looked over at a nightstand.

There was another fucking picture of his grandmother and there was nothing I could do to look away. I think that was the moment I knew I was going to hell. I did not know what to do. I just took the dick and stared at her in her eyes. Every shot from the back was making the situation much worse. It felt amazing, but I immediately regretted it. He came, but I didn't because I was too busy mentally writing an apology note to God, seeking forgiveness. He got dressed while I sat on the edge of the bed, looking at those fucking pictures. That was an all-time low for me. Never had I ever been so addicted to dick that I was willing to fuck someone in a dead person's bed, let alone their home. I told him to go ahead downstairs because I had to go to the bathroom.

I reached down for my panties. When I came back up, I saw another photo. To me, that was an omen so I hurried the fuck up, grabbed my shit, and ran to the bathroom. I cleaned off a bit, got dressed, and headed down. When I came downstairs, Vance was finally dressed in his Best Buy uniform. He smirked. I looked at Orlando and he was smiling too.

Orlando helped me put my coat back on and we headed out to the car. That ride ended up being the most awkward ride ever. They were both Jamaican and started talking in Jamaican Patois. At some point, I couldn't understand a word. But I'm sure they referenced the noises I was making while Orlando fucked my guts. You know how when you're at a nail salon, and the women are talking in their native language, but you don't know exactly what they're saying, but you can tell when they're talking about you? That's exactly how I felt.

That was the last time I saw Vance while Orlando and I were together. Afterwards, I would see him often on campus when he visited, and we were cordial. We would check in and we'd be friendly, but a part of me still thought he saw me as the girl who fucked his homie in his grandmother's room.

Part V: Yellow Dick Road

26. Free Agent

∞

He broke my heart. April came around and he was a completely different person. He told me that we just "didn't know each other" and that we "rushed into things"—which was funny considering the fact that during our entire relationship, he claimed that he knew me more than I knew myself, and I wasn't the one who asked to be in a relationship with him.

(Side note: Literally two days before we broke up, I set up a meeting with a friend of mine who worked at Movado to finance a $2,000 watch. God works in mysterious ways, doesn't he?)

I was crushed. I couldn't eat, I couldn't sleep, I cried all the time. I even tried to commit suicide twice; I was going through it. My period just stopped coming all together and I was forced to take birth control because the stress broke me out.

I saw him on campus often. I looked through him as if he weren't there—as if I had never seen his face a day in my life. I was so wrapped up in my depression that I cut everyone off. I stopped taking calls. I skipped classes. I would just sit in my dark room in silence. Days would pass (weeks even) and my blackout curtains would remain undrawn.

After ignoring all of his intentions of communication and him trying to use my best friend, Jennifer as a middle man to check in on me, I had to change. The hatred ate away at me and I needed to forgive him.

I had a change of heart when I started talking to a different guy named Brandon for a while. Honestly, a part of me wanted to use him to forget all about Orlando. When you jump into dating someone immediately after heartbreak, when your heart is still healing, that person will never have all of you—not what they deserve at least. I knew it was too soon; I knew I was still hurting over Orlando, but there were so many things in Brandon I desperately clung to that I never saw in Orlando. He was kind, and thoughtful, and always happy to see and speak to me. He never made me feel bad about wanting to hang out with him, nor did he ever switch the blame on me when something was his fault.

Orlando somehow got wind of me talking to someone new (I'm guessing from his nosey ass friends who had still followed me on Instagram). We got back in contact for a while and things seemed like they were going to change for the better. I was okay with being one of his friends.

One day in May, he texted me and asked if he could come over. I wanted to try the friend thing because I needed time. A part of me still hated him—the other part felt like shit for it. I allowed him to come over, but I told him that we would be strictly confined to the living room area because I didn't want to be persuaded, convinced, or swayed. He was very conniving and emotionally-manipulative.

When he came over, he hugged me like he used to hug me. He wrapped his arms around me and breathed me in. I broke him off of me because I was not ready for that. After five awkward minutes of catching up in the living room, we somehow ended up in my bedroom.

"Do you miss me?" he asked.

I gave in and told him exactly what he wanted to hear. I think he was content with knowing that even after six weeks of not talking, he still had his claws in me.

"I miss you, too," he said. "I miss your smile, your hugs, your kisses. I miss the way you look at me."

I tried to look away but I just couldn't. He had me wrapped around his manicured finger. When we made eye contact, I thought I felt something (like pent-up emotion), but in hindsight, it was just lust.

I started crying. He wiped away my tears from my cheek. He started comforting me and then he pressed his lips to mine.

All of a sudden, he was pulling off my shorts. Moments later, we were 69'ing. I was on top of him, sucking his dick, and he was underneath me pulling down on my clit. I kept stopping because, like I said, guilty pussy-eating is the best type of pussy-eating, and he felt extremely guilty. He was normally terrible at head, but that time was different.

(Side note: 69'ing is honestly the most amazing and humbling sexual gesture to me. It's like someone is completely willing to choose your nut over their breathing—and that's just so romantic to me. I think that was why it was such a huge deal to me. For once, he wasn't being selfish. For once, he was listening to my body and it was beautiful.)

Then I ended up on my back. He was between my legs, holding his body up by his hands and passionately kissing me.

"You sure you wanna do this?" he asked. I nodded while rubbing his dick on my clit.

Before I had time to think, I felt his warm thick dick slowly sliding into me. His breath quivered. My jaw dropped in ecstasy and I arched my neck back.

"I missed you so much, baby," he said softly looking up at the ceiling.

It felt amazing—like we were one. I felt every ridge and ripple of his dick clinging and gliding against my wet walls. For the first time in my entire life, I had allowed myself to be physically vulnerable. I had never experienced raw sex and it was what they had described it as. It was a level of trust I still can't believe I gave to him. He was inside me, as he was, with no barriers.

I felt the smoothness of his dick rubbing up against my insides and then I started crying. It was a silent cry; a tear streamed down the side of my face and landed in my hair. I think I was happy because I was under the impression that this was a form of making up or making it work. He had eventually seen the fear in my eye, and then he pulled out.

He stood up and walked over to my condom drawer and pulled out my bagful of condoms. He stood there far too long. I just knew he was counting them to make sure I hadn't fucked anyone else.

He climbed back inside of me and ran his fingers through my hair. He lifted my head up. He pressed his forehead into mine. We locked eyes and while my face was reacting to every stroke he gave, I watched him bite his lips. His eyes rolled to the back of his head and he opened his mouth. That was his cumming face—a face I knew all too well. I think I was so focused on him enjoying himself that I let my urge to cum subside. I wasn't worried about him—I was worried about making sure that he stayed with me. I wanted him to love me again. I wanted to feel important to him.

When he was finished and out of breath, he fell on top of me and we cuddled momentarily.

I lifted my body up, wrapped myself up in my blanket, and put my back to the wall. I watched his chest rise and fall. I watched the sweat glistening off of him.

"So," I cleared my throat. "What does this mean? What *are* we?" I asked.

He lifted his body up, reached out for my hand and just looked down at it. His silence spoke volumes. He sighed.

"Look," he said as his voiced lowered. "I still don't think we're ready."

My heart started pounding in agony. I stopped breathing because I wanted to make sure that I heard every word that he said.

"I don't think we're there yet," he added.

"But," I said. "We...just..."

"I know," he said. "I just missed you so much, I couldn't help myself. I shouldn't have come here. I'm sorry."

"You're sorry?" I asked coldly and angrily chuckled. "You're fucking *sorry*?" I shook my head and started crying. "The one thing you wanted this entire time, I gave to you. You knew I would and you manipulated me."

He couldn't look me in my eyes.

I sighed.

"Get the fuck out, Orlando," I said and wiped my tears away. "Just go."

He smacked his teeth.

"Is that what you really want?" he asked, pretending like it wasn't already his intention to fuck me raw and to just bounce.

I started sobbing.

"Just go. Don't ever talk to me again." He tried to hug me. "Don't fucking touch me!" he stepped back. "Just…get out!"

I called Malcolm and Jay crying. I called all of my guy friends. All of them tried to reassure me of how good a person I was. Literally, everyone said almost the same thing. That was when I realized I wasn't the problem. All of them suggested that Orlando was probably talking to someone else or had probably already cheated on me considering how easy it was for him to throw me away.

It all made sense. When we were still together, I saw things in his phone that were questionable but I was too afraid to hear the truth or for him to somehow put the blame on me. When I was with him, my self-esteem was non-existent, which could also have been a factor in me staying with him so long. It took me a long time to admit that; he was just a selfish, disgusting, manipulative piece of shit.

In a text message, like the little ass bitch he was, he told me that he just wasn't ready to be in a relationship and that I shouldn't get my hopes up. He apologized and expressed how terrible a person he was. He said that he somehow managed to keep hurting people, and that he hadn't been the same since we broke up.

I had snapped and a piece of me died, right there. I had lost love for missionary. I lost love for cuddling. I stopped writing poetry. I had to let my heart go. For the longest time, I allowed myself to be treated like an option, or something that someone settled for. I allowed people to treat my heart like shit. I thought it was normal to have to beg the person that's supposed to love you to spend time with you and to treat you like a priority.

I was in denial about how fucking awesome I was. I was in denial about how amazing of a girlfriend and confidant I was. I was in denial about how supportive, caring, and loyal I was. I was in denial about how bomb my pussy was. No one deserved me. I was in a fucked up space mentally and emotionally. All Orlando ever did was use me for sex and ask me for money.

So, of course, I immediately ran to dick as I always had with any emotional problem I had in my life. I've learned that the better the dick, the harder the heartbreak, the easier it is to go down that Yellow Dick Road. A part of me actually wanted it to work out, but the other part of me was willing and ready to start a Hoe Draft; so I did that. I ended up treating Brandon like Orlando treated me. He was such a good guy and I can't believe I did that to him. When they say that you become the person who hurt you,

you really do. I blocked his phone number, and then blocked him on Twitter and Instagram.

I was officially on my fuckgirl agenda once again. I sent the inevitable "hey, big head" text to one of the guys Orlando had accused me of flirting with our entire relationship. I'll call him Nathan.

(Side note: Before there was an Orlando, I was momentarily talking to a guy named Nathan. Throughout my entire relationship with Orlando, Nathan kept his distance and respected what Orlando and I had. We would say hi and bye to one another, but he always kept his distance. I had never been a cheater my entire life. Just like everyone else, of course I had many opportunities to, but it's just not in me. I've always been loyal to a fault. If I wanted to cheat, I would've been single. So when I was finally single, choosing Nathan just seemed like poetic justice to me. When the guy I thought I would spend the rest of my life with (Orlando) turned out to be a little bitch, thot season started a little early. They always say the best way to get over a man is to get under a new one— which seemed to work for me every time.)

My only intention with him was to sit on his face, to get dicked down, and repeat. I wasn't trying to get to know him; I wasn't trying to get emotionally invested because I always ended up in the same place.

When Nathan found out I was single again, his whole vibe went back to the way it was before Orlando and I started talking.

(Side note: Nathan was from Baltimore. For some reason, I just could not get away from Baltimore niggas. Kirk was from Baltimore, Stanford was from Baltimore. Peter was from Baltimore. We ended up texting the entire night, catching up and whatnot. This was pretty much the basis of our conversation that night.)

Nathan: So, what happened to your lil yeah? *(Baltimore niggas love the word "yeah", by the way. They use it as a multipurpose term—it can be a response, it can be a noun and a verb).*

Me: Fuck allat, you tryna yeah? *(I had to speak his language to get my point across. "Fuck allat" can be translated to mean "Fuck it/that. I don't want to talk about any interpersonal matter of my life". "You tryna yeah" is a simple way in which to offer and/or request sex. Mind you, I was still heartbroken, so I was on a Yellow Dick Road to Thotville.)*

Nathan: Yeah.

And just like that, the plan was set in motion. We had agreed to him coming over that following Monday night.)

    Two hours before, I was right back to my old ways. I proceeded to the "Three S's". Just like every girl does right before they know they're about to get some bomb dick. I shat, I showered, and I shaved. I was twerking in the shower because I just knew Nathan was about to dick me all the way down. I hopped out, dried off, and twerked in my bedroom too!

I was making things clap that had no business clapping! I was excited because it had been a while since I had new dick. I got dressed in my "In-House Dick-Getting Attire".

(Side note: For those of you that don't remember, it consisted of a matching bra and thong set, a pair of leggings (booty shorts), a crew neck sweatshirt (or a tank top/cami, t-shirt, or sports bra when applicable), and a messy bunny (or high ponytail if desired). In that case, because it was the perfect weather, I substituted the leggings with some booty shorts, and the crew neck sweatshirt with a t-shirt. Everything else was just the same.)

I lit a couple candles to set the dick-getting mood; I played a Trey Songz station on Pandora. I put my hair in a high ponytail (because I specifically wanted it to be pulled). I needed to be **fucked**—nothing more, nothing less. I texted Nathan nonchalantly (even though I was pressed).

"Wya?" I texted him.

"In ur building," he replied.

I started grinning so hard that my cheeks hurt. He was about to dick me down! I would finally get to get the dick I had missed out on when I started dating Orlando. Nathan was the dick that got away (or so I thought). Whenever I requested a picture of his dick, he would always say "you just gonna have to see". He spoke so highly of his dick when we first started talking, and I was going to meet it face to face!

"Ard bet," I replied. "My room is #404 A."

So I rushed to put my face on. I even brought out MAC for the special occasion—even some highlight **and** a contour! (If I knew then what I know now, he didn't even deserve Black Opal makeup, to be completely honest.)

Nathan was supposed to come over at 9 pm. 9:30 rolled around, then 10 o'clock.

I sent him a slew of 😒 emojis because I figured he had stood me up, and I had never been stood up. I didn't know what to do about the situation.

But then again, I couldn't even be mad because I was so excited about the dick. I knew he was going to bless my guts. He assured me that he was on his way, but that he was in his friends' apartment, turning up. I told him that the door would be open.

Thirty minutes passed and I felt myself falling asleep to "Martin" reruns on TV One. I took my shorts off and got back underneath the blankets. I made sure my little booty was poking out the side of the blanket, just waiting for him whenever he decided to fucking drop by. It was around 11 o'clock when I heard a knock on my bedroom door. I'm a light sleeper so I popped up, readjusted myself, fixed my hair, and lied back down.

"Come in," I called out in my attempted sexy voice.

He walked in and closed the door behind him.

"Wassup?" I asked.

"Ain't shit," he replied. "I was coolin' wit my niggas."

(Side note: Just for future reference, guys, that is the most annoying fucking response ever).

He came around the side of the bed and looked at my ass. I was pretending to be sleepy and unaware. Then he slapped it. That only made me wetter.

"Stooooooop," I whined out.

"But you don't want me to," he replied with a smirk on his face.

He was right. I didn't want him to.

Then all of a sudden, I was kissing this nigga, which was a huge deal! His tongue work during that kiss really fucked my head up. I was pressed. If he could do that well with my lips, imagine what he could do with my….lips (get it?).

We had finally come up for air. I randomly pointed at my thong.

"Isn't my thong pretty?" I asked in amazement.

I was trying to give him a hint to take them off of me.

"Yeah," he replied. "It's sexy. Where you get 'em from?"

Before I could answer, he started rubbing on my clit through my panties, pretending to be interested in where they were from.

I started moaning and trying to say "Victoria's Secret", but I just couldn't. When I'm horny I can't really think straight. He maneuvered his middle finger into my pussy while rubbing on my clit with his thumb. He brought his finger back up; it was soaked. The light from the TV was reflecting off of my juices.

Then he put his finger into his mouth and smiled again (I told you, big girls just taste sweeter).

"Lay the fuck down," he demanded.

"Why?" I replied while saying *Yes daddy* in my head at the same time.

Then he tried to shove two fingers into my pussy. I grabbed his wrist.

"Chill," I giggled out.

Then he put his fingers back in and started slow-fingering me—moving his fingers up and down inside of me, tickling my g-spot. I think I probably saw God. Keep in mind that the entire time, my thong was still on. He had just slid them to the side. I kept trying to push his hand out (but he was too strong) because it felt *too* good. My pussy always gets extremely sensitive when there's a new gentleman caller around her.

"Move your fucking hand," he commanded.

"Or what?" I replied.

He came back up, kissed me, and said it again.

"Move your fucking hand."

I bit my lip and obliged him. He twirled his fingers inside me, then pulled them out and lifted me up. I was damn near doing a headstand. His mouth still hadn't touched my pussy. He stopped trying to be Hulk and slowly let my body down.

Then he yanked my legs closer to him. I was prepared for the head! You know when they yank your legs, it's about to go down! He devoured my pussy. He started growling and I got a little scared. I had an out of body experience while I was having an out of body experience. I saw myself getting the fucking work! Actually, I saw myself *see* myself getting the fucking work! He was slurping and sucking and slobbering. I was trying to run away into a corner, but he was not having it. He kept pulling me right back in. He pulled his phone out of his pocket and I thought he was going to start recording us. I saw him tap a couple buttons and his phone started vibrating, continuously! He was using his own phone as a vibrator and focused it on my clit.

I squirted momentarily, and he pressed the phone down harder on my clit and moved it around. I squirted some more and he caught all of it! An Otterbox case was an amazing investment—honestly, truly. If it weren't there, his phone would have been on the fritz.

My knee kept rubbing up against his dick and I could make out a little bump, but figured it was a keychain or something. I wasn't really paying attention.

I started begging for the dick!

"Fuck me!" I cried out. "Take your fucking pants off!"

I told him condoms were in in the top drawer. I was ready to make this happen. He walked over toward the television, opened the drawer, and pulled a condom out. He pulled his pants down. He had a Hank Hill from "King of the Hill" butt!

I had an array of different sized condoms in my condom bag, so when I saw him pull out a Magnum, I was squealing on the inside! There I was, sitting there—pussy drenched, just anticipating the dick. He started stalling and wasting time. He plugged his phone into my iDock and started blasting music.

He turned around. Everything from that moment on was in slow motion. He had a little chicken nugget! I figured that he wasn't hard all the way, so I walked over to help him out. I grabbed his dick and it was stiff and hard. I was so hurt. I felt betrayed. I was so weak! I tried not to laugh but I've never been the bigger person (physically, yes; mentally, no). A little laugh came out but I played it off as a cough.

My knees kissed the floor and I tried to suck his little bink bink. It was so sad! He could tell that I was struggling! I know I'm *amazing* at head, but his dick was too little for me to work my magic! It was already too late; I had already committed to it. I was down there for five minutes, trying to stretch a strawberry into a Twizzler. He loved it. He started moaning and holding onto my ponytail. I was sucking on a pacifier. I was so upset.

I felt let down because the whole semester before, he was talking his dick up! It would've been completely different had he kept it honest with me. It wasn't that his dick was little, you guys. As you already know, I've been in entire relationships with guys who have had shrimp dicks.

The thing that turned me off was that he completely lied about it. Nikki went completely dry, and that never happens. If I'd have known what to expect, I probably would have been okay with his situation.

"I'm about to cum," he groaned out.

"No, you're not!" I yelled out.

I had just knelt down there and raised that bitch from the dead!

By the time I got lockjaw, his dick had grown another inch. I was still pretty bummed out but it was too late for me. I somehow managed to get wet again when I realized it would still have been considered "out of spite" sex. I had to disconnect myself as far away from Orlando as I could. I figured it was worth a shot.

Emotionally, I was going through some shit, so I had to bust it open for one nigga, or three, or five.

We started doing missionary, but I was not feeling it. That was the only way I could get maximum dick from him, though. He suggested that we do doggy-style. In any other circumstance, I would've totally been down, but I knew I was not going to feel anything. I ended up giving in and agreed to turn over on my stomach.

I didn't even bother arching my back. He started "hitting" it from the back; I was fake-moaning because even in my time of sexual need, I care about people's feelings. He started growling again and after two of the worst minutes of my life, it was finally over. My soul was officially dead.

(Side note: He never spoke to me afterwards. I guess he felt embarrassed about the whole situation. He spread rumors about me around campus. He told people that I was fucking him on the regular while I was with Orlando and it just brought unnecessary drama into my life. The next semester, I saw him at an Economics panel discussion. He looked at me, I looked at him, we had eye contact for a few seconds and that was that. At that moment, I thought about all the things that he had said about me and all the lies he spread. I became livid and started tweeting the story of us about my worst sexual experience. To my surprise, it went viral. That's when it all started—so I guess I can thank him for my success.)

27. Baby Mama Drama

∞

July, 2015

    Months had passed, and I managed to build up my roster. I set up a rainbow of dick appointments for my return to school in September. Life was good. I had reconnected with another guy I was talking to before I met Orlando. For a long time, he was trying to shoot his shot, but when he finally did, I was with Orlando. For the sake of the story, I'll call him Byron. I wasn't really trying to talk to him because he had a daughter and a bad relationship with her mother.

    I knew this because she stabbed him and got him jumped. I had met her a few times because she dated Jay for a bit (which we'll get to). Byron and I mainly just fucked but he always wanted more. I was being a fuckgirl and a product of fucked up relationships.

    I wasn't really trying to get into anything because I had just gotten over Orlando completely. Byron's dick was sub-par but I didn't want to add to my body count. One day after work, Byron told me to come over. He told me that he still had his daughter but reassured me that by the time I got there, her mother would have picked her up already. It wasn't that I didn't want to meet her, I just thought it would've been inappropriate for him to introduce his daughter to someone who may very well be temporary. We weren't there.

I didn't think anything of it. So I rushed home, hopped in the shower and washed my ass. Then I got dressed in my (Summer Season) "On My Way to the Dick Attire".

(Side note: For those of you that don't remember, it consists of black leggings, a black baseball cap (preferably by Nike), some black Adidas or Nike slide on flip flops, and a t-shirt. The key is to be inconspicuous and not to draw any attention to yourself.)

Then I put my face on. So I pulled up to his house, thanked my Uber driver, and got out. It had to have been at least two hours since I last spoke to Byron. I figured his daughter was gone.

I knocked on the door; he pulled the curtain back at the window to see who it was. He smiled and unlocked the door. The door opened and there he stood. I noticed someone two feet tall peeking from behind him, clinging to his leg and smiling.

I immediately worried. It's not that I don't like kids, kids just don't like me and I never knew why. I'm fun as hell! Aunt Smillee is lit! Byron hugged me and put his hand on his daughter's shoulder.

"Jas," he said. "This is Miss Tiy. Tiy, this is Jasmine."

I was nervous because kids and I have a love-hate relationship. I'm fine with that. So I bent down and pretended like I wasn't uncomfortable.

"Hi cutie," I said.

She stared at me like I was crazy. I reached my arms out for a hug, but she walked away. I looked up at Byron and scoffed. He started laughing.

"Yo, I'm sorry," he said. "It takes her some time to warm up to people."

I was not trying to hear it.

"Byron, where is her mother?" I asked. He could tell that I was irritated.

"She'll be here soon," he said. "I promise."

I rolled my eyes and took my shoes off in the mudroom. When we walked into the house, Jasmine was sitting in front of the TV, combing her doll baby's hair. Byron locked the door behind us and walked toward the kitchen. I followed him. He was not about to leave me alone with his demon child! I am not nor have I ever been anyone's stepmother.

He took a load of clothes out from the washing machine and placed them into the dryer. Then he put a new load in. I looked back at Jasmine.

He came up from behind me and hugged me from the back. He kissed me on my neck. I turned around and kissed him on my tippy-toes.

"Go get to know her," he motioned toward Jasmine.

I looked to the side and shook my head.

"No, seriously," he said. "If me and you ever become more than just fucking, y'all gotta bond."

He was a really good guy, but he was getting too comfortable. Little did he know, any chances of us ever becoming anything were about to be ruined by his daughter.

In hindsight, the fact that we weren't even officially dating should have been a tell-tale sign of it being too soon for me to meet his child, but that's just me.

So I walked toward the living room and he slapped me on my ass to wish me luck. He went to go wash dishes. I sat down on the couch and Jasmine ignored me as she continued combing her doll's hair. I was on the couch seriously trying to figure out what to say. What's your favorite color seems a bit cliché for me.

From where I was sitting, I could see into her bedroom. She had a Hello Kitty chair in the corner and a Minions blanket set on her bed. Then a light bulb went off.

"Who do you like better?" I asked. "Hello Kitty, Dora, or Minions?"

She stopped combing her doll's hair, looked at me, then went back to playing with her doll.

Meanwhile, I was sitting on the couch stressed out trying to maintain my composure. Talking to a four year old should not be this fucking stressful! Five minutes passed silently. She was still sitting on the floor and I was on the couch uncomfortable. I was ready to go home.

Out of nowhere, she came and sat next to me.

"I like your makeup," she said smiling and touched my hair. "And your hair."

My face lit up. She was so precious. Before I could say anything, she threw a curve ball.

"But you're not as pretty as my mommy," she said. "My mommy said you ugly and fat."

That was when I realized Byron was telling people about us. This little girl was all of 3 or 4 years old and she was insulting me like a pro. (In a different world, and if she were twenty years older, we would have been best friends. Honestly, truly.)

Of all the people Byron could have told about us, he decided to tell his bipolar ass baby mother! She got back down on the floor and picked her doll up again.

"Y'all good?" he yelled from the kitchen. I just nodded, but in all actuality I was coming up with an exit plan.

I squinted my eyes in confusion.

"What did you just say?" I asked her.

Holding onto her Dora the Explorer doll, she lifted her head up and looked me dead in my eyes.

"I *said*," she replied, "you're ugly and fat."

All I could do was blink incessantly. I took a couple breaths. Usually, I had no problem fucking anyone up, but there is a minimum age and height requirement. In efforts to teach this little girl a lesson in manners and respect, I replied calmly.

"Jasmine, hunny," I said. "That's not very nice."

"I don't care," she replied. Then she went back to playing with her dolls.

I had to calm down. I felt my insides burning. I felt my face getting hot. Because I'm childish, I really had to think about what to say. I didn't want to hurt her feelings. I just took a deep breath and forced a smile.

"Jas, hunny—" she interrupted me.

"My name," she paused, "is Jasmine."

I touched my temples with my hands and leaned back.

"Okay, Jasmine," I said. "It's not ladylike to be rude."

She reached her hand out, palm facing me.

"Don't talk to me."

I sat on the couch flabbergasted. I sighed and kept talking. Jasmine started humming over me. I snapped. That was it. I looked back into the kitchen. Byron was still doing dishes. I leaned into her.

"Your mommy's a hoe and her pussy smells like Tilapia."

Her face froze.

I thought she didn't understand what I was saying, so I had to dumb it down for her.

"She's ugly and dumb," I added.

Jasmine's eyes grew wide and her jaw dropped.

"Daddy!" she yelled out.

I reached for my purse, dug out $5 and reached it out to her. She snatched it out of my hand. By that time, I was out of $55 for below average dick. The Uber ride there was $50.

Byron walked into the living room and wiped his hands on his shirt.

"What, Jas?" he said.

I pulled my phone out and pretended to be preoccupied by it, but my soul was sweating. I was asking God not to allow this little girl to fuck up my consistent (although terrible) dick. She looked at me, I looked at her, she looked at me, I looked at her. She smiled and looked at Byron.

"Daddy, can I have some juice?" she asked then smiled at me.

"You thirsty, bae?" he asked. I looked up from my phone.

"No, I'm good," I replied.

"Come get your juice, Jas," he said.

Jasmine ran behind him to the kitchen. She was making her way back into the living room with her juice but Byron wasn't having it,

"No, drink it in here," he said to her sternly. "You like to spill shit."

A few seconds later, Jasmine was in my face dancing and teasing me with the $5 I had just given her. I didn't care about the $5, she was just bad as shit. I was so angry. Me, being the childish individual I am, I bucked at her and she fell back onto the floor.

She stood up, ran up to me, and slapped me in the face. I was frozen.

I felt my fists ball up and my eyes open wide in disbelief. She stuck her tongue out and kept dancing. Then, she came back around and prepared to slap me again. I grabbed her wrist and squeezed it.

Her eyebrows slanted in pain.

"You gonna stop?" I asked.

She starting crying and nodded her head.

"Yes," she said.

Then she came in closer, opened her mouth, and tried to bite me.

I held her arms at her sides and squeezed harder.

"You gon' stop now?" I asked.

She nodded her head again and started pouting.

I let her arms go. She fell down on the floor and looked at me with a hateful look. Then she flipped me off with her little middle finger. I leaned in again.

"Do you want me to tell your father?" I said vindictively.

I won't hit a child (that's not mine), but I *will* fuck their father on their Minions blanket! I *will* sit him down on their Hello Kitty chair and suck the life out of his dick! I *will* be face down, ass up on their Dora the Explorer rug. I was just waiting for her to try me. I was fed up at that point,

"Byron," I yelled out. "Come get your child!"

As soon as I finished my sentence, he got a call from his crazy ass baby mama saying that she was down the street.

He told Jasmine to go get her things ready. She rolled her eyes at me and ran to her bedroom. Byron sat on the couch beside me.

"What happened?" he asked. "How'd it go?"

I scoffed and leaned back.

"So, she likes to put her hands on people, doesn't she?" I asked.

He knew exactly what I was talking about.

"Damn," he said. "I'm sorry. That's her mother's fault."

Speaking of the devil, there was a knock on the door. He got off of the couch and called for Jasmine. I took that time to take my mace out of my purse because I knew she was crazy. I was too exhausted to fight anyone because I had just gotten off work. I wasn't up for it.

He opened the door. I was ready. She walked in. My mace was in my back pocket. I stood up and faced her.

"Hi Shameka," I said with a smirk on my face.

I folded my arms. I was trying to be polite, but maliciously, you know?

She looked me up and down and turned her head, trying to ignore me—just like her bad ass daughter. Then she finally acknowledged me.

"So, you da bitch Byron talkin' to now, huh?" she asked.

Byron shook his head and stepped in between us.

"Yo, chill," he said.

"S," I said, "You the bitch that gave Byron and my brother gonorrhea, huh?" I replied.

Byron's head snapped back at me.

*(Side note: Remember the white girl I told you guys that Jay was talking to while I was with his sister, Bianca? She was fucking Byron, Jay, and a whole slew of niggas at the same time. She ended up giving them **all** gonorrhea.*

You know that one white girl in the hood that everyone calls "White Girl"? That was her. She was a hoe. She had at least three different baby fathers.)

She inched closer to me. I stopped leaning on the couch and adjusted my clothes. Byron put his hand on her chest and pushed her back.

Shameka was ready to fight. She did not expect Byron to stand up for me. That's how good the pussy was. Byron looked at me and pointed to his bedroom.

"Go!" he yelled at me.

I rolled my eyes because he had me all the way fucked up. I stood there and kept my arms folded. I was not going anywhere. Jasmine ran up to Shameka and hugged her. Shameka looked at Byron and laughed.

"You really fucking her fat ass?" she asked.

"Fucking it, sucking it, licking it, sticking it," I added.

Her nostrils flared. She ran at me. Byron grabbed her by the arm and yanked her toward the door.

"Yo, get the fuck outta my house," he said.

Shameka tried to run at me again. This time, he literally picked her up and walked her out of his house. Jasmine started crying. The fact that he kicked his child's mother out for coming at me disrespectfully weakened my knees and moistened my painties. (You know you're a fucked up person when drama makes your pussy wet, by the way.)

He came in and walked Jasmine out. Then he came back to get her car seat and set it up and in Shameka's car.

I watched from the living room window as he knelt down and hugged Jasmine. He buckled her in and gave her a kiss. Shameka glowered at me. I was about to fuck her ex (and child's father) in her daughter's bedroom. Life was good. When they pulled off, she gave me the finger (like mother, like daughter).

Byron walked back into the house and it was obvious that he was pretty upset with me.

"Why the fuck you do that?" he asked. "You know how she is!"

He slammed the door behind him. In all actuality, he didn't give me enough credit. It's not like he had to call the police or anything.

He started charging toward me.

"I've been wanting to do this since you first got here," he said as he picked my big ass up.

He threw me on the couch and pulled my leggings off. He didn't even ease into it, he just shoved his finger into my pussy. Me seeing how he handled Shameka kind of turned me on so my juices were already flowing. He started ramming his finger in my pussy. There was no mercy. He was upset. My juices were splashing everywhere. He came back up. He bit me on my neck and literally ripped my shirt open.

He pulled my bra cup down and pulled just enough titty out to see my nipple. He grabbed my boob and started sucking on it. He pulled his finger out and pulled the other titty out. He shoved his face in between them and lightly twisted on my nipples as if they were volume buttons. And then he started biting on them lightly which actually felt pretty good. He kissed between my boobs and all the way down to my naval.

He looked up at me and slowly let spit drip from his mouth down into my pussy. He lifted one leg up over his shoulder and rubbed his face into it. I pulled the hood over my clit back and he knew exactly what to do!

He moved his tongue up and down, side to side, in circular motions. He started spelling his name on my clit. Then he started sucking on it gently, then harder. He spat on it and swirled his tongue around. Things got too intense, so I had to kick him off.

We were going to fuck on his daughter's Minions blanket even if it meant me avoiding and holding onto my nut! I don't care nor did I care about how petty it was. If I couldn't hit the little bitch, I was going to cum all over her blanket. I mischievously came up with the perfect scheme to get him into her bedroom.

"I want to fuck everywhere in here!" I said. "Let's start in the hallway."

He picked me up again and walked me over to the hallway. Her bedroom was right there! I was so close. I pulled his pants down and started sucking his dick.

It wasn't the biggest one in the world, but he tried really hard. Then he shifted me onto my knees.

I turned back around and told him to go get a condom.

"Can I just stick the tip in?" he asked with puppy dog eyes.

I looked at him as if he were fucking retarded. Little did he know his entire dick felt like the tip so I wasn't really interested in hearing his bullshit. He knew that I knew that he knew that I knew that his pull out game was very weak and Jasmine was a testimony to that.

He realized I wasn't about to give in so he got up and ran to his bedroom. He was back within ten seconds. There I was, ass up on the hallway floor, trying to sneak into a 3-year old's room. That was officially a new low for me.

He slid the condom on so quick that I had to double-check because I didn't want a Jasmine coming out of me nine months later.

He slid it in. I let out a fake-moan because I care about people's feelings.

"Harder," I said.

When he used to hit me from the back really hard, it felt good but he would always bruise the back of my thighs and my ass-cheeks. I kept inching into her bedroom on my knees. I had to keep the arch serious so that he wouldn't notice anything was going on.

After about ten good pumps (I can't say that I would call them strokes), I was leaning over her little bed. The games had just begun. He lifted my leg up onto the bed because apparently that would help me feel more of him. The thing is, it didn't help at all; it made it much worse.

Then eventually, he told me to get onto the bed. My pussy juices were dripping all over that little girl's blanket. My mission was complete. If that wasn't enough, we ended up on her bed. He was sweating ferociously (and I know this because it was dripping on me). I put my head on her pillow.

For a while there, I sort of felt really bad about the entire situation. Then I remembered how pretty I was and all the terrible things I had done in my life and the guilt washed away from my body.

He pulled out and told me to sit on his face. I'm going to give you guys a moment to guess where his naked ass sat down. In case you were wondering, he plopped down on her Dora the Explorer rug! The plan was going too well! Karma really has no age discrimination. So I sat on his face and rode it for quite some time. He was tongue-fucking my pussy!

I started fucking his face, lifting every ten seconds to make sure he was still breathing, you know? Then I got off of him and told him to stand. If you know me, then you know that it was not about to stop there. I meant to do damage. I looked around the room pretending like I didn't know where I wanted him to sit down. The only options were the bed, which we had already handled, and her Hello Kitty chair. I was trying to get to maximum surface area! I was not leaving until every single place in that room had been fucked on. I rubbed my chin to pretend like I was thinking hard. Then I looked over at the chair and smiled.

"Sit in the chair real quick, babe," I said. (Did I use the fact that he wanted to be with me to manipulate him into playing a part in me acting out my pettiness? Why yes, yes I did.)

He sat down and I sucked his dick. (Correction, I tried* to suck dick.)

So I started sucking on his little D battery for about two minutes. The sweat on his stomach was slapping up against my forehead.

He finally came, but I kept going because I wanted to give him the motivation to finish me off as well. I hadn't cum yet. Apparently, if you're still sucking the tip after a guy has already cum, it's really intense.

Then his phone started ringing, and he got me off and ran to it. I knew exactly who it was. When he walked out of the bedroom, I stood up and picked up my clothes.

I put my hand down in my pussy and wipe it on to the door handle, the chair, her nightstand, her drawer.

I know, I know. It was a terrible, childish, petty thing to do. But I knew exactly who was calling. Sure enough, it was Shameka calling him because Jasmine was crying.

Apparently, she missed him and would not stop crying. He came back into the bedroom. By that time, I was already dressed and ready to go. He asked if I wanted to go with him to pick her up again.

"Hell nah," I replied. "But you can drop me off at home before you pick her up."

I was not about to spend $100 on trash dick. That was where I drew the line. He got dressed and we headed out. He dropped me off, kissed me, and gave me a hug.

After that, Byron and I probably hung out two or three more times after that.

I ended up dealing with another nigga with a child that month who was a football player at Bowie. We fucked in his grandmother's bed, but don't worry, she is very much so alive!

We also fucked at his house once, but I won't go into detail because he was a really good guy.

28. Head & the City

∞

August, 2015

I was working at a cemetery in Arlington and I was making so much money that I didn't know what to do with it. My best friend, Jennifer and I kept saying that we were going to go to New York before school every year I knew her, but we just never got around to doing it. The money I was making changed everything.

I hated my job, but I loved the money. I had reconnected with a childhood friend (we'll call him Roger) from middle school right after Orlando and I had broken up. We spoke that entire summer while I rode faces. We had "dated" in middle school but he was another lame who lied about stupid shit, and to be completely honest, he was just creepy. He even dated my best friend from middle school because she "reminded him of me"—I know, lame, right?

Then we started dating again my senior year of high school. My friends fucking hated him. Right before I went off to college, he broke up with me because he wanted to cheat on me. Those were literally his words. He couldn't do a long distance relationship, and I didn't really want to so God was looking out! I didn't want to break his heart. When we got back in contact on 2015, he told me that letting me go twice was the biggest mistake he had ever made.

I had agreed to being friends with him, but he didn't believe how much I just wanted to be single and figure out who I was as a person. Because I had already been exposed to fuckboys and because I had recently became a dedicated fuckgirl, it was too late.

I had asked him at the last minute if he wanted to come to New York with us and he cleared his entire weekend up just for the occasion. He was annoying as fuck, but he was everything that I needed at the time. I needed someone to confuse. I needed someone to hurt the way I was hurt. I needed someone to fall in love with me the way I had done all too often, just so that I could pull it from under them in the end. I didn't want to admit it, but I was still healing.

We met up at Union Station and caught the Megabus to New York. When we arrived at our hotel, we showered and headed out to Times Square.

After shopping for hours and stuffing our faces at the Hard Rock Café, we went back to our hotel room. By that time, it was around 9 o'clock. Jennifer stayed in the room because she was cramping and on her period—she was severely PMS'ing. I just didn't have time for it.

So, Roger and I went down to the pool. If you're thinking that he fucked my brains out in the pool because no one was around, and that I rode that dick like a soldier in the jacuzzi, you'd be wrong. He had made absolutely no moves and I just wasn't used to that. I'm not saying that I had the juice, but I certainly had iced tea that a lot of guys wanted to drink.

When we got back to the room, it was almost 11 pm. I got into the shower and washed the chlorine out of my pussy. Something deep down inside of me told me that my pussy was going to be eaten, regardless of the fact that he made absolutely no advances. So, I shaved and finished up. I walked out of the bathroom, walked into the bedroom, and kept the door cracked (he was is in the living room and I wanted to give him a show).

So when I came out of the bedroom, I sat on the couch, and threw my legs across his lap nonchalantly. His dick started getting hard. We were sitting on the couch reminiscing, laughing and catching up on old times.

I accidentally moved my legs on purpose, but he just wasn't getting the hint. Things got boring as hell. In the mist of the awkward silence, I fell asleep on him. Keep in mind that the entire summer we talked, he talked his game up. I was so over it.

Probably an hour later, something told me to open my eyes. When I finally opened them, he was in my face, eye to eye.

"I want to eat your pussy," he said.

I sat there for a couple moments, pretending like I was actually thinking about it. But in all actuality, he didn't have to ask me twice. I was ready to take my thong off. I started standing up to help him out, then he stopped me.

"Before we start," he said, "you have to listen to me". His voice grew more serious.

He gave me this huge spiel about how I better not run and this, that, and the third. The more he spoke, the drier I got. He was literally talking for five minutes but my only concern was figuring out what that mouth did. That was literally it. I didn't need an introduction.

"Tiy," he said. "I'm going to be the best you ever had, I promise."

"I doubt that," I said with a smirk on my face.

"Okay," he said. "But you're wrong, though."

I rolled my eyes and smiled.

"Anyway," I said.

"Okay," he said. "If I'm not, I get to eat your pussy again." I nodded. "And if I am," he added, "I get to eat it again.

I took another couple moments to "contemplate"—I didn't want him to know that I was excited about it.

He stood up off the couch and reached for my leggings at the bottom. I was ready for it. It would have been the first time in at least a month. I tried helping him by pulling them down a bit, then he grabbed my hands and put them to the side.

"I got this," he said. "Just relax."

I never understood why niggas always feel the need to tell me to relax when all I was trying to do was help them stuff *their* face with *my* pussy. I *was* relaxed. So he slowly slid my leggings off, then slowly slid my underwear off. I grew anxious and antsy. What was taking him so long?! He got down on his knees and slowly put my left leg onto his right shoulder, and my right leg onto his left.

I waited, and I waited, and I waited. He kissed on my inner thighs, then lower and lower and lower. He was teasing me and it made me cringe and he knew what it did to me. It was torture. I wasn't used to this type of foreplay. I didn't deserve that. He stuck his tongue out and slid it from my clit down to the opening of my lips. He brushed up against my taint. He began French kissing my pussy, ever so softly. Roger was killing it! He was knocking everything out of the park! He was checking everything off of the list. Clit sucking: check. Taint rubbing: check. Tongue-fucking: check.

He started slurping up all of my juices, then he let them trickle down from his mouth onto my clit, and gobbled Nikki up. He slurped the spit up again. My body shook. I was ready to tap out less than twenty seconds in.

"Spit on it," I moaned out.

And he did; the spit splattered onto my clit.

He could not slurp and swallow fast enough the way my juices kept flowing out of me. The couch underneath me was completely soaked. He slid his bloated fingers into my pussy. To be honest, it felt like a dick. Like I said, I was into big boys.

I kept trying to run away but he kept pulling me back in. The angle I was sitting in was pretty uncomfortable and my back started to hurt. But honestly, he had made it all worthwhile. I started grinding on his face. I put my hands on the back of his head and pushed it down deeper into my pussy. His head was not going anywhere anytime soon. I could tell that he couldn't breathe so I eased up and let go. He was committed to the cause—and the cause was the eating of my pussy. He sucked in some air and went back to work. He moved his head back and spat onto my pussy again. Then he licked every single spot he could find spit on. Then he went back to eating my pussy like it was nothing.

I'm really starting to think that my pussy has steroids in it because every time a nigga eats it, they feel the need to lift me up, and I'm much too big.

He flipped my entire body upside down. I was getting my pussy eaten out upside down on a Marriott couch while my best friend was in the other room, sound asleep. This was the life.

Getting your pussy eaten at a 180 degrees is very life-changing. All of my weight was resting on my neck, and I honestly would have been okay with becoming paraplegic at that very moment. I couldn't breathe, but I didn't need to. He held me up by my waist and stomach, so I figured I was in pretty good hands. My tits were in my face. Fortunately for me, he got tired of holding me up. He slowly let me down told me to lay sideways on the couch. I saw the TV reflecting off of his forehead and realized that he was sweating. He was really putting in the work.

He handed me a pillow. That was the moment I knew that he was very serious about making me cum. I was lying in a wet spot, looking up at the ceiling, trying to slow down my breathing. I looked over and saw him take his shirt off because it was completely soaked. He came back onto the couch, spread my legs open, and started going ham. It got so intense that I literally had to push his head off and almost climbed over the fucking arm of the couch to get away. But he yanked me back and held my hand's underneath me with one hand. Then he put his arm behind my knees and pushed them into my chest. I could not go anywhere.

Have you ever cooked your ramen noodles too long and then they become mushy but they're the last ones so you have to eat them anyway— but then you try to fix it up by adding some butter instead? That's what him tongue-fucking my pussy sounded like! At that point, I couldn't even scream considering the fact that my knees were in my chest!

I tried to get my words out to tell him to stop. I was too big for that shit! My knees should not have been in my chest! Eventually, he got the point and slid my body to the side again, got back on the floor, and put my legs over the shoulders. Half of my body was off of the couch, the other half was sliding off. I kept trying to pull myself back up.

"I got you bae," he said.

It took me a while to realize what he had called me and I told myself I would come back to that and correct him. But my mind was in a thousand different places.

So he started pivoting my hips and rubbing his face all in my pussy. He shoved his thick ass finger back in again then pulled down inside of me and shoved another in. He started sucking on the clit again. The flick of his wrist was stupendous. I felt it— like a river rushing out of me. I snuck my leg off his shoulder to kick his fingers out. Then he started tongue-fucking my pussy again.

His lips were glued to my pussy. All of my weight was on his neck. I felt and heard my cum leave my body—it squirted out of my pussy and flooded into his mouth. That cum came all the way from my soul. He swallowed the entire thing. I literally begged him the entire night for the dick but he refused to give it to me. He claimed that he only came to New York with one goal in mind and he had finally done it.

After a while, I ended up falling asleep and I felt him trying to cuddle with me. He honeslty repulsed me, but I was too tired to tell him no.

I woke up the next morning, showered, went to breakfast, came back and he ate my pussy again!

Jennifer walked out of the room and we froze dead in our tracks! My legs were literally in the air. She rubbed her eyes and went into the bathroom. Then he went back to work. I tried to contain myself because she was up. She came back out of the bathroom then we froze again. She closed the bedroom door and we proceeded.

I asked him for the dick again and he rejected me. Never had I ever been turned down for dick. And then it hit me, he had a little dick. Whenever the head was too good to be true, the guy that was giving me head almost always had a little dick. You do the math.

Eventually, he wanted be more than friends but I was a fuckgirl and didn't want to be with him. The thought of it honestly repulsed me. I stopped taking his phone calls, I stopped answering his Oovoo calls, I stopped texting back. He lied about stupid shit and it just made him look even more lame, and I wasn't feeling it. Honestly, I wasn't even feeling him.

29. Captain Fuckboy

∞

It was Mid-August, 2015. I was getting used to being single, but I kept being reminded of my ex, Orlando because I saw him on campus all the fucking time. Roger would come over often to hook me up, and by "hook me up", I mean "eat my soul".

Back in February of 2015, I was taking my trash out and blasting "Odio" by Romeo Santos featuring Drake. I was singing my heart out, and out of nowhere, as I was coming to the corner of the hallway, I bumped into this guy. We caught our balance, he cracked a side smile, and I went on my merry way. I had to keep it short because I was in a relationship with Orlando. When I'm with someone, out of respect for my partner, I avoid having unneccesary conversations with the opposite sex.

The second time I saw him, I was playing the same song in the elevator. I was singing in Spanish and everything. When the doors opened, it was the same guy getting on, while I was getting off.

"Oh, so you speak Spanish?" he asked.

"Yeah," I replied. (I'm fluent in it.)

"Oh true," he said. "I'm Puerto Rican. We should hang out some time and talk to each other in Spanish."

I was still in a relationship and I felt disrespected. I had heard about him and how much of a fuckboy he was so I wasn't interested in hanging out with him. I am not nor have I ever been a cheater, so I politely declined and curved him.

One day, Orlando and I had had a terrible argument before my shift in the cafeteria. When I got to work, I was mad as shit, irritated, and ready to get off. My last hour rolled around and I looked up and saw the same Puerto Rican nigga standing in front of me asking for extra food (I was a food server). I made his plate and handed it to him. He took the plate, thanked me, and came back ten minutes later.

"You know what I like," he said, smiled, and licked his lips.

I ignored his lame ass line and made his plate again. That very same night, he decided to slide into my DM's, knowing I had a boyfriend, which I reminded him of every time he flirted with me. He told me that I looked cute that day. I called him out on his bullshit because I definitely looked like shit that particular day at work because I had been crying all day. We ended up having a short conversation, but I kept trying to remind him that I had a boyfriend.

Lo and behold, I found out that he was from Baltimore—and it all made sense. He was a fuckboy a a half. It was confirmed.

So when he asked me when we were going to chill, I told him probably never considering the fact that I wasn't single.

"No one has to know but you, me, and these four walls," he replied.

Obviously, niggas from Baltimore don't know how to be curved or told "no". In their minds, you're getting dicked down regardless of your relationship status. I politely told him to go fuck himself and exited from the conversation.

Let's flash forward to mid-August. I moved into my dorm a couple weeks earlier. There were other students in the dorm because most of the athletes were able to move in early as well.

On move-in day, Captain Fuckboy and I saw each other in passing; he lived in my building. That night, he slid into my DM's for the second time; this time, I was single and ready to mingle (and by "mingle", I mean "ride dick").

Long story short, he got my number and we started texting. One night, we ended up planning to chill. I proceeded to the first "Three S's" of the semester.

I put on light makeup and waited for him to show up. I left the door open. When he finally came into my apartment, I was pretending to be doing homework. He sat down at my desk and asked me who my roommates were. After telling him their names, he realized that he knew them very well (not sexually; they were all just really good friends). Neither of us wanted anybody in our business.

When my roommate walked out of her room, she heard his voice.

"I know that's not who I think it is," she said peeking into my room. "What you doin' in here?" she asked with a smile on her face in a Jamaican accent. "Why are you messin' with my roommate? She don't want you in here."

They walked out of my room and went into the living room. My other roommate joined in. They knew each other very well because they were all athletes. Apparently, all of the athletes at Bowie were more than acquainted with one another. He played football (and ran track) and they played volleyball and (and also ran track).

He stepped back into my room and we had to come up with a plan.

"Shit," he said. "So, what you wanna do?"

"Just go back to your apartment," I whispered to him. "I'll just meet you there in like ten minutes. I doubt your roommates are gonna know me," I added. "I be in the cut."

"Ard, Ima leave the door open" he replied and snuck out of the apartment.

Less than ten minutes passed and he was rushing me to come over. He told me his room number and I realized he lived on my floor. When I got to his apartment, I opened the door. One of his roommates was in the kitchen and I knew exactly who he was—

he used to fuck my old roommate. I saw another one sitting in his bedroom and realized he was a co-worker of mine. I looked to my left and my lab partner was walking out of his bedroom. He looked up and smiled. He gave me a hug..

"Wassup Tiy?" he asked. "What you doin' in here?"

"I'm here to help Santos on some homework," I said unconvincingly. "Which one is his room?"

He looked me up and down and shook his head smiling.

"But, where is your backpack?" he asked.

He had caught me red-handed. All I could do was smile and flip my hair. We both laughed and he pointed me to Santos's bedroom.

(Side note: Everyone knows everyone at Bowie. I don't know why I ever thought I would've been an exception.)

I closed the hallway door on his side behind me and knocked on his bedroom door.

"Come in," he said.

I walked in and closed the door. He was sitting on his couch watching ESPN. He looked up at me.

"Wassup," he said.

I looked around his room and tried to decide where to sit. I was trying to pretend to be innocent, as I always have. It wasn't my intention to fuck another Baltimore nigga. He looked at me like something was wrong with me. He was surprised that I was actually nervous. Shit, I was surprised too.

"So, you just gonna stand there the whole time?" he asked.

I rolled my eyes and sat down beside him.

"So," I said. "I know your roommates".

He looked at me.

"How well?" he asked.

"Too well," I explained.

He looked disappointed, then I realized he probably thought that it meant that I had fucked them before. I had to explain that it wasn't like that.

"Ohhhhh," he said relieved.

So, we watched ESPN for a while, then I got bored because I didn't understand a word they were saying. Sports is like a foreign language to me.

"So," I said. "What you wanna do?"

He looked at me and raised an eyebrow.

"What you wanna do?" he replied.

I bit my lip and looked down at his basketball shorts, trying to make out his dick print. He could tell what I was looking at. He looked down at his dick, then looked back at me. He smirked.

"You tryna yeah?" he asked surprised.

I looked to the side, then back at him.

"Well, duh," I said. "I didn't shave my pussy for nothing."

He clapped his hands and rubbed them together

"Bet!" he said excitedly.

He immediately started pulling his pants down.

"Wait!" I said. "Wait! Before we start, if you want me to suck your dick, it's gonna be with a condom on. I'm telling you right now."

He looked down at his dick in disbelief.

"Yo, you serious?" he asked as if he were insulted.

"True story," I replied, nodding my head.

I don't play that shit. I had heard a lot about athletes, so I wasn't taking any chances.

"But, I'm clean" his tone heightened.

"Well," I replied. "Where are your papers, then, homie?"

He sucked his teeth.

"Well, can you at least suck the tip or suck it for a lil' bit?" he begged.

"No," I replied and clicked my tongue. "I'm not gonna do that, sorry."

He dropped his head in defeat. I felt bad for the kid, I really did. But it was more important for me to protect myself than to be sucking his dick without a condom on, *especially* knowing that he slang dick all throughout Bowie Place (the nick name for my dorm).

"You're not my nigga, Santos," I said, chuckling. "And I've heard about y'all football players. I'm not finna risk catching **anything**."

After his minor temper tantrum, he realized that I was so entirely serious and was not budging. He smacked his teeth again. I sat on the couch, unbothered and played in my hair.

He walked over to his dresser and pulled out a few Magnums. The corners of my mouth pursed up because the last few times I had seen a Magnum wrapper, I was utterly disappointed and betrayed by little dicked niggas. I was prepared for the worst. He pulled his pants down with his ass facing me. He started putting it on and kicked his pants off.

Before he turned around, I was doubting his dick size. My spirit just *knew* it was going to be disastrous. And then he turned around. He was struggling to get the condom on, adjusting it and so on. Then he let his dick go and it was a sight for sore eyes! I heard angels singing in my ears. It was almost as though a glimmer of light radiated from his crotch. Have you ever seen an empty paper towel roll? That's how thick his dick was! Have you ever seen a 1.5 liter bottle of Fiji water? That's how long it was! I wanted to cry right then and there, but I had to play it off as if I had seen bigger—like I wasn't impressed!

In my mind, I was praising the Lord and thinking about all the good he had done for me! I tried not to smile, or smirk, or squeal because I didn't want to scare him—so I kept it cool. I was so excited to get his dick in my mouth—probably too excited, now that I think about it.

You should already know that this story is about to take a turn for the worst. Just kidding, there was absolutely, positively nothing that could possibly go wrong with his dick! His dick could have fed an entire starving nation! His dick could have caused world peace! His dick could have cured Depression.

He looked down at his dick, then looked up at me and smiled. Then he stood with his hands on his hips and held his head high, in a Superman stance for an uncomfortably long time. He knew his dick was big and he was not ashamed to admit it.

"Come here," I said.

He walked over toward me, dick bouncing *everywhere*! At that point, it was up close and personal. I saw his dick pulsating; I saw the linings of his veins. I saw his life flowing from one vessel to the next. It looked like an abstract work of art, the way his blood came rushing to his dick.

I reached for it, but he caught me off guard and flexed his dick muscles. He made it bounce. I stared in awe and astonishment.

The time had come to say goodbye to my vocal chords for the first time in a long while. I just knew that once I shoved his dick into my mouth, my wig would pop off. I took a deep breath. The entire time we texted beforehand, I talked my mouth game up; now it was time to pay the Piper. I had to let him experience what this mouth could do. He just didn't know. He just didn't fucking know. He just fucking did not fucking know.

There was no way to predict how he would react to it because it would've been my first time (of many times) sucking his dick. All of my relationships started with sex, so I had to be extremely careful not to make it too good, but good enough.

(Side note: The key to sucking dick effortlessly is anger. Every time I sucked dick, it made it so much easier and so much more pleasurable for him if I imagined that they had already done me dirty—like they flushed my makeup down the toilet, or they set my weave on fire. Anger has a positive correlation to how good the head is. It's science. I just thought you should know that. So guys, whenever you want some bomb ass, fire ass head, just be sure to piss your girl off beforehand. You're welcome.)

    I swallowed his entire dick to the extent that his dick was at least three inches down my throat. I felt him in my chest! At the same time, I was pushing on his ass-cheeks because I had to make sure he wasn't going anywhere. He was going to get that head. After deep-throating for a few seconds, I'd feel my eyes bulging, my forehead getting hot, and my lungs collapsing. I literally felt the oxygen struggling to get to my brain. So, every once in a while, I had to pull it out so that I could breathe.
    I was slobbering, bobbing, choking, stroking, popping, and locking. I was pulling out all of my tricks. Spit was dripping down my neck onto my t-shirt. The entire thing was soaked. I started humming on the tip; yes, humming. Those vibrations really catch someone off guard every time. He was moaning—they weren't normal quiet moans, they

were overwhelmingly loud moans. He pretty much single-handedly ruined the lie I told to his roommates about me helping him with his homework.

I stopped sucking his dick and popped it off of my lips. I looked up at him.

"Fuck my mouth," I said out of breath, with mascara running down my cheeks and snot trying to make its way out of my nose.

He dropped his jaw and his eyes grew wide.

"Just hold the back of my head," I said, "and fuck it, damn."

So he did it and I could barely breathe but then again, is the head really good if you *can* breathe? I loved every moment of it because giving head only makes my pussy wetter. I don't know why, it just always has.

You know when you're really thirsty and reach for a tall jug of water, so you gulp all of it down in seconds? That's what him fucking my face sounded like!

At that point, my entire shirt was soaked. The inner thighs of my leggings were soaked too. He pulled my head off of his dick by my hair (almost pulled my wig off, too).

"Take your pants off," he demanded.

I was low-key irritated because he interrupted my dick-sucking. But I obliged him anyway and took them off.

"Sit down on the couch real quick," I said to him.

He plopped down. I bent over his lap and continued sucking his dick. My ass was up, my pussy was dripping, my oxygen flow was cut off. I was choking and my makeup was in shambles.

He reached for my ass.

"Come in closer," he said while I was **preoccupied with sucking his dick**.

I moved a couple inches closer in and went back to sucking. Keep in mind that he was so adamant about not having his dick sucked with condom on, and I had him moaning like a little bitch!

He pulled the back of my thong up and down and listened to the clicking noise it made. Then he slid them to the side and wiggled his finger in while I was sucking his dick. He slapped me on the ass and told me to lift my leg up onto the head of the couch.

I was sucking his dick, worried about making him cum and he wanted me to do fucking yoga at the same time! There was just too much going on—I did it anyway, though.

He slid his fingers down onto my clit and starting sliding them slowly up and down it. He maneuvered a couple fingers inside my pussy and proceeded to rubbing his thumb on top of my clit. I wanted nothing more than to take in the pleasure, but I was trying to get something done. I came up for air for a bit, still stroking on his dick. I looked around his room and realized I could have really gotten some good interior decorating design ideas from him. His room was nice, for a guy. He had the standard posters of bitches with fat asses and fake titties and cars—you know, the usual, but the décor was nice.

He started getting closer to my g-spot. I hopped off of the couch and took my shirt off.

"Give me the dick now," I demanded while wiping away all the spit on my face.

He stood.

"Turn around," he said.

"Well, shit. Where do you want me to go?" I asked.

The bedrooms in the on-campus apartments were small as hell. He pointed at the couch again, even though he had a whole ass bed literally right next to it. I turned around and put my knees onto the couch. I looked back and saw him changing the condom. I had to get my arch ready; I wanted to really wow him. I had to make sure that E equaled mc^2. It was too serious. He came back over to me and slipped his thumb under my thong strap and played with my asshole.

I reached for them.

"You want me to take 'em off?" I asked.

"Nuh uh," he said. "Stay just like that."

He slid the strap to the side and slowly glided his paper towel-sized dick into my pussy. I winced and screeched out. He shushed me. I groaned and dug my face into the couch to muffle the sound.

He pulled back out and started playing in my juices with his dick. He smeared it around, then started slow-stroking.

Have you ever made macaroni and added about seven different types of cheeses and stirred with your handy dandy wooden spoon? That's exactly what his dick sliding in and out of my pussy sounded like. My groans slowly turned into my moans and shuddered tones. Then, out of nowhere, he started fast-stroking at the speed of light. I stopped breathing to take it all in as his thighs slammed against the back of mine.

He was fucking my guts and I didn't have a care in the world. It didn't even matter that he was a fuckboy, his dick was making up for all of that. My head started hitting up against the wall. **BLAM! BLAM! BLAM! BLAM!** To me, it was worth getting a concussion; that's how good his dick was.

He pulled his dick out.

"Get on the bed," he shouted out.

I don't think I've ever run so fast in my entire life, but in the span of .568 seconds, I was on the bed, assuming the position.

"Get that arch right, baby girl," he said to me as he stroked on his dick.

He starting ramming and slamming my pussy! I was trying so hard not to let my arms give in. While he was impaling my vagina, I couldn't help but wonder what it was that I had done to him. What did I do to deserve being punctured in my fucking spinal chord? I can't lie; it hurt so good. If push came to shove and I ended up in a wheelchair, at least I would have gone out with a bang. He pulled out again.

"Lay on your back," he called out.

A part of me was sad because missionary and I had a love-hate relationship (and it usually dealt with people that I used to love but now hate). I wasn't prepared for what was to come.

I lied on my back.

You know when you're about to fry some chicken wings, and you fold the wing back before you dip it into the flour? That's what he did to me! He took my legs and put them behind my ears. He placed all his weight on my legs while he fucked me, and I couldn't go anywhere! Then he let one leg go and I put it behind him. I felt **everything**. Nikki was squeezing hard on his dick (unintentionally). When a vagina feels threatened, it strangles anything within three feet of it.

Then he looked me in the eye.

"You ready?" he asked out of breath.

"Huh?" I said.

He began stroking faster and moving his hips clockwise and counter-clockwise! I couldn't breathe! He was making sure that he touched every single nook and cranny of my walls!

I started rubbing on my clit and staring into his eyes. The average girl probably would have fallen in love with him right then and there, but I was immuned to the fuckboy virus. He put a pillow underneath my head and I fell down ontop of it.

My eyes were in the back of my head when he lifted my legs straight up into the air and crossed them. He continued stirring the macaroni with his wood (if you know what I mean).

Do you know what the stroke feels like when your legs are crossed over one another like two bent back paperclips? Do you? It feels heavenly and incredibly sinful at the same fucking time! He bit my ankles and I didn't even care! Whatever he had to do to get his nut, I wasn't even mad at him.

"I'm about to cum!" I screamed out. "Right there, just like that. Don't stop!"

"I'm not," he said. "Shut up!"

When I'm about to cum, I'm very loud! I finally came and my legs started shaking. Then he came and his dick pulsated inside of me. It was magnificent.

He started slow, slow-stroking (those are the best strokes). Then he stopped stroking and pulled out. I lied there for a couple seconds trying to get right with Jesus before I made any movement.

I took a deep breath and somehow got enough energy to get up and get dressed. We gave each other a high five. Then I tried to head to the door but he grabbed my arm. I turned back and fell into him.

"Don't fuck nobody else but me," he said.

I awkwardly puckered my lips and squinted.

"Yeah, okay," I replied sarcastically and dipped.

On my way back to my room a couple doors down, I did some reflection and knew for sure that fuckboys have and always have had the best dick. Kirk was one thing, but Santos solidified it for me.

He had the type of dick where all he had to do was sit there and be hard.

When I closed the door behind me, I saved his number in my phone as "LDN" (Long Dick Nigga). I couldn't let go of him just yet.

The next day, I couldn't walk. He ruptured my cervix or pierced my soul—one of the two. He made my period come three days early; how fucking rude.

He was geniunely a terrible fucking person, but the dick was too bomb. Once, he even yanked my wig off while we were fucking and threw it onto his head! Like I said, the dick was too bomb to let go.

30. Kappa Style

∞

September, 2015

When I was still working at the cemetery (July 2015), Jeremy (the Kappa from Thomas and Asia's New Year's party) kept posting some depressing shit on Instagram because his aunt had died. I reached out to him to let him know that, even though we weren't close, if he needed anything or anyone to talk to, I would always be there to listen. That's what being a caring fuckperson is all about.

We pretty much texted the entire summer, but I kept my distance because I was under the impression he was Orlando's friend, and I thought it was a trap. I wanted to keep it strictly platonic, but every chance Jeremy got, he would always make the conversation go left. He was a typical light-skin nigga, with typical light-skinned tendencies.

One day in particular, we were on the phone and he asked me what I was wearing and I had to put him in his place because I wasn't really with the shits because the break-up was still new to me.

"You're basically my ex's friend," I iterated. "Why would you ask me that?"

In my eyes, the people that had attended the New Year's party were all pretty close. They were all friends, or so I thought. Well, he put me in my place!

"Look," he said, "I don't fuck with Orlando, nor have I ever fucked with him. I can't stand his ass, to be honest. I only know him through Thomas, that's it."

(Side note: Orlando and Jeremy were both in Thomas's wedding and Orlando was the best man. Jeremy felt salty about that whole situation, which perpetuated his hate toward him. Apparently, Orlando was a terrible best man and he planned everything at the last minute—typical.)

As soon as I heard that, my eyes lowered mischievously. It was on!

"Oh, is that so?" I probed.

"Yeah, man" he replied.

"Well, shit," I said. "You hate him, I hate homework; let's make it happen." (I know the two have absolutely nothing to do with the other, but that's how much I did not give a fuck at that point.)

Long story short, we started sexting—nothing major, just ass and dick pics, the usual. We planned on meeting up at my school the next time he came back down from New York.

That time had finally come. School had officially started and it had been in for a week or so. Jeremy texted me one Friday night randomly asking what I was doing later on. He was back in town to handle some family issues.

He asked me if he could come through later to hang out.

"Sure," I replied. He had snapchatted me the dick for so long and it was finally time to meet the little buddy in person! I was excited because I had gotten so used to fucking Santos (Captain Fuckboy) since I had moved in and the new dick was calling my name. I needed a vacation from fuckboy dick and he was cool as hell. I don't know why I thought the most appropriate alternative was to fuck a fucking Kappa, but it made sense to me at the time and I went with it. It was kind of like a dick-cation, sponsered in part by Kappa Alpha Psi. By the way, while I have the time and your attention, I would just like to thank all the Nupes, nationwide; Jeremy was very well taught.

The entire situation was just messy, but I'm a messy bitch, so it seemed a bit apropos. The whole time I was with Orlando, two of his friends liked me, he got into an argument with another friend about me, I had a crush on one of his friends (who, if he put it down, I would've gladly picked it up and swallowed it whole immediately), and if that wasn't enough, I was about fuck his best friend's friend. Messy was an understatement, but I didn't give a single, flying, sparkling fuck. Old McDonald had a fuck, but I did not. Mary had a little fuck, but I did not. Humpty Dumpy sat on a fuck; I was too busy trying to sit on faces, honestly.

All of my homework was done two weeks in advance. My time management skills are spectacular, just so you know. I would schedule time for head from Roger, coversations with family members, homework, and dick. My calender was literally color-coded and everything. The key included "J" for Jennifer (my best friend at the time), "H"/"R" for head from Roger (who would drop by occasionally to eat from my soul), "Shamp/Con" for shampoo and conditioning day, "D" for dick (mainly from Captain Fuckboy), "F" for family phone calls, and "HW" for homework.

My life was a mess, but a dedicated, organized, thotty mess, you know? I checked my calender and sure enough, it was a "D" day. Captain Fuckboy and I had a fucking schedule. So, I had to come up with an excuse to get out of our fucking appointment for that night. I told him I would take a rain-check; he was pretty pissed, but by now, you know that I didn't care.

Jeremy told me he would come around 12 am, and I was cool with that. I tidied up my room a bit, and proceed to the "Three S's" as per usual. Instead of the shaving however, I naired because I heard a few things about Kappas and their…talents.

I wanted to see what all the hype was about. I was dancing and twerking in the shower, making up an "I'm about to get some dick" song; I was celebrating. I hopped out of the shower and twerked a little bit more on account of the splendiferous dick-cation coming my way. I put on a thong and a matching bra, some booty shorts and a t-shirt. I put my hair up in a bun and did my eyebrows. I didn't really need to put on the full face because the school year had barely started and the stress acne hadn't really come yet. By the time I was finished, it was around 11. So, I made some tea and watched reruns of the Golden Girls.

(Side note: Blanche is low-key my spirit animal—so is Rose, and Dorothy.)

I was sitting on the bed, drinking my hot tea. I decided to FaceTime my cousin, Alysha to tell her all about the tea.
"Hello," she answered.
"Okay," I said and put my tea to the side. "On a scale of hoe to thot, how slutty of me would it be to fuck Orlando's friend?"

(Side note: Alysha was my moral compass—whenever I thought about doing something stupid or crazy, she was usually the one I ran it by to make sure that it wasn't too much.)

"Honestly, Tiy," she said. "Fuck Orlando's punk ass. You're not with him, so you have no loyalty to him anymore."
I nodded my head in complete agreement. I pointed at the camera.
"That's why you my nigga," I expressed.
"Ard," she said. "Now, go forth and get dicked down."

I laughed.

"K," I said. "I'll call you after."

I blew her a kiss and hung up. I never called her after. I don't understand why I always tell people I will, knowing damn well I won't.

Around 12:30, I received a text from Jeremy telling me that he was in the parking lot. So I grabbed my ID because I would need to sign him into my building. Then I started dancing while sliding on my "I just fucked your friend in my shower flip-flops" flip-flops.

I headed down the stairs and as soon as I got closer to the front door, I noticed a guy standing there. I looked pass him, looking for Jeremy. Meanwhile, the guy was staring at me like he knew me. I just smiled and waited some more. He waved at me and gestured for me to come closer.

It was Jeremy! I didn't recognize him—maybe I was too dickmatized to notice his face. Maybe too much time had passed since the last time I had seen him. I should have clicked more on his IG page. He was far less attractive than I remembered, probably because I was drunk when I met him. I sighed and walked closer to the door, trying to hide my disgust.

You know that smile white people make at you when you walk pass each other—the one when they purse and hide their lips, but they're still smirking? I was doing the white person smile.

"Heyyy," I said awkwardly and gave him a side hug.

I gave the security guard our ID's and signed him in. Then he buzzed us back into the building. We got to my room and I was trying to rush him in. I didn't want my roommates to see him because, he was just... I don't know. He wasn't ugly at all, but damn. There was just something about him that didn't sit well with me.

We walked into my room and sat down on my bed. For some reason, age became a topic.

"I feel old," he said. "I'll be 31 in October."

I pursed my lips again trying to process what was just said. I was twenty-two, twenty-fucking-two! I literally felt my facial expression change. It couldn't be real! I waited for him to laugh and tell me he was joking, but that time never came. It was as if after that moment, everything he said to me was not processing.

I know the phrase "the blacker the berry, the sweeter the juice", but did that also mean "the older the berry, the sweeter the cum"? My soul let out a silent cry, but no one came to rescue me.

I figured he was a little older than me, but god damn! Compared to me, he was relatively supposed to have his life together, not fucking fuckgirls in college!

He was funny though, so my reservations about his age eventually subsided. Over time, the whole age thing didn't really bother me because I could relax around him. We ended up watching Comedy Central for a while.

"So, I saw Orlando recently," he said.

I turned my head to him.

"Okay...," I replied, waiting for there to be some point behind him telling me something that I didn't care about.

"I saw his new girl," he said. "She's ummm..."

"She's pretty, right?" I added. He chuckled.

"Ummm," Jeremey said. "I'm gonna go with 'Fuck no' for 200, Alex." I shook my head. "That bitch looks just like him."

I leaned back and started screaming laughing because it was true. She did favor him. I knew it was wrong, but like I said, Jeremy was funny as hell.

(Side line: I wasn't trying to be mean because I'm not a shallow person. When it comes to things like that, all that matters is what's on the inside, but Orlando definitely threw a curveball. I was shocked myself. She wasn't the prettiest flower in the rosebed, but she seemed like a nice girl from what I had heard. Everyone and their fucking mom thought it was important to tell me about her, but I truly didn't give a fuck. Who was I to say that the girl didn't have a great personality? Orlando didn't really care about looks. His dating history before me (of the girls I've seen) weren't all necessarily photogenic.)

"Don't say that," I said and cleared my throat to stop my laughing, "She's pretty in her own way. Let lil' homie live."

He looked at me and smiled.

"You're pretty," he said. "Actually, you're fucking beautiful, if I might add, but that bitch…was definitely a downgrade."

I wanted to be happy for Orlando, but when Jeremy put it like that, he really put things into perspective. I tried to change the subject because I've never really been into gossip, especially with people I don't know or about people I don't give a fuck about.

Jeremy caught me off guard with the whole "beautiful" thing. It took me a while to realize that he had actually paid me a compliment.

"Nah," I disagreed. "I'm not even close."

Then, he light-skinned me, you guys! He took me by the chin, looked deep into the depths of my soul, and said the magic words again.

"You're beautiful."

He didn't know how royally he had fucked up. As soon as he said that word, I was wet (well, actually, I was wet when I saw the dick print in sweatpants, but we'll go with the first one).

(Side note: you know that saying "guys only think with their dicks"? When I was single, Nikki did the thinking for me. I was truly a nigga at heart. After being fucked over by so many people that you love, you just lose your emotional humanity. I always fucked with people heavier than gravity, and that was my problem. I gave them too much of me. I made it my mission to never go through that again.)

We ended up play-wrestling, then he climbed on top of me. I tried to make it seem like I wasn't trying to fuck him, but it *was* a "D" day. He started rubbing on my pussy through my shorts. I bit my lip.

"I'm sorry," he said, "Ima chill."

He eased up and got off of me. I came back up and fixed my bun.

He looked at the tv and I looked at him.

"So what you wanna do?" I asked.

"Honestly?" he asked. I nodded. "I really just want to eat your pussy."

I couldn't even come up with words to reply to his request. All I could do was raise my eyebrows.

"Would you be cool with that?" he politely asked.

"I don't see how that would be a problem," I replied. I tilted my head. "Is that like a Kappa thing, or…?"

He smirked.

"We'll just have to wait and see, now, won't we?" he said. "You've never been with a Kappa, have you?"

I shook my head innocently. He gave an evil smile.

"What should I do?" I asked.

"Just lay back and relax" he replied.

He placed his hand on my chest and of course, I started being difficult. I wanted to egg him on; I wanted him to get frustrated and to be rough. He pushed on my chest again.

"Just lay back. Ima be gentle," he reassured.

I didn't want him to be gentle, though! I wanted him to fuck my shit up! I finally lied back. He got off of the bed to take his shirt off.

He climbed back on, bent one leg, and kissed my knee. Then he kissed my inner thigh and put his lips to my pussy through my shorts. He started munching on it **through my shorts**!

He reached for the top of them, and because I'm such a helpful person, I lifted my body up to help him out. He threw them onto the floor.

"You put these on for me?" he asked while rubbing on my clit through my panties.

"Maybe," I moaned out, nodding my head.

"So you did, huh?" he asked in a low tone. He kept rubbing on my clit. "You're wet as hell!"

He continued rubbing and teasing me. It was a lot more foreplay than I was used to. Santos and I normally just got right down to business. He licked my pussy and slurped my juices **through my thong**! He held the thong to the side with one hand and slowly slid a finger in. Then pulled it out and slid two in. He pulled them both out and put his fingers into his mouth. His eyes lit up. He had finally tasted the Juicy Fruit.

"You taste amazing!" he said. Then something about him changed.

He ripped my thong off and pushed back the hood of my clit. He licked the clit one time. I felt his spit glide down my clit and into my pussy.

He was taking his time, and I grew more irritated by the second. Then he pulled the skin back even more to expose my clit completely. He started sucking on it hard, but not too hard to get a knee to his face, you know?

My back kept arching and my toes kept curling. He slid a finger in again and my pussy clamped down hard on it. I tried running, but that was short-lived because the back of my head hit the wall. He stopped sucking and held his head up.

"Yo," he said. "You good?"

"Yeah, yeah, I'm good," I said breathlessly. "Just don't stop!"

I grabbed him by the back of his head and shoved his face back into my pussy. Then he slid his tongue in and started wiggling it inside of me. It was slow and passionate.

Have you ever had head so good that you'd pretty much be willing to do anything— like be his baby's mother, or meet his parents, or suck on his balls? I was willing to do all those things and more. He came back up and bit my inner thigh. Then I reached toward where he had bit me and wiped some of it off with my finger and put it in my mouth. Big girls honestly do taste better. We're filled with Cinnabon icing and strawberry drizzle. After a while, it was just a beautiful mess. It got into his hair, his beard, his mustache, his eyebrows.

He started shimmying his entire face into Nikki. Then he started sucking on my clit again and fingering my pussy faster. I came almost instantly and squirted a little bit. I heard it leave my body but my bed wasn't that wet.

Then it finally hit me. He caught it. He caught it all. He did not spit one time. He swallowed all of me. He caught a breath but then he went back to eating. And I came again. And he caught it all, *again*.

I couldn't take it anymore. I put my feet on his shoulders and literally kicked him off of me. That was the moment I finally understood—NUPE: Nasty. Ugly. Pussy. Eater. Can we all just take a moment to give a round of applause to every man in crimson and cream? They are really out here changing the world.

I couldn't quite possibly process the fact that he had chosen my cum over air. I was flabbergasted. I was changed. He was such a gentleman. He grabbed both my legs and put them over his shoulders. Then he caressed them. Do you know what a tongue in your pussy feels like at 90 degrees? Do you know what it feels like to be treated like a right angle?

I let out a low grunt and then it just...shot out of me like fireworks on the fourth of July. It splashed everywhere; I looked up at him and his mouth was wide open. He was literally collecting it in his mouth. And then I heard him gulp—he fucking **gulped**. I sort of felt like a water fountain, but a water fountain squirting out cum, you know?

He came back up to my face and kissed me. I couldn't say no—not after all he had done to and for me. He was literally drinking my juices. I licked his face. He light-skinned me again and looked into the pits of my soul. Then he smirked—he didn't say a word. He got up and went to the bathroom.

I sat up. I just sat there in my cum. I didn't even care anymore. I managed to stand up and walk over to my closet to retrieve my towel.

When he opened the door, I was sliding on my shower flip-flops again.

"What you doing?" he asked.

"About to get in the shower," I replied exhausted. He giggled.

"No you're not. I'm not done yet."

"The devil is a lie," I replied.

He literally almost caused me to have an aneurysm and he wanted to put me through it again!

He walked up to me and pushed me up against my closet door. He kissed my neck and rubbed on my pussy.

"So," he said softly. "You're not gonna let me finish?"

I reached for his dick.

"I don't want your tongue anymore," I said. He looked down at my hand. "I want your dick."

"Fine," he said in a conceding tone. "Get on the bed."

He pulled a condom out of his wallet. He put the corner in his mouth and ripped it open. He pulled his pants down and took his boxers off. He put the condom on and came to the bed. He pushed me down and climbed between my legs. He eased it in, and moaned. He pulled it out and teased my clit with the tip. He slid it back in and I gasped. He grabbed me by my neck and started slow-stroking. Slow missionary is actually pretty amazing when someone's trying to squeeze the life out of you with their hand. The sound just intensified everything—and so did seeing the white light.

He kissed me again and bit my bottom lip. He let my neck go and started massaging on my clit while he fucked me. He came in three minutes. I couldn't breathe, or think, or move. He pulled out and fell beside me. He caught his breath while I stared up at the ceiling.

"How was it?" I asked.

He put his index finger up to me and implied that he needed a moment. He started a slow clap. I rolled my eyes and smiled. He turned over and wrapped his arm around me.

"What time do I have to be out by?" he asked.

I wanted him to leave. That was my rule. You come, you cum, you go. But when I looked at my phone, it was 4-something in the morning. So I gave in and let him stay anyway. My dorm's rule was that the guest had to be out no later than 8:30 am, but I told him it was 7:30.

"You can stay the night," I said, " but you have to be out by 7:30 or I get a fine." Then I paused for a moment and came up with a better lie. "Oh, shit," I added. "It has to be before 7:30 because I have Econ class." I didn't have any Saturday classes, and my Economics class met on Mondays, Wednesday's, and Fridays.

Eventually, I felt bad, but being fucked over by so many people really changes you. It makes you heartless. I left him on the bed and hopped in the shower. When I came into the room, he was knocked out. I got dressed and sat on the edge of the bed. Then he woke up.

"I'll leave around 7," he murmured. "Is that cool with you?"

"Yeah, that's fine," I replied calmly. I lied down at the opposite end of the bed.

"You're not gonna sleep up here with me?" he asked.

I had to think of a lie.

"I would," I said, "but I feel like I'm catching a cold. I don't want to be all in your face and get you sick."

"I don't mind," he said. "Get yo' sexy ass up here."

"Well, I snore really loud," I added. "I sound like a grown ass man" (which was actually true).

"I'm a heavy sleeper," he replied. "So, I don't mind."

"I normally sleep at this end anyway," I said. "It's cool."

He eventually caught the hint and dropped his head down on the pillow. He fell asleep but I barely slept. I set an alarm for 7 am on my phone. When he woke up, I was already dressed in "class" clothes. I was really committed to this lie, you guys! I even put my backpack on. We walked down the steps and I signed him out. He hugged me and offered to drive me across campus to the business building for class.

"Nah," I said. "I need the exercise anyway."

Things got a little awkward because he started to actually like me. I was preoccupied with being a fuckgirl. I wasn't looking for anything with anyone. I was honestly content with being a five-foot-tall piece of shit, but I promise I didn't stay that way much longer.

31. Mitosis Osmosis

∞

Late-September, 2015

It was the third week of school and my first biology test was less than twelve hours away. I never took notes in biology class; half the time, I didn't even know what the hell the professor was talking about. Science has never been my strong suit, unless we're talking about the science of sex.

The night before, I rushed to Blackboard and lo and behold, there were notes on every chapter. But even with the notes and the book right in front of me, I still didn't understand anything. I sat at my desk accepting the fact that it was all over for me. After hours of trying to memorize the processes and order of cell division, mitosis, and meiosis, there was nothing I could do.

I almost gave up but after reviewing the syllabus, I found out that tests made up 60% of our overall grade. There would only be three tests, no quizzes, no homework. I knew that if I were to have failed that test, there would have been no way for my grade to recuperate. What sense does that make! Why would any professor only give out three tests and make it damn near worth your entire grade! I sat at my desk for hours. I had to rest. I was stressed out and needed a movie break.

I threw "Easy A" into the DVD player. By the time it was over, it was 2 am. I stared at my Biology book and wondered if college was really worth it. I was really contemplating flipping bricks and whipping shit. I walked over to my bed and lied down just contemplating about life.

Stripping, pimping, and trapping didn't really seem all that bad. I figured if I saved my money up and invested properly, I could live a pretty comfortable life. I dozed off and when I woke back up, it was 3 am! My test was scheduled for 9 am! I was fucked for sure.

I figured maybe if I got in the shower, it'll all come to me like an epiphany. I was hoping that everything would make sense. Have you ever been so overwhelmed that you ended up doing other shit instead of what you needed to do? It never helps, though. Once you come back to reality, it's still there, just like herpes.

I jumped in the shower anyway and thought about my life and all my bad decisions. I was having a mid-life crisis in the shower, letting the water wash away my sins. I just couldn't think straight. Then, while rinsing my pussy out, I kind of got horny. I don't know, it was just something about the water splashing up against my clit that did something to me.

I took care of myself and I came in the shower. I got out, dried off, and sat in my chair. Then I picked up a pen, closed my eyes and wrote down "prophase, metaphase, anaphase, telophase, cytokinesis". Then I opened my eyes, looked at the book and cross-referenced. I had memorized all the phases of a cell division cycle. The concept of chromatids, animal cells, human cells, and plant cells all made sense to me.

It wasn't the first time I had procrastinated, but it was the first time I had actually understood a concept that well. The one time I masturbated while stressed, all of a sudden I understood biology? I was going to take that and run with it. By then, it was 3:45 and everyone in my apartment was asleep.

I'm sure God wanted me to be successful, so he put Santos in my life to help me in my time of need.

I picked up the phone and called him. It rang and rang and rang. I started getting nervous but then he finally picked up the phone. As soon as I heard his voice, I was relieved.

"Was good, ma?" he asked with a hoarse voice.

I could tell he was getting some good sleep, but I didn't give a fuck.

"What you doin'?" I asked innocently.

He sucked his teeth as if to imply that I knew what he was doing at 4 o'clock in the morning (which I did, but I still didn't give a fuck).

"Can you come over real quick?" I asked. He sighed.

"Ard," he replied. "I'm on my way."

I almost cried but I kepy my composure.

"K," I said cheerfully. "The door is gonna be open."

We hung up. Then I took a moment to thank god for all the good he had done for me lately. Then I put on a pink t-shirt, a thong, and some Pure Seduction. I didn't even bother putting on pants because it was Santos and we fucked on the regular. I walked out into the kitchen, poured some water into my mug, and put it into the microwave to make some tea.

I knew once he'd come into the apartment, he would see me in my thong from the back. We both lived on the fourth floor and he was only a few doors down from me. They always say keep your friends close, and your enemies closer; I like to keep the dick even closer than that.

I heard his flip-flops flopping down the hall, getting closer to my apartment. Then I heard the front door open. I looked back and smiled.

"Hey," I said.

He stretched his arms, wiped his eyes, and yawned. I pulled my mug out of the microwave and dipped the tea bag into it.

(Side note: I never fucking got around to drinking that damn tea.)

He came up behind me and wrapped his arms around my waist. Then he kissed my neck.

"You smell good," he said.

"Thanks?" I replied awkwardly, blowing on my tea to cool it down.

Then his tall ass wrapped his arms around my shoulder/chest and rested his chin on top of my head. I tilted my head to the side.

"What you doing?" I giggled out.

It was too cute and I had to stop it immediately. He was getting too comfortable around me. I had to make it clear that we were not about to be booed up. We were nothing more than fuckbuddies and that's just what I needed—it couldn't be anything else. He wasn't shit, I wasn't shit. We couldn't be not shit *together*. Then he finally let up and I put my mug back into the microwave to keep it warm. I felt his eyes looking at my ass. I looked back and sure enough, he was staring at it and biting his lip. I turned back and put the box of teabags back into the cabinet.

All of a sudden, he slapped my ass. I giggled, only because I wanted the dick. I reached for the sugar and he came back up behind me and put his hands on my waist. I felt his dick on my butt—well, technically, it was my back because he was tall as fuck. There's no better feeling than having dick on your butt, by the way (unless the dick is inside you, but you get the point).

I turned around and put my arms up on his shoulders. He picked my big ass up and put me on the counter top. I pulled him closer in by his basketball shorts. He took that opportunity to try to kiss me. At first, I tilted my head back and tried to miss it. Then, I gave in because I figured if I rejected his ass, he would throw a temper tantrum and leave, then I would have to call a former fuck-buddy, and I didn't have time for that. It was getting down to the wire.

So I kissed him (and by "I kissed him", I mean "he kissed me"). It was cool, I guess. I could taste the fuckboy in his saliva. I bit on his bottom lip and he pulled me closer to him by my waist. He started fingering me on the kitchen counter while I rubbed his dick through his shorts. Neither of us really cared that he knew my roommates and that they could have walked out at any moment. It was going down.

He slid my thong to the side and slowly slid his dick in. He started slow-stroking me on the counter! After two or three strokes, I realized something felt different. It felt like skin. How did I miss that? Could it have been because it way past my bedtime? I started freaking out and pushed him out of me. I punched him in the chest

"What the fuck did I tell you about that shit!" I yelled out.

(Side note: He would normally come over my place with a condom already on, ready to fuck my brains out.)

He tried to play it off like he had forgotten.

"Oh shit," he said, grinning. "I wasn't thinking. I forgot."

I knew he was lying, because ever since he had brought me his STD screening results, he kept begging for me to let him fuck me raw. I scoffed, jumped off the counter, and headed to my room.

"Let's just go to my room," I said angrily, "You ruined it."

He followed me to my bedroom and shut the door behind him. I sat on the bed Indian-style and looked at my tv trying to calm down. He sat down in front of me.

"You mad at me?" he asked.

I rolled my eyes. He turned his body and yanked my legs open. Then he lifted my legs up. He went to town. After five seconds, I wasn't mad anymore. He shoved his tongue into my pussy and started tongue-fucking me. He moved my legs all around, spread them, closed them, bent them, rested on them. He put his hands under my ass and pushed me up onto my head. He spat on my pussy, then I felt it drip down my ass crack. He caught it once he saw it crawling down my back.

Then he let my legs go and let them fall over his shoulders. He lifted my fupa up and tried to make me fall in love with him. He kissed my clit apologetically; I could tell he was truly sorry.

(Side line: Much like girls being angry and giving the best head, when guys are apologetic and feel guilty, that's when they really give it their all.)

He lifted one leg up and flipped me around. My ass was in the air and he was eating me out from the back! He grabbed my arms and pulled them behind my thighs so that I was facing him. I could see between his legs.

Then he let my hands go and trusted me to maintain the position. While he was eating away at my insides, I noticed him pulling a condom out. He was finally being a good boy. He opened it, then slid it on with one hand, and started rubbing my clit with the other. He stopped eating, spat, and ate again. Then he did it all over again! He slapped my ass and stood up. He pushed my arms forward.

"Arch your back just like I like it," he said.

Then he slapped my inner thighs further apart. It was time! He put his dick into his hand and guided it in. He stroked his dick slowly a few times, then started whaling on Nikki like she had stolen something. It was so bad, my ass-checks started burning from his thighs slapping them so hard. But I liked it, so I shut my ass up and didn't complain.

Just when I thought he was slowing down, he'd speed right back up! I told him to spit on it again, so he stopped stroking but left the dick still inside. I felt a warm liquid slide down my crack and ooze down into my pussy. He pulled his dick out completely, spread my cheeks and ate my pussy from the back again! I froze up and fell forward! I almost hit my fucking head on the wall .Then he slapped my ass again.

"Nuh uh," he said. "Don't run now."

I screamed out in pleasure. He wrapped his arms around my waist and locked me in. I couldn't run anymore.

I came so hard, I started crying. Tears literally started streaming down my face; it was that intense. My legs were numb and my back hurt. He came, but Santos was always ready for another round. He pulled out and plopped down on the bed. He lied back, on his elbows.

"You tryna ride?" he asked.

I squinted my eyebrows and tried to figure out how to get the fuck out of the situation.

"Yeah, hold on," I said. "Come here real quick."

I honestly didn't feel like riding. I didn't stretch for the occasion, nor did I drink Gatorade.

He inched closer to me. The plan was to suck the cum out from under his soul so that he would forget about the whole riding proposal.

I stood up off the bed and got down on my knees. I opened his legs up and pulled his thighs into me. I pulled the condom off and spat on his dick while he held my bun. I stuffed my mouth with his dick. I started gagging, slobbering, and choking. Within 45 seconds, he had clocked out. He came, I swallowed it, and I kept sucking. His legs started shaking underneath me. He lifted his body up, then fell down. I wore the kid out, and finally let his kids swim around in my stomach for the first time ever—that's how much I did not feel like riding.

He started falling asleep.

I cleared my throat unnecessarily loud.

"So, what you bouta do?" I asked uninvitingly.

"Huh?" he murmerd out.

He clearly was not catching my drift, so it got a bit awkward. I was trying to kick him out politely, but he wasn't getting it. Don't get me wrong, he came rushing to a damsel in distress at 4 am because she needed dick. He was appreciated, but he was breaking my cardinal rule.

I shook him and he woke up.

"Come lay with me," he said. I scratched my neck nervously.

"I have a test to study for," I said and pointed at my desk, "so, Ima be over here."

He sucked his teeth and fell back asleep.

I stayed up until 8 am studying. Then I hopped in the shower, got dressed, and woke him.

"You gon be gone by the time I get back, right?" I said. He nodded his head and buried it back into my pillow.

I think he thought I was joking, but I was dead ass serious.

I walked across campus to the science building and took my test. I scored a 92%! Ninety-fucking-two percent!

Who knew that dick from a fuckboy was a major key to success? I sure as hell didn't.

32. Dapper Dick

∞

Late-September, 2015

It was the fourth week of school and I was doing what single girls did: getting their guts fucked. One day on Twitter, a fine specimen of a man decided to confess to me that he had a crush on me, which we all know was code for "wanting to fuck". The day started like any other day. I woke up in pain after a night of fucking Santos. I hopped in the shower, brushed my teeth, and got ready for class. When I was trying to figure out what to wear, I heard a ding on my phone. I was notified that someone had sent me a DM on Twitter.

I looked at the notification and it read:

"@_____ (his username): Would it be crossing the line if I asked you to sit on my face?"

I was caught off guard. I immediately unlocked my phone and went to his page to further investigate. I wasn't familiar with his handle—he was under the radar. For the sake of the story, it would be sufficient to just call him Mr. Dapper because he was beautiful and looked amazing in suits. After stalking his Twitter and looking him up on Instagram to find photos, I was in love with every physical feature he possessed. I had to slap myself because what I was seeing could not have been real. He was perfection. But then I found out that he played football at my school and my heart sank into my vagina.

(Side note: Don't get it confused or twisted; I never approached nor did I reach out to him. I never approached anyone that I've dealt with in my entire life, now that I think about it. I wasn't the ideal move-maker. They always seemed to approach me. I never knew if it was because they were curious about what it would be like to be with a BBW or if they had already known what was up (or what was in, if you catch my drift).)

Don't judge me, but I must admit that I had relations with one too many football players on campus—or two, or three too many. Santos played football, Nathan (Lil' Bink Bink) played football, both of the baby fathers I dealt with earlier that summer played football, and here he came. Let's just say that all but one of those instances ended well, so I wasn't really excited to meet him. I was, however, excited to sit on his beautiful face.

"I don't see how that would be a problem," I replied with a swiftness.

Actually, it was more so Nikki who sent it. Let's just clear that up right now. Eventually, he got my number and he called me. We talked for a while.

"Ever since I first saw you," he said, "I had the biggest crush on you."

"Mhmmm," I replied.

"No, seriously," he reassured. "I been wanting to ask you that for the longest time."

"Is that so?" I replied unconvinced. "How do you have a crush on me and you've never even seen me on campus?"

I didn't believe a word he was saying. I had seen him on campus but I doubt that he saw me at all. I was always in the cut, I minded my own business, and I laid low. I tried to catch him in a lie, but then he was able to tell me what class I took my first semester at Bowie—it had easily been two years.

"Weren't you in Bob's public speaking class two years ago?" he asked.

"You remember that?" I asked surprised.

"Yeah, but you were quiet, though."

He wasn't lying! I literally only fucked with a handful of people. He was able to spit up facts; he had actually liked me but he had never said anything until now.

(Side note: I never understood why niggas did that to me. They would go an entire semester feeling the kid, but wouldn't say anything until it was too late. Just for future reference, guys, if you like a girl and you want to throw the dick at her, don't wait forever. She might want to pop her pussy for you. You never know until you try.)

I was embarrassingly excited about the entire opportunity. But I had to play it off like I didn't really care. He was just...perfect. He was buttermilk biscuit fine (and you know big bitches love butter, and biscuits)! I honestly can't remember what we spoke about because I was focused on introducing him to Nikki, but we had a pretty decent conversation.

His verbiage and articulate tone was refreshing in a sense. I barely heard that on campus, as most of the guys that attended were from Baltimore (city) and DC—mainly hood niggas. Don't get me wrong, I love hood niggas as much as the next girl, but to a certain extent, I was bored with them. There was something about his accent that I just couldn't put my finger on. For some reason, I couldn't place it.

He told me about his recent injury (which I won't disclose for the sake of his privacy) and about how much he had missed football. His major was Criminal Justice, or Business, or Business Medicine—it was definitely one of the three. Whenever I asked a football player what their major was, they always seemed to pick from that list of options. It was always the same for them. The entire time we were on the phone, I was zooming into his Twitter avi, trying to make out his dick print. I wanted to make sure I wasn't wasting my time. Most of the guys I've dealt with at Bowie, for the most part, had little dicks, and a 50-50 chance was not at all reassuring. I could see a faint print, but at that point, it didn't even matter to me anymore.

For the first time in a long time, I was actually the one to make the conversation go we left. The conversation went too good—and the nigga in me just couldn't have that. I didn't want to get to know him, I didn't care about his hobbies, or his dislikes and beliefs. I honestly, truly, wholeheartedly just wanted to fuck. I wasn't looking for a relationship at all and I damn sure was not in the market for any new friends (fuck-buddies, however, were an exception).

"So when can we arrange my face-siting appointment?" I reminded him. He chuckled.

"Well, what does your schedule look this week?" he asked.

I explained to him that I was pretty free. I had a couple tests coming up, but I was acing all of my classes at the time.

"Whenever you're ready for me is cool for me," he said in a sexy voice. "Then you could do that favor for me."

"Chillllll," I drew out. "You're not ready. You've never been with a big girl."

"Actually," he said. "I've been with a few."

"Is...that...so?" I asked surprised. "Tell me m—"

He cut me off.

"But I have to warn you, though," he said. "Since my injury, you gon' have take it easy on me for now. But in a month or two, I'll be good. Then you can go ham."

His injury was pretty serious. So many things started going through my mind when he reminded me of his injury. Would there be a safeword? Would there be a nurse with him? Would I need his written consent? If, God forbid, involuntary manslaughter would be a result, could I live with myself? Could I survive prison? So many guys claim that they can handle dealing with a big girl until the fat rolls come out, or until their face starts turning blue because they wanted her to sit on their face. What would happen if he got lost in the sauce? What would happen if I bounced on his dick too hard and broke that bitch in half?

I just didn't know what to do. I kept suggesting to him that we hold off until he was completely healed and not a liability. He just would not give in. He wanted to do it. I felt concerned about the situation at first, but then I realized that I couldn't get in the way of destiny.

Who am I to turn down a buttermilk biscuit fine nigga? If he wanted to practice his cunnilingus skills on me, what type of animal would I be if I took that away from him? If he wanted to see how many licks it took to get to the center of the Cinnabon roll, I would help him find out. If it was his time to go be with the Lord, so be it. I was doing him a solid—if he had a death wish, that was not my problem. The Bible said to love thy neighbor; it didn't necessarily say anything about loving thy neighbor's dick, but that was my interpretation.

Maybe he wanted to be able to relate to Drake when he said he liked his girls BBW—because we *do* actually suck you dry and go with you to California Tortilla—or Qdoba, or Chipotle. I'm not picky.

After a complete hour of debating back and forth, I gave in and agreed to have him come over to follow through with my face-sitting appointment. He drove a hard bargain and he was pretty convincing.

The next day, I wrote, edited, **and** revised a paper, did my laundry, cleaned my room—I was being incredibly productive. There is nothing more encouraging than and uplifting than sitting on faces (well, as a college student, anyway).

I headed off to the bathroom to perform my rituals. He was so fine that I actually considered **and** agreed to him coming on a "shamp/con" day, which is a sacred day for a natural/transitioning girl! Normally, on "shamp/con" days, I would wash and deep condition my hair, curl up with some chamomile tea, and read a book or watch the Golden Girls because, stability. But being dicked down was higher up on the priority list that particular night. I put on my go-to "In-House Dick-Getting Attire" (with a t-shirt and booty shorts). I put my hair up in a high ponytail and lathered my body up in the Pure Seduction body lotion and body spray. I put my face on—not too much, not too little.

I told him to come through around 10 and there I was, still waiting at 10:30. He texted me and told me he was on his way up. My roommates were in the kitchen cooking something, which I was trying to avoid because they normally cooked around the same time. I was worried because they were about to find out that I had the juice and that getting niggas was nothing to me. I don't like people in my business. It was nothing against them, I was just typically a private person.

I got a text that said that he was at the door. I sprayed Pure Seduction on once more and headed for the front door. I opened it up and my mouth watered. Buttermilk biscuit fine was an **understatement!** He was pink Starburst fine. He was blue Jolly Rancher fine! He was hot cocoa with marshmallows on top during a snow storm fine! He was Slurpee on a summer day fine! He was A1 sauce fine. He was homemade banana pudding fine! He was adorable, but sexy at the same time. I was trying to maintain my cool because my roommates were in there.

I would have saved him the trouble and fucked him in the kitchen had they not have been there. I tried to act all nonchalant.

"Oh hey," I said casually as if I hadn't been waiting for him for half an hour.

He licked his lips.

"What's beautiful," he said.

I noticed that he was a little out of breath because he had a boot on his foot. I let him step in and pointed to my room. He walked in front of me.

Meanwhile, I could feel my roommate looking at him in shock. I looked back and sure enough, they were both drooling. He was *beautiful*. They were probably wondering how in the hell I managed to pull this one—shit, me too! I never really knew or understood how a girl like me managed to pull niggas like that without **any** effort at all. I'm not that cute, my hair is uneven, and half of the time, I look dusty and homeless.

I closed my door behind us and he put his keys and phone on my desk. Then he asked if he could sit on my bed. He acted so shy and it was so cute. He wasn't aware that I was about to suck the shyness out of him.

I really just wanted him to sit down and to stop acting like it was hard for him to pull bitches.

"Stop acting shy," I whined out.

He laughed and sat down.

"I can't help it, though."

I changed the subject before he even thought about saying that Godforsaken word again.

"You're from Baltimore, aren't you?" I asked.

"Yeah," he replied.

"The county, right?" I added.

"How'd you know?" he asked surprised.

You all should know the answer to that question.

"I can hear it in your voice," I said. "But it's really subtle, though."

He smiled. It was perfect—his teeth were white and everything. He had me imagining what my pink would look like on his white. I passed him the remote.

"I don't really watch TV," I said. "You can put on whatever you want."

Of course, he turned on fucking ESPN—typical football player. It eventually got quiet because he was so into the TV.

"So," I asked after five awkward minutes of silence. "What position do you play?"

He told me and I nodded my head as if I knew exactly what it meant.

I sat on the edge of the bed, pretending to be innocent. We went back to watching the TV, and in my peripheral, I saw him looking back and forth at me and the TV. Another fifteen awkward minutes went by and I just couldn't take it anymore.

"So," I said and turned my head to him, "what about all that stuff you were talking about on Twitter? Is that still open?"

He licked his PEL's and bit his bottom lip; just like that, I was soaked. I reached for his sweats and tugged on them. He lifted his body up to help me out—such a gentleman He was about to dick me down, but he was doing so extremely politely. Out flopped a huge beautiful masterpiece. I almost cried out. I jumped back and put my hands over my mouth. I was flabbergasted. It was like Christmas morning came early. It was like payday—or the last day of your period. Fighting back tears, I was ready to be mouth-fucked. I licked my lips.

He managed to take his sweatshirt off and that was when I knew God was real, because he took his time with him. He had abs for days. He had abs for Stanford, Orlando, *and* Bianca. He was like the Oprah of abs. *You get some abs! You get some abs! Everyone gets some abs!*

He was the finest nigga to ever enter my bedroom and he was completely naked. He had a tattoo on his chest; it could've been a name or a scripture, I can't remember. He had thighs like a God, a smile of a conman, the face of an angel—but an angel whose face you're about to sit on, you know?

I normally pulled 7's, 8's, and sometimes 9's. He was a solid 13. I did a mental exercise to prepare myself. Then I dove head first, without hesitation. I spat and then I swallowed him whole. Then I came back up for the tip and started jerking him off at the same time. I rubbed on his balls with my other hand. I deliberately choked on his dick so that it could get really messy. My t-shirt was soaked and my hands were pruned.

His head kept popping up and down from the pillow. He was gasping and moaning. He stopped breathing a few times. I was going in. He was so fine that I did something I didn't even do for Santos when I first met him. There was no condom on his dick. I was being an idiot—which is never okay. He threw me off. I even sucked on his balls! I was literally gargling on spit—that's how messy it was. I didn't care that a portion of my bed was soaked. He reached for my head like most niggas do. Then he hesitated.

"Go ahead," I said.

It's a good thing I didn't have a wig or weave on/in because that shit would've fallen off. I had put in so much work that my ponytail had gotten loose. He grabbed my hair and wrapped it around my fist because he saw I was struggling to keep my hair out of my face. He had full control. I saw the TV's light reflecting off the spit on my hands, his balls—it was just a beautiful wet mess. I came up to catch my breath.

"Sit on my face," he said.

"Huh?" I asked disoriented.

"Just come here," he said.

I popped up like a dick at 4 in the morning. I stood up and looked at his boot. I was left there wondering how I was going to go about doing this. He tapped on his shoulders and told me to swing my leg over and sit. It was harder than it sounded. He could tell that I was nervous. I was not trying to go to jail. I took a deep breath and climbed onto the bed, stood over him, and knelt down. I was facing his dick and managed to sit down without incident.

Barely settled, he wrapped his arms around my back. I couldn't go anywhere, and you know how much I love to run. Sooner or later, we were 69'ing. I was really trying to reciprocate, but when the head is too good, you just have to stop and take it all in. I started twerking on his face. Then I stopped because I needed to focus on his dick.

He was tugging on my clit with his mouth. He started tongue-fucking me. He spat and I felt it drip back down. I started deep-throating him for ten seconds at a time. I hummed simultaneously. Apparently, it felt good, because as soon as I start doing that, he lifted my big ass up and put me on my hands and knees. He was being a little too rough and doing a little too much. I was worried he was going to end up hurting himself. I was on my hands and knees, waiting for him to bless me with the dick. He got on his knees about to fuck me from behind. I was ecstatic. Then I remembered I never watched him put a condom on. I looked back.

"If you need a condom, they're over there in my drawer," I said. Then I thought about it. "Actually, I'll get it for you."

I was about to stand up and he stopped me.

"Uhn uh," he said. "Stay right there, just like that. Keep that arch just like that."

I got nervous.

"Ummm, sir?" I said quietly.

He rubbed his dick into my juices then smeared some onto my asshole. He lightly pushed on it.

"Wrong hole," I called out. He shushed me.

He slid his dick down my taint and half-way into my pussy. Then he tried to reposition his body to get better leverage and all hell broke loose.

He put all his weight on one knee—the very same knee he had just gotten surgery on. The knee that literally still had stitches in it. He fell back and winced. He was in so much pain. I was nervous and freaking out, wondering what I had done. I started sweating.

"I'm okay," he said.

"No, you're clearly not okay," I replied. "What happened."

"I put all my weight on my leg," he said. "I fucked up. You can ride, though."

I looked at him, then looked at his knee, then looked back at him.

"Nah, I'm good," I replied.

I didn't need any further injury on my conscience. I told him we could finish up in a couple weeks. He frowned.

"Okay," he replied.

I gave him a massage and rubbed around the stitched area, thinking about how I could cheer him up.

"Fuck!" he screamed out and hit the wall. "I'm sorry about that."

"You don't have anything to be sorry about," I said.

He was genuinely down.

"Well, can I at least finish sucking your dick?" I asked.

He looked up at me surprised and his face lit up.

I shoved his dick in my mouth and finally finished him off. I swallowed him up. He needed a few moments to recuperate. He kept telling me I was the best he had ever had, which is always my goal. Another man satisfied, another blueballs avoided, another wet dream unhad.

I reached my fist out, and he bumped it—it was cool as hell. I helped him get dressed and walked him out. He hugged me.

(Side note: Eventually, he started playing games just like every other nigga I had dealt with. Even when I made it my mission not to give a fuck about people, I ended up getting hurt.)

I ended up hopping in the shower, brushing my teeth, and getting dressed again. Then I called Santos over to take care of me, which he always did. When he came over, he commented on ESPN being on my TV, and asked who I had over, which was none of his business. To spare his feelings, I told him that it was the same channel he had left it on the last time he came over. That was the last time we fucked.

The next morning, I realized that I was too far down the rabbit hole and needed to get out. I had **two** niggas come over the night before. I needed to take a break. I started a sexual sabbatical immediately. I allowed myself to become sexually anorexic. Slowly yet surely, I found myself and figured out a way to let all of my pent-up anger and hurt inside me go. And then I met a girl.

33. What Goes Up

∞

Early-October, 2015

At the beginning of my sexual sabbatical, I started to become whole again. I was happy—genuinely happy for the first time in a long time. I started eating regularly. I was no longer always angry or upset. Jennifer could say any of my exes' names without me getting upset or feeling hurt—I was back. Graduation was months away and I couldn't wait to be gone. One day on Snapchat, I was watching peoples' stories, and I noticed a girl who, for all intents and purposes, I'll call her Dayja.

(Side note: She had attended Bowie State the semester before but decided to uproot her life and move to Georgia to go after her dreams. I never understood why people do that—why they think packing up and moving to New York or LA or ATL without a single plan would somehow make all their problems go away.)

She was a stud whose laugh I would soon fall in love with. She had posted a video on Snapchat asking anyone that knew me to tell me to hit her up because she had finally worked up the courage to make a move. Funny thing is, she supposedly had a crush on me the entire time I was with Orlando, but she never spoke to me, not even a hello. It was by chance that I was on Snapchat that day because I rarely used the app.

I heard her say my name as clear as day. When I inquired about it in her DM's, she admitted that she had been crushing on me for quite some time. Then she asked for my number and I gave it to her.

After a few weeks, we ended up talking—trying to figure out every possible thing about each other. She seemed different, and money-driven. She was goofy and always knew how to make me smile. She actually tried to understand who I was deep down. I knew I liked her when I spent all day thinking about her and wanting to be on the phone with her all the time. I spoke to her about my worries and fears, and she actually listened and gave me amazing advice.

After much discussion, we decided to link up. She drove ten hours to see me. I had been sex-free for weekss, and I felt like a completely different person. I was excited to finally meet her and to hug her.

I decided to end my sabbatical with her, and only her. So, I did the "Three S's" for the first in a while. She must have been special, because I brought out the Lancôme for her even though she did not deserve it! Not because the sex was whack, but because she ended up wiping it off while play-fighting.

She texted me to let me know that she was walking into the building. So I went down to sign her in. It was awkward for a little while—it had been a long time since I had dealt with a girl, so I didn't know what to expect. She was supposed to be staying the weekend with me, so a lot of things could've happened.

When we walked onto the elevator, she looked at me and wiped my makeup off. Yes, the makeup that I spent thirty minutes doing beforehand. Yes, the foundation that cost me $50 that I only used for rare occasions and formal events. Once we got to my room, she made herself comfortable.

"Can I have a kiss?" she asked.

"Nah," I replied pettily because I still felt a certain way about her wiping off my makeup.

She sucked her teeth and pulled her phone out.

"I'm about to FaceTime you so it won't be awkward," she said as if that would somehow change something.

Keep in mind that she was only three feet away from me. Even though I shouldn't have, I accepted her FaceTime call.

"Can I get a kiss through the phone?" she asked.

I laughed in her face and shook my head.

"Nope."

So I hung up on her and continued making up the rest of my bed. She pulled me in and kissed me.

"So you just gonna hang up on me, huh," she said.

I nodded my head and she kissed me passionately. It was the type of kiss you had to catch your breath afterwards. She bit on my lip and I bit on hers. We ended up on my bed, just chilling. I turned off the TV and got on Twitter on my phone. Then she started complaining and demanding my full attention. So I turned my phone on do not disturb.

Dayja had the nerve to snatch my phone out of my hand. She walked over to my desk and emptied her pockets—then she placed her keys and our phones on the desk. She noticed I had spearmint gum in my mouth and she asked for a piece.

In no time, Dayja began pulling down my pants, and slid my thong to the side. I hadn't had head in what felt like forever. I almost forgot what it felt like until she dove her head into my pussy. I arched my back as the tingling sensation caught me off guard. It felt cold as hell. Now I knew how it felt to chew 5 Gum. She began sucking on my clit and every time she exhaled, I felt a gust of wind. I pulled the hood back to be helpful, but she kept shooing my hands away.

She got so fed up that she yanked my hands and put them under my ass. I started moaning and screaming. My roommates were outside pre-gaming for a party, but ask me if I cared at all. I came not once, not twice, but three times! My fluids jolted from my body into her mouth and she just never stopped eating. After she tortured my pussy, I couldn't move because all my energy had gone into pushing her off of me.

She came up to me. I managed to lift my entire body up and started kissing and licking all over her face. It had been so long since I was able to taste Nikki! I was just so happy to be back. Think about the fact that even without penetration, I came three times.

She pulled a doozy on me and ended up back down in Nikki. Don't ask me how, because I honestly can't tell you; it all happened so fast. I guess the first time was a warm-up because she started fingering and sucking the soul out of Nikki. So after I pretty much died, had my funeral, and climbed out of the ground, she had finally stopped.

I reached out for her hand and she gave it to me. I shoved her fingers into my mouth and watched her face light up when she noticed my nastiness.

"Come with me to my car real quick," she said as I lied back in the bed.

"Why?" I replied.

"Just come with me," she said. "I gotta get my luggage, and some other stuff. It's really important."

Eventually, we ended up outside and it was below freezing. It was so cold that the pussy juices crawling down and dangling between my legs froze up and became ice cycles. We fetched her suitcase from the car and ran back to the apartment.

As if three times wasn't enough for her! She wanted to shoot for a world record. Another round of cream came out of me. Then my body went limp and she came up and lied beside me. She was exhausted, but walked over and pulled out a strap-on. After helping her set it up, I was ready.

She shoved it in and I flinched. It was too big.

"You're going to have to spit on it or something," I cried out.

She spat on it and started rubbing on my clit to get the juices flowing. Then she eased it in, and I relaxed my walls as it entered. I'm not going to lie; it started to feel pretty good. Then it started to feel great. Then it started to feel amazing!

She flipped me over on my stomach and I assumed the position. The arch was just perfect, at $f(x) = 69x^2 + 69x + 69$. This arch was serious!

The dildo started pushing against my cervix but I soldiered on and maintained that arch. When I say her stroke game was something to be reckoned with, and was better than some other niggas I had ever dealt with, I mean that. Girls just know how to please other girls.

When she pulled the dildo out, I turned around and started sucking on it, and I couldn't have been happier. I crammed it into my small mouth and stretched my lips as far as they could possibly go. She kissed me and looked me in my eyes.

"Sit on my face," she said. I obliged her and started sucking on the dildo as she drank my soul from out of me. She shoved her fingers into Nikki while sucking on my clit. I moaned and stretched out toward the ceiling. A queef came out and I hoped off of her face. I petered in a corner until she got up and put her arms out.

"Oh, my God," I cried out. "I'm so sorry!"

"It's not a big deal," she replied. "It happens."

A huge part of me was embarrassed but the other part of me knew that some air must have gotten trapped in Nikki when Dayja was fucking me with the anaconda-sized dildo. I had lost count of the number of orgasms I had that night, just know that it was a very, very warm welcome back into the sexually active population.

When we finally finished, I lied down on her chest, and we…cuddled. We actually cuddled and I didn't try to get out of it.

"Your pussy is our pussy now," she said.

We laughed, but I never realized how serious she was.

She made me fall in love with everything about her. The difference between her and everyone else was that she had actually become a really good friend and never tried to pressure me into doing something I didn't want to do.

One month later, I practically begged her to be my girlfriend on all realms of social media. My sexual sabbatical really toned down my fuckgirlness and helped me find clarity. It seemed like everything happened for a reason and brought me to her. For the first time ever, I had allowed myself to be that vulnerable—imagine that. To think it all started with a little hoeness.

34. Must Come Down

∞

Dayja was everything I was afraid of her being. I watched her fall out of love with me. The distance perpetuated everything and we just grew apart. I felt more alone than I did before I took my sabbatical. She had pretended to be something I needed for so long, and then, when I had finally found out the truth, it was too late.

She was irresponsible. We dated less than a year, and she had had over five jobs within that time frame. She didn't understand commitment. She was money-hungry. You know the type—the ones always looking out for a get rich quick scheme. I remember her telling me about her doing Forex once upon a time and that should've been a red flag.

She wasn't just broke, money-wise, she was intellectually broke. Although very business-smart, she never understood the concept of persistence. If something didn't work out for her, she always gave up—which would explain why she quit so many jobs.

Dayja not only tried to pretend to be something she wasn't in front of me, she did it in front of others as well. When she'd visit me or I'd visit her, she'd be so concerned and focused on the wrong things. She never wanted anyone to see that she was struggling even though that's all she ever did. It was so bad that whenever we'd go out, she'd have me sneak her my credit card just to make it look like she was the one that was paying. She was prideful—and that was her downfall. Dayja never liked feeling like she depended on anyone or like she was a burden, when that's all she ever was.

She didn't save money; she threw it away on get rich quick schemes that were basically pyramid schemes no matter what way you looked at it. She was amazing at making people believe what they wanted she wanted them to.

Eventually, she signed up for this travel club that would pay out $200 a month if you signed up three or more people. She was living on $200. A month. In Atlanta. She would flex on Instagram and Twitter all while depending on free food through the "Give and Get" promotion on UberEats, but that's none of my business. When she was unsuccessful at that, she would call me, crying about how she hadn't eaten in days, begging me for money. This had become a habit.

By June, I was completely out of love with her. I still loved her, but I couldn't see myself spending the rest of my life with her at all. We were just two different people. I had goals, and plans, and was actually working on them; she just felt entitled to everything.

We never had sex. Literally, the only time we had sex was the first time we met in person, and it only made me hate her more. I lasted an entire year without feeling wanted. I was frustrated, and sexually-deprived, but I never cheated, because I'm better than that.

She, however, did cheat. And to this day, she denies it. In the beginning of June 2016, she and I took a trip with my cousins and my aunt to Fort Lauderdale, Florida. I thought the trip would somehow put a spark back into our relationship. I thought it would save us, but it only made me hate her even more.

Dayja acted distant. It just wasn't the same, you know. She had gotten in the shower and I took that time to go into her phone. My accusations were proven. I opened a thread, headed straight to the multi-media section, and saw nudes for days. To my surprise, she had received them from a light-skinned BBW that wasn't me. When she got out of the shower, I confronted her about it. She laughed in my face and denied up and down even though the proof was *literally* in my hand.

I think a part of me stayed with her because it was the longest relationship I had ever been in and I couldn't bear seeing myself single and alone after so long, even though that's exactly what I had felt for months. It's like I didn't know how to be single anymore.

I remember crying almost every night from February to May because all she ever did was ignore me. She acted as though communication wasn't the most important thing in a long distance relationship, when it's really do or die.

I'm not going to sit here and act like I was innocent throughout the whole thing. I enabled her, and I let ignore me out of fear of being single. I still haven't forgiven myself for that to this day. I can't believe I was so desperate.

I decided to visit her one last time to end it the right way. We were like strangers. We spent the entire weekend doing everything she wanted. She was a part of a traveler's club through a clothing company co-owned by a famous rapper—but I saw through it. It was nothing but another pyramid scheme. The fact that we had spent so much time running around, getting things done for the sham of a business and not spending quality time together really did it for me. Within the last few hours of my stay, I asked her if we could at least spend the rest of the time talking, but she claimed that she was tired and that all she wanted to do was sleep.

I flipped. I screamed and yelled at her. All the things I had pinned up inside of me was finally coming out. I was telling her about how terrible of a person she was and explaining to her why she had nothing and no one. She just stood there, looking past me with a blank face.

I can't remember what it was that I said in particular, but I opened my mouth again and she began grabbing my bags and throwing them out of her room. I felt disrespected. She reached for another bag and I yanked on it. We tussled over it for at least thirty seconds. She dropped it and my zipper burst open forcing clothes out.

I looked down at my bag as tears streamed down my face. I wasn't sad, I was *angry*. Have you ever been so fucking angry that you began crying? I looked back up at her.

"You're a shitty person," I said to her calmly. She laughed and looked down at her nails not saying a word. "You're going to live in this roach-infested apartment building, starving every day for the rest of your life and there's nothing you can do to change it. You're a loser. You are a nobody and you don't know how to love. Your family won't even take your calls." I giggled as I packed my clothing back into the bag.

(Side note: If there's anything I knew about her, it's that she took pride in her cleanliness. I was going after her pride—I was going to make her feel shittier than she had made me feel for so long. She had to move into a roach-infested apartment building after taking a hit financially. She depleted all her resources—it had gotten so bad that her parents or grandmother wouldn't even take her calls. She was a burden— and that's all she knew how to be. I refused to help her out

because I just didn't have love for her in me anymore and I still felt like shit about it.)

She charged at me. Her face was blank, her nostrils were flared, and her eyes were wide. She grabbed my wrists and we fell down onto the floor.

"Get off of me Dayja!" I screamed out, trying to tear my wrists away from her.

She squeezed my wrists harder and I snapped. I started whaling on her. It was like all the hatred I had built up inside of me was finally coming out. How do you treat a person who helped you out of the darkness only to drop you back into that very same darkness on their own accord? I was hurt and felt betrayed. She had grabbed me and after that, I saw red. I didn't care that I was blackening her eye or clawing for blood from her face. The moment she grabbed my wrists, I had a flashback—it took me to a place I'm still not strong or brave enough to share with you all. Just know that it took me to a very black place and I felt like I had to defend myself.

I stopped hitting her when the pain of having four of my nails broken outweighed my fear. The entire time I spent hitting her, tears flushed out of my eyes. But when it was all over, it was like a metamorphosis. The last little bit of anger, love, and pity I had for her…it was all gone. I literally felt nothing.

"Are you done?" she asked as her head rested on my breasts.

My breaths slowed down.

"I wasn't even going to hit you," she said. "I was going to grab you and kiss you."

She had the worst timing. Of all the chances and opportunities she had to prove to me that she still cared, it was too late. I watched as her cheekbone began swelling up. I didn't feel sorry or apologetic because she knew the way she came at me wasn't appropriate.

"Dayja," I said monotonic, "just...get off of me."

I couldn't even look her in the eyes because it was finally our time.

I sat at one end of her bed and she sat at the other. We sat in silence for at least twenty minutes, gathering our thoughts about what had just happened.

"Look," she said. "We both know there's no way we can possibly come back from what just happened."

I nodded.

"You're right," I said. "I just...didn't expect it to end like *this*."

"I just," she said, "don't want to be with you anymore."

"I don't want to be with you, either," I said softly. "We've grown too much apart."

"Absolutely," she said.

"So where does that leave us?" I asked.

"Friends, I guess," she said.

I shook my head.

"Nah, I don't think so," I replied. "I honestly don't even want that. We just…aren't the same people we were when we first started."

She walked over to my side of the bed.

"Can I least get a hug?" she asked.

I sighed loudly and shook my head once more.

"Not right now," I said. "I'm gonna need time."

She agreed. Moments later, we were walking downstairs to her car on our way to the airport. We spent the entire hour-long ride in silence. When we got there, with only thirty minutes before my flight departure, she decided to drive to a parking lot where you could see planes taking off.

"What do think?" she asked, looking in amazement as a plane took off.

"What do you mean?" I asked.

"About this spot," she said. "It's pretty cool, right? I parked here and waited for your plane to land when you first got here."

"Okay," I said nonchalantly.

"Do you want to go back?" she asked.

"**Yes**," I replied boldly.

She was trying to make conversation when there didn't need to be any. The both of us deserved nothing but silence. I didn't want to be in the car with her longer than I needed to be.

"Can you just take me to the entrance, please?" I asked.

She took the car out of park, reversed, and we drove away. When I arrived to the front of the airport, I got out as soon as she braked. I yanked the trunk door open and pulled my suitcase out. She put her hand over mine.

"You need help with that?" she asked.

"No," I said, "I'm good."

She sucked her teeth and stared at me.

I rolled my eyes and let my suitcase go. She closed the trunk and walked me into the airport.

"Wow," she said as she handed my suitcase over to me, pursing her lips. "This is really it, isn't it?"

I raised my eyebrows in "no shit". She reached her arms out at her sides and stood there with her head tilted requesting a hug. I leaned in and she held me for the last time. She breathed me in and lightly hugged me by my lower-back. I tried pulling away lightly, but she didn't catch on. I placed my arm between us and pushed her body away.

"I have to go," I said as I looked at the time on my phone.

"Well," she said, "you don't have to call me, but can you at least text me when you land?"

I shrugged my shoulders carelessly. She dug her hands into her front pockets and leaned back on her heals and then forward on her toes one time with a side-smile. It was…awkward. Like two strangers in the center of an airport asking for directions.

I walked away from her and said nothing more.

I looked up in a corner and saw her looking at me from a mirror facing the entrance. I never looked back at her. I didn't want her to think that there was still love when there wasn't.

That was the last time I saw Dayja. I ran to my terminal and got on my plane just in time for takeoff. The entire flight, I didn't cry, or weep, or fret. I was….happy. I was…free.

Part VI: Who Would've Thought?

35. Love at First Fuck

Early-October, 2016

After a year of going without sex and watching someone I would've done anything for fall out of love with me, I was officially single. For a couple months, Dayja and I tried the whole "friend thing", but the love was already lost.

I had finally got the keys to my first apartment and I was so proud of myself. All of the hustling and bustling and grinding and sleepless nights had finally paid off.

It had been a while since I had exercised my juice, but I never lost it. It was just in the freezer—had to let it thaw out. One day, I posted a photo on Snapchat, telling people to send me a confession and I had no choice but to reply to all of them.

In came Vance (yes, the very same Jamaican guy who was Orlando's friend from chapter 25!) with

"I've low key wanted you and wanted to taste you 👀."

"Since when?" I typed back. "Lol why? I ain't shit."

"Honestly, since you and O but that was the bro," he replied.

"👀," I messaged. "Why'd you never say anything?"

"I was never really in the position to," he responded.

"True," I sent. "Well, are you still hungry?"

"I could always go for a meal," he messaged.

The thought hadn't really crossed my mind that one of my exes was one of his good friends. We're too old for that—it really shouldn't matter.

I'm just going to keep it OG 100 with you guys, being that I was in my own apartment, I just knew my lifestyle was about to change. Translation: I was going to be dicked down, licked down, sucked down, fucked down, 25/8. I honestly, truly did not give a fuck. I was single, he had lips and a tongue and a dick, I had my own place, and we were going to make it happen.

I was committed to finding a contender to help me break in each and every inch of my apartment: my kitchen counter, my bed, my shower, my couches, etc.

It had been a year! A fucking year! Dayja and I had had sex literally for the first and last time in

October of 2015, so my walls were probably on opposite sides of one another; fuck, my hymen had probably re-developed!

So, we had finally decided on having him come over on a Saturday morning, bright and early because his headlights were busted and he didn't want to get a ticket. By the way, bright and early means 7 am. Now, for those of you who may think that 7 am is a bit too early for a dick appointment, I think not! *Dick is life. Dick is love. Dick was sent from above. Dick does not have business hours.* That's just life.

Keep in mind that it had been a year since anyone had played with Nikki. I had some…things to handle. I'm not saying that I had completely stopped shaving, but this called for a celebratory wax! It had to be perfect! Nikki needed a quinceañera—a welcome home party so to speak.

So I called Su at the spa down the street from my house after I got home from work and she was able to squeeze me in. Considering that it had been roughly 365 days since my last "3 S's" ritual, it felt a bit nostalgic. I was singing to Nikki in the shower. I was giving her a pep talk. We joined together in prayer so to speak. It was extremely spiritual. You never realize the tolling effects not having sex for a year does to your mind, spirit, body, and soul until you go through it.

At around 6:30 am, I got a FaceTime call from him letting me know that he was already in his car, on his way to me. When we hung up, I started twerking in the shower, singing, washing my hair, just having a grand old time!

Twenty something minutes rolled by and I heard the buzzer go off. I reached for my phone and it was 6:59 on the dot! He was determined. I hopped out of the shower, ran to the monitor, and buzzed him in. I wrapped my towel around me and ran to the front door.

I swung the door open and I was greeted by his smile. He was perfect. He had a fresh cut. And for the first time ever, I had realized that his eyes were hazel. He was looking delicious.

He didn't say one word. He just stepped in, yanked my towel off of me, sat me on the arm of my couch, and dropped his keys to the floor. Then he started eating me out. I didn't even get a chance to dry off and he just started blessing me! Talk about "top of the morning"! I could only handle thirty seconds because the angle just wasn't working out. He lifted me up and started kissing me. You know how I am about kissing guys, but there was just something about him that I trusted. I hadn't tasted myself in what felt like forever, but I tasted sweeter than I remembered. He stopped kissing me and paused.

"Nah," he said. "I want some more."

Before I could even reply, he pushed me back down onto the couch and wrapped his arms around my stomach. He slipped his tongue down into my soul and I had to stop him because I just couldn't breathe.

I lifted up.

"Well, hello to you, too," I said out of breath. "Damn."

He smirked and wiped his lips.

"Oh, my bad," he said. "How you doing today, beautiful?"

I think we were a *bit* past that, wouldn't you think?

Long story short, we ended up in my bedroom. I was so excited to suck dick after a year of being away from it! Nikki was already drenched. I pushed him onto the bed shyly. He took his shirt off. For a while, I admired his tattoos. Then I crouched down and went to work for the first time in seven dog years! I got a special treat when I found out that he was uncircumcised. I don't know about you, but I absolutely adore them! They're fun. It takes a certain type of female to be comfortable not only sucking them, but knowing *how* to and what certain tricks to use.

Like the lady I am, I politely pulled the foreskin back, spat on his dick, slurped it up, and got to sucking. I don't even think his dick was in my mouth for two seconds before he started moaning. I snatch souls for a hobby, so you know how I am. You know, as simple as it may sound, whenever a guy says "oh, shit" during head, he really means "marry me". I'm just saying. I was going absolutely, positively ham! I was making it supercalifragilisticexpialidociously sloppy! This wet work was one of my bests! It was definitely one for the books! I was putting in work like I had never retired. I was really giving it to him. Honestly, truly, he had received the best head I've ever given thus far in my life.

    I wouldn't be surprised if he actually died a few times. His body would tense up often and then he would drop back down to the bed without letting out a peep. I started humming when his tip was in the back of my throat. His voice went up a few octaves. I inhaled his dick. I was gargling on my own spit. I was jerking it at the right rotation. After he just couldn't take it anymore, he pressed on my shoulders and I eased up. He stood, still jerking off.

    "Get on the bed," he instructed.

    "Yes sir," I said, grinning.

    I thought he was preparing to give me back shots and then bounce. Boy, was I wrong! I got my arch right.

    "No, no, no," he said. "Not yet. Get on your back."

    I backed up onto the bed a little too far and he yanked me closer into him. He slowly dropped his head into my pussy and stared at me as he ate me out again. Soul: stolen. He sucked on my clit ever so lightly and then he started tugging on it! He actually knew what he was doing. It was like my body spoke to him and he spoke to it. This was no run-of-the-mill head. His tongue knew me better than I knew myself, honestly. He guided my feet onto his back and put his hands onto my waist and held it. Passion.

He wasn't like the other guys. His main focus was trying to please *me*. He started neck-rolling in my pussy. It was too good. This was some "nut in me" type of head! I lost my marbles! I know that in other chapters, I explained that I had cried a few times during head, but I was literally *bawling*! My tears were in my hair! My eyes grew puffy! I kept trying to inch away from him but he would just pull me in by my waist. I had to stop him before I agreed to letting him impregnate me.

Apparently, I tasted like "heaven" to him—like a sweet drizzle. My legs shivered. My heart pounded. My soul left my body. My tears streamed. My voice was gone. My pussy throbbed. My life was over. I was ready for his dick. Nikki was soaked. Vance came up and his entire beard had been moisturized by my juices—I could even see its curl pattern. He started climbing onto the bed. I looked at his dick. There was something missing.

"Ummm sir," I said. "Where is your condom?"

He looked down at his dick and looked back up at me, smiling.

"See," he said, "the thing is—"

My eyebrows furrowed.

"The thing is that you've got me fucked up," I thought to myself.

He saw my facial expression change.

"It's not even like that," he said. "I get soft in condoms. The skin always folds back down."

So, I thought up a proposition that I just knew would fuck up his plan to persuade me to letting him fuck me raw.

"If you can provide me a signed copy of an STD screening administered and/or read less than three days ago," I said confidently, "you can fuck me raw."

He didn't say anything. He just smirked as if he had a trick or two up his sleeve. He hopped off of the bed, put his joggers back on, grabbed his keys, cracked the door, went to his car, came back to my apartment, opened the door, took his shoes off, walked back into my bedroom, handed me an envelope, started taking his clothes off, and looked at me from the edge of the bed, smiling.

For the first time ever, someone had made me eat my words. Of all the times I had said those very same words to niggas that have tried the same thing, it had **never** gone down like that! Guys would normally suck their teeth in defeat and reach for a condom!

What were the odds!? What were the fucking odds that he would have had a fucking STD screening literally days before seeing me? HIV/AIDS: negative. Chlamydia: negative. Gonorrhea: negative. Syphilis: negative. Herpes: negative. Trichomoniasis: negative. Signed: 10/14/16. He came over October 15th!

I had always heard that once you have unprotected sex, you immediately fall in love. I wasn't in the mental or emotional space to be falling in love. I immediately started sweating. I couldn't breathe. I hadn't planned on that outcome. I womaned up. I had made a promise and I never break them. The reason I never make promises is because they mean so much. I thought I had the upper hand but then he called out "checkmate".

He had actually come prepared. It was like he just *knew* I would say that—like he knew it would take more than a promise that he was "good". Half the time, niggas self-diagnose themselves by whether or not it burns when they pee after sticking their dick into God knows who.

"Okay," I said. "I'm ready."

He climbed on top of me and tried to stick it in. It was just too painful. It was far too tight. It was like I had gotten my virginity back or something. My pussy was tighter than a sewin installed by a hood rat with six kids, no edges, and endless food stamps! My pussy was tighter than a wealthy alt-right white guy being told by a renowned scientist that everyone comes from Africa. It was tighter than my mom's lips when I was a kid and would embarrass her in public knowing that she was planning on fucking me up when we got home. My pussy was tighter than a straight guy's butt cheeks bending over to pick up the soap he had dropped in a prison sower. My pussy was tighter than a bitch that spent two and half years with a guy only to become his baby's mother, while she watches him marry a girl after being with her for only six months. I needed time to prepare.

"You sure you wanna do this?" he asked, looking at me.

The thing that was different about him is that he was actually looking me in the eyes when he asked that. He wasn't just asking it to ask, he actually waited to hear my response. I nodded. He wasn't a fuckboy— anymore, at least, and not to me.

We tried to get his dick inside of me for a good two minutes. Then we finally succeeded. I screeched out. It felt like he had ripped through my soul. Once he finally got in, things were a bit slippery. The worst part wasn't the fact that he was in me as he was; the worst part wasn't even the fact that he stared into the depths of my soul. **He intertwined his fingers into mine!** I had to close my eyes because we couldn't do all three at the same time! I didn't want to be in love just yet.

When he first started stroking inside of me, his voice shuttered. I had finally realized what the hype was all about. Raw sex was the best thing ever since fucking sliced bread! It's emotionally stressful—but at that point, I didn't even care. I felt every ridge of his dick rubbing up inside of me just right. It sounded like we were on the set of a Kraft Mac & Cheese commercial. It was beautiful. I wrapped my legs around him and clenched onto his back. I scratched him up. I sucked him in further and I watched his eyes roll into the back of his head.

He pulled out, slapped me on the clit repeatedly, and turned me over. He pressed down onto my back with one hand and held onto my bra with the other. He started ravaging my shit! I couldn't run. In hindsight, telling him that I was a runner during Facetime calls probably wasn't the best call on my end. We had later found out that I had started bleeding. But it wasn't period blood—just the type of blood you lose when your hymen breaks for the first time. He was stretching me out! He was opening up parts of me that had been closed away for twelve months.

My arch was on point! He slowly slid his dick in from behind. His voice shuddered once more.

"Oh my God," he called out.

That thing was clenching! Every time he entered me, it felt like a stab into my guts. He fit me just right, but a couple inches more than just right. His dick poked the bottom of my heart—that was how he stole it. He was really piping me down! Sooner or later, my moans turned into cries, and my cries turned back into moans. It's hard to explain, really. I buried my head into a pillow.

"Nuh uh," he said, yanking the pillow away from my face.

He pounded harder and I couldn't even be mad. It was the best sex I had ever had.

Vance pulled out.

"I'm about to cum," he groaned out.

I hopped off of the bed and turned him around, facing me. I sat him down. He was jerking off but I slapped his hand away. I took control. I stroked his dick and sucked it at the same time. I paused on the sucking and began licking on his balls. He had shaved those too! I let his dick go and allowed him to continue jerking himself off. You have to warm up to a guy and see what they like first. You have to observe how to flick their wrist when stroking on their dicks. I had to pay attention.

I stuck my tongue out and caught his cum and it squirted to the back of my throat. He squeezed his tip for the last time and the last little bit of him came out. I licked it up. He lied back and started sucking air in through his teeth. I kissed his dick almost as if I were sending our future kids off to school.

He didn't say a word. We were too busy processing how amazing our first encounter was. Who would've fucking thought?! We were compatible in more than one way and it had finally hit us. God put Orlando into our life just so that that amazing sex could happen. He does and always has worked in mysterious ways.

Vance put his arms over his face. I watched as his stomach danced up and down. He tried catching his breath. I always wonder what guys are thinking at that very moment in time. I wasn't done, so I went back to sucking.

"Tiy!" he screamed out.

He *literally* shrieked. His voice got so high! I like to consider it an accomplishment of mine—having a guy hit notes Mariah Carey often sang!

Vance literally had to push me off. Apparently, it was "too sensitive", whatever the fuck that means.

When I stood up and saw a red spot on the bed, I had finally realized I was bleeding.

"Oh my God," I cried out. "Why didn't you tell me I was bleeding!?"

He tried to calm me down and explained that it was absolutely normal that I bled after a year of no sex.

"I expected there to be some blood," he said.

I sighed, relieved. Why didn't God put him into my life beforehand!? Most guys would have gotten freaked out and rolled out without hesitation. But he remained calm. He pulled me in by the chin and kissed me again. It was weird, but it was pretty cool. It felt right.

I hopped in the shower. About ten minutes later, I heard a knock on the bathroom door. He came in and joined me. We ended up having sex in the shower. It was heavenly. It was divine. There's just something about having my face slam up against body wash that really did something to me, you know?

When we got out of the shower, we ran back to my room, and fucked once more (for a fucking hour!). He had made me sit on his face for a good fifteen minutes.

And then we…fell asleep, side by side. He guided my head onto his chest, and he wrapped his arm around my back and I just listened to his heartbeat. We cuddled and it just…felt right, you know? For whatever reason, I felt safe in his arms—like I belonged there or some philosophical shit.

We had really tired ourselves out. We slept for about three hours. By the time we woke up, it was around noon. I opened my eyes and he was just staring at me, smiling. Drool was on his chest and I popped up embarrassed.

"I'm sorry," I said, wiping it off his tattoo.

"It's cool," he said softly.

"Did I snore?" I asked, putting my hair up in a ponytail.

He grinned.

"Yeah," he replied.

I giggled.

"I snore like a grown ass man, don't I?" I said.

"Son," he said, "I felt you in my chest! You shook the whole bed! You were like (he started mimicking how snores sounded and it was extremely guttural!)."

I burst out crying laughing! It was a laugh that came from deep inside of me. I hadn't laughed like that in months. He was roasting me, but in a cute way, you know?

"It was cute, though," he said.

I smirked and subtly rolled my eyes. He tapped his chest prompting me to lie back down on it. We just lied there. He rubbed the back of my neck and traced his fingers up and down my back. I wasn't nervous or worried at all. It didn't feel weird or awkward.

We spoke for hours about what we wanted to be and what our worst fears were. We revealed our biggest secrets and our greatest accomplishments. We talked about where our past relationships went wrong—what our strengths and weaknesses were. No one's ever opened up to me like that before in one conversation.

He wasn't trying to impress me. He wasn't trying to be something or someone he wasn't. It didn't feel like he had anything to hide from me. He didn't tell me that he "wasn't like these other niggas".

Moments later, we heard keys jingling, and then we heard the lock turn in the living room. I looked at my clock and it was 3!

(Side note: I had totally forgotten that my family was supposed to come over for a small dinner! I was supposed to be hosting them that night and I hadn't even started cooking. I was in a trance—dickmatized. Word to the wise: **never** *give your parents a key to your place!)*

I hopped up in a panic and closed my bedroom door. I explained to him what was happening. He got dressed. If it were just my mom coming over, I honestly wouldn't have given a fuck. She would've been relieved because she couldn't bear thinking about me eating pussy. But, my 80 year-old grandparents were with her. I couldn't introduce him as someone who was just fucking their granddaughter's guts! I somehow managed to get him to climb out of my window and over a fence. On his way out, he leaned in, and I leaned in, and we kissed. It was so sweet.

    I reached for my towel and wrapped it around myself. I opened my bedroom door and my mom asked why I was naked.

    "I was about to get in the shower," I said nonchalantly.

    We hugged. My grandfather greeted me with an awkward waved and my grandmother walked up to me and gave me a hug. Then she kissed me on the cheek. **I had been slapping Vance's dick all over my face not too long ago!** My poor nana. I still had dick on my breath.

    The whole night, all I could think about was him. All I wanted to do was talk to him and hang out with him. I wanted to be surrounded by him, and I wanted him to be surrounded by me (or Nikki). It was love at first fuck, honestly, truly.

36. Plan B Chronicles

∞

Late November, 2016

    We were sexually, spiritually, and emotionally compatible. Go figure. We had both admitted to being fuckpeople at the same time, but for whatever reason, we crossed paths at just the right time.

    We had had conflicting schedules. I was only able to see him a few times a week as he was working part-time and going to school at Morgan State in Baltimore. As long as he dicked me down a few times a week, I was good. The addiction had creeped back up, but the good thing is that it was with one person who was consistent for the most part.

    My life had done a complete 360! My tweets became more positive, I had more energy, my skin was glowing, and my hair was growing. Good dick and conversation will do that to any girl! Everything about him was just what I needed: his smile, his conversation, his dick. Have you ever loved someone's dick as much as you loved your mother? Anyone? Okay, I guess not.

    He makes my heart melt and my knees weaken. He's Jamaican and absolutely gorgeous. He has eyes make me wet on the spot. He's finer than baby hair.

His dick is smoother than a baby's bottom. By that time, he had had my soul in his back pocket for a solid month. I was losing my mind. I was a zombie. I wasn't used to dick that good, that often. I was a mix between Britney Spears in 2006 and Whitney Houston in 2005.

    I was going to be seeing him on Monday night! We always started each other's weeks off the right way! The entire day at work, I was extremely ecstatic. I was twerking in my office, in the bathroom, the hallway, and even in the elevator. My lunchbreak came around smoothly. Noon had come so fucking fast! I headed downstairs to the deli in my building. Then I got a call from "Daddy" (his name in my phone).

    My makeup was popping, my hair was popping, my titties were popping; honestly, the only thing that wasn't popping was my pussy because I was in public. I picked up on the first ring! It wasn't even a full ring, come to think of it. It was like a milli-ring. That's how you know they have you hooked!

    I answered.

    "Hey daddy," I said quietly.

    "What are you up to, beautiful?" he asked.

    I told him that I was getting my lunch. I sat down at a table. He just stared at me though the phone, licking his lips.

    "What," I asked self-consciously. "Do I have a booger in my nose or something?"

He just laughed.

"You're just so fucking beautiful," he said calmly.

I just blinked and wrinkled my eyebrows. I didn't know what to say to that, and I still don't when he says it.

"Babe, stop," I whined out. "No, I'm not."

I tried changing the topic quickly.

"What are you doing?" I asked.

"I just got off the phone with my dad," he replied.

"Oh," I replied nervously. "How did that go?"

"Amazing, actually," he said. "We were talking about you."

My eyes grew wide. My mind started wandering. I didn't know what to expect. The last time he had spoken to his dad about me, he told him that I had his son falling hard. It made sense. Our connection is unlike anything I've ever found in my entire life. We just make each other happy.

I smiled awkwardly.

"Soooo," he said. "My dad suggested something that I want to try out."

I pursed my lips.

"And that is…" I said, waiting for him to fill me in.

"We should try to go a day without having sex and see how that goes," he said. "He's worried that we might be too dependent on sex. If we can be around each other and not fuck, then we'll know for sure it's real."

"Oh my God, babe," I said excitedly. "That's such a good idea."

I was dying on the inside, though. How in the world did he expect me to be around him and not taste his cinnamon toast dick?! How would he manage being around me and not sticking his dick into my Pillsbury Dough pussy?! It was **impossible**. Shit, I made it a whole year without sex. I knew him. I knew my will was strong. I was a bit worried that our sexual chemistry was stronger, though. I just *knew* he would not be able to fade it.

Long story short, the rest of my day was pretty depressing. I was excited to have him inside of me. I had even waxed Nikki! I had thongs and handcuffs set out on the bed so that when I got home, all I had to do was shower, wash my hair, and brush my teeth. I had even tripled up on water and fruits. My taste would've blown his fucking mind! But it was all for nothing. At least I was going to be able to see him and hug and kiss him. That was all that mattered.

When I got home, I showered and got dressed. I still put on thongs just in case and I put on porn star makeup just to tease him. I wanted to see how strong his will was. I was going to put him through hell.

At around nine, I got a call from him. He told me to come outside because he wanted to go grocery shopping. He wanted me to make my specialty: chicken and shrimp alfredo. He said that if he couldn't eat my, pussy, he had to settle for the next best thing.

I put on my handy dandy winter season "On my way to the dick" (with a jacket, leggings, and UGG boots) attire because it was a little chilly outside. I hopped into the car and he just stared at me. I put my seatbelt on and watched him look at me through my peripheral.

"Why are you doing this?" he asked.

I smirked.

"Why, whatever are talking about, Daddy?" I asked innocently.

"Okay," he said. "Bet. I see how it is. You wanna play that game, huh? Cool."

The Giant was only a five minute ride from my house. It felt thirty minutes, though. He put his hand on my thigh and started inching it closer to my crotch. When I moved his hand, he touched my tits. I was trying to hold my ground. I was not going to be the one to fold!

Once we got to the grocery store and got out of the car, he slapped my ass and walked behind me so that his dick was on my ass.

I pushed the cart around, focused on getting the right ingredients. Meanwhile, he kept touching me inappropriately and kissing me on my neck from behind. We rang our things up and headed back to my apartment. He sat down on the couch in the living room and watched TV. I headed to the kitchen. I took the food out of the bags and went to my room to change into shorts because it was hot. I had my heat on for him because he's not used to the cold on account of him being from Jamaica.

The options were as follows: booty shorts, slutty booty shorts, and super saiyan slutty booty shorts. I went with the slutty booty shorts—had to keep it classy. I came out in a pretty much see-through tank top and some booty shorts. My ass was hanging out the bottom. This was war and I never play fair.

I came out of the hallway, walked through the living room, and walked past him. I didn't look back but I could see him looking at me from the reflection in the kitchen window. My friend, Tamara ended up FaceTiming me, so I of course I was going to spill all the tea.

There are two French doors in my kitchen—they separate the living room and kitchen. I closed them because I didn't want him hearing our conversation. I started telling her about the agreement that Vance and I had. She told me about her day. Then, I heard the doorknob turning on the kitchen door. Vance walked in.

"Can I help you, sir?" I asked, washing the chicken and shrimp.

"I'm about to help you cook, bae," he said.

I watched him walk over to the sink and wash his hands. That got me so wet! I was cutting up the chicken and peeling the shrimp. He poured coconut oil into the skillet and began adding seasonings so that they would start roasting. It was so adorable. I had to give her a heads up that he was now in the kitchen.

"So, tell me about your boyfriend," she said. "What does he look like?"

As soon as he heard that word, he walked up behind me, put his dick on my butt, and went out of his way to reach around me to get a spatula out of the drawer. We had never formally discussed becoming official just yet. We were just warming up to one another. We didn't want to rush into anything—that's where most people go wrong.

He just stood there, dick still on my butt. I leaned over the counter and started twerking on him, I didn't care. It was kind of cute. He pulled on my hair and spanked my ass. Tamara was still on the phone! I had my phone resting on the counter, trying to have a regular conversation with her. Meanwhile, his dick was throbbing on my butt cheeks!

Then, I walked over to the stove and threw the chicken and shrimp into the skillet. I reached out for the spatula. He just stared at me and licked his lips.

I just knew something was about to go down. He couldn't hang. He walked up to me, pushed me up against the wall, and pinned my hands up to my head with one hand.

"Sir," I said, clearing my throat. "What you doin'?"

"What you mean?" he asked, acting oblivious.

He just grinned as our eyes met. He leaned in. I thought he was trying to give me a kiss, so I puckered my lips out and closed my eyes. He aimed straight for my neck!

Long story short, he lifted my tank top up, pulled one of my titties out, and started sucking on one of my nipples. Tamara was still on the phone, asking why it had gotten so quiet. I was moaning underneath my breath.

There was no going back! I pushed him off of me and put my titty back into my bra. I continued sautéing the shrimp and chicken. He caught my drift and started preparing the noodles.

"Tamara," I called out. "I'm gonna have to call you back."

Shit was about to get real. I just felt it.

Finally, dinner was prepared. We made our plates and ate in front of the TV. He sat on the couch and I sat between his legs on the floor. By the time we finished, it was around 11:30. I stood, took our dishes into the kitchen, and dropped them into the dish-washing bucket.

I came back into the living room, sat beside him, leaned on his chest, and started fondling with his nipples. Whenever his nipples are touched, or rubbed on, or licked on, his dick gets rock hard. Did I use that against him? What type of person do you think I am? Of course I did!

He grabbed my wrist and placed my palm on the center of his chest.

"Bae," he said. "We're just chillin'. Chill out."

I backed off. I dozed off on his chest.

Midnight rolled around and he woke me up. I looked up and he kissed me. I was soaked!

He looked at his watch.

"Well, would you look at the time," he said. "It's midnight. It's a whole new day."

"You're absolutely right," I replied, yawning.

He stood up, readjusted his joggers, and yanked me by my legs. The back of my head hit the wall. His head was always worth the concussion, though. I saw stars, unicorns, leprechauns and whatever the fuck. It didn't matter to me—I was ready.

He separated my legs, looked in amazement, slowly slid two fingers in, pulled them out, and separated them. My juices retracted and slid down his knuckles. I was nice and wet. Sometimes I'm a creamer. Sometimes I'm an oozer. Sometimes I'm a squirter. This particular night, I was an oozer.

I saw my clear juices sliding down his palm.

He tried eating my pussy with my shorts still on, but it just was not working out. So he ripped them off of me. Those were my favorite slutty shorts, and he just tore them to shreds.

He dove in. I arched my back.

Whenever he eats me out and I moan, he ends up moaning with me! That's the best feeling in the world, it truly is. It's like he gets pleasure from pleasuring me and I think that's why we're soulmates—because I'm the exact same way. I pushed him on the forehead just so that I could catch my breath and readjust my position. When he goes in, he goes in.

Within a span of three minutes, I had easily cum three times in his mouth. Three times. Three minutes. Can you imagine how much energy that took out of me!?

He got up, wiped his mouth, and sat beside me like nothing had happened.

"Sir," I said, confused.

I looked at him flabbergasted and out of breath. He smiled.

"What?" he asked. "We just chillin', remember?"

"I'm sorry, what?" I said irritated. "So, what you're saying is that you just spent all this time getting me extremely horny and now you're not going to give me the dick?"

"Pretty much," he said. "Haha."

"Hee hee, shit," I said. "Take your dick out. You're getting fucked. I'm serious."

"Nah bae," he said again. "We're just chillin'. I just wanted to taste you real quick."

I nodded my head, got on top of him, and started grinding on his dick with no underwear on. I could feel that he was hard through his pants.

Still grinding, I reached behind me and played with his balls. I had to warm them up. He was done for. He held his head back, moaned, and dropped his jaw in ecstasy. He sucked he teeth, lifted my big ass up off of him, and threw me down onto the couch. He shoved his tongue into my pussy. Have you ever had head so good that your eyes rolled so far back in your head that you saw the wall behind you? I mean head that just sent you floating?

My body went limp. He lifted my legs straight up and pulled his pants down. He slid his dick in. The first stroke gave me chills. I got goosebumps. But it was just warm enough to melt my insides. He spread my legs open and came down to kiss me. He alternated between fast strokes and slow ones. He kept having to stop because he didn't want to nut. After ten minutes went by, he started moving his hips from side to side. Then he did this lift up and pull down thing inside of me! It was the kind of movement that made you realize why so many women go to prison after killing their boyfriends for cheating.

He had given me my soul back for a split moment all just to take it back away. It was nothing but the devil's work! I opened my eyes and saw him watching me make faces. We locked eyes and he lifted my head up and held me by the back of my neck. It was so passionate. He was fucking the shit out of my mother's daughter, but he was doing it so romantically.

He pulled out and slapped his dick on my clit! He lied back on the couch and told me to ride him. I got worried. Big girls aren't really the best riders. I mean, riding is cool and all, but I need to ride before any other position. Big bitches can ride for a good five minutes, and that's if you do the appropriate stretching beforehand.

"Actually," he said. "Put that ass up real quick."

I assumed the position. As soon as he took my hair into his hands, he shoved his dick in. I saw my life flash before my eyes. He was showing absolutely no mercy. He was giving me a spinal tap for real! These weren't standard little back shots! He was trying to break my back!

I had eventually gotten tired of him assaulting my vagina like that. No pussy should be subjected to that sort of violence. I fell forward, turned around, and pulled him onto the couch. I straddled him. I saddled up and bounced on his dick like a pogo stick. I grinded my hips, sucked him in, and kissed on his neck at the same time. He was throbbing inside of me.

When I slowed down, he dropped his head back and wrapped his hands around my waist. I held my hair up in a makeshift ponytail and rode him with no hands! I felt celestial—like a higher being.

I caught a cramp and as soon as I felt myself making ugly faces, I had to turn around and twerk on his dick reverse cowgirl. So I spun around with the dick still inside of me and dropped my feet to the floor. I spread my legs and got into position. I was twerking as if my life depended on it. I was doing everything right. I was riding, sliding, grinding, winding, slipping, gripping, dipping, *YOU NAME IT!*

I was fucking it up. He was moaning, damn near crying. I had eventually gotten tired. I had given him the best ride I had ever given. I gave him a solid eight minutes—and that's above the big girl maximum! I had a good six or seven grinds left in me, so I stretched them out and slowed them down.

I dropped to the floor because my legs went weak. I turned around and cleaned his dick off with my mouth. While I was sucking and stroking, he hit me with a doozy.

"Bae, let's go in the room so we can fuck *for real*," he said.

What the fuck is "fuck for real"?! I had exerted all of my energy with that ride and he wanted to "fuck for real"?

By the time we got into my room, it was already 1 am and I had to be at work at 8 am that morning. Yet and still, there I was, cum down my throat, hair everywhere, makeup gone, pussy drenched, legs shook.

We fucked four more times! My headboard was in shambles. By the end of the third time, he pulled out and almost did not make it. Some of the cum had gotten on my clit and dripped down inside of me as he jerked off to finish himself off. I'm paranoid as fuck and that was enough for me to want to get a Plan B contraceptive.

"Well, since we're getting Plan B anyway," he said, "can I shoot up the club real quick this last round?"

I rolled my eyes and I agreed.

That last round, we strictly made love. He intertwined his fingers into mine, tongue-kissed me, held my head, and looked into the depths of my soul. The last few strokes, his voice broke, his body shivered, and his tone went up octaves (plural). I saw his cumming face and I paid attention to the signes. I started doing my kegals, squeezing him with my vaginal muscles.

"Fill me up, daddy," I cried out. "Cum in me baby."

He groaned out and held his head back up to the ceiling. I felt his warm cum enter my body for the first time ever and his dick pulsated inside of me. I felt the light pressure of his cum squirting into my insides. I understood it now—how so many people fuck around and end up having kids. Having raw sex and cumming together, with no barriers between the two of you is the best feeling.

After we came, we got dressed, and quickly ran to the Rite Aid across the street from my house to get a Plan B: One Step pill. At the register, the cashier had jokes for days as if Vance's kids weren't swimming around inside of me, heading towards my ovaries.

When we got back to the apartment, we literally dropped down onto the living room floor. I swallowed my pill without water and we fell asleep right there. We woke back up at around four, he got into the bed, and I took a quick shower. I joined him minutes later. We had both woken up late as fuck. That's what we get for playing with temptation.

37. For An Audience

December 5th, 2016

One day, I went with Vance to handle some business. He was in a suit and tie, just looking like a fucking snack. I just couldn't keep my eyes off of him.

When we began heading our way back, I just watched him drive. We held hands. The way the sun bounced off of his caramel skin, the way the light hit his hazel eyes, the way the bass in Kevin Gates' music vibrated in my seat just got me hot. He reached over and started rubbing on my pussy through my slacks. I was done for. I leaned my chair back and let him do what he does so well. He knows my body more than I know myself. Moments later, I was gushing.

"Babe, I'm horny," he said, steering the wheel and playing with my pussy at the same time.

I bit my lip and began rubbing on his dick.

"Is that so?" I asked.

"You're not about that life," he said. "Chill."

My face dropped unamused. I felt attacked. I felt triggered. Of *all* the incredibly disgusting, filthy, experimental things we've done to each other (including being newly inducted members of the Red Towel Gang!), he accused **me** of "not being about that life"?!

    I wasn't having it! I rose up slowly, so as to not draw attention to us. I unzipped his pants and pulled his beautiful, stiff dick out through the pee hole in his boxers. He slid his seat back a bit. I shoved him down into my throat. I rotated my wrist around his dick while tugging on it with my mouth simultaneously. He moaned out. He pressed down on the back of my head and it was breath-taking. (By the way, I don't think any of the phrases I've used thus far fit as perfectly as that one just did—just saying.)

    For a moment, I got away with it, but the car was just too low for us not to draw attention to ourselves. I came back up in my seat and jerked him off. I wanted to be spontaneous. Eventually, I tucked his dick away because there were too many cars that could've easily seen in.

    When we got closer to my house, we were hungry, so we decided to stop by Qdoba. We got two burritos, but a burrito wasn't the only thing I had a taste for. The pool was open on that crisp winter morning—and by "pool", I mean "my throat". I wanted the kids to come over and take a swim.

    I gave him turn-by-turn directions to a parking lot I knew would be empty. We pulled into the parking lot and drove up four or five flights. There were barely any cars that far up. But for safe measure, we went all the way up to the roof, drove over into a connecting parking lot and parked in a space with a beautiful view of the Silver Spring metropolitan area.

I smiled with my bottom lip tucked away in my mouth. I took my shoes off and dropped them. I yanked my coat off and tossed it into the backseat. I slapped my hands and rubbed them together. It was time to prove to him, for the thousandth time, that my mother didn't raise a punk!

I leaned forward, got on my knees, and told him to push his seat all the way back. We listened to the whirring of the seat gliding.

"Keep going," I said, waving my hands as the seat fell back. "All the way. Almost."

He pressed the button again, and there was nowhere left for the seat to go.

"Perfect," I said.

I reached for his belt and unbuckled it.

"Take it *all* off," I said demandingly.

Without saying a word, he lifted his body and pulled his pants and boxers down to his feet in one swift motion. Then he lied back. I took his dick into my hands, placed my head above it, and let spit slowly drip down on it. I stroked it gently up and down with both hands going about at opposite directions. I wanted to taste his dick—it had been so long. Granted, it had only been twenty minutes, but still.

I took one hand and cupped his shaven balls. I caressed and rubbed on them in a clock-wise motion. I lifted his shirt up and gently kissed his stomach. I moved my head lower and kissed his bald pubic area. I kissed on the base of his dick. I pulled the foreskin back and licked from the base to the tip.

I gobbled his dick up and took in all his moans. I moaned with him. I lifted my left hand up and massaged his nipples through his button-up shirt.

And then, something happened. Something changed. It felt like someone had stood in front of the sunlight that pierced into the car from the back—like we weren't the only ones on that level. Something told me to hold my head up.

I raised my head up, still jerking him off and noticed an old, short, white guy peeping into the back window. We locked eyes and I panicked. He dropped his sunshades from his forehead and stepped to the side. I noticed that he was in the parking lot attendant uniform, but he didn't have a walkie talkie, or a clipboard, or a fucking pen and pad to at least write down our tag number in his hand. He held nothing but air! He was honestly, truly enjoying the free show.

I gasped.

"Babe," I said nervously. "We have to go."

"Why," he moaned out, confused.

"Babe," I reiterated. "We have to move right now. Look."

I pointed at the parking lot attendant just looking into the car from the side. Vance tilted his head to the side, noticed him, started the car, and we sped out of there. **He was driving with his dick out and his pants around his ankles!** I couldn't complain because it was honestly a beautiful view, but I was shook! I was in shock, literally. My hands were shaking, my pussy dried up, and my eye started twitching.

We tried once more when we got down to the bottom floor, but the same old, creepy ass parking lot attendant found us again! We decided that that would be enough spontaneous dick-sucking—at least for that day.

We headed back to my place, which was literally only a two minute drive. We ate our burritos, stocked up on our protein and starch, and fucked for two hours straight.

For some reason, having a minor close call with jail time marinated the pussy in a majestic seasoning because Vance ate me out for at least thirty minutes.

Things between us had gotten more romantic—more intimate. We became closer and found ourselves within each other. We were complete opposites by completely the same at the same time. We never rushed anything; we just let things happen on their own time.

38. *All Tied Up*

∞

December 20th, 2016

And then it happened—that thing love. A man I had known for almost two years was finally mine and we were inseparable. Everything about our time together was magical and spontaneous. Love came like a quiet storm—fast, but peacefully beautiful. I've grown fond of not only his sex, but his conversation, and intimacy. Just being around him affects my energy in the best way. Considering I hadn't had sex with anyone, or been touched really, for a year before we became a thing, let's just say that my confidence wasn't where it needed to be. The first time we had sex, I clung to my oversized t-shirt—I even wore a bra.

There came a time when he got fed up with me trying to hide myself and forced me to take *everything* off before having sex.

"I love you," he'd say. "I love everything about you—everything about your body. You don't have to be self-conscious around me."

These are the things you say to someone you truly love. He wanted me to understand how beautiful I was. He brought me out of my comfort zone. He wanted me to believe that I was beautiful and that I should take pride in my beauty.

"I want to see you," he'd say, rubbing all up and down the folds of my body. "*All* of you."

I've never been with anyone that made me feel as safe as he does when I'm around him. It's like nothing else and no one else matters. No one's ever taken the time to appreciate who I was emotionally and physically. No one saw the damage in me and decided to take it on regardless. This man had truly fallen for me.

One day, Vance and I ended up arguing over FaceTime about which chip was better between Doritos and Pringles. I made my case about how Doritos's Spicy Sweet Chili and original Nacho Cheese flavors will forever be undefeated. He claimed that us "Americans" had fucked up palates and that I didn't know what I was talking about. Apparently, Pringles are a huge thing in Jamaica.

So we did what any other reasonable, 21st century couple would do and took to the internet. We had made a bet—and the loser would be handcuffed later that night for thirty minutes, while the winner was able to do with them whatever they wanted.

Of course, fifteen hundred votes later, I was the victor. I dug out my furry pink handcuffs and set them out for that night's activities.

I wanted to surprise him. So, I pulled out a lingerie piece I had bought weeks earlier. I did it up! The ceremonial "Three S's" had commenced. I hopped in the shower, Naired away my pussy hairs, shaved my legs, curled my hair, and painted my face with sweat-proof AND cum-proof makeup. I doused myself in Pure Seduction spray and body lotion.

He rang the doorbell. The time had come. I grinned and buzzed him in. I flipped my hair, pushed my tits into the bra cups of the lingerie piece, leaned onto the arm of my couch in a sexy pose, and unlocked the door.

He walked in, eyes gleaming. The light from the hallway hit my body just right.

"Damn," he said.

I smiled. He came in for a kiss. I wrapped my arms around his body and squeezed his back. He picked me up and we headed to the room.

Once we got there, we wasted no time at all. He plugged up my phone to my speaker and began blasting "Might Get Pregnant" Apple Music playlist that we had made collectively.

(Side note: This fucking playlist is over one hundred songs long and just might actually get you pregnant. In case you were wondering, this particular playlist currently consists of the following songs: "Inside My Love" by Delilah, "Maniac" by Jhené Aiko, "Speechless" and "That's How You Like It" by Beyoncé, "Come On Over" by Sevyn Streeter, "Bed" by J. Holiday, "Do What It Do" by Jamie Foxx, "Sex Wit You" by Marques Houston, "This Woman's Work" by Maxwell, "Wetter" by Twista featuring Erika Shevon, "Arch & Point" by Miguel, "Do You" by Miguel, "Pussy Is Mine" by

Miguel, "All The Time" by Jeremih, "Body Party" by Ciara, "Tonight" by John Legend and Ludacris, "Love Faces" by Trey Songz, "Neighbors Know My Name" also by Trey Songz, "Pony" by Ginuwine, "They Don't Know" by Rico Love, "Wet The Bed" by Chris Brown, "No BS" also by Chris Brown, "Say It" by T-Pain, "Cece's Interlude" by Drake, "Untitled" by D'Angelo, "Push It" by TWENTY88, "Hey There" by Dej Loaf, "Or Nah" by Ty Dolla $ign, "Falsetto" by The-Dream, "What You Do to Me" by John Legend, "Jungle" by Drake, "Million" by Tink, "O" by Omarion, "Take It Off" by Pharrell, "Sex Therapy" by Robin Thicke, "Teach U a Lesson" by Robin Thicke, "Sweat It Out" by The-Dream, "Nice & Slow" by Usher, "Break You Off" by The Roots, "Dance for You", "1+1", "Rocket", and "No Angel" by Beyoncé, "No.Body" by Wasionkey, "4 Walls" by VEDO, "Loveeeeee Song" by Rihanna featuring Future, "Get It On Tonite" by Montell Jordan, "Naked" by Marques Houston, "Doin' It" by LL Cool J, "Can U Handle It" by Usher, "Back to Sleep" by Chris Brown, "It Won't Stop" by Sevyn Streeter and Chris Brown, "Boo Thang" by Verse Simmonds, "This Love", "One Percent", "Fantasy", "Someone", "Vibe", and "Yours Truly" by Ambré Perkins, "I Love Your Crazy" by Jasmine V, "Suga Suga" by Baby Bash, "Wicked Games" and "High for This" by The Weeknd, "Between the Sheets" by the Isley Brothers, "No Ordinary Love" by Sade, "Touch My Body" by Mariah Carey, "Grind With Me" by Pretty Ricky, "Sex on the Ceiling" by Sevyn Streeter, "Cold Sweat", "C'est La Vie", "Sacrifices", "Ride of Your Life", and "How Many Times" by Tinashe, "Collide" by Justine Skye, "Cross

My Mind" by Jill Scoot, "Say It" and "Mirror" by Ne-Yo, "Any Time, Any Place" and "Warmth" by Janet Jackson, "Can I Take U Home" by Jamie Foxx, "Beautiful" by Meshell Ndegeocello, "No Police" and "So High" by Doja Cat, "Get You" by Daniel Caesar, "A Prince" by Jorja Smith, "Rich $ex" by Future, "Kissin' On My Tattoos" by August Alsina, "Shut It Down" by Drake, "Feel" by Post Malone, "Love Calls" by Kem, "Put It In Your Mouth" by Akinyele, "Bad Intentions" by Niykee Heaton, "Selfish" by PnB Rock, "Panty Droppa", "Jupiter Love", "Dive In", "Scratchin' Me Up", and "You Belong to Me" by Trey Songz, "Trading Places" by Usher, "Worth It" by Young Thug, and last but not least, "Say It" by Tory Lanez. **DO NOT, I REPEAT, DO NOT LISTEN TO THIS COLLECTION OF MUSIC WHILE HAVING UNPROTECTED SEX! YOU <u>WILL</u> GET PREGNANT!**)

I eased up onto the bed. He climbed up on top of me and pressed his lips to mine. His lips were plump and soft. "Jupiter Love" played in the background. He was warm and hard at the same time. He pressed his lips to my neck, then my shoulder, and my collar bone. He pulled down the lingerie and kissed my chest, my breast, and licked my nipple. He pecked my rib, stomach, naval. His lips met my skin again when he pressed them to my thigh and inner thigh. He teased me, and I loved every moment of it. It was a blissful agony. I placed my hand over my vagina. I pressed and rubbed my fingers into my juices through the lingerie. He kissed the back of my hand and slowly guided it away. His tongue replaced my fingers. He unclasped the crotch and slurped me up. The darting of his tongue in and out of me made me see stars.

    I needed release. I let it build up inside of me. Vance licked and stroked his tongue all throughout my quivers. He clenched onto my thighs and pulled me closer into him. It flowed out of me—and he did not let up. He took his shirt off as I watched him through my lowered lids. I couldn't move—I was paralyzed by the pleasure. He leaned toward me in a push up position. I reached between us and guided his solid dick into me. His heat filled me up so deeply. My breath rose as he slowly moved around inside me.

    His hands slid underneath me and cupped my shoulders. He dragged me into him still. I felt the warmth of my breath trapped between my lips and his shoulders as my eyes climbed up the dimly-lit ceiling. He drove deeper and deeper inside of me. My tits bobbed with Vance's pumping. He crouched down, still stroking, and caught one of my hardened nipples in his mouth. He flapped his tongue, circled it, and sucked gently.

    I cried out in bliss. My body melted into the bed as he dropped down inside of me rhythmically. He sucked on my bottom lip. I lightly clawed at his back, and caught sweat underneath my fingernails. I wrapped my legs around his lower back and yanked him in deeper. My clit was throbbing. I felt my walls contracting against him inside of me.

Another orgasm flew out of me as he continued stroking. My wetness was warm against his stomach and pubic area. He took a hand and ran it through my hair to the back of my head and lifted it up. Our foreheads pressed against each other. He winced through each stroke. He panted and clutched onto the back of my neck. He brought the same hand around and lightly pressed down.

"Harder," I called out. "Choke me harder."

And so he did. My head grew hot and my pussy grew even more slippery. I couldn't breathe for a moment, but it was all worth it. He slid in and out of me with both long and short strokes. He let my neck go and spread my legs out. Then he let go of one leg and massaged on my clit with his thumb. He kept stroking. I cried out. It was too sensitive. He flicked his thumb faster and faster. I felt him smearing my juices all up and down my clit. The smoothness of his dick grinding in and out of me was sensational.

My jaw dropped. He kept flicking his thumb.

"Babe I'm about to cum again," I whimpered out. "You want me to cum all over your dick, Daddy?"

"Cum on Daddy's dick, baby," he replied, panting.

I stopped breathing. Air just wouldn't come out. The world stood still. I forced my cum out of me. I came hard. He glided in and out of me.

He held his head back and groaned out. His motion became jerky and less fluid. I fiddled with his nipples. He moaned out louder. The sweat glistened off his body and I watched his face react to me exercising my kegals. He pounded his dick into me again and again.

He pulled out.

"Come on, baby," he said. "Catch it."

I hopped off of the bed and dropped down to my knees. I opened my mouth wide and waited for his creamy cum to drip down into my mouth. And then it happened. I tasted him and it was beautiful. I swallowed him—all of him. He fell back onto the bed. I pounced on top of him and continued sucking. I tasted myself and sucked on his tip slightly.

He screamed out—a part of him died. I popped my head up.

"Oh," I said. "I almost forgot."

I reached out for my handcuffs.

"You ready?" I asked.

He looked up at me and dropped his head back down into the pillow underneath him.

"Babe," he said.

"Yes, sir," I replied giggling.

"Babe," he said again, trying to negotiate.

"A bet is a bet is a bet is a bet," I explained. "C'mon."

He let out an over the top sigh. He was horrified. Every time I suck his dick, I just don't know when to stop. Feeling his dick pulsate in my mouth just does something to me that I can't explain.

I got up and we walked over to the foot of my bed. I handcuffed him to the right leg of the bed. He couldn't go anywhere. His back was on the floor.

I rested on my knees and went to work. I kissed on his chest tattoos. I sucked on one of his nipples and immediately felt his dick growing harder and poking me in the elbow. It was time.

"Go slow," he begged me.

I inhaled him. Swallowed his entire dick and let him hit my tonsils for the fun of it. (Have you ever loved someone so much that you wanted them inside of you all the time? That's what it's like. I just want to touch, and feel, and taste him all the time. I'm addicted to him and he's pretty addicted to me.) He whimpered out, but he took it all. He soldiered through the sticky strokes and the humming.

He was almost there and I didn't ease up.

"Babe," he said, "uncuff me, please."

I gave in. He knew exactly what to do. I was still warming up to learning his stroke pattern. I'd often practice it with him, trying to mimic the rotation, the pull, the squeeze. I watched in amazement as he tugged on his dick ferociously yet delicately at the same time. I took his dick into my hand and repeated the movements I had seen him do. I spat on it and stroked away. Moments later, I felt him pulsating in my grip.

He breathed in sharply and began grunting. I jerked him off while licking on the tip. I made sure the folds of his foreskin fell in just the right spot and that the spit lubricated it enough. My grip around his girth grew more firm and rhythmic. And then his cum sprayed into my mouth in three or four strong squirts. I felt his groans vibrating in the floor and echoing throughout the apartment.

We got back up on the bed and fell asleep roasting each other—calling each other big heads and whatnot. Before I knew it, we were out like a candle, as our playlist pierced throughout my home. It was cute—like I could actually do this for the rest of my left kind of cute.

A few days later, he met my family on Christmas day. It felt right. Of course, it was a bit awkward initially. We had just had sex before making our way over there and a part of me felt like they smelled it on me or saw the guilt in my eyes. At first, he was quiet and acted shy and innocent when we know that this man is just about as filthy and disgusting as I am. They loved him—even my grandparents. Whenever I'm on the phone with them, they always seem to ask me about my "little friend", even though I've introduced him as my boyfriend God knows how many times.

39. Valentine's Day

∞

December, 2017

Valentine's Day had arrived. The white people at my job really stressed me the fuck out. That, on top of trying to run my own business was completely draining. My entire day at work, all I could think about was what was going to happen later that night because it would be my first Valentine's Day in a healthy relationship. I had it all planned out: I was going to start cooking, wash my dishes, hop in the shower, and commence the "Three S's". I was going to put on some lingerie and set the mood with our playlist. It was going to be beautiful.

Right before I got into the shower, I noticed that I didn't have any more toothpaste. It was only around 7 p.m. and Vance normally didn't come over until around 9 after work. I figured I had time to take a quick trip to CVS. When I got back from my trip, as I was walking back to my apartment, I looked up and saw a black guy walking towards the front of our building. I was really trying to figure out which snow-bunny was popping her coochie for a real nigga because I'm the only black person that lives in my apartment building. Then, he turned his head and faced me but I still could not see his face. The closer I got, the more awkward it became. Eventually, I realized that it was my boyfriend and that he was extremely early.

He gave me a kiss on the forehead. It was precious. I opened the front door and we stepped into my apartment. A while goes by. I went to go make my bed up. I walked back into the living room and he wanted me to open up a few presents.

I was flabbergasted. He had spoiled me. I had never gotten a gift for Valentine's Day and it actually made me cry. I literally hugged him for ten minutes straight. He was low-key getting annoyed but I didn't care.

So I walked into the kitchen and started cooking because I wanted to do a candlelit dinner—some real romantic shit. I figured a blowjob by candlelight would really warm the heart.

I made his plate and brought it out. But he wasn't even hungry. Turns out, when I was making up the bed, he was eating leftovers from Red Lobster two days before from when I had taken him out for his birthday. All that hard work was all for naught.

He hopped into the shower before I could. When he got out, his skin was glistening. He was just looking like a five course meal. I grabbed his dick and bit my bottom lip. I was just staring at it. You don't understand how beautiful this man's dick is.

"You tryna to suck you right now?" he asked.

"Boyyyyyyy," I said, pretending to be uninterested. "Yes. Yes, I do. I would like that very much."

I pushed him onto the bed and got ready to go to work. I cleared my throat and relaxed my tonsils. I was pulling out all the tricks. His toes curled at my sides. He ran his fingers through my hair and pressed down. He was face-fucking me. It was so... beautiful. Just feeling his dick throbbing down my throat means the world to me. I started stroking on it and sucking on his balls. That only made it worse. He was ready. I was teasing him.

He told me to hurry up and get in the shower. He wanted to save all his kids for me. For sure, he was shooting up the club. First of all, I would like to take a moment to thank my gynecologist for my prescription to birth control. Also, I would like to mention Rite Aid for filling it. My deepest gratitude goes out to insurance for making it free.

So I hopped in the shower and I was in there for a good forty-five minutes even though I had initially told him I would only needed twenty. Most of that time was spent twerking. I had finally gotten out, dried off, brushed my teeth, and walked into my bedroom. He was on the bed looking like a pink Starburst or a blue Jolly Rancher (whichever tastes best to you). At that point, I honestly just wanted his dick in my mouth, fuck my pussy (see what I did there?). I wanted to gargle his cum— all of it.

I got up on the bed and started crawling toward him sexily. He stood and went over to the wall to plug his phone up to the charger. I felt insulted. Was this really the game he wanted to play? Then he grabbed my phone and plugged it up to the speaker. He started blasting our playlist. That was such a relief; I thought I was going to have to fight him for playing with my emotions. He turned out the light, I turned off the TV. It was time. I pushed him back onto the bed because I wasn't finished what I had started before my shower.

I was necking him down. He was moaning. I was moaning. I was playing with myself while I was sucking his dick. It was sensational. His balls, his dick, his thighs, my arms, underneath him, everything was soaked. My sloppy head is not a game.

He got up, pushed me off of him, flipped me over, grabbed me by the legs, and put them on his shoulders. He kissed my inner thighs and dragged the back of his tongue from my clit down to my taint. Then he dragged the front of his tongue from my taint to my clit. Now, normally, I'm not really into ass play. But the way his tongue tickled up against my hole accidentally definitely worked for me.

He started tongue-fucking me. He was slurping on my clit and squeezing on my thighs. He was, for lack of a better word, serenading my pussy. He was singing lullabies to her. He took his other hand and pulled my hood back. Then he started sucking on my clit with a purpose. I came four times in five minutes.

Half of my soul was gone. Then he stretched my left leg out, then my right leg. He had me spread out like an eagle, then he dug his tongue inside of me. I couldn't talk, or scream.

Out of nowhere, he stopped.

"Come taste this pussy on my face babe," he said.

I hopped up so fast. I was excited. I literally licked every inch of his face. I was in his beard; I licked his cheeks and his nose. I shoved my tongue all in his mouth I sucked on his. And then he entered me. I dropped down. He began slow-stroking. He grabbed one of my breasts and started sucking on my nipple. I felt my pussy clenching down harder on his dick. I'd never really been a fan of making love until I met him. It was romantic. And then he switched the game up on me!

He got me on my knees and started throwing the dick inside of me. These weren't just regular old run-of-the-mill back shots; these were "some I love you, I hate you, I hope you die, I can't wait to spend the rest of my life with you" type a fucking back shots! I fell down into my pillow, face first. I told him to lie down on his back. I wanted to try something. So I hopped on him and I rode the shit out of his dick. I bounced, I thrusted, and I grinded. I was Kentucky Derbying his dick! He moaned underneath me. For the first time ever, I had made myself cum. For the first time ever, I actually wanted to ride him. I don't know where came from, but I know it never left because now I'm addicted.

 We climaxed together and it was magnificent. It was pulchritudinous in every way, shape, and form. Everything about that night was perfect

40. In Conclusion

∞

They say that everything happens for a reason. I want to believe in all my heart that my journey qualifies. Maybe I needed to experience new things and new people. Maybe I needed to get my heart broken over and over again before I realized my worth. I had to find myself. When I finally did, God gave me what I needed exactly when I needed it.

After I finally decided to let go of poisonous people and relationships, after much trial and error, I found happiness. I found a piece of me that I kept losing.

There's nothing wrong with being who you want to be. You have to love yourself first. You have to comfort yourself first. You have to save yourself first. Of course, I did things that most people would not agree with, but I'm the happiest I've ever been in my life. Had I not made the decisions I made, I wouldn't be in the position that I'm in today. I know that for certain. I'm in love with a man who's in love with everything I am. He makes me feel beautiful in every way and I'll forever be grateful to him for that, no matter what comes of us.

He's already undone so much damage from my previous relationships—the emotional injuries that

I've had to walk around with for so many years. Being with him is like finding the perfect dress after wasting so much money and time looking for a dupe that could never compare. I don't feel used or pressured when I'm with him—everything just happens organically.

Some days, we may argue like cats and dogs, we disagree, we have our moments, but we work through them. We work on ourselves and know that what we have is unlike anything either of us has ever come across.

Every decision you make has a domino effect on your life. To you, that may sound like a cliché, but to me, it's my truth. Every petty urge I acted on, every slutty thing I did, every relationship I rushed into has led up to this very moment.

Had I not made the choices I decided to make in my past, I would not be who I am today, and I would never have been this open about my sexuality. You wouldn't be reading these words. This book would not exist if nothing were to have happened with White Boy Timmy. I would never have really gotten to know Ava if I didn't cut all my first friends off. I would never have transferred to Bowie if I hadn't become anti-social.

If I had never transferred, I wouldn't have been introduced to a slew of beautiful fuckboys that ultimately turned me into a fuckgirl. If I wasn't a fuckgirl at the time, I would've been open to dating just anyone. I wouldn't have lost my virginity to a guy, who to this day, could still very well be gay. Had I not given Stanford a chance, we would have neither been together nor broken up. I probably would never have met Orlando if I didn't invited Desiree to my birthday party and befriended her.

Orlando and I would have never fucked in his car had I not still been heartbroken. If Orlando and I had never broken up, I wouldn't have been inclined to fuck Nate (Lil' Bink Bink) out of spite. If I weren't an asshole and didn't laugh at his dick, he probably wouldn't have spread rumors about me on campus, and this book would have never existed!

I wouldn't have dated a girl who didn't have a future. I wouldn't have allowed myself to be manipulated if I knew my worth and hatred wouldn't have filled my body the way it did. Without that hatred, I would have never been able to forgive her.

Imagine if Orlando and I hadn't been a thing—I have no idea how I would have met my boyfriend. I would never have caught his eye; we would have never crossed paths. I wouldn't be dating my best friend—the exact boy version of myself. God works in mysterious ways and I think it's better not to try to make sense of it all.

I would like to say thank you to all the fuckboys and fuckgirls that have entered my life. Without you, this would have never been a thing. To all my little-dicked niggas, you really changed my perspective. To the big-dicked niggas that spent some time with Nikki, you really changed my life. To all my partners with PDL's, you really rocked my world. To all the people that I gave my heart to that didn't know what to do with it, I still have love for you. If you ever need anything, give me a call so I can laugh in your ear. I'm sorry, I'm still working on my pettiness (but then again, who would I be if I weren't petty?).

To the current love of my life, thank you for making me believe that I'm beautiful, and for reminding me of it every day. Thank you for the silent conversations, and for accepting me for who I am. You know me more than I know myself. Thank you for rocking me to sleep, for the forehead kisses, for the hugs that make my heart melt. I know at times I'm a lot to deal with, but you see my worth and you appreciate our future. You're the puzzle piece I searched for in so many boxes, on so many shelves. Thank you for never judging me. Thank you for finding new ways to learn and understand me.

To my readers stuck between a rock and a hard place, the best advice I can give you is to choose your life and not to let anyone choose it for you. Appreciate the little things and *always* remember to make yourself a priority, no matter what the circumstances.

Until next time.

Printed in Great Britain
by Amazon